Muskets & MARTYRS

Muskets & MARTYRS

LINDSEY S. FERA

Copyright © 2025 BY LINDSEY FERA

Editor(s): Colin Mustful and Jenny Quinlan
Cover Illustration: Clara Costa
Cover Design: Merlina Garance
Internal Formatting: allaboutbookcovers.com

ISBN (Paperback): 979-8-9867565-2-3
ISBN (Hardcover): 979-8-9867565-3-0

Pompkin Press
Newmarket, New Hampshire

Pompkin Press

For my 'Jack'

CAST OF CHARACTERS

The Howlett Family

Mr. Robert and Mrs. Margaret (Peggy) Howlett
George Bixby Howlett (from Mrs. Howlett's first marriage to
Captain Bixby), *b. 1751*
Jane Catherine Howlett, *b. 1754*
Annalisa Elizabeth Howlett, *b. 1756*
William Robert Howlett, *b. 1758*
Mary Margaret and Henry Charles Howlett (twins), *b. 1762*

The Howlett Household

Liza, indentured girl from Ireland
Dane and Zeke, hired farmhands

The Perkins Family

Lord John Jackson Perkins II and Lady Elizabeth (Bette)
Bixby Perkins
John Jackson Perkins III (Jack), *b. 1752*
Oliver James Perkins, *b. 1753*
Abigail Louisa Perkins, *b. 1755*
Andrew Richard Perkins, *b. 1759*
Susan Frances Perkins, *b. 1767*
Charlotte Elizabeth Perkins, *b. 1774*
Lord and Lady Brunswick (Aunt Catherine), Lord Perkins's
sister

The late Captain Bixby, Mrs. Howlett's first husband, and
brother to Lady Perkins
Admiral Bixby, eldest brother to Lady Perkins

The Perkins Family Household

Mercy, indentured housekeeper
Wheaton, coachman
Dottie, maid

The children

Thomas John Perkins—*born to Oliver and Jane, March 1776*
Louisa Elizabeth Howlett—*born to George and Abigail,
May 1776*
Robert John Perkin—*born to Jack and Jane, March 1777*
Eliza Perkins—*miscarried to Jack and Annalisa, August 1777*
Frances Howlett—*born to William and Martha, July 1779*
Edward Bixby Howlett—*born to George and Abigail, January
1780, d. March 1780*
Samuel Howlett—*born to William and Martha, November 1781*
Molly Eliza Perkins—*born to Jack and Annalisa, 1782*

Friends and Townspeople of Topsfield

Quinnapin, a Wampanoag Native from Mashpee
Mr. Peabody, Martha's cousin
Samuel Wildes, George's oldest friend *(d. 1776)*
Addy, former housekeeper from Barbados, and Sarah's
grandmother
✝ Captain Gould, captain of Topsfield's militia and owner of
the Whispering Willow Tavern
Martha Perley, William Howlett's wife

Mr. Averill and his son Josiah Averill, Patriots
Hannah French, Lizzie Balch, and Fanny Shepard, gossiping
girls of Topsfield
Elisha Porter, innkeeper at George's tavern

Society of London

Lord Essex, married Abigail in 1775
Sarah, former chambermaid of the Duchess of Devonshire
✝ Georgiana (Gee), the Duchess of Devonshire
✝ Lord and Lady Melbourne
✝ Lord and Lady Jersey
✝ Mr. Fox, prominent member of the Whig Party

Society of Philadelphia

✝ Peggy Shippen (marries Benedict Arnold, *April 1779*)
✝ Chief Justice Shippen, Peggy's father

Continental Army and Patriots

Daniel Bartlett of Menotomy
✝ General George Washington, commander in chief of the
Continental Army
✝ Henry Knox, chief of the artillery for the Continental
Army
✝ Alexander Hamilton

British Army, Loyalists, and Turncoats

Captain Fleming (*d. 1777*)
Mr. Wentworth of Portsmouth
✝ Major General Benedict Arnold

✝ Lord General Cornwallis, British general defeated at Yorktown, 1781
✝ Major John André, British spy, *(d. 1780)*
✝ Lieutenant Colonel Banastre Tarleton "Bloody Ban," commander of the British legion cavalry

✝ *Denotes historical figure*

❧ I ❧
1778-1779

❦ I ❦

ANNALISA
TOPSFIELD, OCTOBER 1778

THE OAK PROVED A vast and sprawling guardian, one that sought to protect and witness Annalisa Howlett's life and tribulations. In wind and rain, in snow and ice, the tree withstood time itself as a sacred observer.

Worn smooth from years of sitting, Annalisa perched on the lowest bough garbed in men's clothes with her musket over her lap. With gunpowder-stained fingertips, Annalisa screwed the lock back into position and placed the soiled cloth into her haversack.

Her musket clean, she leaned it against the branch and stood from the bough. Annalisa made her way to the base of the tree, where she knelt. The unmarked gravesite remained a refuge of peace despite the miscarried daughter who lay buried there: Eliza.

"Sweet girl, how strange I must look to you in these clothes." Annalisa sat upon the cool ground, worrying little for her breeches and wool stockings. "Uncle William is to be married this evening. That means your papa will be here to visit you, too." She hesitated. "You know he must live with his family...and Jane."

She shuddered at the mention of her older sister and withdrew the musket round kept within her pocket. The lead round heavy in her palm, Annalisa rolled it between her fingers, still stained with the dried blood of her shoulder.

"I think had I never fought at Bunker Hill dressed as I am, Lord and Lady Perkins would've allowed your papa and I to marry. We had to elope, you know." Annalisa tucked the round back into her pocket, then drew her initials in the dirt above Eliza's grave. She paused before carving the girl's father's.

J. P.

Annalisa blinked away the sting of tears for the husband she'd lost to her sister. She wiped her face, lingering over the healed scar beneath her right eye. "When this war is won, maybe then we shall be wed. What say you, darling girl?"

Silence pervaded the sacred hollow, and Annalisa stood. "'Tis as I thought. Your papa needs to learn of my secret. But that can't happen, beloved girl. Benjamin Cavendish is my crux to bear. I will not encumber him with the burden of such scandal, one that may endanger him as well."

Her brother's warning vibrated within, as it had these past several years: *"You will be charged with impersonation—and gaoled. At worst, hanged if you're found by the enemy. And I along with you for knowing."*

Annalisa lifted her musket and slung it over her shoulder. William's nuptials approached, and so did the arrival of guests —none of whom could see her masquerading as Benjamin in the refuge of her oak. She stripped from her coat and breeches, her waistcoat, cravat, and shirt, and placed the garments within her haversack. From a large grass frail propped beside her musket, she removed her front-lacing stays, petticoats, and dress—relics of her life outside the Continental Army and the militia.

A brisk autumn breeze puckered the skin beneath her shift as she donned her lady's garments, clothing that defined only part of her waking life—a life she could not fully live and enjoy to her content until the war ended. Already, three years had passed since the opening battles; perhaps many more years remained.

"Annie!" Mary's voice carried beneath the oak's canopy mere seconds before Annalisa's younger sister materialized. "Mamma's been wondering where you were. The Perkinses have arrived."

Annalisa's heart skipped with the anticipation of seeing Jack. She finished pinning her dress, gathered her belongings, and slung the musket over her shoulder.

"Is Will quite ready to marry?" Annalisa asked.

"Of course. Though he's disappointed George and Abbie won't be here to celebrate."

"He knows why they can't be here. 'Tis far too dangerous with Lord Essex in Cambridge."

They walked arm in arm from the protective shade of the tree, and across their family's farm until they reached the barn where William's wedding celebration would be held in tandem with the annual corn husking.

Parked in the drive, Annalisa noted the Perkinses two carriages as another chaise pulled alongside the second carriage.

"Tell Mamma I'll be inside presently." Annalisa kissed Mary's cheek and fled toward the barn.

Inside, she climbed into the garret and hid her haversack in a corner beneath some hay. She hurried back down the ladder and propped her musket on the wall where George's fowler once stayed. The absence of her beloved older brother loomed within the cavernous barn, an echo of the space he'd left when he fled to Portsmouth.

"Miss Annalisa."

Her heart skittered at the familiar baritone, and she turned.

Jack, the father of her miscarried daughter, stood in the barn entryway. His silk breeches clung to his shapely thighs—fitted but without restraint—yet such distractions rarely held hostage her audience quite like the marine-blue of eyes or dimpled smile he so freely offered her.

He removed his cocked hat and tucked it beneath his arm as he approached. "I've thought of you all day." He glanced about the barn, then returned his gaze to her. "I know I shouldn't speak so boldly given our circumstances, but you must know how you occupy my thoughts."

She returned his charming smile. "Likewise, sir."

Jack closed the distance between them and lifted her hand. "I received a letter from the general court. They've accepted my petition regarding Jane's presumed criminal conversation with Lord Essex. I was able to use her visit to Cambridge this past June as evidence."

"Then there is hope your divorce may be granted." Annalisa sighed. "Will you sue Essex, then, for damages done? Or merely challenge him?"

Jack chuckled, then pursed his fine lips to conceal a smirk. "I'd relish in dueling the viscount. But I may retain my gentle-manly honor if I sue him, though I needn't his money, nor the unpleasant salacious gossip of such a case. I know my parents would appreciate my keeping this entire charade as concealed as possible." His thumb rippled across her knuckles. "'Tis a complicated process, dear heart, made more unclear by the revocation of Massachusetts' charter. I've relayed the predica-ment to fellow law students with whom I graduated from

Harvard, and 'tis murky to them as well, whether I should pursue the case in Massachusetts or take it to England."

"England," Annalisa cried. "While we're at war with them?"

"Aye. But there, I may also attempt to pursue annulment through the ecclesiastical courts."

She remained silent, contemplating the possibility of again losing him to the ocean.

"They will grant it, dear heart. Then we, too, may have our day."

"Again." She cracked a smile.

His cheeks dimpled with a crooked grin. "Yes, again."

"I suppose I'm grateful you're a lawyer with an ample inheritance to pursue such a costly endeavor. Such would be nigh impossible for someone of working-class stature." Annalisa softened at his charming affect. "But if you must venture to England—"

"I will take you with me."

Their forms, mere inches apart, drew nearer until the scent of his amber perfume had wrapped itself entirely about her. Without regard for propriety, her lips found his, and the world ceased to turn about them. Sweet and with a hint of tobacco upon his tongue, Jack tasted as she remembered. Swept in the romance of his embrace, they could've been anywhere but her family's barn. If anything, she conjured the night they had eloped to George's tavern in Portsmouth. Jack was her rightful husband, no matter the legality of what the Marriage Act of 1753 had writ into law.

"Annalisa Howlett!"

She pulled from Jack to face the doorway...and the intruder.

2

ANNALISA

TOPSFIELD, OCTOBER 1778

A TALL, BROODING FIGURE loomed in the entryway. His black hair, tied in a queue, swept over his shoulder as he removed his cocked hat and stepped inside.

"George!" Annalisa leapt into her older brother's arms. "Whatever are you doing here? I thought you and Abbie would remain at the Black Water."

"Fie." George bellowed a deep guffaw as he set her down. "I could hardly miss *Wilhelmina's* wedding." He eyed Jack. "Abbie is in the house with your parents, Cousin."

"'Tis been too long." Jack embraced his cousin. "It does me well to see you."

Annalisa appraised her half-brother's commanding form and pondered how alike he must look to his natural father, Captain Bixby, Mamma's first husband, who died at sea. "You look well, Brother. William will be glad to celebrate with you."

George strode toward one of the kegs assembled near the great pile of corn to be husked that evening. Beside the stacked kegs stood a table with cleaned pewter, tin, and ceramic mugs. He retrieved three, tapped the first keg, and poured them each a mugful of cider.

"To William and Martha." George raised his mug. "Sluice your gob, rogues."

Annalisa laughed and clanked her tin cup to Jack's and George's. "To William and Martha."

⁂

THE BARN, FRAGRANT OF WARM CINNAMON, SPICY CLOVE, and woodsmoke, buzzed with murmurs and laughter for the happy couple. Jack's bow glided over his fiddle, and William and Martha spun about the room with rosy cheeks and crooked grins. Annalisa watched her brother and smiled. Her gentle younger brother had been through much, having been imprisoned at Fort Ticonderoga. *How happy he is. He deserves this night more than any of us.*

Abigail's slight hand gripped her wrist. "George is always content to leave me wanting to dance while he drowns himself in cider and ale."

"George has always abhorred dancing." Annalisa laughed. "You know that, friend."

"La!" Abigail's freckled cheeks flushed. "Friend, indeed. You need call me *sister* once you and Jack are again married. He told me about the petition to divorce Jane. I pray the courts grant him thus."

"Jack has much against her in the way she absconded from town with Lord Essex back in June with the children."

"Aye, my Lord Essex, whom I, too, need divorce. He and I have both strayed from our marriage bed." Her friend shuddered, then tucked a loose lock of blond hair into her cap. "Pray, he has much of the same accusations upon me since I abandoned our marriage and leapt the sword with George.

Think you Essex will pursue me and bring me back to his bed and board?"

Annalisa gripped Abigail's hand. "We will do everything in our power to prevent that from happening."

Abigail offered a reluctant smile, then glanced across the room at her brother, who continued to play his fiddle with the other musicians. "Jack so adores music. Would that his son learns to play with as much *joie de vivre* as him."

Jack's adept fingers slid over the neck of his violin. The refined yet coquettish sound sent a quiver down Annalisa's spine. Lost in his playing, her gaze drifted to her older sister, Jane, who nuzzled her son Robby—the boy Jack sired.

"I would coddle and dance with our sweet nephew, but I will not speak to Jane if I can help it," Annalisa said.

"The tart," Abigail sneered. "I can hardly blame you."

"If only your mamma and mine believed the evil she did me and my daughter," Annalisa whispered. "I miscarried Eliza because of the pennyroyal Jane placed in the tea. You were there; you witnessed everything."

Abigail frowned. "I shall never forget that day. I daresay we needn't trust our own mothers. Mine has been most vocal about my returning to Lord Essex despite his cruelty and infidelity."

The room, already warm with the movement of dancers, further heated Annalisa's breast. "But your papa, he couldn't possibly agree with such a notion."

"My papa is the one who agrees with her," Abigail cried. "They've not spoken to me once this evening. Not even to Louisa, their own granddaughter." Annalisa's niece, Louisa, jumped about and danced with the bride and bridegroom.

On his way toward them, George kissed Louisa's cheek, and offered Abigail a mug full of fermented cider. "My lovely mort, you're looking grim. You need more libations."

"Only if it means you'll dance the next with me, George Howlett," Abigail replied.

George's green eyes glittered, and he guffawed. "I'm disguised enough to stumble my way through a reel." He turned and shouted, "Perkins, a cotillion."

Annalisa laughed. "You said a reel, not a cotillion."

With a shrug, George finished his drink, wrapped an arm about Abigail, then hauled her toward the set of dancers.

From the musicians, Jack offered his violin to another, and hurried toward Annalisa. "Dance the next with me, dear heart."

His hand, warm from extensive playing, encircled hers, and he led her to the set lining up in the middle of the room.

"Will it be a reel or a cotillion?" Annalisa asked with a laugh.

Jack shrugged as he stood beside George, who wobbled in place awaiting the music. The first strings sounded, and Jack leaned in. "'Tis George Washington's favorite cotillion, 'Corn Rigs are Bonny.'"

Giddy, and with little regard for the disapproving stares of her parents and his, Annalisa tossed her head back in laughter. She would face the gossiping mouths of their friends and family tomorrow. For now, Annalisa set her sight on Jack and his crooked, dimpled grin.

When the dance ended, they all clapped and Jack tugged her from the set. "Let's to the oak before anyone notices our absence." His deep blue eyes glittered from too much cider.

"You're as disguised as George," Annalisa giggled. "Whatever do you wish of me within the confines of our oak?"

"To hold your private audience before more time is stolen from us."

Tittering, they snuck toward the barn doorway and outside into the chilled October night. Overhead, a near-full moon crested the horizon, illuminating the farm in milky glow. In the dim light, Jack's lips found hers and drowned her in the sweetly fermented cider saturating his tongue. She gripped his coat, pulling him closer.

"Let's to the oak, dear heart." Jack's lips brushed her ear, and she shivered. "Before my father discovers us and accuses me of being a pert jackanapes."

"Fie. Your papa would never use such invective language toward you."

In a mockery of Lord Perkins, Jack tensed his brow and spoke like his father, *"Your behavior was that of a pert jackanapes. For shame, Jackie."*

"I suppose you are rather cheeky." Annalisa pinched his face. "But a jackanapes? If there's one thing you're not, 'tis impertinent."

"If being impertinent means I may spend this moment with you, then let me always be a jackanapes." His mouth drifted across hers, and she closed her eyes, if only to conjure a memory of when those same lips caressed her neck, her breast...

"Soon, we needn't conceal our affection, Annie." Jack pressed her against the barn. "I'll be yours and you'll be mine, and we'll be surrounded by our fifteen children—"

"Fifteen!" Annalisa pulled from him, chuckling. "You'll have me busy, Mr. Perkins."

Jack laughed. "I'll compromise to ten."

"Five."

"As you wish, my darling girl." He found her mouth once more, and she melted against his form. "Please let me have you this night."

His turgid member concealed in breeches pressed against her, and Annalisa tugged him from the barn. "To the oak, then, sir."

The moon as their guide, they crossed the fields until they

reached the shady oak. Beneath its vast canopy, shreds of moonlight streamed through its branches and colorful leaves, many of which carpeted the ground on which they stood.

Jack removed his coat and placed it on a blanket of fallen leaves. She knelt beside him and allowed him to lay her upon the garment. Eager to accept him, she unbuttoned his breeches as he lifted her petticoats. The act, no different than any other intimate moment they'd spent as husband and wife, though brief it was, filled her with desperation. He was her husband, the man she vowed to love and cherish all her days until death parted them.

And yet death had parted them.

At least in presumption when their ship to France capsized and she had been presumed dead.

The zenith of their efforts peaked in an amalgamation of time lost and spent on one another, as Annalisa, with legs wrapped about him, gripped the back of his waistcoat, and he collapsed atop her.

Jack flopped onto the fallen leaves, his chest rising and falling in short gasps. "'Tis unimaginable, our pleasure, Annalisa."

She covered herself with her petticoats and rolled onto her side, facing him. "Would that we needn't conceal it."

"Soon, dear heart. Then we'll give Eliza a brother and sister to watch over." Jack kissed her and buttoned his breeches.

Annalisa sat upright and studied the shadowy space beneath the tree where their daughter lay. "Would that you gave me a child this night."

Jack wrapped an arm about her. "I will pray."

"Pray not to our God. He has done little for us these years."

"I'll pray to whomever listens," he replied. "You know that."

Annalisa studied the perfect symmetry of his face illuminated in moonlight. She kissed the tip of his straight nose and smiled. "We need return. Else we'll be missed."

"One moment more." He glanced at the gravesite that kept their daughter. "She would've been a wonderful sister to Robby."

No amount of bargaining could bring back their miscarried daughter, and no amount of hatred toward her sister could atone for Jane's actions. But her sister remained within the barn with all of town, their families celebrating William and Martha's wedding. They need return, lest they be counted as missing. Gossip enough flew from the tongues of most in town, but they need not add to what most presumed.

Annalisa stood and offered her love a hand. He lifted from the ground and kissed her forehead. "You and I shall marry again, legally. I swear it upon my life and our dear Eliza."

"I believe you, John Jackson."

He grinned and led them from the sheltering sanctuary of their sacred tree. "When we marry, this country will be ours, dear heart. The war will be won and all our efforts will have been worthwhile."

"I pray 'tis so."

They walked in silence until they neared the barn. In the drive, an elaborate carriage was parked that hadn't been there earlier. Annalisa gripped Jack's hand.

"What is it, dear heart?"

She hissed, "'Tis Lord Essex's coach."

❦ 3 ❦

ANNALISA

TOPSFIELD, OCTOBER 1778

LORD ESSEX STEPPED FROM the carriage wearing his finest ditto suit of lavender silk. As he caught sight of Jack the viscount grinned, deepening his chin divot. Jack's grip tightened about Annalisa's hand.

"Mr. Perkins, Miss Annalisa. How pleasant to see you together." Lord Essex bowed.

Jack shielded her from him. "Whyever have you come here, my lord?"

The viscount chuckled. "I was invited, of course. I can hardly refuse an invitation to celebrate young love in marriage. You must know I've also come to collect my wife, your sister."

"Abigail is not here, my lord," Jack lied.

"Of course she is." Lord Essex glared at Annalisa. "She's within, consorting with your brother, Miss Annalisa. Now, if it please you, step aside and allow me to claim what is lawfully mine."

Jack blocked the barn entryway. "I can't allow it of you, sir."

"You dare to insult me, Perkins?"

"If you recall this past June, my lord, you stole *my* wife to your home on Tory Row," Jack replied. "I have as much reason to challenge you, sir, as you have of challenging George Howlett."

"Capital." Lord Essex chuckled. "I don't wish to duel either of you."

Jack's cheeks reddened with indignance. "Then I should like to challenge you, sir."

"Jack, no," Annalisa hissed. "'Tis not worth it."

Mamma and Papa stepped from the barn with Jack's parents behind them. Lord Perkins guided Lady Perkins to greet the viscount, their son-in-law.

Mamma's hand flew to her breast. "My goodness, Lord Essex, how wonderful of you to come."

"What are these scurrilous remarks upon you, my lord?" Lord Perkins asked.

The viscount acknowledged Lord Perkins, then smirked at Jack. "Come now, Mr. Perkins, let's settle this as gentlemen, shall we? I make no claims of taking your wife as my mistress when she visited Tory Row. As you remember, Miss Mary Howlett accompanied her. But may I remind you, 'tis a most natural arrangement for a husband to take a mistress," he glanced at Annalisa, "as you've done here, sir, is it not?"

Jack bared his teeth. "Careful how you go with such polemical rhetoric, my lord. Or, I shall challenge you—"

"Jack," Lady Perkins gasped. "Jane has been a most faithful wife to you."

Mamma added, "You know my Janey. She would never engage in so degrading an act as would compromise her reputation."

"You know 'tis not true, Mamma." Annalisa crumpled her skirts and regarded Papa. "Papa, please listen. You know what Jane did to me—"

"Enough." Mamma grabbed her wrist and tugged her

forward. "Go retrieve Abigail for the viscount, and let this unsavory charade be done. 'Tis your brother's wedding."

Her heart rattled, and she faced Jack's father. "Please, Lord Perkins, do not send Abbie and Louisa back to Tory Row with Lord Essex—"

"Miss Annalisa, I've agreed to stand Moses to the merry-begotten," Lord Essex said.

Jack lunged at the viscount. "That *merry-begotten* is my niece."

Lord Perkins pulled Jack from Lord Essex. "Enough!"

"Louisa belongs to George and Abbie, my lord," Annalisa said. "Please allow my brother the honor of raising his own daughter."

From the dark drive, a horse whinnied, then galloped into the night. Lord Essex turned at the sound and chuckled. "I suppose that was my Lady Essex and her paramour a-horseback."

Lady Perkins bit her lip. "Abigail is no daughter of mine."

Mamma and Papa inched toward the barn door until Mamma extended a deflated gesture for the viscount to accompany them into the barn.

"My apologies, my lord, for such an inhospitable welcome to William and Martha's wedding," Papa said. "Do come inside and enjoy the rest of the festivities."

"We've plenty of libations, and my Janey and Mary will be most obliged to your company, as always, sir," Mamma added, and looked to Lady Perkins. "Bette, will you join us?"

"Yes, of course." Lady Perkins nodded for her husband to lead Jack inside the barn with him behind Lord Essex, Mamma, and Papa. Annalisa followed Jack and his father, but Lady Perkins's hand found her wrist.

Startled, she turned. "My lady?"

Lady Perkins smoothed the wrinkles from her lavender silk skirts. Her blond curls whispered hints of silver, as

Mamma's, but the effect proved regal rather than aged. Lady Perkins adjusted her coffee-eyed gaze, and Annalisa thought she could be looking upon dearest Abigail twenty years from now.

"Miss Annalisa, I want to begin by telling you I'm flattered by your...determination for Jack." A wistful smile lifted her lips. "I don't doubt you may love him—"

"I do, marm, with every bit of myself—"

"Silence." Lady Perkins held up a gloved hand. "You may speak when I'm finished."

Annalisa's breast tightened.

"I've wanted nothing but grand things for my firstborn son." She smiled. "But as he grew into a boy, it became apparent to me he would be uncommonly handsome and a favorite among Society's young ladies. This would be his Achilles' heel, Miss Annalisa. It is a power men hold over us. To detract from this, I needed to secure for him the correct lady, one who would inherit his titles with him; one who could be presented beside him and not dishonor him or his name. A lady who was bred for him."

Annalisa shivered. "Jane?"

Lady Perkins nodded. "Jane. His *wife*."

Her hands trembling, Annalisa's hand slipped into her pocket and fiddled with her musket round from Bunker Hill.

"After the death of George's natural father, my beloved brother and your mamma's first husband, I promised your mother I would marry Jack to her firstborn daughter. 'Twas the least I could do in my brother's absence. So I sent the means necessary to fund Jane's education at Salem." Lady Perkins avoided her stare. "You can imagine my utter chagrin when Jack met and chose you. All our work and planning for naught—" She smoothed her skirts once more. "Forgive me. I don't wish to sound bitter. You are a passionate young lady but your dalliance with Jack must end."

"But he's seeking a divorce—"

"He will not obtain it."

"My lady, how can you be certain?"

"Because Lord Perkins was a magistrate in Boston. He will not let that kind of gossip ruin our family's reputation."

Annalisa crossed her arms. "And what of Lord Essex and Jane's dalliance? Care you so little for that charade?"

Lady Perkins shook her head. "Lord Essex will do as he may, but your sister understands she may not engage with him."

"How can you presume to know the inner workings of my sister's mind? I know Jane better than anyone, and I hardly understand her. But I do know she is conniving and will stop at nothing to gain influence for herself in Society. 'Tis the one thing she's coveted our entire lives. And I know one thing for certain, my lady, is that Jack's inheritance, while ample, will not tempt her so much as Lord Essex's influences in Parliament."

Lady Perkins chuckled. "How little you fathom. Jack is to inherit both his father's and his uncle's estates. Lord Brunswick is dying, Miss Annalisa, and when he does pass, which may be quite soon, Jack will inherit his title as Earl of Brunswick, all his land, and his position in Parliament."

"Then my sister will have reason enough to forgo any dalliance she may have with Lord Essex. Is that correct, Lady Perkins?"

"Quite."

"You are incorrect, my lady. Jane covets Lord Essex's acquaintances and connections in Society...London's *ton*, none of whom are connected to Jack. Jane will continue to consort with Lord Essex, no matter his marriage to Abigail, and no matter her own marriage to Jack."

Lady Perkins sneered. "You will quit your attachment to

Jack forthwith, Annalisa Howlett, and you will marry someone else."

"Marry who, my lady?" Annalisa cried. "Who will have me as I am? Surely, you must know Jack and I created a daughter. 'Twas at your house that I miscarried—"

"Silence!" Lady Perkins's cheeks reddened. "Don't test me, Miss Annalisa. You may have powerful friends from your time in London with the Duchess of Devonshire, but I, too, have connections beyond yours."

"Is that a threat, *my lady*?"

Lady Perkins stepped toward her, close enough to choke Annalisa with her orange blossom perfume. "Refuse to marry, and you shall rue the day you ever set eyes upon Jack."

"And if I do refuse to marry another?"

Her countenance remained smooth, though her cheeks pinked with indignance. "I swear to you upon my own mother's soul, if you do not marry and leave my family be, I will have this entire farmstead burned to the ground."

Annalisa's faced numbed, her anger vanishing. "But my mamma is your f-friend."

"Your mamma owes me a debt, and would never dare question me." Lady Perkins turned toward the barn as Mamma stepped outside.

"Ah, there you are, Bette."

Lady Perkins smiled. "I was just speaking to Miss Annalisa about the fortuitous prospect of sending her to Philadelphia. Lord Perkins has made a friend of Chief Justice Shippen during his time at Congress. I'm certain Lord Essex would accept chaperoning the visit."

Mamma clapped her hands. "Oh, what a wonderful opportunity. Annie, you might meet an eligible gentleman acquainted with the Shippens. An advantageous marriage, indeed. Bette, think you my Mary and Janey may travel thither as well? Mary, too, need be married."

"Of course. Anything I may do to ensure the prosperous futures of your fine girls." Lady Perkins clasped Mamma's hand. "I'm happy to oblige."

Trembling, Annalisa rolled the Bunker Hill musket round nestled within her pocket between her fingers and watched Lady Perkins disappear inside the barn with Mamma. Her family's home and livelihood now rested in the crux of Lady Perkins's threats for her to marry, a stake she could hardly refuse in the light of Jack's divorce crusade. Her own selfish pursuits of love and happiness were now no longer hers, but tied to the well-being of her beloved family and homestead.

A pit formed in Annalisa's stomach for the sacrifice she now faced, one unbeknownst to Jack. And he could never know the terrible threat incurred upon her by his own mother. She could, and never would, place herself between him and his family, especially now that he had a son to raise. If she quit her attachment for Jack, Annalisa could not only save her family's farm, but would preserve the family in which her dear nephew, Robby, lived.

A chilled ebbed its way down her spine at the prospect before her. Yes, she would go to Philadelphia if it was required of her, for she held no other choice, unlike Abigail, who had just fled the farm with George. If only she had gone with them, escaped to Portsmouth and her brother's Black Water Inn.

❧ 4 ❧

GEORGE

PORTSMOUTH, THE PROVINCE OF NEW HAMPSHIRE, NOVEMBER 1778

GEORGE STOOD BEHIND THE green-painted bar at the Black Water Inn. He cleaned a stack of pewter tankards with a linen towel and strained to overhear the murmurs of patrons seated about the main tavern room. Most of these intercourses failed to rise above the constant ringing in his ears—a consequence of war's abuses—which, strangely, piqued his yearning for battle. If only is oldest friend, Samuel Wildes, had not succumbed to his wounds at Kip's Bay. *Wildes would have endured the war to the bitter end.*

A gust of chilled autumn air broke him from his charge as a gentleman, perhaps a few years older than he, stepped inside the tavern and closed the door. He doffed his black beaver felt hat, and bowed. "Mr. Howlett."

"Mr. Peirce." George leaned over the bar to glean a better view of the main tavern room. "Your table is available, sir. Will Mr. Wentworth be joining you?"

"Wentworth is away on business in Philadelphia. Just one pitcher of flip will do." Mr. Peirce tossed two shillings onto the bar and sauntered into the room.

George slid the pieces into his cash box. Peirce and his

friend Wentworth were two of the few patrons who still paid with British coinage. For that, they earned the more expensive rum—six pounds per gallon, to be precise—from the West Indies.

He retrieved the poker from the hearth. Still glowing red, George used the iron rod to mix the rum with his house ale, molasses, and a beaten egg. The beverage nicely frothed, he poured the flip into a pitcher and grated nutmeg over top.

"Flip for Mr. Peirce," George hollered to his potboy.

The young master hurried from the kitchen and retrieved the pitcher from the bar.

Elisha Porter, his hired tavern-keep, followed the potboy from the kitchen and stepped behind the bar. "Are you quite finished, Mr. G?"

"Aye." His friend Samuel still on his mind, George grabbed a bottle of cheap New-England rum from a shelf adjacent to the pewter, and set it on the counter. A swift uncorking, followed by a long pour into his tin cup, he offered Elisha a glass, then toasted to his deceased friend. "Fill to me the parting glass, Wildes." In a single gulp, George downed the measure.

Elisha sipped his rum while opening a large leather tome. His umber fingers grazed the ink until he found for what he searched. "This, here."

George leaned over and read two lines. "Fie. 'Tis what we've been paying since the act of the Assembly established them. The days of paying sixteen shillings per bushel of barley or three pounds a gallon for molasses are long gone." He closed the ledger. "A year ago, our Continental dollars were near equal to the silver pound. This morning, I read in the *Gazette* that four hundred dollars of our Continental paper is now worth one hundred British pounds of silver. 'Tis worthless. Imagine how much more so 'twill be by the war's end."

Elisha removed his new spectacles and rubbed his eyes. "I know not whether we can keep the inn open, sir."

George poured himself a second bumper and silently saluted Samuel. "I thought patronage has been better of late." He peered about the room full of guests, many of whom played cribbage and whist. "There's not a seat to be found. And a few still pay with shillings."

"Yes." Elisha leaned in close. "But we must charge more for flip and mince pies—and ale."

George finished his second drink, then set the cup onto the bar with a clash. He lowered his bass voice to a murmur, "I'm keen on raising prices, but I fear it may ward off our special...clientele. We're the last haven in Portsmouth for these Loyalist reptiles."

He rubbed his forehead as he took in the scene of his largest tavern room. Flames from new beeswax candles danced upon the walls as utterings from Portsmouth's elite filled the smoky air. Down the hall, to the right of the bar and the stairs was a smaller card room and, through another door, a third room of equal size. The second and third floors each contained four rooms for sleeping, usually two to four patrons per room, each paying eight shillings a night; ten if they wished for a hot meal at supper and breakfast.

With a shake of his head, George poured himself a third bumper. "I don't see how we're barely making enough to run this place."

"'Tis the cost of goods, Mr. G. I've seen merchants at the docks increase their prices, and we've done little to augment ours. 'Tis advantageous we host wealthy patrons, but 'tis not enough, sir."

The front door opened, and Abigail hurried inside with Louisa at her hip. She latched the door shut and hastened toward them. Smiling, she sat her basket upon the wooden bar, and their two-year-old daughter beside it. "How good to see you, Elisha."

The tavern-keep nodded. "Ma'am."

"George, look what we've bought today."

Louisa's chubby hand reached into the basket and grabbed a fistful of silky colorful strands.

He glowered. "Ribbons?"

"But look at the assortment of colors," Abigail cried. "Now, I may decorate Louisa's dresses and hats, as well as my own—"

"Pray, how much does a milliner charge for such frivolity?"

Abigail's freckled cheeks reddened. "I paid five shillings—"

"Fie! Five shillings? When I charge eight for a room?" George poured himself a fourth bumper. "You need remember, you neither live as Lord Essex's wife nor with your father's finances to support you."

She crossed her arms. "By the grace of God—"

"Abbie, my inheritance is far from what you're accustomed to. I told you this when we leapt the sword. I'm no plum like the viscount Essex. Neither am I a magistrate like your father. I own an inn—"

"With an inheritance of fifteen hundred pounds per annum." Abigail snatched the ribbons from Louisa's hand and tossed them into the basket. "'Tis more than enough. But if you'd rather I return the one luxury I've allowed myself in months, then I shall."

George ground his teeth until his temples throbbed. The unlikely inheritance he'd received from his deceased father, Captain Bixby, would only get him so far. Yes, fifteen hundred pounds per annum was a heaping of wealth of which he'd never dreamed, nor imagined. But the money wouldn't last forever, not with the inflated dollars he poured into the inn.

Elisha winked at Louisa, then regarded Abigail, who fidgeted with the pins in her bodice. "Surely, there's little need to return your ribbons, ma'am. Mr. G has agreed to raise the prices of ale, mince pies, and flip."

George was about to contest, but the front door opened once more. Another gust of chilly November wind blew inside as his younger brother, William, ushered himself indoors with their youngest brother, Henry, Mary's twin.

"Zounds, *Wilhelmina*!" George rounded the bar, grabbed William's hat, and tossed it.

William groaned, retrieved his hat, and set it on the bar beside Louisa and the basket of ribbons. After acknowledging Elisha, his niece, and Abigail, he scowled at George. "When will you cease calling me thus?"

George guffawed. "'Tis been since you were born, so by my head, never." He then hugged Henry, a strapping young lad of sixteen. "'Tis always jarring to see you, Brother, without Mary beside you."

Henry chuckled, then lowered his hazel gaze. "Aye, 'tis why we came."

Abigail cocked her head. "Is there something the matter with Mary?"

Henry shook his head. "Nothing to fear, per se, but—"

"Annalisa and Mary have gone to Philadelphia with Lord Essex," William cried.

"Well, I'll be damned," George boomed.

"Nothing to fear?" Abigail shrieked. "Henry Howlett, how can you say such a thing? You know nothing of the man he is."

"Peace, Abigail." Henry glanced about the tavern. "Come, let us upstairs to speak privately."

George led them from the tavern, up the stairs to the third floor, and down the hall to the room Annalisa frequented when she stayed. Inside, he latched the door and faced his brothers.

"Now, speak your troth, Henry Howlett," George growled. "I need know what transpired to place our sisters in that cock robin's good graces."

"They traveled thither with Lord Essex and Jane," Henry replied.

"Pray, my brother went with them as well?" Abigail gripped her bodice. "Jack and my father must be with them."

William shook his head. "No, Jack remained in Topsfield. He's awaiting more news from the courts."

George ground his teeth. "Whom are they visiting at Philadelphia that Mother and Pa have deemed worthy of Essex as chaperone?"

"The Shippens," Henry replied.

"They're Loyalist," Abigail said.

"But the Continentals have overtaken Philadelphia," George said. "Benedict Arnold was recently made military governor of the city."

"Aye, that much is also true," Henry said. "Which is why I can trust Mary and Annalisa will not be in harm's way."

"And you say Jane is with them?" Abigail shuddered. "That harpy dares to further cuckold my brother. Would that the courts swiftly grant him the divorce he seeks."

"I've kept an open ear at the Whispering Willow tavern in town," Henry added quickly. "Should I hear of any chicanery regarding Lord Essex and his wavering allegiances from Patriot to Loyalist causes, or of Jane's proclivity for adultery, I will notify whom I must."

George deliberated upon the harried countenance of his brothers and Abigail. They had swiftly escaped William's wedding when Lord Essex surprised them all with his unwanted presence. But now, the dandy prat chaperoned his dear sisters. Surely, the plum meant to study their loyalties and place them in harm's way as a means of retaliation for taking Abigail from him.

George's jaw tightened at the thought of Annalisa, vulnerable and unattached from Jack, at the calculated whim of Lord Essex and his Loyalist Philadelphia acquaintances, the Shippens. Would that his cousin were there to ensure her safety.

❦ 5 ❦

JACK

TOPSFIELD, NOVEMBER 1778

S AT ATOP A MODEST hill, his family's yellow clapboard house rose into view as his coach pulled down the drive toward the carriage house. The ride from New Castle in New Hampshire proved long and tedious, but the home he'd been planning to build overlooking the ocean now had a foundation. If only he hadn't lost these few weeks away from town, and Annalisa. Would that she'd been able to accompany him, to see the summer home he hoped she'd one day inhabit with him.

The horses snorted and snuffled as Wheaton, Father's coachman, handed him from the vehicle. Jack clutched his hat against a blast of November wind as he hurried up the walkway, where Mercy opened the door to the grand house he called home.

"May I take your hat, Mr. Perkins?"

"Thank you, Mercy." He offered her his cocked hat and walked into the parlor.

Lounged upon a blue damask settee positioned beneath two large windows, his younger brother, Oliver, threw down his book and kissed his son Tommy's forehead.

"You've returned. Go give Uncle Jack a kiss." The toddler ran to Jack.

Jack kissed his nephew's cheek. "Young master, you've grown these last two weeks. Were you a good boy for your father and mother?"

"Yes." Tommy offered a meek smile.

Oliver tousled the boy's flaxen hair, an image of his own, then chuckled. "The boy's mother left for Philadelphia a week ago."

Jack's breath caught. "Jane's gone to Philadelphia? With whom? Pray tell, it wasn't Viscount Essex, was it?"

"Aye, of course," Oliver scoffed. "Who better than Lord Essex to acquaint her with Father's friend Chief Justice Shippen?"

Jack burned from the heat rising up his neck. "Where's Father?"

"In his study." Oliver flicked a piece of lint from his breeches. "Brother, all will be well. The magistrates will grant your divorce. They've no reason to deny it."

"Her frequent visits with Essex make her adultery all the more damning. Though, it would be made easier if you would remarry Jane."

Oliver shook his head. "Not after all she's done."

Jack twisted his signet ring. "Jane's character never bothered you before."

"I was a juvenile. I knew little of women or their schemes." Oliver paused. "A lot has changed these eight years."

"Indeed." Jack tugged on his lower lip. "I still struggle believing you're Patriot."

Oliver tucked a strand of blond hair behind his ear. "It took my being left for dead by those I deemed brethren for me to understand I was a mere body to waste in battle. My allegiance to King George made little difference so long as I fired a musket."

Bloodyback bastards. Would that Ollie's defection remain as steadfast as mine and George's allegiance to the cause. Would that Ollie had been a part of it with us from the beginning.

"My boys."

Father strolled into the parlor robed in a black ditto suit with a white silk stock fastened about his thickening neck. Forehead creases and smile lines traversed his face like well-patterned roads upon a storied map. His father's periwig affixed with care, Jack imagined him presiding upon the bench as magistrate at Boston's Queen-street courthouse, now a lifetime ago.

Jack's lips stirred with amusement at the old memory. "Pray, when did you allow Jane to leave for Philadelphia with Lord Essex?"

"I would've written, but I knew it mattered little since he meant to chaperone Mary and Annalisa Howlett." Father sat in his chair by the fireplace and drew up a white clay pipe. After several puffs, a twirl of tobacco smoke encircled Father's head.

Jack rose from the settee. "Pray, what?"

"Aye." Father expelled a tendril of smoke. "Annalisa and Mary Howlett have gone with Essex and Jane to Philadelphia to meet the Shippens."

Heat snaked up Jack's face, and his familial disdain for Oliver resurfaced. He faced his brother. "You knew the vile plum took Annalisa to Philadelphia with him, yet you failed to warn me?"

"Fie." Oliver's cheeks reddened, and he glared at Father. "I knew nothing of the sort."

Jack threw up his hands. "How could you not know? You've been to the meetinghouse this past Sunday. Saw you not Mary and Annalisa Howlett? You should've warned me in the first—"

"I didn't take note of their presence, I swear it," Oliver cried.

Father slammed the arm of his chair. "Enough." He set down his pipe on the cherry-wood table and stood. "I've heard enough. Both of you will listen to me, and you shall heed my warning. Has the viscount made some missteps? For certain. But Lord Essex has come to me and apologized for the incident in June with Jane—"

"But not to me," Jack cried. "He took my wife and son with him to Cambridge. Now, he has endangered Annalisa and Mary by bringing them to a Loyalist home in Philadelphia. I have a right mind to duel him when next we meet."

Father lifted his hand. "The viscount has denied any allegation of adultery, and I do believe him. He has little reason to cuckold his own brother-in-law when he himself has been cuckolded by George Howlett."

"All the more he may wish to slight the Howletts and our family," Jack shouted. "'Tis retaliation to further slander our family's good name."

"I do agree with Jack," Oliver said.

"Essex has little means to cuckold you, Jack. The viscount has explained his financial situation. He is in debt and could therefore not afford for you to sue him for damages in a criminal conversation case. The man humbled himself to show me his accounts ledger. I can't fault a man for his expenses, nor his hubris if he condescends himself for the sake of vanity. He has humbled himself most expeditiously. His taking the Howlett sisters to Philadelphia is as kind a gesture as any I've seen of the man, and I think it best for them to be acquainted with that society. Mr. and Mrs. Howlett agree."

Oliver scoffed.

Jack crossed his arms. "And, sir, what says Essex of his abuses toward our beloved sister, Abigail?"

The roads etched into Father's face twisted. "He denies it, of course. And I'm inclined to believe him, given the circumstances surrounding the merry-begotten."

"Fie." Jack approached Father. "You mean your granddaughter, Louisa? I understand little how you believe the viscount over your own daughter, sir. 'Tis unimaginable. And Louisa is innocent in all of it, no matter her parentage."

Again, Father's hand raised. "Unimaginable or no, the viscount is Abigail's lawful husband and shall decide whether or not he will have Abigail returned to him as his wife, Lady Essex. It would behoove him to maintain the marriage, though he has ample reason to divorce her."

"Then Lord Essex should divorce her for the affair." Jack adjusted the clock upon the mantel before meeting his father's stare. "The courts would grant him such a position, then she may wed George, Louisa's father."

"A position you still seek for yourself, I presume." Father unsuccessfully pulled from the pipe, then set it on the table. "These charades will cease. Abigail's done enough damage to the reputation of this family. As have you. Taking Annalisa Howlett as your mistress? How could you dishonor her in that way?"

"I've not taken her as my mistress—she was my wife, if you've forgotten, sir." Jack joined Oliver by the open windows. Not even the breeze wafting in from the gardens cooled him. "I've been favored by the court at Salem to proceed with obtaining my divorce. I need now decide the proper course to follow. I'm inclined to pursue the ecclesiastical courts at London, followed by parliamentary judiciary court. Then my marriage to Jane may be annulled as well."

Father re-lit his pipe, and a puff of smoke swirled about his head. The tobacco, a once comforting scent reminiscent of Father's study at the Queen-street courthouse, jaded Jack's childhood recollections. Concealing his chagrin behind a stony face, Jack leaned back and eyed Oliver, whose countenance proffered a similar disdain, having, too, fallen victim to Father's demands these few years.

Father's lips pursed as he removed an opened letter from his waistcoat pocket. "If you've well exhausted your hubris, Jack, I've unfortunate news to share." He set down his pipe and removed his spectacles. "Your uncle, Lord Brunswick, has finally succumbed to his long illness."

"How terrible." Jack hastened toward Father and read the letter. "I was always quite fond of Uncle. Pray, was it at least a peaceful passing?"

His father nodded and replaced his spectacles. "So says Catherine in her letter. I don't think you realize what you've just inherited."

"Brunswick's estate." Jack heated beneath his cravat, which threatened to choke him. He loosened the piece with two fingers. "I signed the paperwork. I know what I've inherited."

"Aye." Father grunted. "But with mine when I die, combined with your uncle's—Brunswick's is worth thrice mine—you needn't work a day in your life. You may flit off to whichever estate you choose, be it America or England. You know Brunswick owns at least two properties overseas. As Earl of Brunswick, you may even sit in Parliament, as he did."

The outrage returned to Jack, but this time it engulfed his face, leaving his cheeks hot and his temples throbbing. "Forgive me, sir, but why would I wish to sit in a government that opposes the very one we're trying to build here? That is not a life I wish for myself. I'm Patriot, as are you. As was Uncle."

"Yes, you know where my allegiances lie, but you're a fool if you do not assume your uncle's position of power.

Brunswick was wildly influential in Parliament and among the Whigs. As is Lord Essex, if you recall."

Viscount Essex, the Whig supporter and abusive husband to his dear sister Abigail. The reptile resided at Tory Row, mere houses away from Lord Brunswick and Aunt Catherine. Jack set his jaw, determined to excise Lord Essex from his life.

Oliver asked, "How fares Aunt Catherine?"

"My sister is well taken care of," Father replied. "Brunswick left her their home on Tory Row and a sum of eight thousand pounds per annum in his will."

Jack turned his signet ring. Perhaps with his uncle's inheritance and position in the House of Lords, he could further influence the Whig party. *I can journey to England and complete this divorce and annulment with Annalisa by my side. She knows the Duchess of Devonshire; her husband, the duke, is a powerful Whig supporter.*

His flame brightened at the prospect. Venturing to England seemed more agreeable than not, so long as he could travel with Annalisa and Robby.

Old anxieties from his shipwreck swiftly washed over him. *How can I entertain a trip across the Atlantic after suffering such tragedy two years ago? And can I convince Annalisa to join me upon her return home from Philadelphia?*

Jack shook away the thought and determined to contrive a plan that encompassed his quest for freedom, both in the colony and in his marriage. One that brought Annalisa back to him. He need only tell her the news and book them passage on a ship to London.

6

ANNALISA

PHILADELPHIA, NOVEMBER 1778

TUCKED ALONG THE DELAWARE River with cobbled streets and brick rowhouses, Philadelphia reminded Annalisa of Boston, yet without the bittersweet memories to accompany it. Though she'd only been there twice, she yearned for the town in which she'd first met Jack mere days before the fateful Boston Massacre. Her hands chilled with a frigid memory of the oysters and ice she'd lobbed at the British soldiers that day.

As she and Mary walked arm in arm behind Lord Essex and Jane, no such recollections greeted her in Philadelphia, only new acquaintances and opportunities. *And a potential husband, I suppose.* Her intercourse with Lady Perkins surfaced, melting away the Boston Massacre and that cold March evening with torrid indignation. *No, 'tis for my family I sacrifice myself.*

With her free hand, she reached into her pocket and handled the musket round. A knot of guilt twisted her insides for having left Topsfield without seeing Jack before he returned from New Castle. With not even a letter from her to read, she contemplated the confusion and anxiety he was sure to feel upon learning of her trip to Philadelphia with Lord Essex.

She peered at Mary, who's pleasant countenance bore no sign of trepidation. Her dear sister, though still shorter than she, had blossomed into a lovely young lady of sixteen. Annalisa's heart trembled with the melancholy of having missed Mary's debut last year.

Mary caught her stare. "Think you we'll find husbands here?"

Ahead of them, Jane, clutching Lord Essex's arm, glanced back with a smile. "'Tis only a matter of time, dear Mary. Annie, you too will make a perfect match with some gentleman of Society. It seems you proved your worth quite readily during your stay in London. You've come far from the days of enticing a gentleman farmer from Boxford."

Annalisa bristled, but callously returned Jane's smile. Her "stay in London" with the Duke and Duchess of Devonshire had been an accident following her shipwreck—fortuitous, for sure, but an accident nonetheless. *I'm grateful Georgiana took pity on my unconscious self upon that pier in Calais. Else I'd have perished.*

They arrived outside a three-story brick house, and Jane whirled about. Her face, an ode to Pacioli's divine proportion, lifted into a countenance even more beautiful than nature intended. Her unblemished porcelain cheeks flushed pink as springtime roses.

In her delicate soprano, Jane lilted, "You must put on your finest airs, ladies. The Shippens have been so kind to host us for dinner, and I've been told there will also be eligible gentlemen present."

Ignoring Jane, Annalisa ran her hands over her green silk skirts, her most cherished gown gifted to her by the Duchess of Devonshire. She bit her lip, then quoted Abigail to Mary, "Chin up, shoulders back, and smile."

Lord Essex knocked on the door.

A portly female housekeeper answered. "Right this way, my lord." Taking the viscount's cocked hat and walking stick, she led their party into an ornately papered parlor with white wainscoting, brass sconces, and a dangling crystal chandelier. Stately green velvet curtains draped tall white windows. Dried late-summer roses, stuffed into porcelain vases—no doubt plucked from the vast gardens abutting the home—would have perfumed the room had they visited in summer. Such opulence, reminiscent of Devonshire House in London, rattled Annalisa's breast with a longing for her noble friend, Georgiana.

Chief Justice Shippen, a pale-skinned gentleman nearing fifty, sported a curling white periwig and prominent nose. He rose from a wingback chair and bowed. "My Lord Essex, I am your most obedient servant."

"Sir, you humble me." The viscount returned his gesture, then regarded his party. "May I present Mrs. Perkins—Lord Perkins's daughter-in-law—and her two younger sisters, Miss Annalisa Howlett and Miss Mary Howlett."

Shippen motioned to the lovely young lady behind him. "My youngest daughter, Miss Peggy Shippen."

The girl's rosy complexion and delicately upturned nose certainly rivaled Jane in exquisiteness. Peggy's dark, inquisitive eyes offered a good-natured appraisal of their party as she floated forward, as graceful as the women Annalisa had observed of London's *ton*.

"Miss Annalisa, your gown is breathtaking," Peggy said. "I must have the name of your mantua maker this instant, else I'll go mad."

Jane's full lips pursed, then she smiled; an accomplished mask of pleasantry to conceal her envy—one Annalisa knew all too well.

"I thank you kindly, Miss Peggy, but I unfortunately

can't divulge that information, as I'm ignorant of it," Annalisa replied. "'Twas a gift from the Duchess of Devonshire."

"The Duchess of Devonshire?" Peggy separated Annalisa from her sisters and drew her to one of the green damask sofas. The girl's rose-and-bergamot perfume, similar to the one Abigail wore, wafted over Annalisa as she settled beside Peggy on the couch. "How did you become acquainted with Her Grace? I must hear everything."

Annalisa grinned. "I'll relay all I can, but I say with conviction, the Duchess of Devonshire is a dear friend, indeed."

Peggy squealed with delight. "Lord Essex, what marvelous new friends you've given us." To her father, she added, "Papa, they must meet Major André. Would that the gentleman could pay us a visit from New York. He was one of our most esteemed guests while the British occupied the city. I daresay he's most amiable, is he not, Papa?"

Annalisa prickled at Peggy's wanton mention of a British major and glimpsed Mary, who lingered between Jane and Lord Essex. Her sister's marked indifference startled her even more than Peggy's wagging tongue. *Into the lion's den we've come, it seems.*

"Indeed." The chief justice nodded. "But we've other dinner guests to host this evening, my dear."

Lord Essex settled into a chair across from Shippen. "Who else are you expecting, sir?"

"Major General Arnold, of course—Philadelphia's appointed military governor." Shippen eyed his daughter.

Major General Arnold. Annalisa fiddled with the wampum necklace at her throat as she recollected the major general from Saratoga. She and Quinnapin had set Arnold's leg after his injury at Bemis Heights. *Will he know my face? No, he was delirious with pain. He knew Benjamin Cavendish, not me.*

The housekeeper entered the parlor. "Sir..." She wrung her hands.

Shippen stood. "Well? What is it?"

"Sir, your other guests have arrived."

"Then bring them in, for God's sake."

"Sir, there's an additional gentleman accompanying the military governor, sir."

"A third guest?" Shippen's face reddened with irritation. "Pray, who comes uninvited?"

"G—General Washington, sir."

All redness faded from the chief justice's face. "Quickly, let us receive them. And make sure the general has a place at the head of my dining table."

Annalisa's insides flipped, but Mary's visage remained unaffected as she meddled with a dried flower petal. Annalisa met her sister at the cherry-wood table overflowing with dead roses as Benedict Arnold hobbled into the room on a crutch. With the tips of her free fingers, Annalisa grazed the scar beneath her right eye, now obscured by rouge. Decorated as a lady, it was unlikely the major general-turned-military governor would recognize her as Benjamin Cavendish from Saratoga, or even remember that night after battle.

Her heart rattled as Shippen introduced her, but as Annalisa hoped, Arnold met her with not a second glance, then moved on to Peggy, the obvious object of his attention.

General Washington, sporting his natural hair powdered and tied in a queue, wore the blue-and-buff uniform of the Continental Army decorated with the highest-ranking gold epaulets of commander in chief. His thin lips pursed, though he offered the genteelest manners.

The third guest, introduced to them as Mr. Wentworth, was a handsome young man of about five-and-twenty, with light brown hair and hazel eyes. He kissed her hand, then Mary's, with alarming affability.

"I am your humble servant, my ladies."

Mary curtsied. "Pleased to make your acquaintance, Mr. Wentworth."

"Come, sit beside me." Mr. Wentworth plopped onto the sofa where Annalisa and Peggy had sat.

Mary's face alight with budding fascination, she joined the agreeable gentleman, but Annalisa hesitated. Across the room, Lord Essex and Jane shared an intercourse with Peggy and Arnold while Shippen entertained General Washington with a glass of brandy.

"Miss Annalisa, you must join us." Mr. Wentworth's plea snagged her attention, and she settled beside the obliging gentleman. "There's a good lass. I'm pleased to make your acquaintance, miss."

"The pleasure is all mine, sir." Flooded with his musk perfume, Annalisa returned his smile.

"Is your sister married into the Perkinses of Boston?" he asked.

"Yes, sir," Mary replied. "Lord Perkins used to be magistrate in Boston and is Jane's father-in-law."

"Capital." Mr. Wentworth crossed his legs. "How long are you ladies visiting Philadelphia?"

"A fortnight," Mary replied.

His expression lifted with apparent delight. "Marvelous. I'm here on business from Portsmouth."

"New Hampshire?" Mary's smile glittered.

"Aye."

"Our brother owns a tavern in Portsmouth," she replied.

"Mary." Annalisa crumpled her skirts with little regard for the delicate silk. Perhaps her sister wasn't as clever as they all believed. One handsome man, and Mary's tongue flew about with reckless abandon.

Mr. Wentworth laughed. "'Tis a reputable trade, Miss Annalisa. Dare I presume to know the tavern?"

Mary smoothed her skirts, a worrisome habit adopted from Jane. "I think you should guess it, sir."

"My friends and I frequent the Black Water at Strawbery Banke. Know you it?"

"Yes, sir, quite well," Mary said. "That is the tavern our brother owns."

"The Black Water? How fortuitous!" he cried. "I knew not Mr. Howlett had such lovely sisters. How have I not known you until now? The pleasure in meeting you both is certainly all mine, I'm afraid."

"I make myself scarce at such an establishment," Mary replied. "Mamma requires me to be at home most of the time. As for Annalisa, she's been rather busy these two years, haven't you, Annie?"

"Yes, quite." Annalisa forced a grin, when General Washington caught her eye. "Excuse me." She stood and made her way toward the commander of the Continental Army.

General Washington bowed. "Miss Annalisa Howlett, pleased to make your acquaintance."

She curtsied. "Sir, the pleasure is mine."

"Excuse me, General, Miss Annalisa." Chief Justice Shippen shifted his attention to Peggy and Arnold, who engaged with Jane and Lord Essex.

"Miss Annalisa, Chief Justice Shippen tells me you've made friends of the Duchess of Devonshire." General Washington offered a modest smile. "I'm curious to know how an American lady from a small town as yourself has managed such a task."

"The tale is quite long, sir. I shan't bore you with it unless you insist. But the short version is that I recovered from a shipwreck at Devonshire House in London..."

"I'm grieved to hear this." Washington's jaw hardened. "Was this ship not *Liberté?*"

Annalisa tensed, and she glanced about the room. "Aye, sir."

Washington leaned in close. "The captain, Captain Fleming—"

"Is dead, sir," she muttered. "From what I heard, he died in a duel at a tavern."

The general stiffened. "And your husband?"

Annalisa concealed her grimace behind a forlorn smile. "Was imprisoned aboard HMS *Lively*, sir, while I was presumed dead. After his escape..." Her gazed shifted to Jane. "He married my sister, at the behest of his father, Lord Perkins."

"I see." Washington's mouth curled into a frown. "Quite a journey, miss. You've my sincerest apologies for the trouble you've endured." He hesitated. "And 'twas by divine Providence you met the most remarkable rescuers of an unlikely sort."

"Yes, sir."

The general narrowed his gaze. "Miss, have you any relation within the army? Militia, perhaps?"

"Aye, sir. My brother is Captain George Howlett of Cogswell's regiment—" She stopped, but it was too late. *Two gentlemen here know George. One, the commander in chief of the Continental Army. The other, a Loyalist who frequents George's tavern.* Her stomach twirled as though a rope upon a ship's capstan.

Washington smiled. "One of my most devoted militia captains. Pray, when next you meet him, do give him my regards."

"Of course, sir."

The general faced the room. "I wish to question you further on the matter of your wrecked ship, but all that we speak is of a delicate nature, as you know."

"Yes, sir."

The general kissed her hand before joining the larger party near the fireplace, leaving her nerves to accompany her. Upon the sofa, Mary consorted with Mr. Wentworth; before her, Jane clung to her brother-in-law, Lord Essex. With neither sister to comfort her dwindling reserve, Annalisa studied the one person in the room she meant to better understand.

Peggy Shippen, Loyalist and British sympathizer, clutched the arm of the military governor, Benedict Arnold, the same major general Annalisa had fought beside last autumn at Saratoga as Benjamin Cavendish. *Curious, indeed.*

7

ANNALISA

PHILADELPHIA, NOVEMBER 1778

AFTER DINNER, ANNALISA INCHED nearer to the Shippens' mahogany pianoforte—an instrument certainly shipped from England—in their decorated drawing room. Where the parlor had swallowed her in shades of green, the drawing room's large front windows with cascading blue velvet curtains complemented the velvet upholstered chairs and sofas. From the blue-and-white-striped papered walls hung several paintings of varying sizes; and above the mantel, a portrait of the Shippen family.

Annalisa slipped onto the bench and placed her fingers upon the keys. From memory, she played the first movement of Handel's *Water Music*. Mary scooted beside her on the bench, but rather than enjoy her sister's company, an irate rush singed her breast.

"How could you speak so wantonly of George's tavern to Mr. Wentworth?" Annalisa murmured. "He belongs to a well-known Loyalist family in Portsmouth."

Mary's face paled. "I knew not Mr. Wentworth was Loyalist."

"If he uncovers that General Washington knows George

from his time in the Continental Army, George and Abbie will be in absolute danger upon Wentworth's return to Portsmouth. The Black Water is already a Loyalist haven. If they cannot remain there to hide from Lord Essex, where will they go?"

Mary's pallid cheeks further waned, but she said nothing as Peggy glided toward them from across the room.

"Upon my word, you are most accomplished, Miss Annalisa," Peggy said.

Annalisa fabricated a smile. "'Tis the only thing I'm more proficient at than Jane. I assure you, she's the accomplished one among us Howlett sisters."

"'Tis always the way of the eldest sister, is it not?" Peggy winked, then sashayed from the pianoforte with her glass of Madeira.

Mary stood, smoothing her skirts, and left the instrument to join Peggy and Jane.

In a haze of tobacco smoke, the gentlemen paraded into the room.

"Miss Annalisa plays quite well." A charming grin gleamed across Mr. Wentworth's chiseled face.

Peggy's hand flew to her hip. "*Quite well* is a compliment bestowed upon a third or fourth daughter, Mr. Wentworth. Let us agree she's surpassed proficiency, so much that her playing renders us an opportunity for dancing."

Mr. Wentworth laughed. "Hear, hear, Miss Peggy."

Annalisa caught Peggy's wink as the party guests lined up in the middle of the drawing room. A burst of confidence surged through her fingertips as Annalisa assumed the minuet in Handel's composition.

General Washington promenaded with Peggy, as graceful as any formal dancer. Jane paired with Lord Essex, and Mary with Mr. Wentworth. Unable to join, Benedict Arnold sat near the fireplace across from Chief Justice Shippen, his face warped in envious displeasure. Evident from Arnold's study of Peggy, he wished it were he who danced with her, not the general.

The chief justice left Arnold and made his way toward the pianoforte. "How marvelously you play, miss."

"Thank you, sir."

"You must let Peggy play next so you may enjoy yourself. Certainly, you don't wish to spend the evening stuck upon this bench."

"I'd be glad to share the bench with Miss Peggy."

Though she'd rather play than dance, Annalisa finished the minuet and relinquished the instrument to Peggy. Her father whispered something to her as she sat, and the first notes of *Corn Rigs are Bonny* resonated.

General Washington beamed, and he held out his hand to Annalisa. "Shall we dance this one, Miss Annalisa?"

"I'd be delighted, sir."

The general's favorite cotillion. Jack's words returned to her as she accepted his hand.

Mary paired with Lord Essex, and Jane with Mr. Wentworth, while Arnold watched with bitterness. Annalisa couldn't help but pity the man, though he hardly hid his objective desire. *How is it we ladies are always at the caprice of some supercilious gentleman?*

Glad to dance with the genteel general, Annalisa smiled as they all joined hands, stepped in, then circled the room. They dropped hands from the circle, and she joined with General Washington who returned her grin without missing a step. When Peggy's playing ended, they all clapped.

"Marvelous, Miss Annalisa," Washington said. "What a delight you are. You're certainly your brother's relation. I'll not forget this meeting, nor this dance."

Annalisa curtsied again. "Sir, you're too kind."

After Washington reunited with Arnold and the chief

justice by the fireplace, Mr. Wentworth approached. "Pray, Miss Annalisa, have you a brother who is acquainted with the general?"

Her breast tightened, and she searched the room for Mary, but her sister had been ensnared in an intercourse with Jane and Lord Essex. If Mr. Wentworth asked General Washington, such a revelation would prove disastrous for George and Abigail. As far as she knew, the general knew nothing of Wentworth's loyalties.

"Yes, sir. I've three brothers, but I'm not at liberty to divulge that information presently."

"Peace, Miss Annalisa." Mr. Wentworth's gaze softened. "I mean no harm by it. We are at war, after all."

She stiffened, though returned his smile. "Sir, I know so little of my brothers' offices and how they spend their time, let alone where their allegiances lie. As you may have heard, I spent some time away in London with the Duke and Duchess of Devonshire. Surely, you can forgive a lady's ignorance."

Mr. Wentworth nodded. "Of course, Miss Annalisa. I meant not to insult you after so delightful a dance." He offered his arm. "Shall we dance the next?"

Her heartbeat slowed, and she took his arm. "Of course, sir."

Bottles of wine emptied, and Peggy's playing filled the room with Vivaldi's cadences, enough to detract from Annalisa's harried thoughts of George. In that drawing room, she played the part of an unassuming lady, yet she could hardly dissuade the feeling that masquerading as Benjamin Cavendish proved far less dangerous.

As the clock chimed midnight and Peggy stifled a yawn, Lord Essex addressed the room. "Gentlemen, we mustn't keep these ladies awake much longer."

"The grog flows freely this time of night at the Brown

Dog Inn." Benedict Arnold heaved himself upright on his crutch. "Shall we?"

Her interest piqued. Annalisa lagged behind her sisters and Peggy as they journeyed up the stairs. She lingered on the second stair, watching the gentlemen file out the door and turn right.

8

ANNALISA

PHILADELPHIA, NOVEMBER 1778

WHEN MARY WAS SUFFICIENTLY sleeping, Annalisa slipped from the bedstead and rifled through her belongings. In dark quiet, she pulled on her shirt and breeches, buttoned her waistcoat, and slid on her coat. Her hair plaited into a queue, she donned her cocked hat and sneaked from the bedchamber.

Careful, she tip-toed down the stairs, into the foyer, and outside the Shippen home. She turned right and sped down the cobbled lane until late-night laughter and cheers echoed down a narrow side street. Annalisa glimpsed a sign for the Brown Dog Inn, dimly lit by a solitary lantern. She opened the door, and an odor thick with smoke and fermented hops greeted her.

There, sat about a square table near the crackling hearth, Mr. Wentworth, Lord Essex, and Benedict Arnold played a game of whist. Arnold emptied his tin cup and ordered another from the weary potboy.

Her cocked hat low upon her brow, Annalisa sat at an unassuming table near the three gentlemen she meant to spy. When the potboy brought her a mug of cider, she removed a small glass vial from her pocket and poured the contents into her drink. The elixir, conjured by her dear friend Quinnapin, dilated her pupils, fashioning the appearance of dark eyes far different from the green of her own.

Annalisa drank the cider, made bitter from the elixir, and tuned her ears to the gentlemen two tables over from where she sat.

Lord Essex set down his pewter cup, and cleared his throat. "Arnold, I'm inclined to think a man with your...reputation...must be well received here in Philadelphia, no?"

Arnold grunted. "They've been slow to warm to me, but Philadelphia is agreeable."

"More agreeable than the promotion you deserved?" Mr. Wentworth chuckled.

"Fie." Arnold's speech slurred. "Congress owes me a sum of money for my time in the Continental Army. I'll be damned if they forgo my wages."

"Congress is amidst a battle of their own," Mr. Wentworth replied. "The currency inflation is abominable, but I suspect your most esteemed commander in chief has assured you when there are ample funds, you will be paid."

Lord Essex snorted. "Congress has much to recommend them, but they're sorely lost in this war. The Americans have reclaimed Philadelphia, yes, but the British maintain a stronghold in New York. Unless the Americans can overtake and occupy New York, this war shall lend its favor to Britain."

"But the French have joined our war," Arnold replied.

Mr. Wentworth finished his drink. "Indeed, sir. But Cornwallis is a rather decorated general, who at present, is running the southern campaign for Britain. I suppose it wouldn't hurt Washington to consider tactics other than the capture of New York."

Lord Essex smirked. "But he will not. 'Tis why we must ally ourselves with the winning side, gentlemen."

"Hear, hear." Mr. Wentworth poured himself another drink from the pitcher upon their table and saluted Lord Essex.

Major General Arnold, apparently hesitant to toast to something so treasonous, looked on, though he shook his head. "Gentlemen, if I can convince Miss Peggy Shippen to marry me, I shall be able to garner more influence over this city. Mayhap we need not defect sides."

"Yet," Lord Essex said.

"Aye, sir. Yet." Arnold poured from the pitcher and drank.

"Or she may influence you, sir." Mr. Wentworth laughed.

The hair on Annalisa's arms prickled beneath her coat. Anxious to remove herself from the tavern at once, she stood. The chair squealed behind her, and the gentlemen from the table of offense all looked up.

"Is your lady awaiting you, sir?" Lord Essex bellowed.

Annalisa started and shook her head. "No, sir."

"Then come join us." Mr. Wentworth lost his balance as he offered the open seat at their table.

Arnold recounted the cards as he dealt them. "I can hardly see straight, gentlemen."

Her racing heart slowed as she made her way to their table. They were far too drunk to notice her. Annalisa sat and took the cards offered her.

"Pray, what is your name, young lad?" Mr. Wentworth asked.

"Cavendish," she replied, deepening her contralto to its lowest register.

Arnold lifted his gaze. "I met a Cavendish. The lad set my leg at Bemis Heights with a Native."

"Aye, sir, 'twas my friend Quinnapin and myself."

Arnold scowled. "Would that I could walk without this crutch."

"You asked to keep your leg, sir, a feat which we accomplished far better than your eager surgeon," she replied.

Lord Essex and Mr. Wentworth laughed, and raised their drinks.

"Hear, hear, Mr. Cavendish."

"Indeed, Mr. Cavendish." Arnold grunted. "A feat for which I don't believe I thanked either of you."

Annalisa kept her head lowered in fading candlelight. "No, sir."

"If I marry Miss Peggy Shippen, you and the Native will receive an invitation."

"My thanks to you, Major General."

They played whist in silence a moment or two, and Annalisa glanced up. Each of the gentlemen focused on their cards and paid her no heed. Relaxed, she leaned back in her chair and finished the bitter concoction of cider and elixir.

When the round ended, Annalisa stood, eager to quit their audience before the effects of the elixir had run its course.

"Just one round, Cavendish?" Mr. Wentworth asked.

"Aye, sirs. And I thank you for it." She tipped her hat to them and turned from the table.

"Cavendish—pray, your full name again, sir, so I do not forget you," Arnold called after her.

One foot out the door, Annalisa replied, "Benjamin Cavendish, sir."

⁂

THE FOLLOWING EVENING, ANNALISA WHIRLED ABOUT their chamber like a storm bound for land. At last, she plunged into the chair at the desk and penned a letter to George and Abigail.

Mary opened the chamber door and stepped inside the room. "Annie, we must speak of last night."

"Speak of what?"

"You must know I had no intention of placing George and Abigail in danger."

"It matters little what you intended. You carelessly disclosed George's whereabouts and his profession to Mr. Wentworth in the presence of Lord Essex—from whom he and Abbie are hiding—and General Washington. Wentworth need not learn of George's connection to the Continental Army."

She finished the letter with a temerity she hadn't experienced of herself since Bunker Hill and rose from the desk. Annalisa untied her pockets and tossed them into her trunk, along with her gown and petticoats.

Mary stood from the bedstead. "I'm sorry. I didn't realize General Washington knew George." Her slender, deft fingers unlaced the stays from Annalisa's torso.

"I'm glad I'm here, then." Annalisa sat on the bed they shared. Her anger waning, she yearned to share all she had learned last night at the tavern with Mary, but her sister knew nothing of her cavorting as Benjamin Cavendish—a dangerous charade Annalisa meant to keep to herself.

She shuddered from a cold November breeze slipping into the room and slid beneath the coverlet. Mary quickly joined.

"I'm glad you're here, too." Mary faced Annalisa as they lay beneath the blankets. The light of a solitary flickering candle on the bedside table illuminated her sister's face.

"We must be more cautious, Mary. We can't have another mishap like last night. We were lucky to have adverted chaos, but next time we might not be as fortunate."

"Pray, how did you know General Washington was acquainted with George?" Mary asked. "Had I known, I never would've spoken out of turn."

"George told me."

Mary knew nothing of Benjamin Cavendish and the time she'd spent in the Continental Army with George and Quinnapin, though her sister had learned of her bouts with the Danvers militia.

Her lips taut, Annalisa remained silent.

"What plagues you?" Mary asked. "I can tell you're anxious."

Mary may have blundered, but she was still astute as ever, and Annalisa, far from fooling her. "I'm anxious to see Jack on our return home. He may be cross with me for not leaving a letter upon our departure."

Her sister's face softened. "He could never be cross with you, Annie. I'm sorry you cannot be married—that you must see him with Jane." The upward lilt of her sister's reply preceded an abrupt pause, her lower lip protruding slightly as though in thought.

The air between them grew thick and heavy, like the boughs of their sacred oak hundreds of miles away in Topsfield, those same sheltering arms that protected the space of Annalisa's sweet daughter. But in recognizing an unspoken insight from her sister, Annalisa cajoled Mary with a glance.

"Annie, you'll find what I've to say rather disagreeable, but you may not disagree."

"Go on."

Mary licked her lips. "What if you eloped again?"

Lady Perkins's threat echoed in the back of her mind, and Annalisa shook her head. She could hardly tell Mary that she held no other option but to pursue marriage with someone else to save their farm.

"I just wish for you to be happy," Mary continued.

"I know. And I've loved Jack my whole life. To quit him feels like losing a part of myself. But I must."

"Why? Jack will be devastated."

"Because..." She could never relay Lady Perkins' threat to Mary. Nothing good could come of it. "Because he is married to Jane and they share a child together. And I doubt the courts will grant him the divorce he seeks. There is little evidence to show Jane has truly committed adultery with Lord Essex."

Mary frowned. "You speak rationally."

"I must."

Her eyes closed. Annalisa imagined the dreaded conversation she would have with Jack: a litany of reasons they should not, and could not, be together. Her heart twisted in an agony she'd not felt since her first days in London when she believed herself widowed. An image of Jack with Jane on the night they conceived Robby blew in, a storm much darker than the one that had capsized *Liberté*. The winter storm that had sunk *Liberté* and pelted her with sheets of ice similarly froze her heart until she no longer acknowledged the pain of quitting her attachment. All that remained was the burning, bitter anger of her scorn, a betrayal she'd not entirely forgiven of either of them. Yet Robby need be blameless. But this anguish paled in the light of Lady Perkins and her heartless betrayal that would ruin the very livelihood of her family.

In the light of war, peril lurked at every corner. As if her worries could hardly cease at Lady Perkins, her thoughts turned to George and Abigail. Mr. Wentworth would be traveling back to Portsmouth tomorrow. No doubt the gentleman would regale her brother upon his return visitation to the Black Water.

9

GEORGE

PORTSMOUTH, THE BLACK WATER INN, DECEMBER 1778

A BURST OF WINTRY AIR whisked inside the Black Water Inn. George, hovered over the bar, shifted his gaze to assess the entering patron. The hope of Annalisa or Jack materializing quickly faded as Mr. Wentworth stepped into the foyer.

"Wentworth, 'tis been weeks since last we've seen you," George said. "Mr. Peirce has stepped away but expressed he'd be returning within the hour."

"Capital." Wentworth removed his hat, tucking it beneath his arm. "I've not seen him, either. I've been away on business." He slid coinage across the bar before sauntering toward the sizeable hearth where his old friend had left a deck of playing cards and a cribbage board.

Grumbling to himself, George poured a bumper of rum, saluted his fallen friend Samuel, and downed the measure before ordering his potboy to ready a pitcher of flip for Wentworth.

"Mr. Howlett, there's four shillings here," the potboy said.

George retrieved the coins and made his way toward

Wentworth with the pitcher of flip. "'Tis only three shillings, sir."

Wentworth held his stare. "For your *loyalty* to Portsmouth's patrons. I know the value of a shilling, sir. As do you."

A chill snaked down George's back. "Aye, sir. I do."

He turned toward the bar when Wentworth added, "I met your sisters at Philadelphia, sir. Lovely, and much alike you, particularly the older unmarried one."

Georged spun around. "Tread with ease, sir."

Wentworth chuckled. "I meant no offense." He poured from the tankard and sipped the flip just long enough for George to itch with irritation.

"Anything else I may offer you, sir?"

After another long swig, Wentworth set down his tin cup. "Mayhap an audience with General Washington. I heard a relation of yours is acquainted with the American commander in chief."

George managed a dark chortle. "A relation of mine, sir? Surely, you jest." He turned and strode back to the bar.

"When next I meet Lord Essex, I'll be sure to give him yours and *Mrs. Howlett's* regards, sir," Wentworth called after him.

At the mention of his Abigail, the ringing in George's ears silenced and the bustling tavern halted. His hands and face numbed with Wentworth's thinly veiled threat. *How does the reptile know Abbie is Lord Essex's lawful wife?*

Before further engaging the dandy, George hastened from the bar and into the kitchen, where his potboy worked the hearth. "Where's Elisha? I need him presently."

Elisha stepped from the pantry. "What is it, sir?"

"The squeeze crab, Wentworth. He knows."

"Knows what, sir?"

George cornered his tavern-keep. "He knows I'm Patriot,

that I know Lord Essex, and Abbie was...*is*...his wife, that this place...all of it, is a ruse."

"How, sir?" Elisah adjusted his spectacles. "Perhaps you're stricken with an anxious mind. Is the ringing in your ears profound?"

"Fie." George growled. "Damn it all! The cock robin knows. We must leave—at once."

Elisha's hand rested on George's shoulder. "Peace, sir. If you flee now, all will be the more apparent, I promise you. Come, let's upstairs and discuss our options rationally."

George bared his teeth. "I'm selling the Black Water, and there's not a damned thing that dilberry, Wentworth may make of it. I'll leave him a fart catcher to whomever offers me the best price. I need to run a Patriot establishment elsewhere. Topsfield. I need to return home."

☙❧

January 1779

IT HAD BEEN YEARS SINCE GEORGE LAST HOSTED A gathering; Jack and Annalisa's elopement in September 1775, for which only tavern patrons had been present. This occasion, however, required some panache—according to Abigail —something George readily lacked. At her behest, they had decorated the inn for the season and overpurchased enough food to entertain their friends and family for Twelfth Night. It was the least he could do to placate the disagreeable news he was soon to bestow upon everyone.

From the kitchen wafted aromas of savory mince pies and clove-spiced wassail. Plenty of inflated dollars had purchased the overpriced goods, but it mattered little; Congress had done nothing to deflect the issue that would've been the final nail in his tavern's coffin were it not for that Loyalist dilberry Wentworth.

George swallowed over the thick lump in his throat. His inheritance had put him ahead of the curve for years—until now. The war for independence had run him dry, which, he presumed, was the fate of many taverns and inns. Life in the militia had seemed far simpler when he was captain of Cogswell's. Despite his daughter, Louisa, and his hasty union with Abigail, he still yearned to return to it all.

Though many men did, he could hardly bring his wife and daughter to join the Continentals. Abigail would wilt under the half rations and life as a camp follower. But neither could they remain at Portsmouth. With dwindling money and suspicious ears, he couldn't allow Wentworth the opportunity to garner information, nor risk his family's safety if Lord Essex unexpectedly visited.

George clenched his fist as he wiped clean a pewter mug, a routine task which, in its mundane and thoughtless way, brought him small comfort.

"George, have you finished with that?"

Abigail's voice encircled him. She stood in at the base of the stairs in her crimson silk Christmas gown trimmed with lace and ribbons. Rather than return her smile, he frowned. *She would never survive in Washington's camp.*

"Aye."

"Why do you scowl? We're hosting Twelfth Night. Let's celebrate, please, before we relay the news."

George shook his head. "I loathe selling the Black Water—"

"But Mr. Peabody has offered handsomely."

How little she knew of what had transpired to initiate the transaction. George reached for a bottle of rum. With a swift uncorking, he poured himself a bumper. It was true, Mr. Peabody had offered far above his asking price for the tavern—thanks to Elisha—so much that George could now afford to buy the Whispering Willow in Topsfield without haggling Captain Gould. *The ultimate plan, should Jack agree to help.*

"To the Black Water." He raised his drink and downed the measure as the front door opened.

Annalisa, Mary, Henry, and Quinnapin, along with William and Martha stepped indoors. Jack and Jane followed with Oliver and the boys, Tommy and Robby. From the bar, George hollered a brisk "hello" and resumed wiping clean his mugs and tin cups.

"Welcome." Abigail glowed as she greeted their friends and family, not once revealing her apprehension about the sale. "We've wassail and food aplenty."

But George dawdled at the bar until everyone settled about the room, and his potboy rushed about serving wassail. As he scanned the room, Annalisa caught his eye and hurried toward the bar.

She leaned over the ledge. "I'll take a bumper of rum with you, Captain Howlett."

George smirked. "Aye, Private Cavendish."

Annalisa raised her glass. "Hear, hear."

They saluted and drank. When they finished, she offered her cup for a refill. "To you telling me what's been plaguing you this evening."

"'Tis coming." He poured a second bumper for her, then himself. "An announcement, of sorts."

"Abigail is with child." Annalisa laughed.

"Well, I'll be damned." George guffawed and choked on the rum. "No, thank God. Louisa is plenty for us, presently."

"I was worried for your disagreeable countenance in making such an announcement." Annalisa returned her gaze to the room. "Since I've uncovered 'tis not an untimely niece or nephew, what is this news?"

Unable to withhold the information, George leaned in. "We're selling the Black Water."

Her cheeks reddened. "'Tis Wentworth, isn't it?"

"Aye. As your letter warned. 'Twas a matter of time, Little One."

Annalisa bit her lip. "Where will you go?"

"Charleston. We plan to visit Addy and Sarah."

"Oh, George." Annalisa frowned, though he suspected she understood the necessity of their escape from Portsmouth. "What will I do without you and Abbie?"

"This was bound to happen, with or without Wentworth's interference. The inflation has been a pittance and thorn in my side for months. Truly, I couldn't afford to remain open much longer, and Mr. Peabody made a handsome offer. Wentworth's discovery only hastened my need to sell." He chuckled. "Perhaps I should thank the dilberry."

Annalisa offered a sad smile. "Would that you could move back to Topsfield."

"Not while Essex remains in the province, the reptile he is. But I have a plan."

"Do tell."

George picked at the wax clinging to the bottle of cheap New-England rum. Annalisa lifted her glass to him and he poured her another. *If only she'd been born a brother, then we could enlist together.*

"I plan to buy the Whispering Willow from Gould."

"Capital." Annalisa sipped the rum. "But who shall run the tavern while you're in Charleston? Have you anyone in mind?" She winked at him.

George studied the main room. Jack sat at a table near the roaring hearth with Robby on his lap. Quinnapin sat beside him. Across from Jack, Oliver shuffled a deck of cards with his son, Tommy. Jane played whist with Mary and Martha at another table while Henry beat William at a game of cribbage at a third table.

"You wish to run my tavern, but I would never ask it of you," George said. "You need a husband."

"Fie." Annalisa finished her rum. "I can run the tavern as Benjamin Cavendish."

"Damn, Cav," George growled. "You promised me you'd never again wear his breeches."

"I know I did, but I uncovered some unsavory news while at Philadelphia."

He bared his teeth. "You didn't."

"I did. I sneaked out to a tavern where Wentworth convened with the likes of Lord Essex and Benedict Arnold himself."

"Well, I'll be damned." George poured them both another bumper of rum and leaned in close. "Do tell."

Annalisa downed the measure and sucked in a breath when Jack approached the bar. His hand grazed her arm, and she smiled at him. "Sir."

"I hate to interrupt, but your intercourse appeared far more engaging than the game I was playing."

Annalisa licked her lips, and George wondered if she'd relay her tale to Jack, who still knew nothing of her bouts as Benjamin. "When we were in Philadelphia, I witnessed some scandalous charades of Lord Essex."

"Pray, did he engage with Jane in a criminal conversation?" Jack asked.

Annalisa flushed. "No...not to my knowledge, though I shared a bed chamber with only Mary."

Jack pursed his lips. "Very well. Go on, dear heart."

"Wentworth is a proclaimed Loyalist; we've all known that," Annalisa said. "But he toasted Lord Essex to sharing allegiance with the winning side, meaning the British. Lord

Essex readily returned the toast. We all supposed him a supporter of the Whigs, but I fear he is easily swayed."

"And of Arnold?" George asked.

Jack's eyes rounded. "Benedict Arnold was there as well?"

"Aye." Annalisa swirled the remaining fluid in her cup and drank. "He did not readily join in their toast, though he did grin and offer something about marrying Peggy Shippen."

"Think you Chief Justice Shippen will allow his daughter to marry a major general of the Continental Army?" Jack asked.

"I daresay he might."

"This is quite the speculation, Little One," George said. "One that should be offered to Henry."

"Pray, how came you by the scene you witnessed?" Jack asked.

Annalisa bit her lip and peered down. "I...had retired for the night but had forgotten my reticule within the drawing room. As I made my way downstairs, I overheard said gentlemen with their port assembled in the parlor."

Jack smiled, and brushed a kiss against her forehead. "Clever, my darling girl. When you've finished, do join me by the fire. I so wish to play you in cribbage."

"Of course." She returned his grin, which amply faded as he returned to his table by the hearth.

George poured himself another bumper. "And when will you tell him about your muse, Cavendish?"

Her cheeks paled. "He can never know, George."

"Never?" George tsked. "He will find out, Little One. I only pray for your sake he is as kind and generous with you as always."

Annalisa leaned close and whispered, "He dueled me at Saratoga. You know this. He will never forgive me these lies— the years of lies and danger I've placed not only myself in, but you as well."

"Aye. And I've warned you for years to hang up the breeches, yet you persist. I only pray I'm still alive and well should you one day be uncovered by the enemy. They will hang you, you know. The British will hang you for a spy, and as a woman impersonating a man."

Annalisa's jaw set. Though she said nothing, she nodded.

The tavern door opened, and in stepped a young gentleman with curling black hair, dark eyes, and regular features. George hastened around the bar to greet the man, who removed his hat and immediately smiled at Annalisa.

"Mr. Peabody, thank you for coming." George shook the man's hand, and gestured to Annalisa. "May I present my sister Miss Annalisa Howlett."

Mr. Peabody bowed. "The pleasure is entirely mine, miss."

"How good of you to purchase this place from my dear brother," she said. "Come, I will introduce you to our family and friends."

With Mr. Peabody now present, George held little reason to withhold the news much longer. His friends and family assembled before him, ready with glasses to toast Twelfth Night, he held Abigail's steady gaze, then addressed the room.

"Rogues and family, I'm delighted to inform you we're selling this beloved establishment to Mr. Daniel Peabody," he gestured to William's wife, "Martha's generous cousin from Boxford—whom you've just met. Abigail, Louisa, and I will be leaving this place within a fortnight."

The room fell silent, and Louisa wailed. Abigail scooped her up and fled the room, and Annalisa followed them.

With everyone's eyes upon him, George raised his tankard and locked his gaze with Jack. "Sluice your gob, abrams."

10

JACK

THE BLACK WATER TAVERN, JANUARY
1779

JACK SET ROBBY IN Jane's lap, passed Mr. Peabody, and hastened toward George as Annalisa fled after Abigail.

"Explain yourself, Cousin."

George poured himself a dram and downed the amber liquid, an act reminiscent of Jack's days in mourning when he believed Annalisa dead, dark days he never need revisit.

"It seems two-fold I've been ousted from this place," George said. "That Loyalist cad Wentworth offered me some well-timed threats, which came as an opportunity to sell the Black Water Inn. In fact, I welcomed it."

"Ah, I see. Then he's uncovered the nature of your allegiance."

George grunted and replaced the stopper into the bottle, then placed it upon the shelf above the bar. His green eyes, so alike Annalisa's, glimmered from too much grog.

Jack rested his forearms upon the bar and peered into his empty tankard, but he no longer wished to celebrate with cider or ale. "Where will you go?"

"Charleston," his cousin replied. "We'll visit Addy and Sarah as long as we must."

"I imagine you'll be paid handsomely for this place," Jack said. "Should you not consider investing in another property? Cousin, your inheritance is generous. I can't imagine it wouldn't cover the cost of acquiring a smaller tavern or—"

"The Whispering Willow," George murmured. "I should like your assistance in acquiring the Willow back from Gould."

Jack vibrated with a flicker hope. Buying the Whispering Willow from Captain Gould would bring George, Abigail, and Louisa home to Topsfield. "I can speak with Gould on your behalf—"

"Precisely." George smirked and removed the cork from the bottle of rum he'd just replaced on the shelf. He poured them both a small amount to toast. "I wish to run a Patriot establishment to garner as much information as I can on these Loyalist reptiles and that squeeze crab Lord Essex. I want to see them all burn."

"Peace, Cousin." Jack choked on the rum and set it aside. "We're soldiers, not spies."

"Aye. But Wentworth has driven me from here. I wish to see him suffer. Same with Essex. You heard Annie's story. He clearly defected, and it sounds like even our own Benedict Arnold may consider the same. Dilberries, the lot of them."

Jack bit his lip to hide his smile. George's bear-garden jaw often ran rampant when he was wrapped in warm flannel, as he now was.

"Offer Gould something he can't refuse," George continued, his words beginning to slur. "Is that understood, Perkins?"

"Aye." Jack nodded. "I'll require Mr. Peabody's price for the Black Water."

"Come, let's draft the paperwork. The Willow will be

mine again. Topsfield is ideal. It may be landlocked, but it abuts Ipswich. 'Tis safe and unassuming. No one would suspect information bleeding from such a small, unremarkable town." George bared his menacing teeth and leaned against the bar. His breath reeked of sugary rum. "I want eyes and ears in Topsfield, and the Willow may be a haven for Patriots. I know Annie wishes to run the tavern, but I want it in Henry's hands. Henry is clever and has connections elsewhere. He may do what he wishes in my absence, but by the devil's cock, if I return to Loyalists at my inn, heads will roll."

The hair on Jack's arms raised beneath his coat. *What connections does Henry have, and where?* With a purse of his lips, he shoved away thoughts of espionage. "I'll to Captain Gould immediately upon our return to town."

George removed himself from the bar, and Jack followed him from the main tavern room, around the stairs, and into the smaller rear tavern room. A modest fire lapped the bricks in the hearth, casting smoky shadows of his cousin's towering form as he crossed the room and rested at one of the wooden tables. Jack sat across from George, presented him with a small stack of papers, an inkwell, and quill.

George scribbled upon the page. "Tell Gould 'twill be my one and only offer."

Jack peered at the offer and quirked a brow. "That is generous. I can't imagine the old man would refuse it." He withdrew a blank page, dipped the quill in ink, and started to draft a purchase of sale.

"That is my hope. This is the final time I purchase a tavern of any sort." George leaned back in his chair and clasped his hands behind his head. "I need to ensure Abbie and Louisa are properly cared for should I fall."

"Fall?" Jack looked up and set the quill aside. "You plan to rejoin the army in Charleston, don't you?"

George's frown deepened. "I've not told Abbie, and I

don't wish for you to relay it, either. I haven't even told Annalisa. But I must join, Cousin, while we're still at war."

"But we could be at war for several years to come," Jack replied. "And we escaped with our lives. Please let that be enough. We can't continue to tempt divine Providence. I don't wish for any of us to suffer Samuel's fate."

George's face hardened. "Would that it were me instead of Wildes. I still can't understand why I was spared and he fell at Kip's Bay."

"Because 'twas God's plan."

George's deep chortle filled the room like hot tar. Jack shuddered at his cousin's sardonic laugh, an echo of the Sons of Liberty's cheers at their administration of the modern punishment upon the old Loyalist Mr. Chatham on Boston's Long Wharf.

"You still believe there is a God after all you've seen and experienced?"

Jack chewed his lip, considering the tragedies of the last few years. "I know not what I believe anymore. But I must pray to something. How else may I endure this life? How else may I hope to one day marry your beloved sister if I do not have God at my side? He's undoubtedly tested me, but I've found one truth in it all: I won't succumb to the fate of war; I won't let myself become a martyr for Washington's army or Congress or Clinton and his Redcoats...because dying is easy, George; *living* is much harder."

They sat in silent stillness until Jack finished the draft. He turned the document for George to read, but his cousin returned the page having only glanced at it.

"I trust you, Cousin." He rose. His lofty form hovered over Jack and cast a dark shadow over the purchase of sale. "I'll not die a martyr for Washington. I'll die for the birth of this country."

"Zounds." The chair squealed behind Jack as he stood.

"You are the father of my beloved niece, brother of my dearest Annalisa, and husband by common law to my sister—you will not die, George Howlett. Not for this country, not for your own glory. I will not be left in this world without you, and neither shall the women we love."

His speech flew from him as though he were Father seated upon the bench at Boston's Queen-street courthouse. Perhaps it was the way he scolded his cousin, or perhaps it was his polemical tone, but George's heavy brows furrowed as a sneer danced upon his lips.

"Of all the rogues I thought would understand my plight—"

"I do understand it," Jack cried. "What I can't understand is this nonchalance for martyrdom. From where does it come? Why now? You've a family. *My* family. I've been through what it feels to be widowed, and I shan't wish it upon anyone, especially not my own sister." Jack folded the purchase of sale and stuffed it into his coat pocket. "I'll finalize this tomorrow morning. You'll meet me here, sign it, and you'll purchase the Whispering Willow back from Gould. When you arrive in Charleston, you will not join—"

"Well, I'll be damned," George roared. "Have I upset you, Lord Perkins?"

Jack stepped back, his breath knocked from him as though George had assaulted him with the force of his fist and not his words. Yet, rather than cower, Jack straightened his coat and added, "'Tis Lord Brunswick, if you wish."

George scoffed. "You speak with your father's invectiveness, *Lord Brunswick*. 'Tis unbecoming of you. You may outrank me in Society, but in Washington's camp, I was your superior." His face hardened into that of Captain Howlett of Cogswell's regiment. "I'll sign the paperwork, then I'll to Charleston with Abbie and Weeza, where I will join the army gathered there. Meet *me* here at dawn, and I'll sign your finalized notes, *Lieutenant*." George quit the room without looking back at him.

Jack writhed inside his velvet coat, a deterrent comparison to his father by the man he'd grown to value most in his life. *That had once been Father.* In a strange twist of fate, his own moral compass pointed ever more in the direction of his rogue cousin than the man who had raised him. Despite the promises he'd made as an heir and first-born son, and a gentleman of Society, Jack could neither hope to be like Father nor be like George, a man of courage and mania abound in one fearless mind.

No, he wouldn't become Father's myrmidon, but neither would he be George's. Jack shook away the ghost of his cousin's words and returned to the table where he'd sat moments ago. With a swift and practiced pen, he redrafted the terms of the purchase and sale, then set it aside for the ink to dry. Beyond this small room, where a dainty fire wobbled and snapped, laughter accompanied the strings of a rough and ready fiddle where Twelfth Night festivities continued without him. Rather than fear his absence, he relished in it. *I may be absent from this colony for a greater cause...*

He stood and folded the dry letter. Placing it into his pocket, he returned to the main room, now brimming with dancing and a large Twelfth Night cake to be eaten with the bean to be found. They had yet to crown a king or queen.

His hopeful gaze fell upon Annalisa as she danced with Mr. Peabody, and Jack settled at a table with Oliver and Quinnapin.

"Where've you been?" his brother asked.

Jack reached for the pitcher of flip and poured himself a tankard. "I've been contemplating my next steps in this journey of life."

Quinnapin's mahogany eyes narrowed with his smile. "And what are those, Friend?"

"I'm determined to live, Quinn. Because this life, no matter how arduous, shall be worth it." Jack sipped the steamy, frothing liquid, and the bitter taste of earth and molasses settled into his stomach. "England. I will venture to London and use my status as the new Lord Brunswick to petition my divorce there."

"And will you take Annalisa with you?" Quinnapin asked.

"Of course." Jack eyed her as she danced with Mr. Peabody. She tossed her head back with laughter, and Jack smiled. "My darling girl loves to dance, does she not?"

"So long as the dance is not a minuet." Oliver continued to shuffle the cards then set the stack between them. "What of Robby, Brother?"

"I may take him with Annalisa and me," Jack replied.

"Good. I feared you would leave him to his mother," Oliver said.

"Hardly." Jack chuckled. "Jane deserves not the honor." When his brother did not return his laughter, he added, "Why so solemn?"

"I've decided to take Tommy and join Abigail and George on their trip to Charleston."

"Zounds." Jack rested his arms on the table. "Why-ever should you go to Charleston?"

Oliver's coffee-colored eyes flashed. "Because I wish to take my son on an adventure, away from the prying eyes of our parents, and the influences of Jane. Should I require a reason other than this? He's my boy, and I shall take him if I wish to."

Jack leaned back in his seat and contemplated this. Legally, it was true; no longer married to Oliver, Jane held no rights to Tommy, even as the boy's mother. *How sad for her, to lose both her sons at once.* As quickly as his empathy surfaced, it vanished in the face of his dear Annalisa, who had miscarried their daughter at the hands of Jane. *My wife, and mother of my son*. With any hope, Annalisa would join him on his venture to London for the divorce he'd been working so tirelessly to obtain.

Quinnapin asked, "Ollie, when do you leave?"

"Sooner than Jane will like to hear," Oliver said. "A fortnight."

Jack studied his wife, who played a game of whist with Mary and Martha, entirely unaware that she was about to lose her children. It was the law, yes, but he could hardly stomach tearing Robby from his mother so soon after losing Tommy to Oliver's travel whims. Jane had committed a crime most vile against Annalisa and their stillborn daughter, but taking a woman's son from her felt similarly wicked, especially as they fought for a country rife with ideals of freedom and equality, a war in which he'd fought. But now, he needed to fight a different war—one within his own family. He needed to help George and Abigail escape to Charleston.

Abigail loitered with Annalisa, who cuddled Louisa, at an open table in a darkened corner of the room.

Jack regarded Quinnapin. "Friend, will you join me?"

"Of course."

They rose from the table and met Annalisa and Abigail in their dimly lit corner. Lifting his niece from Annalisa's lap, Jack kissed the small girl.

"Uncle Jack!" Louisa squished his cheeks between her hands.

He laughed. "My darling girl. How well you've danced tonight. Go find your papa and ask him for a piece of cake." He set her down, and she scurried off to find George. When she had disappeared, Jack focused on his sister seated across from Annalisa. "Abbie, where will you stay in Charleston? Please, let me pay for your rented apartments."

Abigail peered up at him, her dark eyes so alike Oliver's and their mother's. She frowned and searched the room for

George. "I know nothing of the details of our journey, and I'm certain George will be hesitant to accept such a generous offer. With Mr. Peabody's purchase of the inn, he has funds enough for our stay."

"He needs that money to buy the Whispering Willow in Topsfield," Jack replied. "Abbie, your comfort is of utmost importance to me. Please accept my offer for the sake of Louisa."

"I can't tell George."

"Then it will be kept between us."

His sister smiled. "You're too good to me for the shame I've caused our family."

"'Tis no shame to pursue whom you love." Jack clasped her hand, though he met Annalisa's gaze. Her green eyes, so full of life and vigor, dulled in the dim light. "No matter what Mother and Father say."

Abigail laughed. "Even Ollie has reconciled with me. But pray, Jack, how will Ollie leave with Tommy?"

Quinnapin brushed his long obsidian hair over his shoulder. "You can meet Oliver and Tommy at my house when you reach Topsfield."

Abigail's countenance lifted. "We would be most obliged to you, old friend."

"And how do we suppose Oliver will pry Tommy from my sister's cold hands?" Annalisa asked.

Jack bit his lower lip, and looked to Jane who sat with Mary and Martha. "I'll take Jane to Ipswich for new ribbons and a new hat. She can hardly refuse. While we're away, Ollie can take Tommy to Quinn's."

❧ II ❧

GEORGE

TOPSFIELD, LATE JANUARY 1779

GEORGE PEERED BACK AT Abigail and Louisa as he hastened up the path to Quinnapin's modest home on the outskirts of town. Set back from the road leading to Ipswich and quite near the river, Quinnapin's house proved far enough from Lord Perkins's estate and the Howlett farm. Save for Jack and Annalisa, no one else knew they traveled this way before continuing their journey south.

He knocked on Quinnapin's door.

It creaked open, and his old friend smiled. "You made it. Do come inside."

The foyer smelled pleasantly of woodsmoke and sage with a hint of something savory cooking on the kitchen fire. Three rooms of the first floor were furnished with only the furniture and items a solitary man would need. *How lonesome, keeping a home by oneself...yet how freeing.* Quinnapin was widowed, having lost his wife, Weetamoo, at the hands of the Iroquois in New York.

"Come, sit by the fire. I've plenty of corncakes and soup." Quinnapin led them into a kitchen with a large hearth.

"My deepest thanks for letting us stay the night," George said.

Quinnapin held up his hand amidst preparing the food. "No need to thank me. We are brothers."

"A lovely sentiment," Abigail said. "Louisa, say, 'Thank you, Uncle Quinn.'"

"Fank you, Uncle Qwinn!" Louisa shouted.

"Is Ollie meeting us here tonight or in the morning?" Abigail asked.

"On the morrow," Quinnapin replied. "Jack will take Jane to Ipswich to buy new ribbons."

"A reasonable charge," George said. "Then we make haste south."

They ate the corncakes and venison soup in silence. Even Louisa gaggled not a word, as though she, too, felt the weight of their plan lurking in the air. For them to withdraw entirely from the colony was one thing; to take Oliver and Tommy with them was another.

After the low winter sun had set, and Louisa, tucked into her blankets by the fire, drifted to sleep, George and Abigail made their way into town and down the long, shadowy lane to the Whispering Willow Tavern.

George's spirit pulsed at the familiar sight of the yellow clapboarded building that had once been his old Peat Moss Inn, a long-lost lover, now returned to him after years of an illicit affair with the Black Water. Once the war was ended, this would be the place to spend all his days—and end them. If only he'd known it years ago when he sold it to Captain Gould. If only he hadn't been so blind as to believe his prospects of owning a larger tavern in a seaport. Truly, it had been the most expensive mistake of his life.

Thankful for Mr. Peabody and his purchase of the Black Water Inn, George strode up to his tavern and opened the door. His hand lingered a moment upon the chipped and curling red paint. "'Tis good to be back, you old mort."

Near the rear of the main room, Jack, Captain Gould, and Elisha Porter sat about the table George and his friends had so often frequented. How pleasant to see his cousin Jack upon that bench, where across from him Samuel had so often sat. His oldest friend's absence magnified as George closed in on their table.

"Good evening, rogues."

Elisha stood with Gould, and Jack slipped around the table to embrace Abigail.

George shook Gould's hand. "Thank you, sir."

The old man released a gritty chuckle and swiped a hand over the stubble beginning to sprout from his chin. "The pleasure be mine, Captain Howlett." He winked, then returned to his seat and frothy mug of flip.

George and Abigail joined, each pouring from the pitcher. Even Abigail, who at first timidly swallowed the earthy drink, gulped it.

Jack unfolded the final pages of the purchase and sale and spread it across the table. "I need only signatures from each of you gentlemen."

"Where's Annalisa? I thought she was meeting us here to say our good-byes," Abigail said.

"I know not." Jack leaned against the bench. "We've not spoken since Twelfth Night."

"That was a fortnight ago." Abigail's shrill accusation colored Jack's cheeks.

"'Twas not by my design, I assure you," Jack replied. "I've made several attempts to get Annie in my private audience, but Mother has thwarted my visits with requests for me to take Jane to Boxford and Salem and Danvers. I daresay I've not been home most days since Twelfth Night."

"Why do you insist on this hideous marriage to the

woman who murdered your daughter?" Abigail cried. "I was there, Jack. I saw everything as it unfolded that day. Tell me she does not keep to your bed—"

"Peace, Abbie." George tugged her into her seat. The flip had quite gone to her head, but he could hardly contain his emotive wife, nor did he wish to.

"No, she does not keep to my bed," Jack hissed. "Jane is my wife in name only."

"You need sign here." Elisha pointed to the page, eager to commence with the appointed task. George scrawled his name upon the paperwork, as did Gould. The sale was final, but the room sweltered with Abigail's fiery temper.

Jack, cool and reserved, folded his arms. "You know little of my plans, Abbie. Don't dare accuse me of doing nothing to salvage my friendship with Annalisa."

Abigail threw up her hands. "Then what? What is it you've done to remedy your situation? What do you plan? Indulge me, dear brother, and I'll not accuse you of lechery."

"Well, I'll be damned," George grumbled. "Lechery? We all know what befell Jack in his days of mourning. 'Twas hardly lechery."

"Miss Abigail, shall I get you a Madeira?" Elisha asked.

"No, thank you, Elisha." Abigail's tone sweetened like molasses candy, as though she'd not just spat vitriol at her brother.

Jack held his sister's gaze. "For months, I've petitioned the magistrates in both Salem and Boston. They favored my petition, but I've decided to pursue the judicial and ecclesiastical courts in London."

Silence spread across their table like the calm between cannonade within the redoubt at Dorchester Heights. George banked his memories of the Siege of Boston, and returned his attention to Jack.

"London?"

Abigail crossed her arms. "Shall you, too, leave our dear Annie?"

"No." Jack slammed his fist upon the table. "I will ask her to join me. This is my final hope. I pray they recognize my decree and grant the divorce as well as an annulment. It is the absolute least I can do for Annalisa. She deserves no less. And I will wed her here in town, as she's wished. But to do this, I need to attend London and claim my place at Parliament as Lord Brunswick. This is the surest way, I'm afraid."

The rear door to the tavern closed.

At this, Elisha and Gould excused themselves. George, too, wished to follow them. He neither yearned for dramatics nor vitriol; such was to be left to the theatre. He gulped his flip.

Jack's plan silenced Abigail, and she settled into the chair with one hand at her breast.

"London? You mean to leave, too?" Annalisa's voice, a deep and steady contralto, wavered with doubt from behind their table as she lingered near the keg vestibule.

George stood and brought his sister to their table, where she settled between him and Abigail. He poured her a tankard of flip.

Jack lowered onto the bench. "Yes. I meant to say something to our families soon."

"I see." Annalisa drank the flip. "Then we lose more than just Abbie, George, and Ollie. Pray, will you take Jane and Robby with you as well?" She spoke Jane's name with a venom George only reserved for his bitterest enemies, those being the British and that fart catcher Alexander Hamilton.

Jack hesitated. "Just Robby. And you, of course."

Annalisa said nothing, though her lips parted to speak. Jack's head cocked, and he quirked an eyebrow, awaiting her response.

"We'll speak privately, but I can't stay long." Annalisa

embraced Abigail. "Dear friend, please write to me every day, and relay my love to Sarah and Addy. I pray we meet again soon."

"I shall." Abigail brushed a tear from her cheek. "And you must continue to be my eyes and ears for Lord Essex."

"Of course."

When Annalisa regarded George, a familiar tightness closed his throat as it had that morning in August of 1775, when he left her to join the army outside Boston.

"Little One," he croaked. Not one to cry, he bit his cheek. "I'll write to you as well. You have my word."

He stood and pulled her into his arms. The tallest woman he knew, she fit comfortably in his embrace. How he cherished her and their kinship, the one other in his life he loved as much as Louisa and Abigail. Having watched her grow from child to woman, perhaps he loved her a bit more.

From their days in the clearing, where he'd taught her to load and fire his firelock, Bixby, to the day she'd nearly succumbed to her musket wound at Bunker Hill, to the moment he'd acknowledged her as Benjamin Cavendish at Saratoga, they'd been through hell and back together. Before relinquishing his own tears, George pulled away to find Annalisa had stained his coat with hers.

"It won't be long before we meet again, Little One. I promise." The irony of her nickname was not lost on him. But the assurance was made in vain.

"Don't lie to me George Howlett." Annalisa slapped his shoulder. "Though I'd like to believe we'll be reunited before the new decade."

Abigail sobbed. "We shall—1780 is a whole year away. There is hardly a reason we shouldn't be reunited before then."

Annalisa glanced at Jack, then returned her study to

Abigail. "Many months and many miles will part us. You know as well as I how much may happen in a single year."

"Don't speak thus, dear heart." Jack rounded the table and tugged Annalisa into his arms. She flew willingly into his embrace despite her cold reception of him that evening. From the way Jack clutched her head to his chest, George knew his cousin hadn't held her in months.

"All shall end well for each of us," Jack crooned. "I swear it."

"You all promise so much, yet I grieve the possibility 'tis all lies." Annalisa's voice muffled against Jack's chest.

He kissed the top of her head, and George thought she might return the sentiment, but Annalisa pulled away. Swiping her tears, she straightened her shoulders and stood erect.

"My apologies. I've forgotten myself. I must be going." She kissed Abigail's cheek. "Do write." After she kissed George, she added, "And you must stay alive, dear brother."

He straightened at her comment. *She knows I mean to enlist.* "And you must refrain from too many charades," he said. "I know the trouble you and Mary could uncover."

The look she gave him kept the smile on his mouth from sloping. Benjamin Cavendish was their secret to keep, and no one else's. But Benjamin Cavendish was put to bed, not to be seen again.

I hope.

Annalisa slipped from their table toward the keg vestibule, then quit the tavern through the rear door.

"I adore her so." Abigail's eyes flooded. "Would that we could take her with us."

"Perhaps she would rather join you in Charleston." Jack twirled the signet ring about his finger, his gaze fixed on the route Annalisa had left the tavern. Slowly, he met George's stare. "I need to speak with Annie." He jumped from the bench and fled through the rear door through which Annalisa had exited.

※ 12 ※

JACK

TOPSFIELD, LATE JANUARY 1779

JACK HURRIED AFTER ANNALISA.

"Annie, wait."

"Yes?"

A pale winter moon illuminated her cherry-red cloak and face as she stood near her horse.

"I'm venturing to England in springtime," he said. "I hoped you would join me."

She advanced toward him and rested her hand on his chest. The gesture lit a flame within, and he tugged her close enough to breathe in her lilac perfume.

Annalisa rested her forehead against his lips. "I desire nothing more than to travel with you and Robby."

He wrapped his arms about her. "Then please join me. I can't fathom being parted from you again for so long."

"I know." She sucked in a quivering breath, and stepped back from him. "But what if the court never grants your divorce?"

"I—"

"What then?" She lowered her gaze to her hands as she picked her thumbnail, and Jack followed her stare. The absence of his grandmother's gold sapphire ring upon her fourth finger sent a pang through his chest. "Shall I become a spinster?"

"Please don't speak thus. We've time for the courts to—"

Her left hand flew to his mouth. "When this war is through, I wish to be married, to have children...and presently, you can give me neither."

"But I shall." Jack drew her hand from his lips and ran his thumb over her knuckles. "I will marry you again. And I will give you a child. I swear it."

"You already have a child," Annalisa said. "One you created with my sister, if you've forgotten."

His jaw set, taken aback by her comment. "That conception was a mistake. Annalisa, I don't love Jane. I love y—"

"Please don't speak it. I can't rid myself of your betrayal... and hers. I'm tortured by it each time I see Robby. The torment I bear that her child by you still lives, when mine rots in an unmarked grave is unparalleled."

Jack's innards hollowed as he pictured the stillborn daughter he never met, buried beneath their revered oak. He never meant to cause Annalisa anguish, such raw emotional disquiet; and to see her before him a ruptured shell of herself, he could hardly stomach the guilt.

"If I could return to the day you and I set sail for France, I would turn us from the pier and ride home to Topsfield forthwith. But I can't erase all we suffered at the hands of that wreckage, nor the unfortunate sequelae that followed. I take full responsibility for the impudent, disagreeable way I chose to mourn. I thought I'd lost you, and Jane thought she'd lost Ollie when he was reported dead by the British. I assume culpability for my actions, but I was far from my correct state of mind. Laudanum and brandy filled my veins and clouded my judgment—I can't even recall the event. I'm ashamed to admit it, and I've already confessed these sins to you. I swore to atone for them, Annie, and I carry the guilt of Robby's conception with me each breath I take. Please forgive me my sins."

Though she growled and threw up her hands, her gaze hinted at longing. "John Jackson, it takes two to strum, no matter Jane's seduction or your murky, laudanum-induced haze. 'Tis a wonder your member performed in such an intoxicated state of duress."

Jack stepped back, startled. "Aye. It takes two to strum, but I was not myself. Perhaps I'll never be able to explain my sins, but I will die trying to right them. You are my dearest, most beloved friend, my companion, my love..."

Annalisa diverted her gaze, perhaps to conceal the tears spilling onto her cheeks. "I must go."

Until that moment, he'd not allowed himself to consider the English courts might not grant his divorce and annulment or that Annalisa would quit her attachment, though she had plenty of reasons. Overwhelmed by the reality of losing her forever, Jack reached for her.

"Please don't give up on me." His mouth dry, he croaked, "On us."

Annalisa blinked, then wiped her tears. "You've much to prove to me. But tonight, this intercourse has ended."

"Then you will not travel to London with me."

She shook her head. "How can I, Jack? I loathe the gossip in town that I'm your mistress. Yes, a husband may take a mistress, but he needs to be discreet about it."

"You are not my mistress," he replied. "You're my wife."

"Our elopement was not recognized, Jack, and you married Jane when I was presumed dead, a demand I shall never forgive. Your mamma, I shall never forgive her—"

She stopped herself.

"Pray, what has my mother to do with it? 'Twas my father who requested I marry Jane."

"I...thought it w-was your m-mamma."

The stutter. Jack reached for her and enfolded her in his arms. Her head to his chest, his neck warmed at her breath as she whispered the stanza to her favorite poem.

"Would that I could be rid of this terrible stutter," she murmured.

"I imagine the thought of living on a ship for several weeks is disagreeable to you since the shipwreck," he replied.

"Aye, it is."

He kissed her head. "Then I won't request it of you, dear heart." He held her at arm's length. "Just promise me one thing while I'm away."

Her lower lip trembled, though she nodded. "Anything for you," she whispered.

"Do not lose faith in me, darling girl. My love for you is steadfast, and I will not return home without a divorce and annulment. I swear it upon Eliza's soul."

"I believe you."

Annalisa's mouth found his. Impassioned yet quick, she pulled away. The kiss, desperate and hesitant, burned his lips and left him wanting more. Of course, he yearned for the physical intimacy that marriage offered, but so, too, he craved her companionship and their late-night discussions about the war. Her beliefs of freedom and equality echoed his own, ones he meant to live by as both a gentleman and a husband.

"I need to ask you a question," he said.

In the moonlight, a tiny smile danced upon her lips. "Just one before I go."

"Where do you rank truth amongst freedom and equality?"

"Truth in what regard? Truth to information or truth to oneself?"

Jack grinned. "A thoughtful query to my own." He pursed his lips. "Truth to all things, darling girl. Truth in what we say and how we live our lives. They need to be in harmony, do they not? If we mean to live as free and equal."

Her countenance tensed. "Aye, I suppose freedom comes from the release of truths."

Jack held her hand. "Then speak yours to me, Annalisa."

"M-My truths?" She withdrew her hand. "You know all there is to kn-know about me, J-John Jackson." Annalisa forced a smile, kissed his cheek, then mounted her horse and rode into the moonlit night.

❧ 13 ❧

ANNALISA

TOPSFIELD, MARCH 1779

ANNALISA SAT AT THE spinet in her family's drawing room. The late afternoon grey offered little light, though the days fared longer the nearer they drew to April. She rose from the bench and, using a paper spill, lit a candle and returned to the instrument.

From memory, her fingers played the *adagio* from Mozart's Second Piano Sonata, a composition Jack had gifted her from Vienna. Lost in the music, Annalisa conjured Jack's Atlantic-blue eyes the night George and Abigail fled town. His request for truth shook her core. Surely, he suspected she withheld information from him, two issues of which she did: her muse, Benjamin, and Lady Perkins's hideous threat. Two happenstances she could never tell him, no matter his need for honesty. And yet it pained her to withhold such information from him, particularly as he remained candid with her on all things.

The former, a revelation of her being Benjamin Cavendish, could never come at an opportune moment; the charade had endured for far too long and accrued damages that could neither be undone nor erased from memory and time. And the latter, a malicious event with Jack's own mother, could neither end well for Jack nor her entire family. Thus, she could only ever withhold the hideous happenstance from him.

And marry another? The chilling thought constricted her breast. *Mayhap I will confine myself to spinsterhood if I cannot marry Jack.* Lady Perkins's intimidation had come over six months ago; perhaps Jack's mother would be content to merely see her marry no one rather than enter an unwanted, unhappy marriage with another undisclosed gentleman.

With a profound unease, Annalisa finished playing her ode to Jack as Mamma and Lady Perkins entered the drawing room with Mary and a familiar gentleman she'd met at the Black Water Inn, Mr. Peabody.

Annalisa stood. "Mr. Peabody, how good to see you, sir. Pray, are you in Boxford visiting Martha's family?"

"I am, Miss Annalisa. Her family has always been kind to host me."

Mamma offered him a seat on the sofa adjacent to the spinet. "Mr. Peabody, my Annalisa is most proficient at music."

"Indeed, she is, sir," Lady Perkins added. "Miss Annalisa, do continue to play. We so wish to enjoy your music."

Annalisa met Mary's pleading eyes. "As you wish."

She played for another half hour, until Mr. Peabody stood. "I fear I must be going."

"Oh, you must stay for dinner, Mr. Peabody," Mamma said.

"I would, ma'am, but I'm promised to my aunt this evening."

"Very well. Liza will show you out, sir." Mamma called for their indentured girl to escort their agreeable guest to the front door.

When he'd gone, Mamma and Lady Perkins encircled the

spinet where Annalisa sat. Mary, perched beside her on the bench, reached for her hand.

"What do you think of Mr. Peabody?" Mamma asked.

"He's kind, handsome, and attentive." Annalisa's stomach furled as she asked, "Why should you ask?"

Mamma looked to Lady Perkins, and smiled. "Bette thinks he would make an excellent match."

"For Mary?" Annalisa glanced at her sister, who still said nothing.

"Of course not," Lady Perkins said. "You need to marry before Miss Mary."

"Me?" Annalisa jumped from the bench. "But I hardly know the gentleman. And what makes you believe he will want me for a partner in life?"

"Mr. Peabody is looking for a wife now that he bought the Black Water from George," Mamma said. "I heard all about the assiduity he paid you at Twelfth Night."

Annalisa flushed, then ground her teeth. "We danced but twice. There was no assiduity paid, I assure you, marm."

"Janey thinks you will make a fine pair," Lady Perkins said. "It would behoove you to take a husband, Miss Annalisa."

"Why must I marry at all? I may manage the Whispering Willow for George—I needn't a husband if Henry is there to run it with me."

"Absolutely not," Mamma cried. "To think, a spinster! I will not have it. Bette, speak some reason to this headstrong girl of mine. Come, Mary."

"No, Mary, wait."

Annalisa reached for her sister, but Mamma tugged Mary from the room, leaving Annalisa alone with Lady Perkins.

Her orange blossom perfume clung to Annalisa's throat in the same way it had the night of William's wedding. Annalisa recoiled to her spinet bench. As Lady Perkins glared, Annalisa ran her hand over Mozart's music. Upon the front page, Jack's impeccable script read: *For a dear friend, always near, no matter how far—J. Perkins.*

Lady Perkins's gaze followed her hand. "You know you may not marry Jack, no matter his trip to London."

"You made that quite clear last October, my lady."

"Good. You would do well to heed my warning and allow a courtship of Mr. Peabody."

"Or else?"

"Or else," Lady Perkins leaned over the spinet, "You will lose everything."

❧ 14 ❧

ANNALISA

TOPSFIELD, MARCH 1779

ANNALISA REACHED INTO HER pocket and handled her Bunker Hill musket round.

"My lady, do you realize all you're asking of me?"

"And do you realize what I'm capable of, Miss Annalisa?"

Sickened, Annalisa held her face. "What of the daughter Jack and I created? Am I to keep this grave secret from Mr. Peabody? Should he ask to marry me, he will eventually uncover I'm no maiden."

Lady Perkins's countenance drooped. "Leave your concerns to me." As quickly as she'd spoken, Mamma and Mary returned to the drawing room with Jack and Jane.

For the first time in weeks, Jane's rosy cheeks glowed with good cheer as she entered. Anticipating the worst, Annalisa held her breath.

"We've something exciting to share," Jane said.

Annalisa focused on Jack, who met her stare for only a moment before returning his attention on Mamma and Lady Perkins.

"Are you with child?" Lady Perkins asked.

Jane's cheeks flushed a darker shade of pink, then she

shook her head. Annalisa expelled the breath she'd been holding.

"We've been invited to Peggy Shippen's wedding," Jane squealed.

"Whom is she marrying?" Annalisa asked.

"The military governor, Benedit Arnold," Jane replied.

Annalisa's breath caught once more. Peggy Shippen, daughter to a Loyalist family, would wed Continental Army officer Benedict Arnold. She searched for Jack's gaze again to see if he, too, caught the meaning behind such a union—one she'd warned him about at Twelfth Night.

"How wonderful." Mamma clasped her hands. "An advantageous invitation, for sure. Pray, I wonder, was Lord Essex invited as well?"

"I'm unsure, but I imagine he should be." Jane hesitated. "Is Quinnapin about? There's an invitation for him as well, and a man called Benjamin Cavendish. I'm not sure how or why they came to be delivered to us..."

"I'll give it to him." Annalisa reached for the envelope and read the elaborate writing. It was from Arnold himself. Her hand over her mouth, she read: *Mr. Quinnapin and Mr. Benjamin Cavendish.* Arnold remembered Benjamin and their meeting at the tavern.

"Annie, Mary, there's one for each of you as well." Jane handed her a second envelope. As Mary opened and read, Annalisa's heart galloped with each breath.

"Annalisa, whatever's the matter with you?" Mamma hissed. "You look pale."

With little reason to refuse such an invitation from Peggy Shippen, she would have to attend the wedding. *Can Benjamin refuse Arnold?* Surely, the military governor would see it as a slight, but how could she be both herself and Benjamin Cavendish at one event? She peered at Mary, who smiled with ardent candor.

"I'm thrilled," Mary replied. "Mamma, may we attend?"

"We must ask your papa this evening, but I can see no reason to refuse."

"When is the wedding?" Lady Perkins asked. "Jack, will you be quite at leisure to attend? I thought you were soon to be leaving for London."

"My ship sails the second week of May," Jack said. "It would give me great joy to attend."

Mamma led Jack, Jane, and Lady Perkins from the drawing room, and Annalisa returned her attention to the spinet. Mary slid beside her on the bench and rested her chin upon Annalisa's shoulder.

"You seem less than enthused," Mary muttered.

"I'm thrilled," Annalisa replied. "I'm quite fond of Peggy Shippen."

"No, I mean about Mr. Peabody."

Annalisa frowned and said nothing.

"Fair enough." Mary fell silent for a moment. "You'll be interested to know Elisha Porter uncovered a letter at the Willow yesterday. Henry opened it. 'Twas addressed to Lord Essex at his home on Tory Row by a man called Ben Cavendish."

"Aye, odd that." Annalisa's hair rose, and she resumed playing Mozart's music. "What were the contents of said letter?"

"It informed the viscount of George and Abigail's removal to Charleston, but the letter clearly never made it into a courier's hands."

Annalisa's heart thudded. "We must warn George and Abbie."

"The note was intercepted. 'Twas sealed." Mary paused. "Think you this Benjamin Cavendish invited to Peggy's wedding could be the same writer of the letter to Lord Essex?"

"No." Annalisa shook her head. "Why leap to such conclusions when you know as little about Benjamin Cavendish as you do the sender of Lord Essex's letter?"

"It is a strange coincidence I can't ignore, Annie. I shall ask Quinnapin of this Benjamin Cavendish. If he knows Major General Arnold, he must be a Patriot. Mayhap we shall meet him at Philadelphia—"

"Maybe." Annalisa rose from the spinet, the room now silent and closing in on her. Her breath caught in shallow waves, and quickly, she excused herself. She hurried from the room, down the hall, and out the front door.

The chill March air stabbed her lungs like hundreds of steel bayonets, but she ran through the crunching snow toward the oak. When she reached its haven of thick, naked branches, she paced by the trunk until her breath returned to her. *Whoever can be writing as Benjamin Cavendish? And why did they write to Lord Essex? Mary is suspicious; can I trust her with my secret?*

"Annie, whatever's the matter?" Mary, who had chased after her, stepped beneath the tree's shelter.

"You don't know what you speak," Annalisa said.

"Of Benjamin Cavendish or Lord Essex?"

Annalisa paused at the base of the tree where her daughter lay beneath frozen earth.

"Peace, Annie. I'll speak with Quinn about this Benjamin Cavendish." Mary settled on the tree's lowest bough. "Henry's quite certain Lord Essex has defected his allegiance to the British. I can say with certainty anyone writing to Lord Essex must mean to spy for the British, and this Benjamin Cavendish, if it be the same man Quinn knows, could be no different—"

"Fie, Mary Howlett!" Annalisa cried. "I'm Benjamin Cavendish!" She fell to her knees and sobbed. "I'm Benjamin Cavendish."

A thick silence invaded her sacred space as Mary said nothing until finally, she whispered, "You wrote the letter to Lord Essex?"

"No." Annalisa faced her sister. "I never wrote to Lord Essex. I'm no turncoat."

"Then how are you Benjamin Cavendish?"

After a moment of contemplative silence, Mary gasped and jumped from the branch.

"The Danvers militia! You joined the Danvers militia and used that moniker with them. How could I have forgotten it?"

"You were younger than you are now—"

"I'm such a fool."

Annalisa lifted from the cold, wet ground and reached for her. "No more fool than I. You know what would happen if anyone discovered me within the militia...or the army."

"You joined the army, too?" Mary's eyes rounded. "You joined and kept it from me?"

Annalisa nodded. "Aye. With Quinn. After..." She glimpsed the space where her daughter lay buried. "I had to leave after she died, Mary."

"You told us you went to Charleston to visit Addy and Sarah." Her sister's face contorted. "You lied to me."

"I lied to everyone."

"Except Quinn."

"He knew. He helped me bury her. I trusted him with more than my life. I still do. He's the only one, save George and Abbie, who know about my charades as Benjamin." Annalisa hesitated, wishing the next bit to be untrue: "And Oliver."

"And Ollie," Mary shrieked. "Then 'tis only Henry, Will, and I who don't know."

"And Jack," Annalisa said. "And Jane...and the rest of our

families, Mary. Most don't know. And they must never learn it."

Mary twisted her lip. "Are you certain Jane doesn't know?"

"I would never trust Jane with such information." Annalisa gripped her sister's hands. "And you must keep this to yourself. You must take this bit of knowledge to your grave, Mary Howlett. I'll not see anyone I hold dear hanged or gaoled on account of my behavior."

Mary nodded as though finally understanding the danger Annalisa had been a part of these years. "You have my word. I'll never speak of it."

"Not even to Henry," Annalisa warned.

"Not even Henry."

The air between them softened, as though healed by the ancient oak; or was it the gentle spirit of her daughter that quelled Mary's perceived betrayal? Annalisa would never know for certain, but in that moment, the bond between them forged into an unbreakable steel.

Mary held her gaze. "Now, we must configure a way for you to attend Peggy's wedding as both you and Benjamin."

"It can't be done," Annalisa replied.

"Of course it can. I will help you."

❧ 15 ❧

ANNALISA

PHILADELPHIA, APRIL 1779

ANNALISA SETTLED INTO THE sofa. A modest fire lit the parlor of their rented rooms in Philadelphia, the same they'd visited back in November. Her sisters occupied by their needlepoint, Annalisa resumed her book, *The Expedition of Humphrey Clinker.*

"Quinn, when shall we meet your friend Mr. Cavendish?" Jane looked up from her canvas where she embroidered a rose into a handkerchief.

"At the wedding, Mrs. Perkins," Quinnapin replied.

Jane smiled. "I'd very much like to meet the man who helped you set Major General Arnold's leg. Else he may not have healed well enough to marry dear Peggy. Pray, Quinn, is your friend Mr. Cavendish handsome or a man of Society? Annie, you may take a liking to the young sir."

Jack lingered near the fireplace with a newspaper in hand. He peered up and snorted with disgust. "Quinn, what say you of Cavendish?

"I'm hardly the person to say," he replied. "His eyes are dark, his face quite regular, as is his height. I don't believe he's a man of Society."

Jack rolled the newspaper. "Miss Annalisa already knows Cavendish. I've met him as well."

With a gasp, Jane set aside her canvas. "You said nothing, sir."

"'Twas at Saratoga that I met the fellow," Jack replied.

Annalisa bristled. "Aye, Jane. Mr. Cavendish is a distant relation to Papa. I met him when he visited Danvers once. He took a liking to me, but that is all." She caught Jack's stare. "'Twas years ago. We've not kept in touch."

Jane glared at Mary, who perched beside Annalisa on the sofa. "Knew you this?"

Mary shook her head. "Nay, but I'm keen on meeting the gentleman."

A coy smile lifted Jane's lips, and she returned to her embroidery. "Well, since Lady Perkins and Mamma are quite eager for you both to find husbands, mayhap we shall introduce the eligible Mr. Cavendish to Mary."

"I thought Mary had taken a liking to Mr. Wentworth," Annalisa said.

"Fie." Jack tossed his newspaper into the fire. "The Loyalist from Portsmouth?"

"Oh, is he Loyalist?" Mary slid closer to Annalisa. "Maybe I will attach myself to Mr. Cavendish, then."

Jane smiled. "If you meet Mr. Cavendish and take a liking to the sir, I shan't inveigle you otherwise. That leaves Annalisa for Mr. Peabody."

"The Mr. Peabody who purchased George's inn at Portsmouth?" Jack faced Annalisa. "Has the gentleman made you an offer?"

"No." Annalisa burned with indignation. "There has been no transaction between us. I've seen the sir but twice."

"It won't be long before he does. I'm sure of it." Jane smirked. "Jack, your dear mamma and mine have conjured the match. Don't you think Annie and Mr. Peabody would make a blissful pair?"

"Quite." Jack's jaw twitched. "Excuse me, ladies. Quinn, I've a need to satiate my thirst. Care to join me?" He stood, bowed, and quit the room before awaiting his friend's reply.

Quinnapin rose but before leaving, he added a genteel, "Good evening, ladies."

Annalisa threw down her book and jumped from the sofa. The heat of the fire burned her face as she peered into its dancing flames. Beside her, Jane sat so demurely in a chair adjacent the fireplace.

"How dare you?" Annalisa growled.

"I beg your pardon?" Jane tsked. "You've not spoken more than five words to me since summer. I don't wish to quarrel with you any longer."

Annalisa dug her fingers into the fireplace mantel until the tips whitened. Her temples throbbing, she unclenched her jaw.

"Please say something," Jane said. "Anything."

Her neck and face burning, Annalisa released the mantel and faced Jane. "You know very well Jack is soon leaving to pursue a divorce petition from Parliament, yet you speak to him of my marrying Mr. Peabody as though it were more fact than fiction. And this is hardly your worst offense toward me." She lowered her voice. "You wish for me to speak anything? I shall do so plainly. I find you so intolerable I dare believe you the devil incarnate, come to torment me for my sins."

"I see." Jane's bottom lip quivered. "I would never do such evil, Annie. Not to anyone, and certainly not to my sister. I pray you'll soon learn the truth. Then 'twill be you who regrets the dreadful curses you've inflicted upon me without cause."

Jane lifted from her chair by the hearth and fled the room.

Annalisa snatched Jane's embroidery and tossed it into the flames.

"Annie, no." Mary leapt from the sofa and rested a hand Annalisa's shoulder. "Your words were invective—"

"But true. And I will not apologize for this. She may forever rot in an unmarked grave like my daughter she murdered."

"Peace, Annie." Mary led her back to the sofa. "Pray, listen. Part of me wonders if Jane did it. She's always denied it."

"Of course she denies it," Annalisa cried. "She hopes I'll learn the truth, but therein lies one truth: she brewed the tea with the pennyroyal and let me drink several glasses. Abigail was the only other in our party that day and would never do something so indescribably cruel or senseless. Ergo, 'twas Jane. She, and she alone, had reason to end my pregnancy. If I birthed the child, such would've justified Jack's divorce petition to the courts—"

"Albeit in scandal," Mary added.

Annalisa glowered. "After all we've endured, what's one more scrap of gossip? Have we not suffered enough?"

"Patience and fortitude," Mary whispered. "In time, you'll have what you desire. But careful how you go. Jane is hardly clever, but she's calculating."

"Yet you think she may not have poisoned me?"

"She's calculating, Annie. But she's not evil."

Now chilled, goose skin puckered the exposed flesh of Annalisa's forearms. "If not Jane, who else had reason to terminate my pregnancy and nearly end me as well?"

"I know not." Mary inhaled sharply. "Have you ever considered it an honest but gravely misfortunate happenstance?"

Annalisa's face numbed. "*Gravely misfortunate happenstance?*

Speak we of the same devastating event? I thought you sympathetic—"

"Shh. Of course, I'm sympathetic. But I must also consider alternatives if Jane is innocent. 'Tis all I wish to do, Annie—uncover who caused your miscarriage, and why."

Annalisa held her head. "I would spend countless hours of my life poring over the details of that horrid day, but I can't. And come tomorrow, I have far greater things to face."

Mary clasped her hand and squeezed. "Ben Cavendish... and the wedding."

"Aye." Annalisa shuddered, her entire body cold. "We must contemplate a plan for this to work. Else we both shall suffer."

16

ANNALISA

PHILADELPHIA, APRIL 1779

ANNALISA TUCKED IN THE collar of her men's shirt to allow for a wide neckline similar to her chemise, then rolled up the long sleeves. She yanked on her breeches, stuffed the shirt between her legs, and buttoned the flap. Over the shirt and breeches, she donned her stays, which Mary helped tighten about her torso, made bulkier from the breeches. Into the pockets tied about her waist, where she kept her Bunker Hill musket round, Annalisa hid a neckpiece and shoe buckles. Mary helped tie on the hoops over which Annalisa secured her green silk petticoat, then pinned on her formal gown.

With Mary's assistance, dressing took no more than ten minutes, a feat she could never have completed alone. Quinnapin folded and tucked her coat and waistcoat into a haversack while Mary removed two wigs from her travel trunk.

"My wig from London?" Annalisa chuckled. "You would have me wear such a coiffure tonight?"

"Yes." Mary proceeded to stuff Annalisa's tresses into her wig cap.

"Brilliant," Quinnapin said.

"Yes." Mary positioned the lady's wig over Annalisa's head and secured it into place with pins. The second wig Mary had procured—though hadn't revealed how she obtained it—was a men's wig Annalisa would don as Benjamin.

Her coiffure in place, Annalisa peered into the looking glass. She hadn't worn the hairpiece since London, but the style would suffice for tonight's celebration. Fashionable a year prior, Jane would certainly be jealous. The men's periwig, powdered and curled with a queue, would only further enhance her disguise as Benjamin Cavendish.

"I'll be at the ready to help you change at a moment's notice," Mary said.

Annalisa smiled. "You'll be my minutewoman."

Mary chuckled. "I swear to you, not a soul in attendance shall question you." She reached into her pocket and revealed the rouge and white cosmetics covering Annalisa's complexion. "I will touch up your face when you return to your dress, so keep a handkerchief with you to wipe it clean when you change into Benjamin's clothes."

"And my scar?" Annalisa patted the silvery space beneath her right eye.

"'Tis hardly noticeable, especially in this face paint," Quinnapin replied. "I doubt anyone will notice it."

Annalisa skewed her mouth. "Jack and Jane will."

"What did you do to conceal it from Jack at Saratoga?" Mary asked.

"I was covered in grime and gunpowder when I saw him." Annalisa frowned, recalling the duel between her and Jack.

"Jack had been heavily altered by tincture of opium and brandy," Quinnapin said. "I doubt he saw you clearly. But to be certain our plan will work, let's postpone changing you from Annalisa to Benjamin until after the drinks are flowing, and we shall keep to darkened corners of the assembly hall."

"Then I need not make acquaintances of Jack and Jane?" Annalisa asked.

"No. Let them see you from a distance with Quinn and me," Mary replied.

Annalisa sucked in a nervous breath. "Then let the festivities commence."

The assembly room of the Shippens's home teemed with a great ostentation of Philadelphia's elitest peacocks. They saturated the air in orange blossom and musk, far more pleasant aromas than Jane's saccharine lavender perfume.

Annalisa clung to Mary, who drank a glass of claret with Jack, Quinnapin, and Jane. Across the room, Lord Essex loudly flaunted news of his new title as Earl of Essex.

"Did you hear that?" Annalisa whispered to Mary. "Earl? Can you believe that?"

Mary's lips parted to reply but Jane interrupted. "Have you yet seen Mr. Cavendish?"

"I've not," Quinnapin said. "But I'm certain the gentleman shall be here."

In one inconspicuous motion, Jack tugged at Annalisa's skirts and clinked his glass with hers. "You look well in that green gown," he murmured.

"Thank you, sir." She hid her grin behind her glass of wine and sipped.

"I want to apologize for my abrupt departure last night." He continued to speak low. "I know 'tis not your fault our mothers have overzealous plans for marrying you and Mary to some unsuspecting gentleman of consequence. But Mr. Peabody, is he...a contender?"

"I know my mamma and yours would wish it so." Annalisa finished her drink. "There's little I may do to assuage the situation until you've returned from London with your divorce. I will try to thwart it as long as I can."

Jack leaned in, flooding her with his amber perfume. "I'll speak to my mother—"

"No!" she cried.

Quinnapin, Mary, and Jane looked in her direction. Annalisa smiled and adjusted a pin within her bodice. "I'm quite all right."

Jack raised a brow. "That was an emphatic refusal."

"Let's speak privately." She linked her arm about his and let him lead her about the room. "I don't wish to worry you of these things when you've so much to plan for Parliament. Besides, 'tis mostly my mamma who wishes for me to marry. I will speak with her."

"As you wish, dear heart." He brushed a subtle kiss across her hand.

She eased with his arm about her, despite the unfamiliar assembly hall and her plan to change into Benjamin Cavendish later that evening.

"I'm dreading this trip to London," Jack said.

"You will be sorely missed at home."

A beat of silence passed between them while she kept his pace, a cordial, formal partner to pass the time beside him, yet he was far more than that to her and would always be so.

"Indulge me. Just once before I leave for London—"

"Where?" Her heart skipped. "Here?"

"At my apartments or in some darkened corner of an unoccupied room." Jack blushed with impassioned zeal. "Annalisa, I know such actions speak very little of my character, but you must know I find it impossible to regard you as anything other than the partner of my life."

"Such fine words only render your leaving next month that much worse." She hesitated. "And if I coddle our cravings, what shall that make me, Jack? Your mistress; and something I never wished for myself, especially with regards to you."

"You are not my mistress." His lips pursed. "Since the wreckage, I can't help but consider the possibility of my ship capsizing on the crossing..."

Annalisa's face tingled. "I should mourn you the rest of my days." Before they circled the room, she faced him. "There's a hallway. We may find a room to speak more privately."

She led them down the corridor until they reached a blue painted door on the right. She entered, then he behind her. After she latched the door shut, she turned to him, incapable of withholding her tears.

"Please don't leave. If you perish on the crossing, I shall die myself. And if you're gone a twelvemonth, I know my mamma will have me married before your return—"

"Dear heart, peace." Jack held her close.

"Please don't go."

"If I'm to obtain my divorce, Annalisa, I must go."

"You well know I would die for you this very instant than return home and face the possibility of being courted by anyone other than you." She swallowed thickly, wishing all she said weren't true. But it was. And he needed to go to England to receive a divorce from Parliament and an annulment from the ecclesiastical courts. Would he return to find her engaged, or worse, married? All because of his mother.

"Annie, listen to me." Jack's countenance softened. "I'm leaving for England for us. You must delay any engagement until my return. Please, you must."

"I will do my best, but you know nothing of what's at stake." Annalisa choked on the last word, yearning to tell him everything his horrid mother had threatened. She spun from him.

"Annie, you're my heart. I can't spend my life without

you. I won't. With my uncle's title, I'm certain I will be well received at Parliament. You have my solemn vow: I'll not return to Massachusetts until I've a divorce and annulment."

At his fine words, she faced him once more. Jack swept his thumb over the scar beneath her right eye to clear away the droplets. She covered his hand with hers and kissed his palm.

"This is too hard."

"Life is hard, Annie. But 'tis worth living." Driven toward her by the intimate gesture, Jack cupped her face with his other hand. "Stop fighting it, my darling girl. I've never wavered. Whyever should you doubt me now?"

Annalisa shook her head but gripped his wrist. She tugged him forward and blended her lips with his. She sank into his embrace as he kissed her with as much zeal as she remembered of their nightly intimacies as husband and wife. Eager to please, his tongue entered her mouth with a promise to delight her in every way he could. His breeches tightened against his turgid member, Jack pressed himself against her, then reached for her skirts. She longed for him. Craving his touch, his caresses, she parted her legs, and the breeches beneath her skirts tugged her into the moment.

She tore from him.

"I can't." With the breeches beneath her petticoats, she created a sizeable distance between them. "I can't. Not tonight." She needed a reason to refuse him, and she required one quickly.

Jack's head tilted, puzzled at her sudden change of heart. "Whatever's the matter?"

"The m-morbid flux is upon me," she blurted.

He offered his most tempting grin. "You know that never deterred me."

She blazed and adjusted her skirts. "I know, I just...not now."

"As you desire, dear heart." He righted his breeches, then offered her his hand. "We should return."

"Jack—" Annalisa stopped him from moving toward the door. "L-Later. Tonight."

"Only if you'll have me, dear heart. I won't inveigle you otherwise."

"I will have you." She nodded. "Of course I will. Just...give me some time to collect myself. The flux is rather burdensome this evening."

"Of course." Jack kissed her, then led them from the study.

When they returned to the assembly room and their party, Lord Essex greeted them with a cunning grin. "Good evening, Lord Brunswick, Miss Annalisa."

Mary, beside Quinnapin, said, "Annie, you look pale. Are you feeling quite well?"

Lord Essex tsked. "Unwell so soon?"

Jack glared at the earl, then addressed Annalisa. "Perhaps some fresh air would do you good? Would you like me to accompany you outside?"

"No, thank you, sir." Her hasty use of the morbid flux proved beneficial in allowing her to disappear. Pleased with herself, she met Mary's gaze. "I'll have Mary accompany me."

"Allow me to escort you both," Quinnapin said.

They escaped the assembly room and bustled down the long corridor.

Annalisa rapped on the closed door of the room from which she and Jack had just escaped. When no one spoke from the opposite side, they slipped inside, and Mary latched the door behind them.

Immediately, Quinnapin handed Annalisa the elixir from his pocket. "There's enough to last the night."

"Thank you, friend." Annalisa swallowed a mouthful of the bitter fluid, then grimaced.

"That escape proved easier than I thought." Mary helped Annalisa remove her dress without regard for Quinnapin, who quickly turned from them.

"Aye, I told Jack the morbid flux was upon me," Annalisa replied.

Mary chuckled. "Then we should have little trouble declaring your intermittent absence." Her sister quickly sobered, adding, "I can't help but get the terrible feeling this wedding has been contrived."

"Why do you suspect it?" Quinnapin asked.

"Because the Shippens sympathize with the British." Mary unlaced Annalisa's stays. "Yet Peggy is marrying a Continental general."

Breathless, Annalisa stuffed her gown and petticoats inside a wooden cabinet and hid her stays beneath a sofa cushion.

"I snuck out to the tavern dressed as Benjamin that night Arnold, Wentworth, and Essex left after dinner," Annalisa said. "Essex seemed happy to defect his allegiance, and Arnold seemed easily persuaded."

Mary sighed. "Then this marriage is perhaps an indication of Arnold's own intent to defect. Does Henry know? He has a contact who collects information..."

"I told George, but I know not if he relayed the information to Henry," Annalisa replied.

Her men's shirt already tucked into her breeches, she retrieved her waistcoat and coat from Quinnapin and threw her arms inside the garments. Mary removed the lady's wig from Annalisa's head and replaced it with the men's periwig. At last, Annalisa wiped her face of rouge.

"Please tell me I look convincing enough."

Mary stepped back. "Yes—"

"Perhaps from a darkened corner of the hall?" Annalisa asked.

"To be sure," Mary replied. "Quinn?"

He nodded. "Aye. And we'll be quick about regarding General Arnold."

Annalisa inhaled a deep breath then released it through pursed lips. "Then you and Mary should return. I'll find you in ten minutes."

As Quinnapin stepped from the room, he added, "Remember, Annalisa, people see what they want to see. No one here knows 'tis you. They will not see you tonight."

Her nerves heightened, Annalisa paced the dimly lit study and prayed to whomever would listen. *Oh, Great Spirit, my darling daughter, whom I shan't call by name, please let me fool everyone tonight. I must maintain this guise.*

With a final inhalation, Annalisa opened the door.

17

ANNALISA
PHILADELPHIA, APRIL 1779

CHATTER AND LAUGHTER RUMBLED through the assembly hall over bright violins and elegant cellos playing Mozart. Invigorated by her favorite composer, Annalisa stepped into the room with her head poised high. She scanned the crowded space for Mary and Quinnapin, who lingered by the musicians.

"You made it, Mr. Cavendish. We've been awaiting you." Quinnapin handed her a glass of wine. Quickly, Annalisa poured some of the elixir into the glass.

She drank several sips before regarding Mary. "Pray, does Jane see me? Jack? Lord Essex?"

Mary scanned the room from her periphery. "Yes. I'll alert you if they approach." She stepped back and appraised Annalisa. "You do look quite masculine, I must say. From a distance, I'm certain Jane will have no idea you're not some rogue I've just met this night."

Buzzing with wine, Annalisa grinned. "Think you I may fool Peggy Shippen?"

"She knows you far less than Jane or Jack," Quinnapin replied.

Mary's face paled. "Quick, they come this way. Get to."

"Let's pay our respects to Arnold." Quinnapin gestured with a nod for them to cross the room before Jane, Jack, and Lord Essex could join their party.

Sipping her wine, Annalisa followed Quinnapin through the crowd. Relieved to have avoided them, she finished her glass and plucked another from a servant's tray.

Major General Arnold leaned on his cane near a table overflowing with sweet, tantalizing desserts. His prize, Peggy Shippen, clung to his arm as she chatted with Mr. Wentworth. Annalisa's heart skipped at the sight of Wentworth, whom she'd met that same night at the tavern with Arnold and Lord Essex. She held her breath and awaited a lull in their intercourse, then addressed the major general.

"Major General, sir."

The military governor and his bride turned. Arnold's smug face contorted into one of mild disdain. "And you are?"

"Private Benjamin Cavendish, sir. And this is Quinnapin of the Wampanoag Nation. We fought with you at Bemis Heights. We're honored to celebrate, sir, by your request..."

"Yes, the saviors of my leg." Arnold still limped with his cane, much as he had in November, but at least he walked. "Welcome, gentlemen. Please enjoy yourselves."

"Ah, Cavendish." Mr. Wentworth clapped her shoulder. "A pleasant evening to be reacquainted, sir."

"Likewise," she replied. "And my friend, Quinnapin."

"How wonderful to meet you gentlemen." Peggy offered a bright smile and removed herself from Arnold's arm. "How thankful I am to you both for saving my dear husband's leg. Pray, you must dance the first with me." She winked, then returned to her husband, who paid them little heed.

Annalisa and Quinnapin disappeared back into the crowd, and Quinnapin laughed. "Zounds! The gall of that man."

"A self-important reptile," she snickered. "To think, we

traveled from Massachusetts for ten seconds of his time. But I will find Peggy and dance the first with her."

Quinnapin cackled. "Capital!"

Across the room, Mary advanced toward them in a swirl of fine silk. "Did you speak with the military governor and his wife?"

"He was grateful to have us," Annalisa replied. "And Mrs. Arnold is a delight. She asked to dance the first with me."

Mary snickered. "A sordid plan, but one I will delight in watching." Her gaze flickered toward the encroaching gentleman, Mr. Wentworth.

"Mr. Cavendish, I knew not you knew Miss Mary Howlett," Mr. Wentworth said.

Mary curtsied. "How good to see you, sir."

"The pleasure is all mine, Miss Mary," Mr. Wentworth said. "Pray, is your other sister here as well?"

"Miss Annalisa is here, sir," Quinnapin replied. "She's resting, presently."

"Pray, Cav, how do you know the Howlett sisters?" Mr. Wentworth asked.

"They are a distant relation to me, on their father's side," Annalisa replied.

Vivaldi's minuet from the *Concerto in C Major RV 447* filled the assembly hall, and eager guests flocked to the center of the room for dancing. Mr. Wentworth set his gaze on Mary and offered her his hand.

"Will you dance the first with me?" he asked.

Mary hesitated. "Of course, sir."

Annalisa hurried from their group to find the bride, who stood expectantly for her beside Arnold.

"I knew you wouldn't forget, Mr. Cavendish." She held out her hand, and Annalisa led Peggy to the set of dancers.

Her stomach knotted, with Jane so near to her paired with Lord Essex. A notoriously difficult dance, and one she loathed, Annalisa fought the urge to run from the set. Rather, she recalled her days in London where she'd danced plenty of minuets in the lavish assembly hall at Devonshire House.

Annalisa held her head high and stepped in time to the music with Peggy, who, like Jane, eclipsed her in accomplishment. But not this evening. Even as she kept a close eye on Jane as she danced with Lord Essex, Annalisa promenaded down the center of the room, her feet light, and never once losing her count of six. When the dance ended, she caught Lord Essex bow and whisper something to Jane. Annalisa quickly bowed to Peggy, who beamed up at her.

"Mr. Cavendish, how well you dance. You are quite light of foot. Wherever did you learn to dance?"

"You flatter me, Mrs. Arnold. I had a very diligent sister teach me."

Peggy laughed and clapped her hands. "Marvelous!"

Annalisa bowed again, eager to retreat from the set and into a darkened corner of the room. "I shan't keep you any longer, marm. I'm certain you have plenty of partners waiting to share the dancefloor with you."

"You're charming, Mr. Cavendish." Peggy curtsied, then turned to accept the hand of another gentleman.

Annalisa hustled toward her sister, who remained in Mr. Wentworth's audience. From the set, she caught a glimpse of Jane and Lord Essex as they spoke before the next dance started.

"Mr. Cavendish, will you take a turn about the room with me?" Mary asked, breathless.

"Of course." Annalisa held out her arm and led Mary away from Mr. Wentworth.

When out of sight, they slipped down the hall toward the study that kept Annalisa's belongings. They latched the door behind them, and Mary fisted her timorous hands.

"Thank you for saving me from Mr. Wentworth. I fear he knows our family is Patriot."

"He absolutely does," Annalisa replied, removing her coat. She untied her neckpiece and unbuttoned her waistcoat. "And 'tis worse now he knows Benjamin is acquainted with our family and fought for the Continentals."

Annalisa flung off her men's clothes, including the breeches, and donned her stays. Her sister's adept fingers laced them about her slender torso. When she finished, Annalisa salvaged her dress, pockets, hoops, and petticoats from the cabinets. As Mary replaced the men's periwig with the lady's wig, Annlisa tied on her garments. At last, she and Mary pinned on her gown.

"My face, Mary. The paint and rouge."

Her sister removed the cosmetics from her pockets and, using her fingers, hastily made-up Annalisa's face.

"My heart won't quit racing," Annalisa said. "I fear we're in a world of danger."

Mary ran her hands down Annalisa's arms, now encased to her elbows in green silk and lace. "You've done well. I know they must believe Benjamin to be someone other than you. Now, you may enjoy the evening as yourself."

Annalisa sucked in a quivering breath, then released it. The escapade was over. Hopefully, no one would take notice of Cavendish's absence the remainder of the night, though she suspected Peggy might. She'd done her diligence in maintaining the façade while avoiding Jack and Jane, but the game was far from over. Jane would surely have questions about the man she glimpsed from a distance, the man who danced the minuet with Peggy Shippen: Benjamin Cavendish.

$\mathscr{H}$ 18 $\mathscr{H}$

ANNALISA

TOPSFIELD, EARLY MAY 1779

ANNALISA SAT BENEATH THE ancient oak and contemplated the events of Peggy Shippen's wedding. That night in Chief Justice Shippen's study, she would have succumbed to Jack's tantalizing kisses had she not been wearing breeches beneath her skirts. Despite their brief tryst after the wedding, she quaked at the thought of his discovering her ruse. Nearly a decade had passed since she joined the Danvers militia as Benjamin, and four years had come and gone since the battle at Bunker Hill. Jack would never forgive her for withholding such a scheme for so long. Not when he could have been an accomplice to her, like George.

But it was better this way. Jack need not meddle and endanger himself with knowing something so scandalous. The Continentals would gaol her if they discovered her identity while masquerading as Benjamin, a danger George faced for merely knowing and concealing her secret. A fate far worse than gaol, she would be hanged if found by the British. Keeping Benjamin from Jack was the least she could do to protect him.

A cool May breeze rustled the handkerchief about her

neck, and she shivered. Her throat tight with reservation, she drew her initials into the dirt where her daughter lay buried. Beside hers, she scrawled Jack's.

"Here, we may always be together," she whispered. "And you were the proof of our love, my darling."

Salvage all you can, salvage it all, dearest Mamma.

"I'm sorry to intrude."

Startled, Annalisa turned.

Jack lingered in the shade of the tree with Robby propped in his arms. "I came to wish you well."

Annalisa stood and stepped forward to kiss her nephew's forehead. "Safe travels. I'll miss you, little sir."

"I fear he'll miss his Auntie Annie almost as much as I will."

Robby's lower lip quivered. "I miss Aunee Ana."

Annalisa's heart ached at the sound of her two-year-old nephew speaking her name. She'd been absent for his first word, among other milestones, and would certainly miss more while he was away in London. Jack lowered the boy into her arms, and she smoothed his soft chestnut locks from his face.

"I love you, young master Robby. I'll see you again soon. I promise."

If saying good-bye to her nephew proved this difficult, she could only imagine the utter torment Jane felt on this eve of their departure. *Perhaps Jane will feel as destroyed as I was to have lost Eliza.* The thought sat bitterly as she and Jack now occupied the space where their daughter lay. If only she could grip his arms and pull him toward her, tell him how she wished he would never leave and stay forever with her beneath their tree.

"Jack…" Annalisa croaked.

His hand found hers. "What is it, dear heart?"

She softened at the endearment. "I kn-know not what to s-say." *The damned stutter!*

Jack's sad lips smiled, and his thumb swiped the scar beneath her right eye. "Then speak nothing."

As they stood in the silent shade of the tree, something, an essence or spirit, drew their forms together until his forehead rested against hers. With Robby between them, Annalisa closed her eyes and inhaled Jack's amber perfume as it mingled with her nephew's delicate scent. She'd never known babies to smell so wonderful, and she wished she could cuddle the toddler the rest of her days. *Would that we could create another child together, Jack, one we could raise and care for, one who will outlive us and raise a family of their own, one who will love and remember us.*

Salvage it all, Mamma.

Her daughter's sweet voice echoed from beyond the ethers, and Annalisa wondered if Jack heard her. Their foreheads still one, she peered into his deep, Atlantic-blue eyes.

"Salvage this moment," he said. "'Tis what she said."

Tears welled and spilled onto her cheeks. "Then you heard her, too."

Robby's hand reached up as though he meant to grab a hold of someone's hand above them. "I hear. Yiy-za."

Jack and Annalisa stepped from one another, the air thick between them despite the fair, temperate day.

"Robby, do you see your sister?" Jack asked.

The boy's smile sported several small teeth, another development Annalisa had missed. Her breast rattled for the girl buried beneath the tree. Would that her daughter were with them in the flesh to play with her half-brother. Quickly, she handed Robby back to his father.

"We will create another, you and I," Jack said.

"Don't speak thus."

"I've seen it."

Her stomach twisted at his words.

Robby tugged Jack's hair, loosening it from its tie. Jack set the boy on the ground and removed the ribbon. Chestnut locks fell about his shoulders, and Annalisa's heart skipped at the sight of his hair unbound; vestiges of those tresses tossed upon their marriage bed tingled her breast.

"You've seen nothing, John Jackson."

His mouth twisted with an impish grin. "When you call me John Jackson, every inch of me burns. Annalisa Howlett, call me 'heathen,' or one who deals with the devil, but I've seen it." He hesitated. "I saw much during my fits of darkness aboard HMS *Lively*. And a vision of our family is what kept me alive."

Annalisa repressed a shudder at the mention of his imprisonment. She'd renounced God after that shipwreck, and he had, too. But to hear him speak of the devil puckered her skin, though not of fear. Her own draw to Quinnapin's belief in the Great Spirit had given her immense comfort during her days of mourning. In this moment, she craved to tell Jack she saw a future with him, that she, too, had seen their children in a vision. But she hadn't. Only their daughter's spirit. *Why does he see a family with me and I do not?*

Jack licked his lips, then glanced at the ground where Robby played. The boy mumbled and jabbered at Eliza's grave. Annalisa eased at the sight rather than fear it. Her daughter's spirit was benevolent and kind; she would have made a wonderful sister.

"Annalisa Howlett!" Mamma's voice carried on the wind.

She started. "I must go."

Jack frowned. "May the Lord keep you while I'm gone."

"You know I pray little to God."

He chuckled. "I recite those prayers with Robby every night as he goes to sleep."

"Now I lay me down to sleep," she started, and he joined:

"I pray the Lord my Soul to keep
If I should die before I wake…"

Jack cupped her face. *"I pray the Lord my Soul to take."* He finished the prayer, then kissed her. "If I should perish on this voyage, my soul left this earth bonded with yours."

Their lips fused for only a moment, and his hand lifted from her face, leaving her cheek cold and wanting. As Jack collected his son from their daughter's grave, Annalisa pondered how much longer they could display such intimate behavior in front of the boy before he learned to speak all he saw. It was the last thing Lady Perkins needed to hear.

"We need to be careful, Jack."

He smiled. "There is little need. When I return with my divorce, we need never again hide our love."

She returned his smile despite the gnawing culpability burning within her breast. "I pray for your swift return."

"God keep you, my dearest love." He kissed her once more, then slipped from the sanctuary of the oak's branches, leaving her beneath its boughs.

Heavy tears coursed her cheeks and burned her lips. *How can I now meet Mamma?*

Annalisa wiped her face and pressed the heels of her hands against her cheeks to dispel the swelling. Several inhales and exhales slowed her racing heart, and she straightened her bodice. In that moment, she missed her brother George more than anyone else in the world. He would tell her to run, to hide from any fate she found displeasing. He had done just that, himself.

As she stepped from the protection of her tree, Annalisa imagined George and Abigail somewhere in Charleston sequestering Abigail from Lord Essex, and from the threats of Mr. Wentworth and other Loyalists. Espionage was a dangerous game, indeed; one in which her dear brother never meant to partake.

When Annalisa returned to the house, Mamma met her in the foyer with Mary, Lady Perkins, and Jane, whose tear-stained cheeks mimicked the morning dew upon a summer rose.

"I suppose you've said your farewells to Mr. Perkins," Mamma said.

Annalisa flushed. "I have."

"Farewell, indeed." Lady Perkins pursed her lips.

Annalisa met Jane's icy gaze.

"You will pay for this horror," Jane said. "You took him from me—my son and my husband will no longer be mine when he returns from London."

"Robby will always be your son, Janey," Mary said.

"Peace, Janey," Mamma hissed.

"Speak not so," Lady Perkins said. "Let Jack believe what he may. Let him travel thousands of miles for nothing. He will return to you your husband."

Annalisa burned. "No, he won't. There is little reason Parliament won't grant him the divorce. He has plenty of evidence Jane cuckolded him with Lord Essex."

Mamma shrieked, "Annalisa Howlett!"

"'Tis the truth." Annalisa threw up her hands. "A man may take a lover, but a lady may not. 'Tis not my rules, Mamma. 'Tis Society's."

"You hold your tongue, young miss," Lady Perkins snapped. "And has Jack taken you for his mistress?"

"I would never divulge something so vile to you, my lady. Especially not in the presence of my sisters and Mamma."

"Yea or nay, Annalisa Howlett," Mamma sneered. "Have you been taken his mistress?"

Annalisa crossed her arms. "I will never confirm it, nor

will I deny it. It is my private business to know, and no one else's. Besides, I owe Jack—"

"Lord Brunswick," Lady Perkins said.

Annalisa swallowed. "I beg pardon, my lady. I owe *Lord Brunswick* the same decency."

Mamma threw up her hands. "You selfish, ungrateful girl. Have you not seen what this liaison has done to your sister? That your infatuations have taken her son and husband from her? I will never forgive you for this."

"What of the miscarriage your beloved Janey caused of your granddaughter?" Annalisa cried. "What of that horror? Or is it a lesser offense because the child would have been no different than Louisa—a merry-begotten—born of a silly dalliance meant to break apart a marriage that never should have taken place?"

"That is a vulgar thing to say, Miss Annalisa." Lady Perkins rested her hand across her bosom. "The miscarriage was a grievous event that neither involved your sister nor myself. Sometimes, we miscarry, Miss Annalisa. But this marriage between Jane and Jack, however insignificant you deem it, happened. And it will take an act of God to dissolve it."

Annalisa looked to Mary for help, but her younger sister remained silent. "Then I will retreat to wherever George and Abigail have taken up residence."

"You would not dare," Mamma said. "You will remain here, and you will be courted by Mr. Peabody."

Mary gripped her hand. "You needn't leave town, Annie. I need you here with me."

Mary's plea took her by surprise. Annalisa held her imperative stare and knew she meant to keep her safe from any matrimonial agreement with Mr. Peabody so long as she remained in town to help her spy at the Whispering Willow.

They had, after all, come by some information at the Shippen-Arnold wedding that needed to be dispatched.

Annalisa regarded Mamma and Lady Perkins. "If I refuse?"

Lady Perkins smoothed her skirts and maintained a charming countenance, though Annalisa could tell she fumed with indignance. "Miss Annalisa, it would behoove you to comply, lest you wish to find yourself in a gravely unfortunate circumstance. A spinster's life is not one we'd choose for you. Your mamma and myself wish nothing but the best for you."

Though she spoke fine words, the threat in Lady Perkins's glare hollowed the space within Annalisa's breast. She tightened her hand in Mary's and focused on Jane, a withered flower in Mamma's embrace. The sight would have caused any sister to comfort, but Annalisa held Jane's watery gaze with fire.

No, she would not marry Mr. Peabody, not when Jack meant to return with his divorce decree. But she could placate Lady Perkins and Mamma until his return. Anything would be better than allowing her family's farm to burn to the ground.

Now, she need only write to George and Abigail to see if they would host her for a while.

19

GEORGE

CHARLESTON, SOUTH CAROLINA,
MAY 1779

BEADS OF SWEAT TRICKLED down George's temple as he traversed the cobbled streets of Charleston. Grid-like and lined with brick rowhouses, the town was flanked by the Ashley and Cooper rivers until they joined in Charleston Harbor. The setting rekindled in George a vision of a smaller New York—New York with a thick, disagreeable mugginess in springtime. Only divine Providence would tell how he could survive such a place having just enlisted with the Continentals.

As he neared their rented apartments, George conjured the resentful outburst Abigail was certain to offer upon discovering his reenlistment. With a grimace, he slowed his pace. The brick building with blue-painted front door loomed, and within, Abigail and their daughter, Louisa. *A merry-begotten.* Had Abigail not been daft enough to leap the sword with him at Valley Forge, their living together would have been doubly questioned. And yet she remained legally wed to that reptile Lord Essex.

George gritted his teeth, then entered the rowhouse.

Abigail paced the foyer. "Where have you been? 'Tis been hours. Sarah and Addy will be here with the captain any moment." Addy and Sarah's friend, the captain, had been delayed leaving New-England, having made port in Charleston just last week. Of course, this left Abigail no choice but to invite the seafarer to dine, no matter the humble state of their lodging.

George removed his hat and wiped the sweat from his brow. After hanging the hat on a wall hook, he shook free of his linen coat and rolled his billowing sleeves to his elbows. "This humidity is unbearable for springtime."

Abigail took the coat and hung it beside his hat. "You haven't answered me, George Howlett. Where have you been these hours?"

"'Tis no matter. I've returned in time for our company."

Her freckled cheeks pinked. "Have you been with another?"

Already overheated from the weather, his face burned as though he stood over a cooking fire. "Another? Pray, is that what you consider me? An unfaithful lover?"

"'Tis no secret you've been with many." Abigail threw up her arms. "We both know you've an unsatiable lust—"

"Well, I'll be damned." He glimpsed their daughter in the parlor, nodding off on the sofa, and stomped from the foyer to the kitchen to pour himself a bumper of cheap New-England rum. "Unsatiable, she says."

Abigail quickly followed. "George Howlett, look at me."

"Unsatiable? And unfaithful?" He gulped the rum, then glared at her. "How little you regard me."

She frowned. "I do. I just...I know not what to believe when you tell me nothing upon your tardy return home."

"I've not consorted with doxies," he growled.

"What, then?"

"I enlisted with the Second South Carolina regiment." The thick air settled between them. "Are you satisfied?"

Abigail's cheeks faded to pallor, and her lower lip quivered. "You would do that to me?" In an added whisper that sounded more like a hiss, "To Louisa?"

George's face hardened against her powerless expression. "I do this for us. We'll never win this war—or end it—unless we have men to fight it. We learned this up north. 'Tis no different here."

Abigail said nothing. Her incongruous silence—an eerie disembodiment—crawled his skin far more than the outburst he'd imagined.

"Fie! Speak, Abbie."

She shook her head. "I've nothing to say." With a solitary glance at the ceiling, she muttered, "And these cobwebs won't remove themselves. Kitty!" Rather than seek out their lone housekeeper, Abigail flitted about the space as though they were about to host the Prince of Wales and not some unnamed captain.

Unwilling to feed her anxiety, George returned to the parlor and settled beside Louisa on the sofa. He ran his calloused hand over her soft, black hair. "Little mite, you understand your papa, don't you?"

The front door opened, and Oliver stepped inside holding a vase of creamy white southern magnolias. He knelt and handed Tommy the vase. "Go and offer them to Aunt Abigail." Tommy smiled and rushed off to find Abigail in the kitchen. Oliver joined George in the parlor. "Cousin, you're looking rather vexed. Is there trouble in paradise?"

George scowled at Oliver's leer. "'Tis your sister."

Oliver chuckled, then sat in a chair near the unlit fireplace. "To be unattached to a woman is fine, indeed."

Louisa stirred beside George and yawned. "Where is Tommy?"

"In the kitchen, little mite."

The girl slid from the sofa and toddled from the parlor. In the doorway, she met with Abigail and Tommy and the vase of magnolias.

"Ollie, these are perfect, thank you." A floral sweetness filled the room as she set the vase on a table by the window. Humidity stifled every room of their apartments, no matter the proximity to the harbor. A sea breeze only offered more moisture that ebbed from pleasant and briny to the effluvia of low tide.

"I miss New-England." George loosened his neckpiece. "This weather is unbearable."

"Hear, hear." Oliver removed his coat. "I must say, I hardly miss those cold rainy days in spring, but I'm far from used to these oppressive ones."

A knock sounded at the front door.

"They're here! Heavens, does everything look in its place? Kitty, the door!" Abigail smoothed the wrinkles from her petticoat. "That girl is useless."

Kitty, a young indentured girl, sashayed from the kitchen without a care in the world.

"Will you make haste?" Abigail sneered.

"Peace, Abbie." Oliver stood and donned the coat he'd just removed. "The captain is probably of modest means. And you know Addy and Sarah. This dinner should cause you little anxiety."

George adjusted his neckpiece as he crossed the parlor and into the foyer to receive their guests. Beside him, Oliver held Tommy's hand, and Abigail clutched Louisa.

Kitty opened the door.

Sarah and Addy stood on the front steps, obscuring a gentleman behind them. Their umber complexions glowed beneath straw hats decorated with springtime flowers.

Particularly Sarah, Addy's granddaughter, appeared youthful in her finest pink silk dress—a gift from the Duchess of Devonshire.

Addy opened her arms wide. "Georgie." She embraced him. "You're looking well."

"You, too, marm." George kissed her cheek, then led them inside the rowhouse.

The gentleman followed. Nearly as tall as George and robed in a formal blue-and-buff uniform hedged in gold, he boasted a square jaw and long hair laced with grey, tied in the queue of a sailor.

George shook away a sudden chill. Having himself adorned the blue and buff of the Continental Army, it was as though he peered into a looking glass twenty or so years from now.

The man removed his cocked hat and bowed. "Admiral Bixby, at your service, sir."

George's breath caught. *Bixby, 'tis my father's surname.* "Admiral, the pleasure is all mine. I'm Captain Howlett. Do make yourself at home, sir." He led the admiral into the small parlor, then motioned to Abigail. "Sir, may I present my—"

"Mrs. Howlett, if you please, sir." Abigail curtsied. "And our daughter, Louisa."

George sighed, relieved Abigail had chosen to be acknowledged as his wife and not Lady Essex. "This is Abigail's brother Mr. Oliver Perkins, and his son, Thomas."

"A pleasure, Admiral." Oliver bowed.

Addy clasped her hands. "'Tis so wonderful for you to finally meet Captain Bixby—"

"Admiral Bixby, Grandma," Sarah replied.

Addy shook her head. "My apologies, Admiral. This old mind is far from what it used to be."

The admiral sat in a chair opposite George before the

unlit hearth. He crossed one leg, then took up the dram of brandy offered him by Kitty. The poor girl suffered to do everything, including cook their meal whilst watching Louisa and Tommy in the kitchen.

"Bixby—'tis our mother's maiden name, Abigail," Oliver said.

"It is," she cried. "How fortunate. I wonder, are you a relation of the Bixbys at Suffolk? 'Tis where our mamma is from—"

"Abigail, peace," George muttered.

Oliver intercepted, "Tell me, Admiral, when did you make port in Charleston?"

"Tuesday last." Admiral Bixby adjusted himself in the chair. "We had marvelous weather sailing the coast from Providence."

George stiffened. "Providence, sir?" The Royal Navy had been stationed there. His nerves heightened, he leaned forward in his seat.

"Thank heaven," Sarah said. "Your presence was sorely missed these several months, sir."

"Yes, the captain—Admiral," Addy shook her head, "was so considerate to us upon our arrival to Charleston last year. I know not how we would've managed without his generosity."

"It was my pleasure to offer you my humble dwelling," he replied. "I rarely spent any time there these three years. Better to have someone keep it safe and in good hands."

"What fortune," Abigail said. "And to think, you managed to avoid any naval ships on your return to Charleston."

Admiral Bixby laughed. "I sail with the navy, Mrs. Howlett."

George's skin stung. *Then he sails with the navy.* "Pray, Admiral, you sailed from Providence. I knew a man from Providence, a Captain Fleming—"

"I knew Captain Fleming." The admiral's cheeks reddened

and he crossed one leg over the other. A brief smile lifted his lips and he said, "But let's not speak of the war." He raised his glass. "Rather, let's share a toast. To good health and good cheer."

"Hear, hear."

They all saluted, but George drank his liquor with reservation. He'd not cause a fuss at this meeting, but the admiral sailed from Providence, Rhode Island with the Royal Navy, and he knew the villainous Captain Fleming, a turncoat who sailed Jack and Annalisa's ship to Halifax when it had been bound for France. In tandem with all of this, the man bore his father's surname. George couldn't shake the feeling the admiral could somehow be a distant relation. Of course, he could hardly surmise the origin of such a common surname as Bixby, but the irony proved uncanny.

Oliver cast a hesitant glance his way. In that look, George vibrated with a sense of purpose to observe Bixby and uncover what he must. *Chance occurrences are rare.* George lifted his glass and drank. If only Annalisa were there to meet the admiral. Surely, his sister would have something to say, some sort of insight to impose on him. She was, after all, his most beloved confidante and understood his plight to learn of Captain Bixby, his natural father.

Could this man be my father? The hideous thought crossed his mind but once before evaporating into the humid air perfumed with magnolias. *No.* Bixby had been dead over twenty years, or so his mother told him. Such an occurrence would prove more than rare; it would be impossible. Yet, as George had found in his quarter century of living, life was rarely what he thought it should be—a nugget of wisdom he'd imparted on Annalisa. *Would that I could learn from my own advice.* Trite, indeed.

George peered at Abigail, who also studied the admiral with curiosity, and pondered if she held similar thoughts. The more troubling issue than the prospect of this man being some kind of relation was his knowledge of Captain Fleming. *How did he know Fleming?* George hardened his jaw and remained silent. Like a hand of cards, he would keep his observations and accusations near to his chest, but this meeting proved far more than anything he'd anticipated.

20

ANNALISA

TOPSFIELD, JUNE 1779

ANNALISA WIPED CLEAN A stack of pewter mugs behind the bar at the Whispering Willow Tavern, awaiting the courier. Her younger brothers, William and Henry, swept the floor and cleaned the vacant tables of sticky residue from spilled libations.

"I'm surprised that Benjamin Cavendish fellow from Peggy Shippen's wedding hasn't written to Mary," William said.

Annalisa peered up from the tankard she cleaned. "Did she say he would write to her?"

"Perhaps it was Wentworth she expected to write," William replied.

"No, it was Cavendish," Henry chimed from across the room.

Since their return from Philadelphia, her youngest brother—Mary's twin—seemed particularly interested in learning about Benjamin Cavendish.

Annalisa returned to her mug and set it aside with the other clean ones. "I doubt he will write, Henry. She spoke with him briefly that night."

The front door opened, and Mr. Peabody stepped inside. William straightened, setting the broom aside, and greeted the gentleman. "Mr. Peabody, how good to see you, sir. Have you been by the house to see Martha?"

Mr. Peabody nodded, smiling. "I have. I'll be spending the evening with you and my aunt and uncle."

"Capital." William gestured to a vacant table. "Have a seat, and let me get you something to drink."

Mr. Peabody wandered toward Annalisa at the bar. His soft brown eyes met hers with a candor she'd not witnessed in a man since the day Jack departed for London.

"Miss Annalisa, it does me good to see you."

She returned his grin, then averted her stare. "You're too kind, sir." *Where is the courier?* She'd written to George and Abigail weeks prior and had yet to receive a response.

The tavern door opened and closed once more, and Mary hurried inside. "Annalisa!"

Annalisa turned her attention from the man before her as Mary, with petticoats gathered in her hands, shuffled past their brothers toward the bar.

"Mr. Peabody, I apologize for my intrusion." Mary's frantic gaze held hers. "Jane is gone."

William gasped. "Gone?"

"Jane has?" Henry asked.

Their brothers convened around the bar.

"Lady Perkins is presently visiting Mamma," Mary said, breathless. "She said she returned from Ipswich to find Jane gone. Her trunk, everything."

"As in, gone to Cambridge with her latest dalliance, Lord Essex?" Annalisa asked.

Mr. Peabody's cheeks blushed at the conjecture, though he'd heard of the attention Jane paid Lord Essex at Peggy Shippen's wedding—a scandal all of town knew, thanks to Mary's deliberate whispers at the meetinghouse.

"Is it for the scorn she's met in town?" Henry asked. "Surely, she'll return in a few days. Did she not leave a note?"

"She did." Mary's mouth twisted. "She left for England to pursue Jack and Robby."

"England?" William cried. "How will she travel thither alone?"

"She's not alone," Mary said. "Jane wrote that Lord Essex booked them passage."

Annalisa scowled. "Mamma must be in a fit of hysterics. 'Twas bad enough Oliver took Tommy to Charleston; Jack had to bring Robby to London. Now, Jane is gone."

"Aye." Mary bit her lip. "We must go to Mamma."

"And say what?" Annalisa asked. "Mamma and Lady Perkins find little comfort in my company of late."

William tugged her from behind the bar. "Go home to Mother. Henry and I can manage the tavern."

Reluctant, Annalisa followed her sister, though she couldn't help but wonder if Mr. Peabody would rethink his intention to court her in light of her family's latest charade. A small grin lifted her lips as she mounted her horse and rode after Mary. *Thank goodness for you, Janey. You may have just saved me from an unwanted courtship.*

❦

"My Janey!" In the parlor, Mamma wailed in Lady Perkins's arms. "How could she do this to me? To our families?"

"Hush." Lady Perkins wiped Mamma's tears. "All will be well. Jane means only to retrieve her husband and son. She is accompanied by a fine gentleman. I assure you no harm will come of it."

Mamma lifted her reddened gaze. "Annalisa, you did see Mr. Peabody? Oh, Bette, what will I do if the Peabodys refuse this match. They will hear of Jane's departure, I'm sure of it."

"Peace." Lady Perkins held Annalisa's stare with unfeeling, dark eyes. "Mr. Peabody will not be deterred by this happenstance."

"How can you be sure?" Mamma cried.

Lady Perkins returned her softened gaze to Mamma. "The Peabodys, while modest, know better than to ruin a courtship over such silly charades. I will make sure of it."

Her hair standing on end, Annalisa gripped Mary's hand. Her life was no longer her own, but was it ever? She needed to receive word from George and Abigail and journey to them before it was too late. Worse, Jane now traveled to London to ensure Jack would not receive his divorce from her.

❧ 21 ❧

JACK

LONDON, LATE JUNE 1779

JACK TWIRLED HIS SIGNET ring while he waited with Father and Robby for his youngest brother, Andrew, who'd been abroad these last eighteen months.

"Father! Jack!" Andrew, nineteen and full of vigor, slipped through the open front doors of King's College and hastened down the front steps.

"My boy." Father hugged his youngest son, then stepped back to appraise him. "My God, look at you. You've become a man."

"Law school has done me well, I suppose," Andrew replied with Jack's crooked grin.

Jack went to shake Andrew's hand, but his youngest brother pulled him into an embrace. "You look well, Brother. It does me good to see you in such good health."

Andrew's eyes, an amalgamation of light blue and grey, glittered in the London sunshine—a rarity, Jack overheard at the tavern this morning. "And this must be young Robby." Andrew knelt and introduced himself to his young nephew, who had been only a few months old when he departed for London. "Jack, 'tis fantastical how Robby looks so much like you. A job well done, I suppose, as you always appear dashing."

Jack laughed and clapped his brother's shoulder. "Perhaps I look well, but I feel my age."

"At seven-and-twenty?" Father chuckled. "Wait until you're my age. Then you may grieve your youth." Father held Robby's small hand and beamed with pride. "We're only missing Ollie, else I'd have all my boys with me this day."

"And Tommy," Jack added.

Father nodded, looking rather pained. "Of course, young Thomas."

"How is Tommy?" Andrew asked.

"He's a quiet, pensive boy," Father replied. "I quite savor my time with my first grandson. It pains me Ollie's taken him to Charleston."

"Charleston?" Andrew's brows lifted. "You didn't write—"

"We'll discuss it later. Let's return to the inn for some lunch and a proper pipe." Father led them down the cobbled street.

Jack held Robby's other hand, and the boy toddled and tripped until Jack lifted him to keep their pace. He studied his son, who, to his distinct pleasure, looked more like him each day and less like Jane. "Do you miss Tommy and Weeza?"

Robby nodded. "I miss."

"Them," Jack said. "I miss them."

"I miss...fem," Robby repeated in his small voice. "I miss... Aunee Ana."

Jack's heart plummeted. No word for the boy's mother since they left America, but he missed his Auntie Anna.

With two fingers, Andrew pinched Robby's dimpled cheek. "You're quite the fine young master. You're sure to be as handsome as your papa. The ladies will be in trouble."

Jack smirked. "He already gets far more attention than I ever did—"

"Hardly!" Andrew guffawed. "No one, and I mean no one, ever looked twice at Ollie and me. 'Twas difficult growing up in your shadow, Jack. I admit it now, but I wished to be like you in every way. Had you been anything less than the decent and doting brother you were, and the honorable man you've become, it would've been intolerable. I'm grateful for your generosity and kindness in our youth. Pray, what specimen of gentleman can boast both agreeable features and a penchant for treating others as earnestly as you? Surely, it doesn't seem likely one man may be blessed with both qualities."

Jack flushed at his brother's fine words. "I knew not you felt this way."

"And humble," Andrew cried.

Father looked back and smiled. "What is this?"

"Your eldest son and heir, now also Lord Brunswick, is not only uncommonly handsome, but treats others with as much heartfelt dignity and acknowledgment as ever I've seen," Andrew said. "I'm astounded by you, Brother. If I could be but half the man you are, I daresay I could go anywhere in this life."

"Fine accolades, indeed," Father said. "But pray, place no man on a pedestal."

Guilt-ridden, Jack pondered his father's pursed lips and his brother's candid accolades. *I'm hardly as noble as he believes of me. Is his admiration the fantastical raving of a starry-eyed younger brother? Surely, he will come to see I'm no different than any other dishonorable man seeking to divorce his wife for the love of another.*

The chatter of men and clank of pewter filled the tavern at their inn. A potboy served steaming beef mince pies and tankards of frothy ale. His stomach grumbling, Jack cut into his pie, but Andrew raised his mug.

"A toast, gentlemen."

Jack and Father lifted their tankards.

"To our family and the end of the war," Andrew said.

"Hear, hear," Jack muttered beneath Father's grumble. They saluted and drank the tepid ale.

Andrew cut into his pie and chewed with the vigor of a young man still growing into his clothes. "You came all this way to collect me. I'm grateful and quite flattered I needn't travel the long way back to Boston alone. But how fares the colony? I've not heard much since being here, only what the papers write. Much of it is Tory nonsense."

"I'm here to collect you." Father glanced over his round spectacles. "Jack is here to pursue his own ambitions as Lord Brunswick."

Andrew picked a piece of gristle from his teeth. "Yes, I was quite bothered to hear of Uncle's passing. But, Jack, that leaves you quite an inheritance. You needn't practice law in Topsfield anymore. Not that you ever required a way to earn money."

Jack shook his head. "I like to employ my time with fruitful labors. I'm here of a different occasion."

Andrew leaned in and whispered, "Are you here for Congress?"

"He's here to pursue a divorce petition from Parliament, from Robby's mother," Father replied.

"Jane?" Andrew sat back. "You mean to dissolve your marriage?"

Jack swallowed his mouthful of crust, then washed it down with the bitter ale. His conscience thick, and now fearing his brother's scrutiny, he nodded. "Aye."

"Could you not obtain it at home?" Andrew asked.

"I need Parliament and the ecclesiastical courts," Jack replied.

Andrew quirked a brow. "Chicanery?"

"Perhaps." Jack returned to his pie. The filling oozed from the thick crust with a gelatinous quality that, in tandem with the mawkish scent of his ale, churned his stomach.

Father grunted, then pushed aside his half-eaten pie. "Chicanery or not, you seek an unconventional circumstance for your family, Jack, that I do not approve. But I can neither stop you nor deny you."

Anger flooded Jack with unbridled offense. "Your polemical rhetoric neither influences nor alters my conscience, *sir*. I will do as I see fit to correct the constitution of my life and Annalisa's."

Andrew shrugged. "It seems I've missed quite a bit of turmoil at home. I'm not surprised by any of it. But you said Ollie's in Charleston? With whom did he travel?"

Jack quickly relayed the state of their brother and nephew, which only led to a confirmation of Abigail and George's whereabouts, another contentious topic that further emboldened the indignant vein upon Father's forehead.

Father set down his spectacles and rubbed the bridge of his nose. "I'm unsure of where I faltered in parenting, but I assure you I assume responsibility. 'Twas mine, not your mother's."

Jack and Andrew fell silent.

"Sir, your failures as a parent are certainly my failures as a son," Jack replied softly. "I never wished to cause you such trouble. I only ever looked upon you with the same esteem and adoration my own brother looks upon me." He stood. "Excuse me, gentlemen. I've an appointment."

He kissed Robby and quit the tavern as quickly as he finished his ale.

Though Jack had frequented the streets of London eight years ago, they felt as unfamiliar as his new title, the Earl of Brunswick. Wearing his best hat and coat, and eager to speak with whomever would hear him, Jack cajoled his way through the bail dock, a semicircular brick wall in front of the Old Bailey, which had been rebuilt since he'd last seen it in 1771. True, he should have written to obtain an appointment—he had none—but he needed to accelerate the speed with which he filed his petition.

Once inside the stuffy brick building, Jack withdrew the letter he had received upon his uncle's death: a writ of summons to Parliament signed by King George III himself, the very monarch from whom they sought freedom within the colonies. Until America's freedom was granted, Jack would use his inherited title by whatever means necessary.

"May I assist you, sir?" A young man, perhaps a law student or steward of the court, greeted him near the entrance. "Have you an appointment?"

Jack shook his head. "No, I beg pardon, but I'm seeking counsel by whomever might be available presently."

The younger man's lips twirled into a grimace. "I'm afraid all are previously engaged. You'll need to make an appointment, sir."

Jack handed the man his summons to Parliament. "If I may, I'm Lord Brunswick and wish to speak with the first gentleman...esquire, magistrate...whomever might be first available. I'm willing to wait as long as it may take."

"This is most irregular, my lord." The man handed him back the summons. "I'm afraid I can't interrupt the trial, but I can put your name on the list for," his forefinger scanned the open ledger within his arms, "Mr. Brown, esquire, for Thursday next."

"Thursday next?" Jack's eyes widened. "'Tis only Monday. Shall I be grieved to wait over a week to meet with Mr. Brown, esquire? Have you no other available sooner?"

"Magistrate Hornsby may meet with you, my lord, on the thirtieth."

"The thirtieth instant?" Jack asked. Perhaps he would wait

the extra few days if it meant he could meet with a magistrate.

"No, my lord. The thirtieth of July."

"July," Jack cried. "That is over a month from now. I cannot wait until the end of next month, sir."

The young man's face blushed, and he closed his ledger. "My apologies, Lord Brunswick. I do wish there was more I could do to meet your needs."

Jack set his jaw. "Write me in with Mr. Brown for Thursday next."

"Very well, my lord. Two o'clock, Thursday next."

Without wishing the poor young lad well, Jack turned and fled the Old Bailey as quickly as he'd sped there.

JACK

LONDON, JULY 1779

"JACK, YOU'VE MAIL FROM the courier." Father handed him a small stack of letters.

Immediately, Jack recognized the seals, but his heart sank as another day passed without word from Annalisa. Their rented rooms at Kensington were modest but well furnished. He and Father sat in the orderly office, his father at the desk and Jack in a black Windsor chair beside a bookcase.

"Sir, did you recognize the rider?" Jack asked.

Father's lips pursed as he peered over his spectacles. "I did not. Is there a particular London rider from whom you receive letters?"

Jack stiffened at the conjecture. "No, but I'm awaiting word from the Old Bailey. Surely, you'd recognized one of their appointed couriers." He cracked the seal and read the contents with brevity: a message from Jane. She and Lord Essex had taken up rooms at Chelsea. He crumpled the letter. "Fie."

His father looked up. "Foul news?"

"Jane writes." Jack handed the letter to his father. "She and Essex are here in London."

"Here?" His father read the letter, then set it upon the desk. He leaned back in his chair and removed his spectacles. Rubbing the bridge of his nose, he sighed. "She certainly holds on to her frustrations in the wake of your departure with Robby. I suppose, in such a small way, you know she cares."

"I'm the boy's father. I may take him with me as I like." Jack burned. "Shall I now be cuckolded for all of London Society to ridicule me?"

"No." Father reddened. "I won't let that happen."

"'Tis too late. She already crossed an ocean with him."

Father shook his head. "I can't believe your mother allowed this to happen."

Jack cracked open the second letter in his lap. It read oddly. He took the chamberstick from the desk and held the paper to open flame. As the ink of a hidden message appeared between the other written lines, he settled back into his seat.

Sensing his trepidation, Father stood and moved to Jack's side. "What is it?"

"'Tis...unbelievable." Jack looked up. "Henry Howlett writes. He writes of some intercepted mail at the Whispering Willow. A man I know and fought with at Saratoga—he was also at the Arnold-Shippen wedding; I saw him with Mary Howlett and Quinnapin—has been identified as a potential spy."

"Which man?"

"Benjamin Cavendish."

"And Henry discovered his letters to...whom?"

"The letters were addressed to Major General Arnold in Philadelphia. The contents were traitorous."

Father rubbed his temples. "And Mr. Cavendish remains within the colonies?"

"So it would seem," Jack replied. "But it is all nonsensical. Cavendish fought beside George and me at Saratoga. Why should he turn coat, and why write to Arnold? Why would either man risk his situation?"

"Men do despicable things in times of war, Jack. Perhaps he planted himself amongst your militia to gain intelligence. Not uncommon in these times." His father took the letter to re-read. "How came Henry by such information?"

"He and William captured a rider at the Willow. Cavendish must be in Topsfield." Jack expected old feelings of anger for Benjamin Cavendish to resurface, but his chest iced with melancholy. "Annalisa and Mary...they could be in danger if Cavendish is in Topsfield...if the man is truly a turncoat. Mary especially, spent quite some time with the rogue in Philadelphia."

"There's hardly anything we may do here," Father said.

"Perhaps we should return to America in haste," Jack replied.

His father's complexion greyed, but he shook his head. "Lord Essex and Jane have come to London. You must finish what you sought to do here." He rose from the desk with conviction. "Obtain your petition from Parliament, let Jane see her son, then we shall book passage home with Andrew."

Jack tensed at his father's resolve. "You now approve of my decision to divorce Jane?"

Father placed a hand on Jack's shoulder. "The assiduity Lord Essex paid on Jane at the Shippen-Arnold wedding was a bold display I can't ignore. I'm quite shocked by it. I only pray I may be able to right these wrongs I've done you."

"Go on, sir." Jack twirled his signet ring and settled into his seat.

Father cleared his throat. "I know you've never quite

forgiven me for my...request of you. But I was wrong in conceding to your mother's demands that you marry Jane. Let this be my apology to you. And Annalisa. I only pray 'tis not too late."

Despite his father's regret, Jack prickled with an unknown blanket of secrets still withheld from him, questions yet to be answered about Benjamin Cavendish, the lad who entered his life with a burst of tumult at Saratoga, and whom he'd only recently witnessed at the wedding. Now, he no longer trusted Cavendish. *How can such a man cause me such disquiet?* He would have to locate and confront the lad upon his return to America. Hopefully, he'd still be in Topsfield, though Jack could only guess as to where the rogue made his lodging.

Father stood, breaking Jack from his trance. "Come, let's ready for tonight. We've a dinner invitation with Lord Melbourne. No doubt Essex will be present with your wife."

⚜

Jack and his father entered the three-story Melbourne House only moments after the arrival of the Duke and Duchess of Devonshire, to neither of whom they'd been previously introduced.

"Lord Perkins, Lord Brunswick, how wonderful for you to come this evening." Lord Melbourne, an agreeable-looking gentleman of middle age and average height, boasted London's latest fashion. He led Jack and his father toward the Duke and Duchess of Devonshire. The duke's disinterested demeanor propagated the need for his stylish ditto suit, which complemented his lady's highly fashionable silk *robe à la polonaise.*

Jack smiled, eager to meet the influential young woman who rescued his Annalisa from certain peril upon the docks in Calais after their ship's wreckage.

Lord Melbourne gestured to the nondescript duke and his rather popular duchess. "Your Grace, I'm pleased to introduce Lord Perkins and his eldest son, the new Earl of Brunswick."

The duchess gave a flawless curtsy. "How wonderful to meet you, my lords." Her coffee-colored eyes gleamed with a kindness that Jack had only half expected of the young noble; she could be no older than Annalisa. His innards flipped with excitement. *Yet she is exactly as Annie described.*

"Your Grace, the pleasure is entirely ours," Father replied.

The duke, as taciturn as Jack suspected, gave his brief regards, then slipped into the room. When he'd gone, the duchess eyed Jack. "My lords, how is your stay in London? I've been aware of your arrival and have been awaiting our introduction."

"You flatter us, Your Grace." Jack flashed her a charming grin. "We've been busy reuniting with my brother—he's been studying at King's College these last eighteen months—and I've been settling a matter most personal to me with Parliament."

The duchess clutched her breast. "Oh dear, I do hope 'tis nothing too serious, Lord Brunswick."

Jack shook his head. "You needn't worry, Your Grace." He peered about the room, expecting his wife and Lord Essex to materialize at any moment.

"Is there someone you seek, Lord Brunswick?" the duchess asked.

"His wife, Your Grace," Father replied.

Jack added, "She's expected to arrive with Lord Essex."

The duchess gasped. "You're—"

"Shall I get you some wine, Your Grace?" Father asked.

The duchess composed herself with practiced ease and smiled. "Wine would be marvelous, sir." She then tugged Jack aside and whispered, "You're Jack, dear Calais's husband.

Pray, she's to arrive with Lord Essex presently? I can hardly wait for us to meet again."

"Yes, I'm that very Jack." A lump rose in his throat. "But I'm afraid you're mistaken, Your Grace. I was married to Annalisa, and in our time apart, when I was believed widowed, I was made to marry her sister Jane—"

The duchess gasped again. "Yes, that's right. She did write. My poor Calais. The months of recovering, the torment—utter torment—upon remembering herself, only to believe you dead, for her to return home and find you wed to her sister."

Jack warmed. "'Twas unimaginable, I assure you, Your Grace. 'Tis why I'm in London. I decided it would be more fruitful for me to pursue a divorce and annulment here so she and I may again marry."

"Any luck?"

"Unfortunately, no. I met with Mr. Brown, esquire, who was maddeningly unhelpful. The magistrates are rather difficult to gain an audience with, Your Grace."

"Do you mean to file for a criminal conversation case?" She leaned in and whispered, "Can we blame Essex?"

"No, I don't wish for any kind of publicity." Jack fiddled with his signet ring. "Though I have reasonable evidence Essex has been having criminal conversations with Jane now for months. Just the annulment and divorce."

Her gloved hand landed upon his. "Allow me to help. I shall introduce you to Lord Mansfield. He's the lord chief justice and quite possibly the most powerful man in England next to our king. We shall maintain your good reputation, Lord Brunswick."

Jack vibrated with a vivacity he'd not experienced since docking in London. "Your Grace, I'd be most obliged to you."

"I'd do anything for Calais." The duchess peered behind

her. "You cannot possibly understand your good fortune, Lord Brunswick. I see your wife has arrived with Lord Essex. Come, let's greet them together. I've heard much about Calais's sister as well." The duchess winked, then linked her arm with his.

Her kindness washed over him as he eyed the Earl of Essex with Jane and his father. He cared little for Jane's advances when she paid him mind, and he cared even less for her attentions bestowed upon Lord Essex, save for his own good reputation.

"My Lord Essex, our circle is complete now you've returned," the duchess said. "And as earl, no less. Well done, good sir. I heard the news and could hardly wait to congratulate you, my lord."

Lord Essex bowed. "Your Grace, you do me an unjust honor."

The duchess gestured to Jane as gracefully as a dancer. "And I understand this is Lord Brunswick's wife, Lady Brunswick."

"Yes, Your Grace," Lord Essex replied. "Lady Brunswick, may I present the Duchess of Devonshire."

Jane's face blossomed, and she curtsied as though she'd been preparing for this moment her entire life—and Jack knew she had. "Your Grace, it is an honor."

"Yes, I can imagine," the duchess replied. "You're the older sister of my dear friend Calais, as I dotingly call her; Annalisa to you. I adore your sister, Lady Brunswick, and shall not rest until I've helped right the wrongs done her." The duchess smirked at Jack. "Shall we, Lord Brunswick? I've plenty of our circle to whom I must introduce you."

Jack returned her smile. "Lead the way, Your Grace."

When they were beyond Lord Essex and his party, the duchess giggled in a way that reminded him of his Annalisa. Astounded by her ability to transform from influential

Duchess of Devonshire to giddy young lady, Jack joined in her laughter.

"I quite used to adore Lord Essex. He's been a member of the Whig Party since before I married the duke. But," the duchess led Jack to an unoccupied corner, "he's written to Prime Minister Lord North—'tis how he was awarded his earldom."

"'Twas what Annalisa and Lady Essex—my sister Abigail —said they uncovered at his office. Pray, is Essex a turncoat, then?"

The duchess pursed her lips. "You can trust him less these days, so take care. Essex is a powerful man with friends in many places, including the Tory Party."

Her words shuddered his spine, and Jack wished to be as far from England's shores as the winds would carry him. "Pray, when may I meet Lord Mansfield, Your Grace?"

The duchess's hand landed upon his chest. "Please call me Gee."

Taken aback by her friendly gesture, Jack cupped her hand. "Gee. Please call me Jack."

"Jack, I'll write him first thing on the morrow. You'll have your divorce finalized at last."

"Many thanks to you, Gee."

As Jack engaged with the duchess and met her friends, politician Mr. Fox and playwright Mr. Sheridan, he couldn't help but think of Annalisa thousands of miles away, who had, unknowingly, brokered this most unlikely acquaintance. Yet it wasn't until he met Lady Melbourne and her friend Lady Jersey that Jack recalled his trip to London with Oliver.

Jack tensed with the anticipation of seeing Lady Jersey, wondering if she would recognize him after all the years of her other exploits. While hers and Lady Melbourne's affairs were quite known within London's *ton*, he still carried guilt for strumming Lord Jersey's wife all those years ago.

"Mr. Perkins, how *delightful* to meet you again, sir."

He bristled at the voice and turned.

Lady Jersey smirked with her rodent-like face caked in rouge. He hid his grimace as the duchess reintroduced him as the Earl of Brunswick.

Lady Jersey licked her thin lips. "Lord Brunswick, you're as delicious as you were the night you took me at Vauxhall. Perhaps more so."

"'Twas in the dark, my lady. I'm flattered you recall the event, but I must insist it remain a distant memory."

With a coy smile, she moved past him in a gust of lavender perfume, her hand grazing his breeches. The scent, redolent of Jane, left him reeling with discord. As though summoned by the unfavorable memories laden in lavender, his wife—in name only—stroked his back.

"Jack, darling. You look well. How's my sweet Robby?"

The Countess of Jersey, who lingered near a table of desserts, cackled. Unfortunately for her, one agitated glance from Jane silenced her at once. Had such a glare come from a plain-featured noblewoman, Lady Jersey would certainly have persisted in her disgrace. But Jane's beauty far eclipsed Lady Jersey's indelicate presence, an attribute for which Jack had not anticipated being glad. Jane held herself well in the room, as though bred for it. And, indeed, she was, no thanks to Mrs. Howlett.

Jack hesitated before kissing Jane's hand with the formality required of their reunion. "The boy's quite well, I assure you."

Jane stepped closer, flooding him with a lavender wave. "I've missed you terribly. Perhaps as much as I've missed Robby."

He recoiled without altering his expression, a facility he'd learned at court from his law partner, John Adams. "I believe little of what you say, madam. You've deceived me in more ways than I can count, and whether you admit it or not, you shamed me in Philadelphia with Essex and now here, tonight. You know I don't wish to remain married to you, but neither do I wish to be cuckolded."

Jane whispered, "You've not been cuckolded. Lord Essex and I have not been together. He's been a mere friend—and decent brother-in-law, if I must remind you—in bringing me to London. I miss our son." She kept her soprano low to divert suspicion. In fact, she gazed upon him with the same mask of pleasantry he bore. "Divorce me if you must. I shan't resist any longer. But please don't take Robby from me."

Jack's jaw tightened. "We'll speak more later."

"How shall we speak later? You're kept in your rooms at Kensington, and I'm settled at Chelsea."

He stiffened, though she was right.

"Let me join you." She cajoled him with every bit of her agreeable form. "Allow me one chance to grant you an heir—"

"No." A practiced smile danced upon his lips as he glanced about the room. No one suspected their distress. "You've already birthed me an heir. I should like to name Robby the next Earl of Brunswick."

A candid glimmer of relief poked through her rehearsed pleasantries. "I was against it, but our darling boy is deserving of such an inheritance. If you'll allow me to give you an heir to Perkins Est—"

"Annalisa shall birth the next in line to my father's estate." His words crumpled her smooth countenance, but Jane resumed her mask for Society and offered a trained smile.

"Of course."

Jack added softly, "After she and I wed, of course. I owe her at least that."

"If she should continue to thwart Mr. Peabody. Our mothers are persistent, you know." Jane plucked a glass of claret from a passing servant and sipped the liquid. "You know 'twas your mother who determined you and I should marry, yes?"

"Yes. My father relayed as much."

"Your mother promised mine after George's father died that she would marry you to me."

Jack spun his gold signet ring. "As consolation?"

She spoke nothing as her icy gaze scanned the elaborate room. None of London's *ton* paid them any heed, and for that, Jack slackened his posture.

"Every bit of this is your mother," Jane whispered. "Including what your papa did for Lord Essex."

His heart skipped. "What did my father do for Lord Essex?"

Jane licked her rosebud lips. "He paid all of Essex's debts."

"What for? Has he no sense at all? Surely, you're mistaken, madam."

"He paid off the earl's debts in exchange for a seat in Parliament. 'Tis what your mother told me."

"A seat in Parliament?" Incredulous, Jack straightened his coat and retrieved his own glass of claret. Sipping the contents, he suspected little in believing anything Jane said. Yet what she relayed rattled his conscience. "My father relinquished his seat in Parliament years ago. I beg pardon, madam, do I hear you correctly?"

"Yes, my lord."

Across the room, Father convened with Lord Melbourne, Lord Essex, and the Duke of Devonshire—all members of the Whig Party and supporters of America separating from England. Or so he assumed. Father even now approved of his divorce, something he'd ardently criticized until their arrival in London. *Has Father involved himself with men beyond Congress of unsavory politics?* As the lines between truth and fallacy blurred, Jack focused his attention upon the one person in the room his conscience trusted, someone he'd met that very evening: the Duchess of Devonshire.

His darling girl, Annalisa, thousands of miles across the sea, had trusted the duchess. His chest constricted with an even greater conviction to meet Lord Mansfield and obtain the divorce decree, all at the behest of the duchess. Only then could he return home to his beloved.

"One more bit before I take my leave of you, sir," Jane said.

"Go on."

"You may obtain your divorce from me; you may slander my name and Essex's in this pursuit. You may even marry Annalisa when you return home. But you need to know Annalisa is not who you think she is. And when you do learn it, please remember 'twas I who warned you."

Jane dipped a small curtsy and drifted into the assembly hall.

Iced by her unsavory chastisement of his beloved, Jack scanned the room until the duchess rescued him from his own vacillating thoughts.

❧ 23 ❧

ANNALISA

CHARLESTON, AUGUST 1779

AFTER RECEIVING A LETTER from George and Abigail, Annalisa confided in Quinnapin of her intention to journey to Charleston. At his insistence that he accompany her, they decided the venture would be made quicker a-horseback than in a carriage. For this, Annalisa guised herself as Benjamin Cavendish. And after a quick good-bye to Mary, Annalisa and Quinnapin quit town before sunrise. Their venture would take several weeks, but she was no stranger to such travel. And anything was better than succumbing to Mamma and Lady's Perkins's plans to marry her off to Mr. Peabody.

As she suspected it would be, South Carolina proved nothing like she'd envisioned; deeply hot and swampy, yes, but teeming with massive oaks billowing with veils of Spanish moss. The city of Charleston itself, small and quaint and tucked between two brackish rivers, was laid out like a grid, far more organized than the winding streets of Boston.

Annalisa smiled at Quinnapin as they trotted through the streets, destined for George and Abigail's rented apartments. "'Tis pleasant here, despite the heat."

"Aye." Quinnapin wiped his brow, beading with sweat. "This is where the Kiawah, Stono, and Etiwan used to live."

Annalisa frowned. "Dispersed because of us. Like what happened to my grandmama's people."

"Aye. And my Wôpanâak."

Annalisa contemplated the woman from whom she had inherited most of her features: Papa's mother. He faintly remembered his mother and had been told by his father she was Agawam, but according to Quinnapin, Agawam was not a people, but a place. This meant her grandmother was either Pennacook or Pawtucket. And not knowing her truth only added to the cavernous unknown of the woman whose skin and eyes Annalisa bore. A woman she imagined to be both beautiful and fearless.

"Who remains, do you think?" she asked.

Quinnapin hesitated before replying. "The Catawba may have assimilated many. The Waccamaw, the Cherokee, among others."

Annalisa shuddered despite the damp heat. "Would that there be no more displacement of the Native peoples."

"Aye. This land sprawls farther west. Much farther, and is inhabited by thousands."

Her eyes widened. "How much farther?"

"Thousands of miles. I've not been past the eastern mountains myself, but I've heard stories from those who have and met the people west of here, the Lakota, Dakota, Cree, the Ojibwe—there are countless people west of here, the Navajo and Apache of the desert—thousands of miles from here, there are plenty of people who have not yet been displaced by yours."

She uttered a silent prayer to the Great Spirit, then said, "May they never be removed."

He smiled at her. "Creator will decide these things, Miss Anna. Until then, we can only hope to live in harmony."

A regiment of provincial militia marched by, and she added, "Mayhap when this war is won."

They continued in silence until they reached the street described in George's letter and stopped outside a brick rowhouse. Annalisa dismounted her horse and tied him to an iron gate before making her way to the front door. Her body vibrated with the excitement of seeing her most beloved brother and Abigail.

She knocked.

The door opened, and Abigail flew into her arms. "Oh, dearest friend. You've come at last."

Annalisa clung to her longer than was deemed appropriate for her given attire, and the rounded belly between them. She stepped back to assess Abigail's delicate condition and cried, "You didn't write you are with child."

Abigail's hand rested on her modestly round torso. "I wanted it to be a surprise."

"Many congratulations," Quinnapin said.

Abigail led them inside a small foyer. "Kitty is our housekeeper and is entirely useless. I'm so relieved you've come. 'Tis a nightmare running my own home while caring for Louisa and Tommy."

Annalisa clasped Abigail's hand. "I'm glad to help."

❦

THAT EVENING, AFTER LOUISA AND TOMMY WERE PUT TO bed, Annalisa changed into the dress she'd brought with her —riding horseback meant packing light—and settled into the parlor with Abigail and Quinnapin.

"Where's George?" she asked.

Abigail peered up from her needlepoint. "He's training with the Second South Carolina regiment."

"Then he did join," Quinnapin said.

Abigail's brooding silence resonated as neither shock nor resentment. Perhaps it was something she had grown to merely accept from the man she loved.

"Tell me, was your mamma glad to let you travel to see us?" Abigail asked.

Annalisa pursed her lips. "I absconded away without hers or my papa's consent."

"You fled?" Abigail tossed aside her needlepoint. "Your mamma will be furious."

"'Tis the least I could do, Abbie," Annalisa replied. "Your mamma and mine are plotting to marry me off to Mr. Peabody. If I'm absent from town, the proposal can never happen." Annalisa fiddled with her wampum necklace at her throat. "Jack means to return from London with his divorce. I must wait for him. Our mothers are persistent...I can only thwart their scheme for so long. And that poor, silly sir, Mr. Peabody. He is kind and amiable, but I could never marry the man...I could never do that to Jack. I promised him I would not."

Abigail leaned forward and reached for Annalisa's hand. "You are safe, here. I thank God you've come." She shuddered and leaned back in her chair. "I fear I'd suffer the same had we not left Portsmouth. My parents would return me to Lord Essex—"

"Who is now the Earl of Essex, by the way," Annalisa blurted.

Abigail's cheeks paled. "All the more reason for them to send me back to him. More political influence."

"Jack and I could never have done what you and George are doing, Abbie. We tried. We tried to elope, and look where that ended us."

The front door opened and closed, and George and Oliver stepped into the parlor. Annalisa jumped from her seat.

"George!" She flew into his arms.

"Little One."

He smelled of gunpowder, sweat, and rum. *A trip to the tavern after drilling.* She grinned as he set her down and removed his hat. Always towering over any man in any room, he appeared well in gaitered trousers and a blue coat with red facings. She greeted Oliver, decked in his finest linen ditto suit, then resumed her place across from Abigail by the unlit fireplace. George and Oliver received Quinnapin and joined him on the sofa.

"The travel south looks well upon you both," Oliver said. "Pray, was it tedious?"

"Not as tedious had I worn skirts while riding," Annalisa said. That Oliver knew of her bouts as Benjamin Cavendish when his brother Jack did not, plagued her.

George's jaw set. "You rode as Benjamin?"

"I had to. I escaped with Quinn and needed to pack light."

His face, bronzed from the long, hot summer, darkened to an angry shade of cherry. "You fled home?"

"I had to," Annalisa cried, then proceeded to update her brother and Oliver of their mothers' plans to wed her to Mr. Peabody.

George's hardened countenance softened. "Then I suppose 'tis well enough you remain until we hear of Jack's arrival to Boston Harbor."

Oliver snickered and crossed one leg. "Your wicked sister shall finally have what she's deserved since we were wed."

"Would that she marries Lord Essex," Abigail said. "Pray, I wonder if he's yet petitioned for divorce from me."

A wave of relief washed over Annalisa, and she settled into her chair. Unfortunately, the respite proved only moments when she met George's harried stare.

"What is it?" she asked.

"I've joined the Second South Carolina under Lieutenant Colonel Marion."

"Yes. And?"

"I was captain with Cogswell's, but Marion refuses to honor my rank. He did, however, offer me a position to captain a small band of militia in the Lowcountry."

She bit her lip, contemplating this enlistment. While her brother's militia experience in both New York and Boston offered much to recommend him, she knew he would hardly leave Abigail, pregnant, to captain a militia in the Lowcountry.

"Know you anything about the artillery?" Annalisa asked.

George chuckled. "Wildes and I were part of Knox's expedition to Fort Ticonderoga in January of '76. We stole their guns and hauled them back to Boston with eighty yokes of oxen."

"A feat, for certain." Annalisa smirked. "Mayhap you could study artillery. They're the most learned men on any battlefield. 'Twill keep you here in Charleston while Abbie is with child and may lend you an opportunity to garner more information about this Admiral Bixby you wrote about."

"I could not write such scandalous information but, Bixby knew Captain Fleming."

Annalisa's breath caught and she cried, "He knew Fleming? The captain of *Liberté*?"

"Aye, though I don't know in what capacity."

"We must uncover this information, George. Fleming was a turncoat!"

Quinnapin rose from his seat and joined Annalisa by her chair. He rested an arm on her shoulder. "Peace, Friend. There is much we don't know."

"Aye. Quinn is right," Oliver replied. "Any man in Providence may claim to know Fleming. Perhaps the admiral met him at a tavern and beat him in several games of cribbage. We know nothing of their acquaintance."

She settled in her seat but kept her gaze fixed on George. Her brother held her stare with jaw stiff and frowned lips pursed. His green eyes glittered with resolve. Though he remained silent, she knew the gears of his mind turned.

"I'll study artillery, Little One." George's cavernous voice filled the room. "'Twill offer me an opportunity to watch the Royal Navy offshore, and locate Admiral Bixby."

24

GEORGE

CHARLESTON, OCTOBER 1779

IN HER BRIEF TIME in Charleston, his sister altered the course of George's plans, and he was glad to oblige. Together, they procured the books on mathematics he required to learn artillery, quite a different task from commanding a militia. Never a particularly learned man, he rather enjoyed the calculations, understanding them far more readily than Abigail's mood swings. Not to mention, the task proved a welcome distraction from Admiral Bixby. At least for Annalisa.

As he sat with his sister in their small parlor practicing multiplication of fractions, a courier delivered a letter. George jumped from his seat and retrieved the envelope.

"'Tis from Henry."

Annalisa hovered behind him, as eager to read their youngest brother's script. George broke the seal and read:

> *September 4th 1779*
> *Dearest brother,*
> *William and Martha were deliver'd of a Girl,*

Frances Martha Howlett, who was born July
27th. Both Mother and babe are in Goode health.
Will spends as much tyme as he can at the
Willow, but is Devot'd to his young family.
Mary spends much time helping at the Willow
since Annie left, and has been twice visited by
Mr. Wentworth, who wishes to court her.

Annalisa gasped. "Mr. Wentworth has called on Mary twice?"

"There's more between the lines." His chest rattling, George re-read the letter, which offered several gaps between the lines of Henry's writing. Quickly, he lit a candle and held the note aloft of the flame. Henry's invisible ink slowly appeared between the lines.

George read the words aloud:

"Gould and I have continu'd to search for
the wryter of notes to Lord Essex, the
Scurrilous Benjamin Cavendish. Mr. Wentworth
has visited more than twyce since my last letter.
He claims to be calling on Mary, but I suspect
he spies. He saw Benjamin Cavendish at
Philadelphia and knowes the villain. I also
receiv'd worde from my connexion at Oyster Bay
of your Admiral Bixbee. The Admiral knew
Captain Flemming, the captain of Annalisa and
Jack's ship. More to comme.
     Yours +,

H. H."

"Then 'tis wider knowledge that Captain Fleming knew Admiral Bixby." Annalisa gripped her breast. "But Benjamin is thought to be a spy, a turncoat?"

"Peace, Little One." George read the letter again. *Admiral Bixby knew Captain Fleming.* Fleming captained Jack and Annalisa's ship, *Liberté*, bound for France. Paid by the British to alter the course of their ship to British-held Nova Scotia only doomed the ship to wreck off the coast of Halifax. That much they already knew. But Fleming was from Rhode Island and proclaimed to have been involved in the destruction of HMS *Gaspee*, a Patriot endeavor. A turncoat, then again a turncoat. If only the traitor was still living to confirm his connection with Admiral Bixby.

George peered at his sister, who perseverated over the letter and news of her Benjamin Cavendish. He scowled. "Your muse Cavendish is now connected with that Loyalist reptile Wentworth. It would do you well to retire those breeches for good, lest you risk being uncovered—forget the danger of your masquerade."

Annalisa's face paled and she returned to her chair, silent.

Fuming and bursting with questions, George held Henry's letter over the candle and watched the page turn to ash. Guilt-ridden, but still burning with a need to speak with Admiral Bixby, George rose from his chair.

"Where are you going?" Annalisa asked.

George donned his blue coat with red facings—the uniform given him by the Second South Carolina—and said, "To do what I must. Keep to the apartments and relay news of Henry's letter to Quinn, Ollie, and Abbie when they return home. Tell them I'll return as expediently as I may, but I may be gone several days."

"Wait." Annalisa met him in the foyer. "Think you I'm in danger?"

"Keep to your skirts and forget the rogue Cavendish unless you wish to end imprisoned a traitor."

"But...how? Who is using Benjamin's name so scandalously?"

"I know nothing about it, Little One. Only that your charades in Philadelphia have apparently circulated among Loyalist reptiles, Wentworth being one of them. If I were a betting man, I'd say that dilberry Essex plays some part."

He stepped from the rowhouse into the hot, overcast Charleston day. His fowler and cartridge pouch slung over his shoulder, George hurried to the fortified harbor.

HMS *Dover* had been anchored for weeks offshore, her naval crew and captain holed up inside, leaving George to wonder when the rest of her fleet would arrive. It was no secret Lord Cornwallis, second in command to commander in chief, Sir Henry Clinton, made his way south. It was only a matter of time before his regiment met battle against the British here in Charleston. In the months prior, members of the Second South Carolina had seen small skirmishes in the Lowcountry between Charleston and Savannah.

On the banks of the river, George studied the British naval ship for movement. If Admiral Bixby was upon it, he'd have to emerge eventually. Various other sloops and schooners speckled the waters, none of which bore the flag of Britain.

For the next four hours, George sat amidst the earthwork on the riverbanks, watching. He studied the ship until the sun set behind him and lanternlight dotted the deck of the vessel. Rather than return home or to his regiment's garrison, he stationed himself for the night until the following morning, and again into the night, eating and drinking only what he carried, though the gnaw of hunger never plagued him—only a yearning to question Admiral Bixby.

In the twilight of his third night encamped upon the banks of the Ashley River, a modest rowboat floated ashore at low tide containing two gentlemen in hunting shirts. They climbed the riverbanks after securing their vessel, and George loaded his pistol. He half-cocked it as they ascended the crest.

"Hold your fire," one of the men said, raising his arms.

George closed the distance between them. "I shall blow you both to hell if you neglect to tell me for whom you row this vessel."

"We're militia—"

"Lies." George fully cocked his pistol. "You have one more chance."

The first man eyed the other as he reached for his pistol.

George aimed at him. "Retrieve your weapon and I will discharge mine, reptile. I know you're sailors for the Royal Navy. Get me your admiral. Now."

"We can't do that," the first sailor said.

"Then I will put a hole in your leg." George pointed at the first sailor's right leg. "Or perhaps your dominant arm. 'Twill have to be amputated, of course, at this range."

The first sailor glanced at his companion, who shrugged. *Is this King George's fearsome Royal Navy? These sailors can be no older than seventeen.*

"Captain Howlett." A deep voice resonated up the river's embankment, and Admiral Bixby ascended the crest. "Release my sailors. I sent them ashore to Sullivan's Island for water. Needless to say, they rowed upon the incorrect shore."

George kept his pistol fixed, this time on the admiral. "Then you're precisely who I thought you were."

Admiral Bixby, dressed in his blue-and-buff uniform,

stood before him. "Yes, Captain Howlett. I am. And what is your business?"

"I came seeking you, sir." George maintained his aim. "Now, send your men away so we may speak privately. Else I'll blow you three to the devil's den. Or is Davy Jones's locker where you bastards die?"

Admiral Bixby chuckled. "Boys, return to the ship. I won't allow this rogue to harm me."

The two young sailors fled the banks to their rowboat. When they rowed well into the middle of the river, George spoke to the admiral.

"How came you to know Captain Fleming of Rhode Island?"

Admiral Bixby's countenance warped. "I hardly knew the man."

"Answer the question, reptile."

"Why should I? Such information might lead to my death. A denial may lead to the same consequence." The admiral crossed his arms. "What is the benefit to me?"

George ground his teeth, unwilling to relay his information, yet the admiral posed a reasonable question. "He captained the ship that wrecked, along with my sister's and brother-in-law's lives. You said you knew him."

Admiral Bixby's face grew grey in the dying light. "Aye. I knew him."

He sucked in a breath and asked the question he'd been contemplating. "Gave you the order for Fleming to sail for Halifax?"

"Where is Fleming? Can't he answer these questions?"

"He's dead." George fully cocked his pistol. "And you'll meet him soon unless you answer me."

Admiral Bixby paced, unwilling to meet George's stare. "This makes things quite a bit complicated, Captain Howlett. I gave the order, yes. But now, knowing your person, I fear something else."

George's anger bubbled, and he rushed the admiral, jabbing the pistol beneath his chin. "Speak, villain. What else could make you fear me? You have perhaps ruined the lives of both my beloved sister and brother-in-law, irrevocably, and Fleming's blood is on your hands."

"I believe your father was my brother."

His words reverberated over George, and his hand shook. "Do you jest, sir?" The remote possibility of Admiral Bixby being his father evaporated, and his father's ghost, a mere sentinel in George's life, vanished.

The admiral shook his head. "I suspected it upon our first meeting, but it became apparent to me learning of these connections to Captain Fleming and his wrecked ship."

"My deceased father, Captain Bixby, also has a sister, Lady Perkins—"

"Who is also my sister," Admiral Bixby said. "We've been estranged for years." He maneuvered in George's grip. "Come now, you don't wish to murder your uncle."

His hand trembling, George shoved the pistol farther into Admiral Bixby's chin. "How can I believe you? How can I trust all you say, you filthy cockrobin?"

"Ask...your...aunt," the admiral choked.

George released the admiral with a force that collapsed him to the ground. Admiral Bixby held his neck and hacked.

"You're as reckless a hothead as Edward, I'll give you that," the admiral said between coughs. "The same reckless-ness that landed him at the bottom of the ocean with his ship, *the Preamble*."

George's face stung with coldness. *The Preamble*. He'd not heard the name of his father's ship spoken aloud since he met Mr. Hancock in Boston and learned of his father's life insur-ance that had left him a modest inheritance.

"You knew my father intended to work for Mr. Hancock?"

No longer choking, Admiral Bixby adjusted his neckpiece and up-righted himself. "I heard of it. I was stationed in the West Indies at the time. We hadn't spoken in years. Not since he married Margaret...your mother." A shadow of regret crossed his face in the darkness. "What's done is done."

"What do you mean by that?" George barked.

"Leave it, lad." The admiral turned from him and started to descend the bank to his rowboat. "Do give Lady Perkins my regards when next you meet. She's yet to answer my previous letter."

"Come back, reptile," George hollered, but did not chase the admiral. Something kept his feet planted upon the sandy shore. "Why estrange yourself, sir?"

The admiral neither acknowledged nor answered him. He merely stepped into his rowboat and pushed offshore, his face as stone in the dim light. Shaken, George crawled up the embankment and sprinted from the river until he arrived at the lodgings he rented for his family.

In a flurry, he burst inside the apartment. Abigail and Oliver sat upon the sofa with Louisa and Tommy, reading a book. Annalisa and Quinnapin played a game of cards.

"George!"

Oliver helped Abigail stand. "Where have you been?" he snapped.

Annalisa stood. "Did you meet him?"

"We must pack our belongings and leave at once," George said.

Abigail's freckled cheeks rouged. "Whatever for? What have you done now?"

"I met Admiral Bixby. He confirmed our relation."

Oliver's and Abigail's faces paled.

"I knew not Mother had another brother." Oliver regarded Abigail, then George. "Are you certain?"

"Yes. He even knew the name of my father's ship, *the*

Preamble," George replied. "But I trust him little. He's been estranged without revealing why. And he confirmed knowing Captain Fleming—"

"We know this, he told us," Oliver cried.

"He gave Fleming the orders to sail for Halifax," George roared.

"But why?" Annalisa asked.

"He would not reveal that to me," George replied. "We must leave Charleston. Now. Who knows what he may conjure now that I know such information?"

Oliver held up a hand. "You can't just desert the Second South Carolina regiment—"

"I can, and I shall." George turned to Abigail. "Have Kitty pack your things. I'll write to General Washington. Mayhap he can forgive my actions...have me transferred up north."

George sat at his writing desk, pulled a piece of paper, dipped the quill in ink, and scribbled across the page.

"Why bother with that?" Oliver asked. "We should return home."

A knock sounded at the front door, and the room stilled. Abigail and Annalisa grabbed the children and fled the room. Oliver, Quinnapin, and George removed their pistols and closed in on the front door.

Slowly, George cracked the door.

"Mr. George?"

Sarah's smiling face fell.

George sighed, then opened the door for her to enter. Addy ushered inside behind her.

"Whatever's the matter?" Sarah looked to Oliver, who uncocked his pistol and replaced it in its holder.

"We've uncovered some unsavory news about your Admiral Bixby," Oliver replied. "We must leave town."

"Then I'm going with you," Sarah said.

Oliver offered her a small smile, then regarded George.

"You and Abbie may venture to Washington's camp, but I'm taking Tommy back to Topsfield. Miss Devonshire, I would be more than honored for you to accompany me."

Sarah faced Addy. "Grandma, may we?"

Addy nodded. "Phibbah, you know I'll go wherever you go. No matter the place."

"We will return with you," Sarah said.

Abigail and Annalisa reappeared with the children. "Louisa and I will go with George. Wherever he goes, I go."

"But you're seven months pregnant," Annalisa said. "You won't have nearly as many comforts at an encampment as you do here."

"I will not leave him," Abigail replied. "We leapt the sword at Valley Forge. If we must return there, I will."

"We'll ride to Washington's encampment in New Jersey. By the time we arrive, they will be entering winter's quarters," George said. "We leave tonight." He hesitated. "Annie, you and Quinn should return home with Sarah, Addy, Ollie, and Tommy."

Annalisa shook her head. "No, I can't go home—not yet. We've not heard if Jack has returned from London. Might I go with you and Abbie and Weeza?"

"No." George heated. "You will go home, and you will never again don Benjamin's breeches. This is your chance to travel thither with the protection of both Quinn and Ollie." Sensing her trepidation, he wrapped his arms about her. "I will write as soon as we're settled in New Jersey."

25

ANNALISA

TOPSFIELD, NOVEMBER 1779

WITH A RELUCTANT LONELINESS she'd not associated with her beloved town, Annalisa trotted down the narrow familiar lane leading to her family's farm. Trees clung to sparse brown leaves, a final vestige that clung to autumn when the cold air felt quick to welcome winter. Quinnapin took Sarah and Addy to his home on the outskirts of town, along the Ipswich River, while Oliver made his way to the Perkins Estate with his son, Tommy.

Alone on this leg of the journey, Annalisa gripped the reins with the anticipation of a wrathful reception from Mamma and Papa—one her behavior deserved, a behavior, she maintained, that had been necessary. As she neared her family's acreage, she pondered if Jack had returned to town with his divorce granted. It had been six months since he'd left for London, notwithstanding the tedious month-long journey at sea. *Would that he is soon to return.*

The brown clapboard saltbox came into view. A swirl of white smoke piped into the grey November skies from the large central chimney. She turned her horse down the drive, dismounted, and stabled the beast within the barn. The other horses snuffled and snorted within their stalls; Papa was sure to hear. Quickly, she tossed her belongings into the garret and hurried from the barn and up the path to the front door, where she hesitated.

Annalisa sucked in a breath and knocked.

The front door opened, and Liza greeted her. She led Annalisa inside.

"Annie," Mary cried. She rushed from the parlor and embraced Annalisa. "Thank God, you're home."

Annalisa pulled from her sister. "Pray, has Jack arrived home yet?"

Mary's face paled. "Not yet." She licked her lips. About to speak, Mamma, having heard the commotion in the foyer, made her way down the hall from the kitchen.

"Annalisa Howlett."

Annalisa stiffened. "Mamma."

Expecting her mother to slap her, Annalisa closed her eyes, but was enveloped in her mother's rose perfume, then her warm embrace. She eased against her mother and sobbed into her shoulder.

"I'm so sorry, Mamma."

Mamma kissed her forehead, then stepped back. "I thank God you returned."

Annalisa followed her mother and sister into the parlor, where she warmed herself by the fire. Hesitant, she relayed the nature of her visit to Charleston and that George, Abigail, and Louisa were quite well. She bit her lip, concealing the information about Admiral Bixby and Captain Fleming, and George's escape to New Jersey.

Mamma seemed pleased by the news, though melancholy at the continued absence of her firstborn, George. "You'll be glad to hear Mr. Wentworth has been visiting our dear Mary."

Annalisa held her sister's stare. "How fortunate."

"Yes. And now you've returned, I may relay more good

news—Mr. Peabody has accepted our proposal for you to marry."

Annalisa leapt from her seat. "I beg your pardon, marm?"

"Your papa and I, along with the help of Lady Perkins, have secured for you an engagement."

"But I was not here to accept such a proposal," Annalisa cried. "How can you accept him on my behalf? Is my life not my own?"

"Annalisa Howlett, you will marry Mr. Peabody and let poor Janey fix her own broken family. This is the end of it. Your papa and I have declared it so, and the engagement may not be broken. Is that understood?"

Annalisa's face numbed as she searched for Mary's sullen gaze. "Please, Mamma. Jack is to return from London with his divorce—"

"Janey and Lord Essex, as you know, went to London to prevent that from happening," Mamma said. "Now, please, be grateful Mr. Peabody is willing to have you despite your... disorderly conduct of late. He will make a fine husband."

Her fate, sealed in her absence and without having known it, dangled before her like a noose hung from the ancient oak. With every fiber of her being, she needed to end the engagement—and before Jack arrived home to find out. But quitting an engagement was akin to breaking a legally binding contract and would not be taken lightly by the Peabodys or, she suspected, Lady Perkins. Jack's mother was undoubtedly the orchestrator of this grand scheme to end her life before it ever began. And what better way to secure it than in her absence.

I would have fared better here than had I gone to Charleston. If I remained here, I could have refused the gentleman when he asked for my hand.

Her chest tightened. No, she could not have refused him, lest she risk her family's farm burning. Lady Perkins's threats, so idle as they seemed, were very real, particularly in the light of her allowing Jane to travel to London with Lord Essex.

"Come now, don't look so disagreeable." Mamma stood. "I'll have Liza bring you a nice hot cup of chocolate."

When Mamma left the parlor, Annalisa flew to her sister's side and knelt. "What am I to do? Was there nothing you could have said to stop this from happening?"

Mary's countenance stiffened. "I have been coping with my own troubles, Annie. Mr. Wentworth is persistent, and Mamma sees little reason I should refuse the sir."

"'Tis hopeless. We're pawns in their horrid chess game, Mary."

"What's worse is the growing scrutiny surrounding Benjamin," Mary said, "and now myself, for being seen with you at Peggy Shippen's wedding. Henry thinks I may be at risk of being accused of espionage by the Continentals for the British."

Annalisa held her head and paced the room. "This is a disaster. How has it come to this? Who has made such speculations upon Benjamin?" Annalisa threw up her hands. "I fought at Saratoga, Mary."

"I know." Mary stood and met her in the middle of the room. "'Tis our attendance at Peggy's wedding, I suppose. 'Tis what Henry's heard."

"And not even George may help us." Annalisa composed herself. "There is little I may do to assuage the situation. If I may focus on one trouble, I must hope Jack soon returns, else I may have to marry Mr. Peabody."

26

JACK

BOSTON, DECEMBER 1779

THE LAST TIME JACK docked at Boston Harbor from Europe, he found himself swept up in the Sons of Liberty's antics, having partaken in the destruction of the tea. This time, he stood on the pier with Father, Andrew, Robby, and Jane.

He reached into his pocket to ensure the documents from Lord Mansfield had not been displaced.

"They're still there," Jane snapped. "I've not stolen them, as you fear I might."

Jack scowled. "Ma'am, I've endured quite enough of you, if I'm to be frank. 'Twas an unbearable crossing with nothing but your sniveling for Lord Essex for weeks on end."

Jane crossed her arms. "You bade me leave him in London, Jack. He was meant to chaperone my visit, not cuckold you. He is a good man and deserves not your ire."

"The man was abusive to Abbie, and yes, he cuckolded me. He shall return to America of his own will when the courts are done examining him."

Father adjusted his spectacles. "I do think the criminal

conversation case was a bit much, Jack. I had thought you didn't wish for the poor publicity."

Jack bit his lip. "I had no other option when he arrived with Jane to Lord Melbourne's dinner. Sueing him was more honorable than dueling the bastard, was it not?"

Father sighed and shook his head. "Let's return home. I'm quite weary from such a long crossing." He led them to the carriage.

As they sat within the coach, Jack ran his fingers over the smooth parchment tucked inside his coat. Knowing Annalisa was in reach, these last few hours of their journey home to the North Shore of Boston proved more tedious than the five weeks at sea.

When finally they turned down the familiar snow-covered drive of Perkins Estate, Jack's spirit vibrated at the sight of his family's yellow clapboard house. All four chimneys piped white smoke into the December night.

Andrew smiled. "How wonderful to be home."

After greeting his mother and siblings, Jack loitered by the fire contemplating whether he should journey to the Howletts', though the hour grew exceedingly late. Tomorrow was Christmas Eve, the first of Christmastide. He could wait until then to visit Annalisa and gift her the decree, though seeing her would prove the greatest gift of all.

Mercy brought them all a round of Father's best claret, and they saluted to their good health and fortune. Jack's young sisters, Charlotte and Susan, retired for the night when the nursemaid put Robby and Tommy to bed.

Jane, Andrew, Oliver, Jack, and his parents remained in the parlor. Father sipped his third glass of claret before addressing his wife's pressing stare.

"John, why did you not send for the girls and me?" Mother asked.

"Absconding to England was never the plan, Bette,"

Father replied. "I promised you we would return to Topsfield, and we did."

"Not in front of the children—"

"They're adults," Father cried. "Of which you must also learn: Jack and Jane have dissolved their marriage. As of tomorrow, she shall return to her home."

Mother gasped. "You didn't! Of all the things I instructed of you—"

"Peace." Father lifted his hand. "You'll be dissatisfied to know your daughter-in-law cuckolded Jack with Lord Essex. Not even I could stand for such behavior. I'd like to say 'twas I who helped Jack in procuring his decree, but it was the Duchess of Devonshire."

"Lord Essex escorted Janey to England under my instruction," Mother snapped. "She did not cuckold you, Jack. I sent her there to keep your family together."

"Fie." Jack rose from his chair. "I'll not hear another word of it. What's done is done. Jane was never meant to be my wife, and you know it well. Your attempt at keeping us together was in vain. Thanks to the duchess, I've obtained a dissolution of my marriage, including an annulment. The marriage never happened. And that is how I intend to continue with my life."

His mother's lips parted with a sneer, but Oliver jumped to his feet. "Say not another word, Mother. Let Jack have this night to rejoice in being rid of the wicked old harpy."

Jane rose. "I merely acted as you instructed me, Lady Perkins. I trusted you." Tears dripped from her arctic eyes, and she fled the parlor.

"Very well." Mother stood, her face as stone. "Get your rest, Jack. I very much anticipate tomorrow evening's celebration at the Howletts'."

❧ 27 ❧

ANNALISA

TOPSFIELD, DECEMBER 1779

THE FIRST NIGHT OF Christmastide was upon them, and Mamma whirled about the house in a flurry of cedar and mistletoe. Mr. Peabody, Oliver and Tommy, Lady Perkins, and her youngest daughters—Charlotte and Susan—were soon to arrive for the festivities. From the kitchen, scents of cinnamon and clove permeated the air from Liza's baking.

Annalisa sat at the pianoforte in the drawing room. It felt to be ages since last she played the spinet. From the memory of her heart, Mozart's Second Piano Sonata, Jack's gift to her from Europe, flew from her fingertips.

A knock at the door lifted her head. Mr. Peabody entered the drawing room, smiling. "Miss Annalisa, how good to see you."

She stood. "Likewise, sir."

He approached the spinet. "Your playing is quite accomplished. I look forward to listening most ardently when we're married."

Her face warmed. "Sir, I—"

"Please, Miss Annalisa, if I may be so bold." He reached into his pocket and procured a gold and ruby ring.

Her heart rattled. "Sir, I—"

"Please do me the honor of wearing my grandmother's ring."

"I couldn't possibly, sir. Not until we're married—"

"Nonsense." He reached for her hand and slid the ring upon her finger. "It looks well on your complexion."

Annalisa's throat tightened. "Thank you, sir."

Quinnapin and Mary entered the drawing room and sat on the sofa across from the blazing fire.

"Good to see you, Mr. Peabody, sir," Mary said.

He returned Mary's greeting with a smile, then said, "I'm going to help your father and Henry with more firewood. I'll return shortly."

Annalisa waited until he quit the room before replacing her fingers upon the keys, yet she could not play.

Salvage it all, dear mamma. The little voice of her tiny angel daughter spoke from behind the grave, but only she could hear.

"Annie, why'd you stop?" Mary broke the silence. "Perhaps some carols would be nice?"

Beside Mary, Quinnapin sat forward and said, "She hears her."

A lump formed in Annalisa's throat. "Yes."

Quinnapin always seemed to know when her daughter spoke to her from beyond. Perhaps it was because he'd helped bury and guide her spirit to Keihtánit's house. If not for Quinnapin and his generosity in offering his Wampanoag traditions, Annalisa feared to think what she would have done otherwise.

Ignoring Mary's request for carols, Annalisa glanced at her hands, still bronzed from summertime, and the gold ring. *How can I break this engagement?*

Sarah glided into the drawing room wearing a crimson *robe à la française*, one of Georgiana's many gifts to her before they left England. "What do you think, Calais?" She spun about the room and smiled.

Annalisa grinned. "You look stunning."

"I wish to impress Mr. Oliver."

"I think he's already impressed by you." Annalisa chuckled. "But a gorgeous gown won't hurt, either."

"Lady Perkins is here," Mamma announced from the drawing room door, her ivory cheeks pleasantly flushed and reminiscent of Jane's. "Come to the parlor at once."

Annalisa rose from the bench and left the room with Sarah, Quinnapin, and Mary. From the corridor, sounds of a luscious baritone drifted from the parlor, and her heart stopped. As she'd know his fiddle playing anywhere, so Annalisa recognized that voice to the ends of the earth. She stepped into the room full of familiar faces: William and Martha and their baby girl, Frances, who'd been born in late July, Mr. Peabody, Mamma and Papa, Henry, Oliver and Tommy, and the Perkinses with Jane.

When did Jane return from England?

As though no others lingered about the parlor, her focus shifted to Jack. Handsome as ever in his blue velvet coat and breeches, he stood nearest the fire with Andrew and Lord Perkins.

Her cheeks numbed as his deep North Atlantic gaze met hers. Small pieces of his chestnut hair had loosened from its tie, framing his freshly shaved face. One hand clutched Robby's, the other gripped a rolled piece of parchment tied neatly with a bow.

Annalisa's throat clogged. "Do I dream?"

Jack stepped toward her, his lips parted as though to speak, but Mamma parted them as she reached for Jane.

"My Janey." She embraced Jane, then lifted her beloved

grandson, planting a kiss on Robby's round, dimpled cheek. "We're so glad you've returned healthy and unharmed from your long voyage. And how you've grown, Master Andrew."

Andrew laughed good-naturedly. "I'm hardly *master* anymore, Mrs. Howlett. I've made twenty years in September."

"A man you've become," Papa said, a twinkle in his dark eyes. "We're right heartily glad to host you all this evening. Please enjoy the wassail." He gestured to the large bowl of steaming mulled wine Liza had prepared.

Jack lingered beside Andrew, who had grown considerably since Annalisa had last seen him. Without Robby to distract him, Jack tucked the roll beneath his arm and spun the signet ring upon his pinky finger, a habit she knew palliated him in times of distress. But Lord Perkins migrated toward her with kindliness.

"Miss Annalisa. It does me good to see you, my dear."

Lord Perkins's cheeks dimpled with a charming smile, much like Jack's. He motioned for Jack to join them and he did so with alacrity.

Jack lifted her left hand and kissed it. "Miss Annalisa, 'twas a long—" He noticed the ring, and his face paled. At once, he created distance between them. "'Twas a long voyage, Miss Annalisa."

Mr. Peabody joined their party. "Lord Perkins, Lord Brunswick, a pleasure to celebrate Christmastide with you."

Lady Perkins clapped. "And I see Miss Annalisa wears your ring, Mr. Peabody. How lovely. It suits you well, Miss Annalisa."

"Then you've been married," Jack said, his voice cracking on the last word. He regarded Mr. Peabody, hiding his displeasure behind a dimpled grin. "Congratulations, sir." He went to toss the rolled page into the fire.

"No." Annalisa stopped him. "Not married yet. Engaged, Lord Brunswick."

In that moment, she only suspected what it was he meant to destroy but could not bring herself to acknowledge the hideous, cruel truth. The room beginning to darken about her, she inhaled several breaths to ward off the incoming spell.

"You could've told me," Lord Perkins uttered to his wife as he passed by Annalisa.

"Annie, you look pale," William said.

"Calais, sit." Sarah led her to the sofa where Martha sat with baby Frances. Mary and Sarah clasped her hands, unwilling to let her go.

Mr. Peabody knelt beside her. "Some wassail, Miss Annalisa?"

She nodded. "Yes, sir."

He smiled gently. "You may call me Daniel," he whispered.

Her whole body numbed, though she burned for Jack's private audience. She needed to explain herself, the situation.

Daniel returned seconds later with a glass of wassail. With trembling hands, she tried to secure the glass from him but only agitated the steaming liquid. He lifted it to her lips. "There, that's better, no?"

Annalisa sipped the spiced wine, wishing to tear her gaze from Jack's, but she was incapable of doing so. Rather, Jack looked on from the other side of the room, his family and hers buzzing about, impervious to his own paling face. Finally, in an effort made with haste, Lord Perkins, having noticed the scene, retrieved Robby from Jane and planted the boy in Annalisa's lap.

"Your nephew missed you greatly, Miss Annalisa," he said with a hint of hopefulness in his timbre. "Robby, you have a new cousin, too. Miss Frances." He settled his gaze upon William's daughter in Martha's arms. The babe of five months slept soundly, as though nothing could be amiss in the world around her.

Robby beamed at Annalisa. "Aunnee Annie. I miss you."

Tommy ran to her from Oliver and said, "I love you, Auntie Annie."

Her heart swelled with the adoration of her nephews. "I love you boys, too." She met Lord Perkins's doleful stare and sensed his regret—something she'd not anticipated of him. Annalisa kept Robby upon her lap until Daniel was reassured of her well-being, and with a satisfied nod, he left her side to mingle with the others.

"Calais, Jack's uncovering your engagement to Mr. Peabody was always going to be the worst day," Sarah whispered.

Unable to speak, Annalisa nodded.

"I don't see a ring upon Janey's hand," Mary gasped.

Annalisa gaped at Jane, who huddled between Mamma and Papa. Her left hand was hidden. "How did you see?"

Mary replied, "I swear 'tis not there."

"I did not see her ring, either," Martha added softly.

Annalisa rose from the sofa and, holding Robby's hand, brought him to his father. Her heart pounding, she said, "It does me well to see you, Lord Brunswick." The words felt unfamiliar in her mouth as she spoke them.

His jaw tightened. "Likewise."

Hating his hardened stare, she added, "Your son is growing well."

"Indeed, he is."

Annalisa hesitated, awaiting his reply as his lips parted. She glanced at Andrew, who held Daniel and William in conversation, and she opened her mouth.

In unison with Jack, she said, "I'd like to take some air."

They both smiled and stifled a chuckle, all formality between them having dissipated.

"Very well," Jack said. "Let's take Robby about the garden."

"I'll get my cloak." She crossed the crowded room, Jack and Robby close behind her.

When she entered the foyer, Quinnapin stood by the door with her cloak. "Go now, while you won't be missed."

Jack reached for his hat and greatcoat. "Thank you, Friend."

"I'll cover for you. But be gone no longer than a half hour," Quinnapin replied.

28

JACK

TOPSFIELD, DECEMBER 1779

JACK LED ANNALISA AND Robby from the house into the chilled December night. Light snow flurries fell from wispy clouds threatening to obscure a bright moon that had been full the previous night. Still, the moon offered enough light to guide them safely to the venerable oak.

In the deep silence beneath the naked tree's boughs, Annalisa rested on their branch. Jack took Robby by the hand and stood over Eliza's gravesite. His back to her, he withdrew the parchment from his pocket and held it outward. Moonlight dribbled through the branches of the tree, casting an ethereal glow upon the roll. A trickle of flurries stuck to the ribbon tied about it.

His heart bounding, he said, "This is it, Annalisa. 'Twas meant to be a Christmas gift." He turned to face her. "I'm certain you don't wish to know what it is, now."

"Tell me."

His quivered in the moonlight and frowned. "Read it."

Annalisa rose from the bough and met him by the grave. She took the parchment, untied the ribbon, and unrolled the page.

"Read it aloud so our daughter may hear the contents, Annalisa. So all the space we now sit in may be privy to hear what's written upon that page."

The document wavered in her hands. "I cannot."

"Read it."

"N-No, I c-can't."

At her stutter, he softened his gaze. Any other would have looked upon her with unfeeling betrayal, but he couldn't. He need only learn what had led her to accept Mr. Peabody when she knew he would return with this annulment and divorce. "You must. I need to hear you read the words aloud."

Annalisa cleared her throat and read:

"On the n-ninth day of September 1779, R-referring to the decree made in this Cause on the twentieth of J-June 1779 whereby it was decreed that the m-marriage had and solemnized on the nineteenth day of February 1777 at The Perkins Estate in the Province of Massachusetts Bay between John Jackson Perkins III, Earl of Brunswick, the petitioner, and Jane Catherine Howlett Perkins, Lady Brunswick, the respondent, b-be dissolved by reason of adultery committed by said respondent and said petitioner since the celebration of the s-said marriage. The m-motion of counsel made by Lord Chief Justice Lord Mansfield, for the said petitioner, this final decree pronounces and declares said marriage dissolved."

Annalisa wiped her tears. "Jack, I—"

His anger bubbled forth. "I came home, as I said I would, with all I promised. 'Tis more than I promised, Annalisa—Lord Mansfield assisted me in obtaining an annulment by the ecclesiastical courts. My entire marriage to Jane has been erased as though it never happened. I stand here before you an unmarried man." He cleared his throat. "I'm yours, Annalisa, but I've come home to discover you engaged." He pinched the bridge of his nose to ward off unwanted tears. "Why did you not wait for me?"

Her teeth sank into her lower lip as tears streamed down her cheeks.

"Have you nothing to say?" he growled.

"'Twas not something I agreed to. You m-must believe me—"

"My heart is shattered, Annie," he cried. "I know 'tis probably only a fraction of the grief I caused you in siring Robby, but haven't we caused one another enough pain? When will it end? When will you release me from my agony?" He swiped the parchment from her hands and knelt to the ground. Jack tore into the earth with his bare hands and buried the document beside Eliza. When he finished replacing the snowy dirt over the shallow hole, he rested his frozen hands upon the earth. "I swear, here and now, dearest Eliza, if you should listen to bear witness, I shall take no other wife the rest of my days in the scant chance your mother may one day be able or willing to marry me. This is my solemn vow to you, my darling girl."

Annalisa approached and rested her hand upon his shoulder. "Jack, I—"

"Didn't believe me." He peered up at her, defeated. "I pray he makes you happy. You deserve no less." A beat of silence passed between them. "Pray, have you kept my busk? Does Mr. Peabody know of the musket Quinn and I had made for you?" Jack rose to his feet, quickly eyed Robby, who sat watching them in silence from the base of the tree, and faced her. "Does Mr. Peabody know about Eliza? Or our elopement? What does he know about you, Annie? Does he know about Bunker Hill and the round that nearly killed you?"

"I—"

"But does he *know* you, Annalisa? Like I know you? Does he know you don't wish for a man to hold a teacup to your lips like a feeble maid ought to expect? That you're far stronger than that?"

"I—"

"Annalisa, I've known every bit of you." He reached for her hand.

She recoiled. "You don't know every bit of me, Jack Perkins. I daresay you wouldn't wish to. Some secrets belong to a woman's heart that shall never be shared with anyone."

This silenced him, and suddenly, he recalled Jane's attestation at London: *Annalisa is not who you think she is. And when you do learn it, please remember 'twas I who warned you.* His chest tightened as he contemplated all that Jane had warned him, he assumed, unnecessarily so. *Is Jane correct?*

Annalisa reached into the front of her dress and removed the busk he'd carved for her from wood harvested of that very tree.

"I do wear it. I never stop wearing it."

He grimaced. "Even when Mr. Peabody will undress you at night? I honestly feel sorrow for the kind sir."

"Then you would rather I not wear it?" Annalisa handed him the busk. "Take it. You may remember me by it. Or perhaps you should bury it beside the divorce decree and our daughter. Yet another reminder of our fallen romance." She turned from him, but he caught her wrist. At this, she added, "I've not married Mr. Peabody, Jack. We're engaged, and I pray it may be broken."

"Breaking an engagement is akin to ending a contract, Annalisa. Whyever did you enter into this engagement so lightly?"

"I did no such thing, John Jackson," she cried. "I fled town to escape this fate. Quinn and I found George and Abbie in Charleston, and when I returned home, Mamma and Papa—and your mother—had arranged this engagement for me. Agreed to it without me. I played no role in accepting Mr.

Peabody, and that is the truth of it. If you choose to believe me, I pray you will. But if you do not, then I suppose we must part this space as friends."

His heart skipped at the admission of how her engagement came to be. "Then 'twas not by your acceptance this happened? But your parents and my mother?"

Annalisa gripped her cloak and cried, "Your mamma, Jack! Yes, my papa and mamma agreed to it, but 'twas always your mother who inveigled me with her threats."

"Threats?" Jack's chest tightened. "My mother?"

"Please, you mustn't speak to her of it."

He burned with indignation. "What did my mother say to you?"

"'Tis neither here nor there. I shouldn't wish to recount the event. 'Twas most distressing."

"I was willing to tear apart my family for you, Annalisa—I did, and I'll never regret it. I'd do it again, even if it took me back to England. But for my mother to threaten you? Pray, tell me exactly what she spoke to you."

Annalisa licked her lips. "You must swear never to recount it."

"You have my word."

"She told me how Jane was bred for you, how she paid for Jane's education so she might make you a wife..."

"Yes, I know all that."

"I said I would wait for you to return, that I would marry you. Your mother held my private audience and said she would have my family's homestead burned to the ground if I refused to marry someone else. I don't doubt she coerced Mr. Peabody into courting me, the wretch that I am. I'm unweddable, Jack, you know that. She said my reputation precedes me. But worse, she said while I have friends in elevated positions, like the duchess, so does she."

Jack's mouth dried as though he'd eaten cotton. "The wicked harpy."

"That is your mother—"

"I care not."

"Would that I could change it—that I never escaped to Charleston thinking I could evade a marriage proposal. Rather, I never thought my parents and your mother would arrange it for me and accept without my consent. 'Tis unimaginable. And poor Mr. Peabody, too, is a mere pawn in your mother's chess game."

"She's livid I divorced Jane. I can't imagine she'd burn my house down because of it."

"Stop. I know she's a powerful woman, Jack. Far more powerful than I am. I fear risking my family's well-being. What should I do?"

He reached for her and enveloped her in his arms. "My dearest heart, how you've suffered, and I knew nothing of it." He held her head to his chest and kissed her tresses. She still smelled of lilac, and his heart thudded at her familiar scent.

She closed her eyes, and tears dripped onto his coat. Jack swiped them away. Without thinking, he brushed his lips against the scar upon her right cheek. "I'll devise a plan to break your engagement."

Annalisa pulled from him. "What if your mamma destroys the farm if it don't marry Mr. Peabody?"

"She will not. I will make sure she doesn't. And besides, I'm no longer married to Jane. It matters little keeping up the appearance when the marriage is dissolved. My family is broken, and Jane is shamed. As is my mother. There is no other reason for her to threaten you with such atrocities."

Annalisa nodded, lingering a moment as Jack retrieved Robby from the tree. When he turned to her, she held his gaze. *Salvage all you can, Papa.*

"You're right." She drew away from him. "But you must know one more thing before we return."

"What is it?" He ached for her—her touch, her kiss.

"I missed you with every breath I took, the way you enfolded me in the scent of your amber perfume and pipe tobacco. Each time I played Mozart, I heard your charming voice and the way your fingers work the fiddle with such precision and care. Each pamphlet I read of this war, I recalled with great clarity each scar your body bears—"

Before she could finish speaking, his mouth found hers, and she melted into his embrace.

"Forgive me." Jack tore from her, albeit unwillingly.

"I will not. You commit no crime, if only for not kissing me sooner than this moment. But now I may rest tonight having felt your lips upon mine."

Jack groaned. "Annalisa." His tongue swept over his lower lip. "You know I would do much more if I could."

"As much as I wish you would," she peered down at her nephew, "I thank goodness he's too young to recognize our predicament."

Jack frowned. "He's witnessed quite enough for one night. Come, let's retire indoors. This December chill has penetrated my insides. I can only imagine what 'tis done to the boy."

29

ANNALISA

TOPSFIELD, DECEMBER 1779

THEY HAD CERTAINLY OVERRUN their half hour of privacy. Hopefully, no one had taken too much notice of their absence. Annalisa followed Jack from their tree with little Robby, who peered back at her and smiled.

"Aunnee Annie. Wiza wuvs you. Wiza wuvs Papa."

"You mean Weeza?" Annalisa asked, though the boy hadn't seen his cousin Louisa in many months.

"No," Robby said. "Wiza."

"Eliza?" Jack asked.

Robby nodded.

Jack held Annalisa's stare as though their daughter had spoken through Robby. "Strange he should know her."

"Stranger things have happened, Jack."

Robby continued, "She wuvs my sisser."

"You haven't a sister, Robby," Jack replied.

"No." Robby shook his head. "Mowwy is my sisser."

"Mowwy?" Annalisa crinkled her nose, unsure of how to pronounce the name her nephew spoke.

"Mary?" Jack asked. "Your Auntie Mary?"

"No!" Robby cried.

"Molly?" Jack asked, unnerved.

Robby smiled. "Yes! Mowwy!"

Annalisa shook her head. "There is no Molly. I'm sorry, darling boy."

Jack reached for Annalisa and tugged her aside before they entered the house. "Did I get you with child before I left for London? Did you miscarry another daughter?"

She startled at the question. "No, I would've written. I seem incapable of bearing children. If 'tis Robby's sister, she will be born of your loins, not mine."

"Or Jane's," they both said.

"Did Jane lie with Lord Essex?" Annalisa asked. "Is she with child?"

Jack shook his head. "I know nothing for certain."

Annalisa sighed. "Then maybe he speaks of Jane's unborn daughter—one she hasn't yet revealed. Three children with three fathers. Mamma will be thrilled."

"And mine." Jack chuckled.

She opened the front door to her house and led them both inside. "Abbie is with child. Or was so when I left Charleston. She may be delivered of the babe by now."

"Wonderful news. And George?" Jack followed her into the parlor, where Mary sat with Quinnapin and Henry.

Annalisa settled into a chair beside the fire and Jack into the one across from her.

"He and Abbie left Charleston for New Jersey the same time I returned home," Annalisa replied. "George met his uncle, Admiral Bixby—"

"Admiral Bixby? Mean you to say I've another uncle?" Jack asked. "Why has George not written to tell me?" A ghost of regret washed over his face. "Would that I could join him."

"It came as a shock to me, too," Annalisa replied. "As well as Abbie and Ollie."

Quinnapin stood, joining them. "Cornwallis's army is in

the southern colonies. 'Tis only a matter of time before George sees more battle."

Daniel Peabody entered the room with a steaming mug of wassail.

"There you are, Miss Annalisa. You must be chilled." He offered her the drink and stood beside her. "I'm rather cold myself."

"Thank you. 'Tis quite nice after being outside." She sipped the wine.

Jack rose from his chair by the fire. "Mr. Peabody, please sit."

Daniel smiled. "Thank you, Lord Brunswick." He exchanged places with Jack, reheated his hands, and peered out the window. "It is rather lovely, all that snow falling."

Mary nodded. "I do love a pleasant snowfall."

"This could be the last Christmas of the war," Daniel said.

"How do you suppose?" Henry asked.

Daniel shrugged. "I don't, Master Howlett. 'Tis just my hope this war should end swiftly. I'm loath to think of all the children being born into such tumult. Such uncertainty and hardship plagues us all. We're lucky to be as self-sufficient as we are on our farms. At the very least, the Black Water is faring well in Portsmouth."

"Speaking of taverns," Henry said. "Jack, I've come by some information at the Willow you may find interesting."

Annalisa held her breath and eyed Mary, knowing perfectly well the information her brother was about to divulge.

"Go on, Henry," Jack said.

Henry rose from the sofa and joined Jack and Quinnapin by the fireplace. "I've uncovered several dispatches indicating Quinn's friend, Benjamin Cavendish, is a traitor, that he spies for the British."

Jack's eyes rounded, and he regarded Annalisa. "Knew you this about Mr. Cavendish? Quinn?"

"No, I hardly spoke to him at Peggy's wedding," Annalisa said quickly.

"Me either," Quinnapin added.

Jack addressed Mary, "Miss Mary? I saw you spent quite some time with the sir."

Mary shook her head vehemently. "No, of course not. I was shocked to hear such discourse about such a kind young man."

"The rogue," Jack cried. "I dueled the poor lad at Saratoga, but I never once considered him a threat to the cause. Maybe those unassuming are the ones we should most fear, Henry."

Annalisa shuddered, unable to bring herself to speak on behalf of her other self, the one bit of her that she continued to keep secret from Jack, the part of her she shared with George, who now encamped in New Jersey. Even now, as she stuffed Benjamin Cavendish into the deepest parts of herself, she couldn't rid the dreadful feeling that beset her each season: this could be their final Christmastide together.

II

1780

30

GEORGE

MORRISTOWN, NEW JERSEY, JANUARY
1780

GENERAL WASHINGTON DOTTED AN *i* and crossed a *t* while George stood by and watched. Being reunited with his commander in chief, and with that fart catcher Alexander Hamilton always by his side, reminded George of his days in New York with Samuel and Bartlett. Those days somehow seemed simpler, days digging trenches, drinking wibble around the fire, and fighting Bloodybacks; before Samuel lost his own battle and succumbed to his arm amputation after the battle at Kip's Bay. George's throat tightened at the memory of leaving his oldest friend at the sick tent to be buried the night they evacuated Long Island.

He studied his commander at his desk: the tight line of his mouth and hardened jaw hinted at a man worn down by years of leading an army destined to fail. Despite this, Washington's shoulders remained square and stable, as though he intended to carry the weight of this war until the very end, as he had the night they escaped Long Island by a miracle of fog.

"Pleasure to have you sign on, Major Howlett." Washington handed George the ledger. "I can't promise when you shall receive your payment from Congress, but you will be compensated, sir. I'll make certain of it."

"Sir?" George started. He'd been promoted from captain, something he'd not anticipated upon re-signing.

The general frowned. "Is there an issue, Major?"

George shook his head. "No, sir. I'm flattered by the promotion." He scribbled his name across the page.

"Quite." Washington poured sand over the ink. "Hamilton and I are right heartily glad to have your experience in these trying times. Your wife will receive half rations while she's at camp. Should you fall in battle—"

"She has forty-eight hours to remarry or leave the army," George replied. "Aye, sir. I recall it well."

"You shall have command over whatever's left of Cogswell's."

George suppressed a grimace, wondering if he might be able to join Henry Knox and the artillery. He'd have to find old Knox and plant the seed. "Thank you, sir."

The aide-de-camp poked his head inside. "Sir, Major General Arnold wishes for your private audience."

Washington replied, "Send him in."

Benedict Arnold entered the office guided by two Continental Army officers. "Sir, I wish to discuss the nature of my court-martial—" Arnold paused when he noted George lingering near Hamilton.

Quickly, George bowed to Washington, gave a scant acknowledgment to Hamilton and Arnold, and quit the head-quarters. *Court-martial? What has Arnold done?* George wrapped his wool cloak about him as a wintry gust tipped the cocked hat from his head.

Inside the shared log cabin, Abigail clutched her stomach and cried, "George Howlett, remove this child from me."

"Is the babe coming?"

Having never witnessed the barbarity of childbirth, the

sight of Abigail's wet, reddened face was enough to make him wish to never again put his pego inside her. How could such pleasure lead to this much agony?

"What does it look like?" she screeched.

"'Tis Major Howlett now," he muttered. "Let me fetch a midwife."

"I care not what to call you. I need Annalisa. Get my mamma!"

George hurried from the cabin, which housed ten others. The last time he camped at Morristown, he'd been a single man with only Jack for company. Now, he returned to New Jersey with his small daughter and pregnant wife, now in labor. How things changed in three years' time. At least they were under the army's protection and far from Admiral Bixby and the Royal Navy at Charleston.

In the wild, whipping wind, George ducked in and out of every cabin. "Is there a lady present? Any midwives here?"

The men of Washington's army often traveled with wives and camp followers, though not every lady proved knowledgeable in childbirth.

"I can deliver the babe," a woman said. She appeared older than he, perhaps forty or so. She left her husband's cabin with his permission and retrieved another camp follower to assist her.

The woman rattled off a list of items to the second woman that she would require to bring the babe into this horrible, wintry, and diseased world. Eager to flee Abigail's screams, George barreled from the cabin once more.

"The girl," the first woman said. "Please, take the girl with you, Major."

George returned for Louisa and held his three-year-old daughter beneath his arm. The poor little mite sniffled and coughed against the ice and snow whipping her face. He tucked her against his chest, inside his cloak.

"All will be well, little mite. Mamma will be all right."

"She is sick," Louisa wailed. "Let me help."

"There's nothing you can do, Weeza. Not yet. You're too little to help." He kissed her forehead. "Come, let's see if we may find Henry Knox."

Forty-eight hours of blizzard dropped over four feet of snow, but as the storm made its welcome exit, George's son arrived to clear skies and a snow-laden camp. The boy was crowned with a head of black hair, like Louisa, and, against his better judgment of keeping the child nameless until his first birthday, George called him Edward Bixby Howlett, for his natural father.

George crawled into the wooden bunk beside Abigail, who slept, nestling the children between their warm bodies. Louisa's teeth chattered against his chest as he wrapped the thin blanket about them. He brushed her black hair from her forehead and studied her face beside Edward's. The babe, with his cone-shaped head of black hair and swollen face, slept peacefully at Abigail's breast.

"Papa, I'm hungry," Louisa whimpered.

"I'm sorry, little mite. We've eaten all we're allowed today." He continued to smooth the hair from her face until her green eyes closed. When he was certain she slept, he closed his eyes, vowing to write home on the morrow.

❧ 31 ❧

ANNALISA

TOPSFIELD, MARCH 1780

ANNALISA POKED AND STIRRED the charred logs within a large brick hearth at the Whispering Willow. Glowing embers recaught flame, and she chucked a new log into the fire, followed by another. The blaze danced within its brick home, warming her face and neck. She wiped her hands on her apron and returned to the bar, where Henry and Mary convened. They whispered amongst themselves.

"Any word today?" Annalisa asked.

"From whom?" Henry asked.

Annalisa narrowed her gaze. "From your friend at Oyster Bay."

Henry returned to cleaning a mug. "I have no friends outside of town, you know that."

Mary giggled, then whispered to Annalisa, "No, his Oyster Bay contact has not written."

"Why must I depend on Mary for honest answers?" Annalisa grinned, satisfied.

She grabbed a linen towel and wiped clean the sticky bar. Behind her, Mr. Averill played "Cold and Raw" on his guitar. The absent strings of Jack's fiddle magnified in his solo instrument. When she finished cleaning, Annalisa poured herself a mugful of ale and sipped a good measure of the liquid. The morbid flux was upon her with a vengeance, cramping her insides and leaving her bloated within her stays. She meant to quell such symptoms, as later that evening, they would celebrate three birthdays—Jack and her two nephews, Robby and Tommy.

The front door opened, and a gust of wintry wind blew into the tavern. A courier with a letter offered it to Henry's outstretched hand. Her brother glanced at the address and handed it to Annalisa.

"'Tis for you, from George."

Henry then poured himself a tankard of ale, and Mary leaned over Annalisa's shoulder to read the letter.

> January 19th 1780
> Dearest Little One
> Abbie was deliver'd of a son in January. We call'd him Edward Bixby Howlett for my Natural father. I wish to relay that Mother and child are well, but the Wintyre has been Harsh. Rations are scant. Abigail is unayble to feed Edward well and WeeZa looks quite thin. I feare the worst. I think it best Abbie returnnes to towne with the children while She can.

Mary held the letter to a candle flame, and the rest of his note appeared between the lines of his wobbling script. Annalisa gripped her skirts as she continued to read.

> Benedict Arnold has been court-Marshalled

for exploytation. He has Apparently used his Status as an Officer for financial Gayne. He has Been found Guilty of minor accounts. I Trust the man little.

More to come.

Yours &c.

G

Her heart in her throat, Annalisa handed the note to Henry, who read it in seconds. "I'm sensing a tergiversation of the party aforementioned." He took the letter to the fire and dropped it into the flames. The pages curled and sizzled, quickly blackening to ash. "Pity about Abbie and the children. Pray, think you we should send Jack to retrieve his sister?"

Annalisa gripped Mary's hand and met her anxious stare. "No, don't trouble him with such news."

"Oliver, then?" Mary asked.

Annalisa's lips pursed. "He shouldn't have to leave Tommy behind."

"Who better than her own brothers to rescue her and the children from Morristown?" Henry asked. "Jack's been there before and knows the way."

Annalisa's lips parted to speak when Jack, draped in his navy-blue cloak and black cocked hat, stepped inside the tavern in a gust of wintry air. His cheeks pinked from the bitter air as he smiled at her. The tip of his hat angled over his left eye, he lifted it from his head and drew nearer the fire where Mr. Averill played his guitar.

"I'm a bit early to the festivities." He offered a dimpled a grin.

Annalisa circled the bar to meet him and smiled, hesitant

to taint his birthday with news of Abigail's turmoil at Morristown. "Happy birthday, sir."

Jack spun her around, their noses nearly touching, then left her by the fire as he sauntered to the bar to greet Mary and Henry. "How do you do, Howlett twins? It does me well to see you."

"Likewise, Lord Brunswick," Henry replied. "An ale for you, sir?"

Annalisa met Mary's stare, and Jack turned to meet her gaze. "Only if Miss Annalisa joins."

She faltered, crumpling her skirts. "I was just about to return home before the—"

"One drink." Jack extended his arm to her.

"One drink." She rejoined them at the bar but took her mug to George's old table adjacent to the keg room. Jack and Mary left the bar and slid onto the bench.

Jack lifted his tankard. "To our continued good health."

"Hear, hear."

They saluted and drank. When Jack set down his cup, his tongue swiped away the froth from his upper lip. Annalisa crossed her legs against the burning rush upon remembering his tongue as he tipped the velvet. Her face flushed at the memory, and she wondered if he, too, thought of their intimate moments as frequently as she.

She looked up from her tankard and caught him staring.

He smiled. "Are you quite well, Miss Annalisa?"

The sound of that formal address upon his familiar baritone tortured her in ways she never knew, perhaps worse than all she'd endured in battle as Benjamin Cavendish. *Does he mean to taunt and torture me coming here, all debonair as though I have no betrothed?* Yet Jack's charm radiated from his person as though it were that blustery March day in 1770 when she'd met him.

Were it not for her brother and sister, and Mr. Averill

with his guitar, she would have sat upon his lap without fear or reservation. Annalisa envisioned the heat of his thighs, his hands upon her, his growing arousal beneath her derriere...

"I cannot finish my drink." She stood.

Jack abandoned the table forthwith, all allure fading from his countenance. "Are you unwell?"

"I am."

"Upon my honor as a gentleman—"

"I need air." She stepped toward him and muttered, "You know me, Jack Perkins." Caught in a tantalizing haze of his amber perfume, she closed the distance between them and whispered, "I'm not of sound mind to refuse you."

"Let me at least accompany you outside." His hand upon her back, he led them into the chilly March twilight.

When they were outdoors, Jack said, "I swear I'll not compromise you while you're engaged—"

"I wish you would," she said. "I can't guarantee I'd refuse your advances. Fie! I'd welcome them upon the floor of the tavern were Mr. Averill and my kin not present to witness it."

A glimmer of desire returned to his gaze. "I apologize for teasing you so."

"You tease, but 'tis I who must return home to my parents until I'm married in springtime. You may milk your Thomas with memoirs of our intimacies, but I must share a bed with Mary."

Jack turned from her. "I know your agony well. But I never strummed Jane but for the one night Robby was conceived. Pray, have you shared no intimacies with Mr. Peabody?"

"He's made no advances upon me."

Jack wound his arm about her waist and pulled her through the snow-shoveled path toward the wood, where he leaned her against a thick oak. Pressing himself against her, he whispered, "If you'll have me now, I will take you." His lips found her neck, and he kissed her to her chin.

"The morbid flux is upon me."

"You know that never deterred me."

Dazed by his familiar scent, she closed her eyes and sighed. "I thought you would not cuckold Daniel."

"'Tis not cuckolding him if I cannot get you with child," he murmured.

She chuckled. "What rules are these? Have you created them?"

Jack's mouth found hers, and he bit her lower lip. "They're mine. If your betrothed will not have you, then I offer myself to you, darling girl."

Annalisa had never considered offering herself to Daniel. The thought humiliated her, as the act of intimacy with anyone other than Jack seemed foreign. Never had she conjured such perfection in two bodies entwined as one, as she had with Jack. All awkwardness of girlhood had dissipated from the first night he offered himself to her; and he'd never given her reason to doubt him or his love as he worshipped every inch of her for the entirety of their short marriage.

But the seeds of honor and doubt crept in as Jack gathered the layers of wool petticoats and found the space between her legs. Still, she persisted, aching for his touch.

"Jack. People are to arrive for the event."

"We're not to be seen from here," he crooned.

His fingers caressed her until she panted against his lips. "I'll go off if you continue like this."

"Then go off, my darling girl." His tongue found hers. "You know it pleases me to gratify you."

It had been ages, eons, since he last touched her or delighted her in any way. And it took very little to contain her. At the culmination of his efforts, her fingers dug into his hair and she gasped with ecstasy.

The moment spent, Jack fused his lips to hers. "Would that I could take you home tonight."

The passion between them spent, she shivered against the night encroaching upon them. In the twilight beyond the wood where they dwelled, the last of family and friends arrived for the birthday celebration.

"We can hardly appear at your celebration now."

Jack cupped her face, though her teeth chattered. "Listen to me, Annie." His thumb swept across her cheek. "You should never feel shame for our love. It is something beyond ourselves. I can't explain it, even to myself. Everyone, everything, is beyond it. I am bound to you, flesh and blood, as is my soul beyond the here and now. How should we expect any other to understand this?"

She trembled in his arms. "I know not."

He kissed her lips, her cheeks, her forehead.

Annalisa buried her face in his cloak. "I love you, Jack Perkins, with every bit of me."

"And I love you." Jack smiled. "Let's return to the Willow."

◈

THE WHISPERING WILLOW CROWDED WITH FRIENDS FROM town, family, and the other the birthday boys, Tommy and Robby, having arrived with Oliver.

Mr. Averill played his guitar, and Jack quickly joined with his fiddle, filling the smoky room with reels and jigs. For the first time in weeks, Annalisa appreciated the genuine smile upon Jack's face as he laughed while his young son gleefully clapped to his music. At George's table, Mary rocked and bounced baby Frances while William led Martha in a dance to

"Dribbles of Brandy." Lizzie Balch and Ezra Kimball joined, along with Martha's brother, Isaac Perley, Fannie Shepard, and that disagreeable hag Hannah French. Oliver drew a laughing Sarah into the set of dancers, and from the bar, Andrew Perkins clanked tankards with Henry.

Weary of sitting and buzzing with flip, Annalisa reached for her nephew Tommy and spun him about the room.

"You've another lad who wishes to dance with you, Miss Annalisa," Jack called to her over his playing.

She peered behind her and met his gaze. He gestured to Robby, who toddled toward her with arms outstretched. Annalisa scooped her other nephew into her arms and kissed his cheek. "A kiss for the other birthday boy. Shall we dance, Master Robby?"

"Yes! And Tommy, froo."

Annalisa reached for Tommy's hand as she hoisted Robby onto her hip and they danced amongst the others. When Mr. Averill and Jack finished the song, everyone clapped, and Josiah Averill replaced Jack on the fiddle.

His cheeks flush with joy, Jack joined Annalisa and the boys. He ran his hand over Robby's hair and kissed his forehead. "You've grown quite big, you know. Do you know how old you are?"

Robby shook his head. Jack leaned in close, whispering, "Are you...three?"

Robby's toothy grin widened. "Yis. I'm phree." He glanced down at his brother. "And Tommy is..."

"Four!" Tommy shouted, holding up four fingers.

Jack and Annalisa laughed. Their solemn little first nephew was usually softspoken and quiet.

"And pray, how old is your papa, Robby?" Annalisa glanced at Tommy. "How old is Uncle Jack?"

"Uncle Jack is...old," Tommy whispered.

"Old!" Jack guffawed, reminding her of George. "I feel old, though I'm unsure eight-and-twenty constitutes as such."

Annalisa shook her head. "Hardly. You've still much life in you, sir."

"Life or virility?" Jack winked.

Her face warmed. "Both."

Jack studied her a moment. "Boys, I should like to dance with Auntie Annie for this next one."

Sarah approached with Oliver. "I'm looking for a dance partner. Would either of you wish to join me?"

Tommy nodded. "I would, Miss Sarah."

"There's a good lad." Oliver swiped a gentle hand over his son's blond head, then plucked Robby from Annalisa. "I'm happy to take this one from you while you dance, Miss Annalisa."

She took Jack's outstretched hand. To their left, Quinnapin and Mary lined up; to their right, Ezra Kimball and Lizzie Balch. The fiddle and guitar played, and Jack threw his head back in laughter. He'd certainly had enough ale for the two of them, and his friends offered pints, none of which he refused.

"As one of the guests of honor tonight, I daresay I've the most agreeable lass in this tavern." Jack's comment came as he passed her in the dance, his hand joined with hers.

Annalisa couldn't help but smile as she rebuked him. "Hush, Jack Perkins!"

"'Tis Lord Brunswick now," Jack replied, then whispered, "and you, my dear, shall be my countess."

Annalisa pursed her lips to conceal the giggle that was sure to escape any moment. She eyed Lizzie, who bit her lip and made eyes at Ezra.

Jack continued, this time loud enough for Ezra Kimball to hear: "And once you're my countess, we'll make an army of little earls and countesses to overtake our families. Then we may retire in our seaside home at New Castle."

Ezra's heavy brows lifted. "This feels vaguely familiar to the Strawberry Festival of years past."

Not entirely humiliated, Annalisa recalled the event Ezra referenced, the night Jack confessed his love to her. She could hardly bemoan the memory, though this time she was no longer the maid she had been than night. Such was lost to her now, but she rejoiced in Jack's joy, no matter the consequence of his speech or who heard him.

The dance ended, and he kissed her hand, his lips lingering a moment too long upon her knuckles. "Miss Annalisa." The address seemed to sober him, and he stepped away from her, quick to return to his fiddle playing.

"Jack, wait." She tugged his coat sleeve. "Let me get you some cider."

He smiled. "The keg is quite hefty. Allow me to help."

They fled the crowded dance space and snuck into the vestibule where Annalisa had often spied on George and his friends. Alone with the great kegs stacked about the small, dimly lit room, Annalisa pulled Jack toward her and fused her lips to his.

His hands cupped her face, and she melted into his embrace. If not for the ample guests within earshot, she would have had him there in that very moment, and she suspected he would have accepted her most readily. His breeches taut with arousal, he pressed against her and groaned into her ear.

Annalisa nibbled his earlobe. "Lord Brunswick, you've had much to drink this night. Think you're able?"

Jack hoisted her onto a keg and spread her legs beneath her skirts. "Oh, lass, I'm able."

"Annalisa?"

William's harried voice carried into the vestibule, and

Annalisa tore herself from Jack a moment too late. Her younger brother hauled inside the keg room and grimaced. "Zounds, Annie!"

Jack approached William. "'Twas my fault—"

"Fie! None of that. Mr. Peabody is here. Get to."

Annalisa and Jack hauled from the vestibule and parted as Mr. Peabody advanced toward her.

"Miss Annalisa, Lord Brunswick?" Daniel's dark gaze darted between them.

"How good to see you, Mr. Peabody. I was just wishing to speak with Lord Brunswick about a matter most concerning." Her mind whirled with a reason to have been alone with Jack in the vestibule and she blurted, "Sir, I wished to tell you sooner but Abbie was delivered of a son and is unwell."

Taken aback, Jack's brows raised. "George wrote?"

"Aye, from Morristown."

"Morristown, New Jersey?" Jack leaned in close and whispered, "Annie, do you jest?"

She frowned and shook her head. "I didn't wish to spoil this evening. George wishes for Abbie and the children to be carried from there before illness takes hold."

His face paled. "Then I must go to her."

Daniel interjected, "Allow me to help."

"I cannot allow it, sir," Jack replied. "'Tis my sister."

"But Miss Annalisa is my betrothed." Daniel rested a hand upon Jack's shoulder and Annalisa couldn't tell if the gesture proved candid or a threat. "Her family is also mine, my lord."

Jack stiffened. "Sir, I can't allow it of you."

"And Mr. Howlett is soon to be my brother-in-law," Daniel replied. "Please, allow me to go. It would offer me the opportunity to prove myself to your family."

Annalisa's throat closed. "I...I know n-not what t-to say."

Jack led Mr. Peabody from the rear of the tavern to George's table, where Annalisa watched them convene for nearly an hour. Were it not for the scrutiny of her muse, Benjamin, she'd have left herself that night to retrieve Abigail and Louisa from Washington's camp. But as such was the determination of men, Mr. Peabody established, against Jack's resistance, it be he who goes to Morristown. When Jack could be neither persuaded nor convinced, Mr. Peabody fled the tavern with a promise to return with Abigail and the children.

"A fool he is." Jack joined Annalisa at the bar. He cradled his face in his hands. "A stubborn donkey who wishes only for George's admiration and nothing else. It should be me going, Annie. Not him. 'Tis but a fool's errand."

Her conscience swelled with guilt. "I should go to Morristown. George is my brother."

"Fie." Jack lifted his head and held her stare. "Speak not of it." He tucked his thumb under her chin. "I'll seek Mr. Peabody on the morrow and convince him otherwise. You will remain here. Safe."

Annalisa bit her tongue against the rage building within. She could absolutely ride to Morristown and retrieve Abigail and the children. But in the little time she knew Mr. Peabody, she suspected the silly sir had already left town and would be nowhere to be found come morning.

32

ANNALISA

TOPSFIELD, LATE MARCH 1780

A FORTNIGHT AFTER MR. PEABODY left town to retrieve Abigail, Papa met Annalisa in the drawing room. His dark, heavy gaze fell on her with sorrow. "I've no way of breaking such foul news to you, Daughter."

She rose from the spinet. "What's happened?"

"I'm afraid Mr. Peabody's been...delayed in New York."

Her heart galloped. "How did you come by such information, sir? Is he unharmed?"

"A letter was delivered written by Peabody himself. He claims he's been imprisoned by the Continentals."

Annalisa flew past Papa into the hallway. "Mary!" She ran down the corridor until she reached the front door. "Mary?"

Her sister materialized from the parlor. "What is it?"

"I'm going to the Perkins Estate. Mr. Peabody's been imprisoned by the Continentals." She fled the house for the barn, where she tacked up her horse, then rode down the narrow lane.

ANNALISA ARRIVED AT THE PERKINS ESTATE FAR QUICKER than her thoughts carried her. She knew not what to say when she arrived, but she was received by Mercy into their parlor. Jack, Andrew, Oliver, and Quinnapin—who was visiting—greeted her with unparalleled charm.

"Miss Annalisa." Jack kissed her cheek. "It does me well to see you."

"My papa's received a letter from Mr. Peabody. He's been captured by the Continentals and taken prisoner," she said.

"The Continentals?" Andrew cried. "Is he a turncoat?"

"Where?" Quinnapin asked.

Jack said, "I will find him at once—"

"Don't be a fool," Oliver replied.

"He's in New York," Annalisa said. "But I can't understand why the Continentals would capture him."

Jack clasped her chilled hands, and she wished to take refuge in his arms. "I'll find him. I promise you I will."

"'Tis too risky, Jack," Andrew said. "And you've your son to consider."

Annalisa met Jack's stare. "You needn't put yourself in danger. Not for me."

"I fought with the Continentals. I'm sure there's been some kind of misunderstanding." He held her gaze, his hands still enclosing hers. "I'd do anything for you, Annalisa."

"What of Abigail?" she asked.

"You're a fool if you think you will uncover Mr. Peabody," Oliver said. "At what camp do you suppose you'll find him?"

"I will do what must be done," Jack replied. "I know men at West Point. Perhaps he's been taken there."

"Abigail still needs someone to bring her home..." Annalisa's voice petered off into nothingness as Jack consumed himself in an argument with Oliver and Andrew.

If only George were there, he'd undoubtedly offer himself to seek Mr. Peabody in New York. Of their circle, no one knew the place better than he, but he remained at Morristown with his ailing wife and children.

If Jack abandoned town to find Mr. Peabody in New York, someone else needed to rescue Abigail from the horrors of the Continental Army's winter quarters. A surge of courage flooded her, and she caught Quinnapin's study from across the room

"I will leave on the morrow," Jack said. His attention returned to her, and he drew up her hands. "You have my word, Miss Annalisa. I'm certain Mr. Peabody's imprisonment with the Continentals was a grievous misstep. He is a good man—foolish, for certain—but a good man. And I will return him to you. Ollie will leave for Morristown and retrieve Abigail and the children."

Annalisa withered at the gesture, noble as it was, while their intent to break her engagement by springtime haunted her conscience.

"Ollie, you will leave Tommy?" Annalisa asked.

"No, I will go," Andrew said.

"Andy, will you shut your potato trap and give your tongue a holiday?" Oliver barked.

"Fie!" Quinnapin stood. "Allow me to bring Abbie home. 'Tis the least I may do; I have no children." He held Annalisa's stare, and she knew he meant for her to join him as Benjamim Cavendish

☙❧

Two days after Jack left Topsfield for New York, Annalisa, Mary, and Quinnapin devised a tale that would take them from town to fetch Abigail and the children.

Mary presented a false letter to Mamma written by Peggy Shippen Arnold, inviting her, Annalisa, and Quinnapin to visit Philadelphia.

"Of course," Mamma cried. "Why, Mary, maybe Mr. Wentworth will be present as well. 'Tis been ages since he last called on you. I was so certain he was about to make you an offer."

Jane flounced into the parlor with Robby. "Am I not included in this invitation? Has Mrs. Arnold so soon forgotten me?" She snatched the letter from Mamma and read. When she finished, she tossed the page, allowing it to land on the floor. Her face twisted, she settled into the chair by the fire. "I suppose news of my divorce has spread to the middle colonies at last."

"Fie, Janey," Mamma hissed. "You're to remain here. You've little ones to care for."

Annalisa bit her lip to suppress a chuckle. Mamma rarely spoke against Jane's convictions.

Her older sister threw up her hands. "And you're quite well to allow Annalisa to tag along with Mary and Quinnapin when her betrothed is imprisoned by the Continentals?"

"Annie could use a distraction from the disquiet," Mamma said. "And I'll not limit poor Mary. She is still unmarried and looking to be courted. One never knows the opportunities that abound in higher Society. Yes, Mary?" Mamma returned to her needlepoint in the second chair opposite the fire. "I trust Mr. Quinnapin very much to chaperone them well."

33

ANNALISA

NEW JERSEY, LATE MARCH 1780

THEY ARRIVED AT JOCKEY Hollow just before nightfall. The late-March wind whipped, and snow-drifts, several feet high, encapsulated the large log cabins of Washington's encampment. The scene reminded Annalisa of the winter Jack had been ill at Valley Forge, the winter he'd nearly succumbed to death. She shook away the horrid memory yet couldn't help but ponder Jack's whereabouts in New York.

It didn't take long to locate George, or Major Howlett—a promotion he'd neglected to write in his sparse letters—within one of the log cabins.

Annalisa stepped inside and gagged. The fetid stench of ten others huddled within their wooden bunks burned her nose and roiled her insides. Nearest the stone fireplace, her older brother scratched his stubbled face. He rubbed his eyes, as though to confirm all he saw.

"Little One." George scooped her into his arms, and she wrinkled her nose against the body odor and illness, a diseased amalgamation of scents she'd not appreciated since the sick tents at Saratoga and Valley Forge.

George held her at arm's length. "Look at you. I thought I told you no more Cav."

"I had to." Annalisa pursed her quivering lips. Shadows danced and flickered over the hollows of his cheeks, now peppered with two-day-old stubble—the army was only ever allowed three-days' growth—and in the firelight, an oily sheen reflected his long black hair tied in a queue, which lacked powder and crawled with mites. He scratched his scalp, waiting for her to speak.

"Oh, George," she whispered. "'Tis far worse than I imagined."

His jaw stiffened. "You've no idea." Quickly, he greeted Mary and Quinnapin, who'd stepped inside behind her. A ghost of concern haunted Quinnapin's face, and Mary cupped her mouth.

"Where's Abbie?" Annalisa asked. "Where are the children?"

George led them to the opposite end of the cabin. On the lowest wooden bunk, Abigail huddled with Louisa and a small babe.

"Abbie?" Annalisa's throat clogged, and she swiped away her tears.

Her friend's matted blond head slowly turned. "Annalisa?"

Annalisa knelt. "Shh."

Abigail's bottom lip split when her mouth parted with a smile. A droplet of blood pooled before she licked it away. "Oh, Cav. How wonderful to see you." A lone tear trickled down the side of her ashen face. "This is Edward. He...he won't latch and suckle anymore."

"We've tried everything, but there's no food," George said. "I've gone without so Louisa and Abbie may have something, but 'tis not enough." He gripped Annalisa's arm and pulled her close. "I never should have brought them here."

"Hush. You knew not what this would be," she replied.

"Blame not yourself. Congress must answer for this hideousness." A burning rage melted her insides, and she balled her fists. "How could Congress allow this the state of Washington's army? How can we ever suppose to win the war with men in this condition?"

George massaged his temples. "Washington is as despondent as I. And come spring, you're quite right to purport our devastation against Cornwallis's and Clinton's armies. We've nothing left. Thousands have died, succumbed to illness, starvation, or both. Many more have deserted, and rightfully so." He hesitated, as though to suggest he, too, considered desertion over death.

Quinnapin's hand reached for George's shoulder, the part of him that once filled his coat with broad muscle. Now, his wool frock hung from his six-foot-four frame as upon a skeleton. "We're here, Brother. We're going to bring Abbie and the children home."

"Would that you could join us," Mary said. "Please come home with us, George."

He shook his head. "Admiral Bixby is in Charleston. Here, I have the protection of the army. And when spring comes and we leave this fetid cesspool, I'll find my uncle and challenge him for consorting with that reptile, Captain Fleming."

Annalisa shuddered and pulled her cloak tightly about her. Despite the wool stockings and breeches encasing her frigid legs, she missed the layers of quilted and wool petticoats.

"Then the admiral must also know Lord Essex," Mary muttered.

Abigail turned within the bunk. When she repositioned Edward, she placed his little face to her breast. "Come now, you must suckle."

The babe's face, looking quite ashen, did not change with her movement. Her hand stroked the baby's head of downy black hair.

"Edward?" Abigail's guttural cry echoed from the deepest part of her that Annalisa understood all too well. Grief, wholly harsh and inexplicable, and something no mother should ever experience, gripped her as she lunged into the bunk and held Abigail. Edward had passed into the ethers and now belonged with Eliza.

"He's...gone?" George choked on the last word.

"Mamma?" Louisa's exhausted little voice chimed from the space between Abigail and the log wall. But her mother said nothing as her wails faded to shattered whimpers. She had nothing left, not even to cry. George removed Annalisa from the barracks and replaced himself beside Abigail.

Annalisa found Mary and Quinnapin clutching one another between the set of bunks. All had fallen quiet despite the other soldiers abound. Her sister's sobbing into Quinnapin's chest did nothing to conceal her anguish, nor should it. But Annalisa, who masqueraded as Benjamin, bit her tongue to assume the stoicism of her guise, though her heart wrenched and ached for Abigail and George. Such misery could not be bestowed upon any person, but had befallen those dearest her, and for that, with the guilt of losing Daniel to the Continentals—and Jack to finding him— Annalisa knelt to the floor. She held her face to conceal her silent sobs. Not a solitary good thing had come of this cursed war for independence.

⁂

IN THE GUSTY WINDS OF APRIL, GEORGE HEAVED HIS SPADE into the earth to bury his son, Edward Bixby Howlett. *Always risky to have named a babe before his first year of life.* Mary gripped Abigail and Louisa while Annalisa and Quinnapin stood by as George spoke a few words of the son he and Abigail had lost.

"When I helped Miss Anna bury her daughter, we placed

her facing southwest," Quinnapin said gently, "so she would make it to Keihtánit's house, where there is bountiful harvest, ample game, and always pleasant weather."

"Yes." Abigail sniffled. "I should like him to go there."

Quinnapin regarded George. "When *Wôpanâak* bury a child, the father cuts a piece of his hair to leave with the dead."

George said nothing as he removed his knife and sliced a long black tress from his head, which he draped over his son's infantile chest. Mary held Abigail and Annalisa cradled Louisa. Nothing could redeem the moment, not even the sprinkle of early spring sunlight upon her nephew's tiny gravesite, a space startlingly similar to Eliza's final resting place. And yet, as Quinnapin spoke his native Wampanoag, a surge of hope filled Annalisa.

Salvage it all, Mamma. Edward is with me. We never want for anything.

George and Quinnapin replaced the earth over the boy's body, planting him as though a seed, as she and Quinnapin had done with her daughter beneath the ancient oak.

"*Wachônuq ahkee,* the earth takes care of him," Quinnapin said.

Abigail sank into the melting snow, still encased in Mary's arms, but George quickly scooped her from the earth.

"Abbie, you are too indisposed to ride," he said. "The journey to Topsfield is long from here."

"Pray, is Philadelphia far?" Mary asked. "Mayhap we shan't lie to Mamma at all and take Louisa and Abbie to Mrs. Arnold to convalesce."

Annalisa sought George's harried stare. His jaw hardened. "'Tis a day's ride at most. But I like not for them to recover at the Shippens'. Benedict Arnold was court-martialed here not three months ago."

"Peggy is a kind and amiable young lady," Mary said. "I

should think her quite willing to take us in until Abbie is well enough to return home."

George regarded Annalisa. "What say you, Cav? You've met the doxie. Is she worthy of caring for my family?"

Annalisa bit her lip. Peggy Shippen Arnold had been generously accommodating, but riding south, and out of the way, seemed ridiculous when they could ride north and find lodging somewhere in New York or Connecticut. Yet recuperation at an inn proved less ideal than a well-established home in Philadelphia, complete with servants.

"Mary, write to Mrs. Arnold. Tell her we're seeking convalescence of your sister-in-law, and that Quinn and I shall accompany you as chaperones. Pray, is the major general still at camp?"

George shrugged. "He's been offered command of West Point. I think he may have refused the post there."

"Then we'll employ our plot without his consent," Annalisa replied.

34

JACK

NEW YORK, APRIL 1780

RIDING INTO BRITISH-HELD New York City would have been daft, too daft given Jack's own reputation as an escaped prisoner of HMS *Lively*. For all he knew, his imprisoner, Lieutenant Dickens, still hunted him despite the leg injury Jack had inflicted upon him in the Publick House at Sturbridge—the same night Captain Fleming died.

Haunted by that event, Jack rode north to West Point, a Continental Army-held post and the most likely place to find Daniel Peabody. His anxiety for being uncovered by Lieutenant Dickens diminished, Jack no longer donned his bauta mask from Venice for travel. Perhaps he feared the lieutenant less than other things, like discovering Daniel Peabody's disposition. How could he tell Annalisa the condition in which he might find her betrothed, if at all?

The thought both worried and thrilled him. *I am a scoundrel if I should rejoice in poor Mr. Peabody's demise.*

If only George were with him on the quest. Having marched hundreds of miles with Washington's army through New York, his cousin knew the colony far better than he. Despite this, Jack persisted, guided by his conscience and unyielding love for Annalisa. For the sake of duty, he would bring her betrothed back to her.

Situated atop a plateau on the west bank overlooking the Hudson River, Jack appreciated why General Washington had so revered West Point as a stronghold. Losing such a post to the British meant relinquishing control of the river, thus cutting off New-England from the rest of the colonies. Jack recalled Benjamin Franklin's political cartoon of the colonies drawn as a severed snake; New-England was the snake's head. *Remove the head, end the war.*

"Your papers, sir."

Jack had neither papers nor orders allowing him entry to West Point, only the sturdy reputation of his cousin Major Howlett, down at Jockey Hollow in New Jersey. "I've none, sir, but I'm seeking a prisoner who may have been taken under false pretenses."

The soldier on duty scowled. "No orders, then I may not permit you entry, sir."

Jack straightened his coat. "I understand, sir, but I'm Lord Brunswick, brother-in-law to Major George Howlett. We fought at Lexington and Concord with militia, and again at Bunker Hill. We also saw battles at Saratoga in '77. I swear to you, I'm no British spy—"

"Save your breath, my lord." The sentry held up his hand. "No orders, I may not admit you. Carry on."

"I implore you, sir. Write to Major Howlett—he's encamped presently at Jockey Hollow. He will substantiate my tale."

"Very well, sir." The soldier gazed forward, impervious to Jack's plight. "Good evening."

Jack turned from the entry, mounted his horse, and rode down the road. He would have to wait until the soldier on duty changed—a tiresome and tedious task.

As the early spring sun faded below the horizon, a chill

crept into the air. From the river, the chirp of peeper frogs resounded, reminding him of pleasant spring evenings in Topsfield. In the twilight, Jack rode a quarter mile from West Point, where he set up camp for the night. There, he would take rest until dark, then resume his mission at the fort.

AFTER TWO MORE UNSUCCESSFUL ENCOUNTERS WITH THE guards at West Point, he introduced himself to the new soldier on duty just after midnight.

"Sir, I'm Lord Brunswick, and I'm seeking aid in finding a man who's been wrongly taken prisoner."

The private, a short, rotund soldier no older than he, scratched his ear. "You speak of finding a needle in a haystack, my lord."

Jack quirked a brow at the familiar accent, then squinted in the moonlight. "Bartlett?"

Bartlett's gaze rounded. "Lieutenant Perkins?"

"Thank God, 'tis you," Jack cried. "Will you admit me into West Point, please?"

Bartlett fiddled with his facings. "I—I'm certain I may not unless you have papers, Lieutenant Perkins."

"I haven't any papers," Jack replied. "But you know me. We fought together with Howlett—who is now a major and presently encamped at Jockey Hollow—"

"Is Major Howlett in trouble, sir?"

"No, 'tis a different friend who was captured prisoner, wrongfully. I need to scour your gaol for him, please."

Bartlett hesitated, peering about him in the darkness. "Whom do you seek? I may post a notice for said prisoner if you like."

"Mr. Daniel Peabody of Boxford in the Province of Massachusetts Bay. The man is not a soldier, but allegedly was taken captive in New York. He runs and owns the Black Water Inn at Portsmouth."

Barlett adjusted his coat. "We've a few new prisoners recently taken. Let me take you when my relief arrives."

Jack clasped his hands. "Thank you, Bartlett. I'll be in yon woods, waiting." He hurried from the gate and slipped from the road. There he remained for two hours, watching, until another soldier relieved Bartlett. Jack hurried back toward the gate, where Bartlett lingered with the other soldier.

"This way, Lieutenant," he said and ushered him within the fort.

Jack followed Bartlett down a long, dimly lit corridor flickering with lanternlight. The smoky scent of campfires mingled with woody cedar, but as he neared the gaol, a sour putrescence overtook any pleasantness in the air.

Bartlett unlocked the cell and opened the iron door. Jack suppressed a shudder at the sight, his own imprisonment and torture aboard HMS *Lively* returning to him. He swallowed over the tightness in his throat and stepped inside the darkened cell.

"Mr. Peabody?" Jack squinted to see the faces of those imprisoned.

One man huddled in a blackened corner lifted his head. "Lord Brunswick? Or do my eyes deceive me?"

Jack's chest rattled at the sound of Mr. Peabody's croaking voice. "Sir, how came you to be in this place? Are you a Loyalist?"

Mr. Peabody rested his head against the wall as though too fatigued to move. "No, I'm no Loyalist, Lord Brunswick —" He hacked, a debilitating cough Jack recognized from his time at Valley Forge. "I spoke…the wrong name, my lord."

"What name?" Jack hastened toward him and knelt. "What name landed you in this ungodly place?"

Mr. Peabody hacked again, and Jack offered him his handkerchief. The poor, wretched man held the linen to his lips until specks littered the white with red. "Benjamin... Cavendish. I thought he a friend...of yours and the Howletts."

"Benjamin Cavendish?" Bartlett whispered from the cell entryway. "I knew him, too, sir."

Jack's face numbed. "Cavendish, you say." He left Mr. Peabody for Bartlett, who awaited him by the cell door. "You must release this man at once. I can attest to his good nature. He is no Loyalist."

Bartlett recoiled. "He claims to know Private Cavendish. I heard he's wanted for treason."

"What for?" Jack asked. "What are Cavendish's charges?" He loosened his neckpiece from the rising temperature.

"I know not the specific charges, my lord, only that we've orders to arrest Cavendish or any other knowing the lad."

"Has Mr. Peabody been questioned? Has he given any reason to suspect he knows Cavendish intimately? Or well?"

Bartlett shook his head. "I know not, sir. I was not the one to question him—"

"I want him released at once, Bartlett."

"I'm afraid I can't take orders from you, sir," Bartlett replied.

Jack ground his teeth. "Damn it, Bartlett. I fought at Lexington and Concord and Bunker Hill. I killed Hessians with General Washington on Christmas Day in '76. I suffered at Valley Forge and fought at Saratoga as a lieutenant. I, too, was imprisoned, taken aboard HMS *Lively*, where, by the grace of God, I escaped. You know me, Bartlett. Upon my honor as a gentleman and officer of the Continental Army, please release this man."

Bartlett swallowed, slowly nodding. "I believe you, Lieutenant." He bustled into the cell. "Mr. Peabody, with me, sir."

Jack hastened to Mr. Peabody's side and aided him to his feet. The poor man coughed into Jack's handkerchief, expelling more blood. "Come now. Let's put many miles between us and this place."

Annalisa's betrothed staggered from the cell gripping Jack's arm. "My thanks to you, sir. I'm forever...in your...debt, my lord."

Jack cupped Bartlett's shoulder. "Thank you, Bartlett. I'll not forget your kindness, nor your assistance in this matter."

Bartlett shook his hand. "Of course, Lieutenant. Let me escort you back."

Jack assisted Mr. Peabody down the long corridor with Bartlett, then beyond the confining walls of the inner fort. When they reached Jack's horse, he aided Mr. Peabody atop the beast, then climbed up behind him. They wouldn't be able to ride too far in this darkness, nor too fast with two grown men upon one animal, but they could venture far enough from West Point to spend the night at an inn.

As he focused on delivering Mr. Peabody home, Jack's thoughts turned to Benjamin Cavendish, the unassuming fiend whose reputation had led Annalisa's betrothed into a Continental Army gaol; Cavendish, who continued to be a thorn in his side, was accused of treachery.

❧ 35 ❦

ANNALISA

PHILADELPHIA, MAY 1780

ABIGAIL'S FRAILTY LEFT THEM no choice but to venture south to Philadelphia. At least there, in the comforts of the Shippen home, she and Louisa could convalesce.

"I think the less time we remain here, the better," Mary whispered.

The door to the Shippens' drawing room only slightly ajar, Annalisa—dressed as Benjamin—rose from her seat beside Mary and closed the door.

"Why? The Shippens have a goodly reputation—albeit as Loyalists—and have offered to help." She returned to her space on the sofa. "Abigail and Louisa will recover better here than at home. You know that, don't you? Abbie can't return to the Perkins Estate. She must stay with us. Lady Perkins will not have her in their home."

Mary bit her lip and studied the empty drawing room for eyes or ears hidden within the walls. "I fear for our reputation. You remember what Henry said. We're being scrutinized within our own circle for this kind of acquaintance. 'Tis by the grace of God we entered and fled Morristown with as much ease as we did."

Annalisa's jaw tightened. "I know."

"Particularly Benjamin," Mary added. "You read those letters. Who could be slandering Benjamin's name? I think about it constantly and can't conjure a single person."

It was true. The letters bothered Annalisa, too, but she could hardly let them rule her conscience. Abigail and Louisa were quite unwell, and if masquerading as Benjamin proved the safest option to guide them home, she would do it no matter the consequence.

"I fear the Continental Army very little, Mary. George's reputation alone would be enough to release us of any accusation. 'Tis the British I fear. If uncovered by them, 'tis the gallows we'll see."

Mary held her hand. A thick, unsettling silence oozed between them as the weight of such consequences amassed to dangers beyond their grasp or comprehension. Considerations for Mr. Peabody, supposedly gaoled, pummeled forth, and Annalisa wondered if Jack had been able to locate him. Or, was he, too, now imprisoned?

The door to the drawing room opened, and Mary released her hand. Peggy stepped inside with her husband, Benedict Arnold, and Quinnapin.

"Oh, Miss Mary, how good to see you again." Peggy embraced Mary, then smiled at Annalisa. "Mr. Cavendish, a pleasure."

Annalisa bowed. "Likewise, Mrs. Arnold."

"Gentlemen, shall we spend tomorrow gaming?" Arnold asked.

"Much appreciated, sir," Quinnapin replied. "'Tis been many months since last I hunted for sport."

Arnold clapped his hands. "'Tis settled. Tomorrow at dawn." He quit the drawing room at an alarming pace, given his invalid leg and use of a cane. Yes, she and Quinnapin had saved his leg from amputation at Saratoga, but it seemed to never entirely heal.

Annalisa chewed her lip to hide her smirk. Quinnapin quite detested the nature of gaming, and his snide tone had wholly surpassed the military governor, who was now beyond earshot and down the hall.

"My dear husband is right heartily glad for your visit, Mr. Quinnapin, Mr. Cavendish. And of course, I'm so very pleased to offer Lady Essex and her daughter a place to recover from that horrid winter camp." Peggy shuddered. "My husband had nothing but ill words to describe the conditions when he stayed in December."

"He visited General Washington?" Mary asked.

Peggy twisted her skirts. "Yes, in some capacity." She hesitated, then murmured, "He was court-martialed, but nothing became of it."

The hair rose on Annalisa's arms beneath her coat. George had mentioned the event but spoke nothing else of it. *If given the proper timing, and enough liquor, will Peggy reveal more?* George also mentioned Arnold being offered command at West Point. Such left Annalisa pondering how much Peggy could be trusted, if at all. And in that moment, she glimpsed Mary, whose hazel eyes bore the glint of unease.

What if Peggy's marriage to Arnold is a ruse? What if she wed him to obtain intelligence for the British?

Her own lies weighed down on her. Jack knew nothing of her rescuing Abigail and Louisa; neither did he suspect her crimes as Benjamin Cavendish. As the secrets piled upon one another, the dangers of being uncovered by one of these two warring armies at last seemed tangible.

Days turned into a week, and Abigail regained her strength, both of mind and body. Annalisa snuck down the corridor to her room and knocked.

"Abbie."

The door opened, and her friend greeted her with Louisa. "Come in, friend."

Annalisa slipped inside rose-scented room and closed the door. "Oh, Abbie, you're looking much better." They embraced, then she knelt to kiss Louisa. "You, too, little one. And I think next week might be someone's birthday."

Louisa giggled. "I'm four, Auntie Annie."

"A big girl," Abigail said. "Auntie Annie's birthday is the twentieth. She'll be four-and-twenty."

"Four-and-twenty?" Louisa's eyes rounded. "You're old, Auntie Annie."

"Weeza," Abigail hissed. "That is rude. Apologize at once and come here to let me tie your stays."

"I'm sorry, Auntie Annie." The girl, since age three, had donned stays and a dress, no different than what any lady wore. Annalisa smiled, though she wished to cry. Her young niece so resembled George with his green eyes and black hair, yet her porcelain cheeks started to freckle, as Abigail's. *My own dear Eliza would've been the perfect amalgamation of Jack and me.*

"Auntie Annie, why do you dress like a boy?" Louisa asked.

"Weeza, I told you never to mention that," Abigail said.

"'Tis fine, Abbie." Annalisa knelt. "You've much to learn of our world, Weeza, but a lady can only do so much. If I dress like this, people think I'm a man and treat us differently. Especially if we're traveling with Uncle Quinn. If highwaymen think there's two men in our party, we needn't trouble ourselves as much along the road to home."

Louisa studied Annalisa a moment. "Will you marry Uncle Jack?"

Annalisa stiffened under the girl's study. Perhaps her niece and nephews absorbed far more than she'd previously surmised. "One day, I hope." Her throat tightened thinking about Mr. Peabody, perhaps lost forever as a prisoner of war, a victim of the times.

Abigail kissed Louisa and took her to the chamber-maid down the hall.

Dinner passed as any other formal event: two hours and no less. After the meal, Annalisa and Quinnapin remained at the table with Chief Justice Shippen and Benedict Arnold to drink port. Giddy for only a moment to remain among the men, Annalisa sipped her drink and watched her sister and Abigail conform to ladies' rituals as they retreated to the drawing room with Peggy. Her entire life, she'd been relegated to the parlor or drawing room while the men drank their port and spoke of things not meant for ladies' ears.

Eager for Arnold to wag his boastful tongue, Annalisa offered him a third glass of port. He drank the contents heartily.

She sucked in a breath to muster her courage. "I heard you were offered command of West Point, sir. My congratulations to you. Pray, when will you take up your command?"

"Thank you, Private Cavendish." Arnold shifted uncomfortably in his seat. No doubt his leg bothered him. "I've not yet accepted the position. If I do, I will relocate next month."

"Surely, you must accept it, sir," Quinnapin said. "Is there any reason to refuse such a prestigious position?"

Arnold's jaw twitched, and he sipped his port. "No, no reason at all. Except my own unwillingness to leave my wife in Philadelphia, should she refuse to relocate with me."

Annalisa finished her drink laced with Quinnapin's elixir.

The harsh, bitter fluid thawed her insides and left her light-headed.

"I think 'tis a marvelous promotion, Arnold," Chief Justice Shippen replied. "And Peggy will be thrilled to join you on this journey."

Arnold smirked. "Then there you have it. You've all convinced me."

Quinnapin raised his glass. "Hear, hear."

They saluted to Arnold's promotion, but Annalisa focused on the wry smile dancing upon his lips. Something felt amiss, but she couldn't discern what.

Annalisa stood, her head swimming with port. "Gentlemen, I think I'm about ready to join the ladies."

Arnold chuckled. "Yes, too much male company never does me good." He followed them into the drawing room with a strained hobble upon his cane.

In the drawing room, Mary sat beside Abigail while Peggy played her English pianoforte, a similar mahogany piece to the one decorating the Duchess of Devonshire's drawing room. Resisting the urge to displace Peggy from the bench, Annalisa joined her sister and Abigail.

"Ladies."

Abigail smirked. "Mr. Cavendish, how good of you to join us."

"You look entirely aglow with spirits, sir," Mary said with a light chuckle.

Annalisa nodded. "Aye, wrapped in warm flannel if I'd had another."

"Look at Peggy," Mary whispered.

Annalisa returned her gaze to the pianoforte and the young lady who played its ivory keys. Vivaldi's decadent cadences of "Spring" flowed from her accomplished fingers, yet only a lady learned in observation would notice the dried streaks of tears upon her cheeks.

"Why was she crying?" Annalisa murmured.

"A letter she received from an *old friend*." Mary's brow lifted. "A Major André."

"British?" Annalisa muttered.

"Yes."

Annalisa withheld her gasp and stood with nonchalance. She cleared her throat and circled the room, seeking the silver tray of brandy lingering between Benedict Arnold and Quinnapin. She retrieved a glass and sipped the amber liquid. Its smoky essence burned her throat down to her stomach, the same way it had when she learned of Jack's affliction with opium and brandy. Since then, she'd not seen the drink in his hand. Struck with guilt, she downed the measure, exchanged a few words with Quinnapin and the major general, then returned to her sister and Abigail upon the sofa.

"Pray, did she show you the letter?" Annalisa whispered.

Abigail nodded. "Yes."

Peggy played for at least another quarter hour when her husband excused himself to retire for the night. He hobbled from the room with Chief Justice Shippen, and Annalisa stood once more, waiting for them to pass down the hall and beyond earshot.

"Let me coax it out of her." Annalisa made her way to the pianoforte and leaned over its glossy finish. "Mrs. Arnold, your playing is far more accomplished than Miss Mary's sister, Miss Annalisa."

Peggy's countenance lifted. "I remember Miss Annalisa and her playing. She was quite good. You flatter me, sir." She reached for her glass of claret and finished it, the music halting for mere seconds before the resounding *adagio* of Mozart's Second Piano Sonata filled the room. The sound of Annalisa's most beloved composition tightened her breast with vestiges of Jack. She studied Peggy's slender fingers as they pranced about the pianoforte's white-and-black keys, the gold ring upon her left hand gleaming with an emerald stone. "You look as though you've been crying, Mrs. Arnold. I pray 'tis nothing of consequence."

"How kind of you to notice."

Annalisa held her breath, hoping she hadn't exposed herself with such a study.

Peggy peered at her for only a moment before returning her gaze to her hands. "I'm quite well, I assure you, Mr. Cavendish."

"I gave my heart to a lady once. I'm remiss to admit she quite damaged it," Annalisa replied. "I should think if I saw any lady looking as sullen as you do now, I should be right heartily convinced of her affection. Madam, is it the major general? Do you grieve his injury?"

"I love my husband, sir. I want you to know that—"

"Peace, Mrs. Arnold. I meant nothing by it."

"I only wish for him to know and adore my dear friend as much as I do."

Annalisa swiveled around the pianoforte and slid beside Peggy on the bench. "Your dear friend?"

"He, too, is an officer," she whispered.

"Ah, I see." *She must speak of this Major André.* Annalisa's heart fluttered within her bound breast at Peggy's veiled admission. "On my honor as a gentleman, I'll not speak a word."

"Thank you, Mr. Cavendish." Peggy's lips curled. "I'd nearly forgotten how delightful you are. Such kind, dark eyes...I feel I can trust you."

"You flatter me, Mrs. Arnold." Annalisa stood. "By your leave, madam."

Peggy abruptly rose. "Miss Mary, Lady Essex, I should like to dance with Mr. Cavendish. Mr. Quinnapin, choose your partner, and the omitted lady shall play for us."

Quinnapin lifted from his chair by the fireplace and

extended his hand. Abigail and Mary whispered amongst themselves, then Mary accepted him while Abigail exchanged places with Peggy at the pianoforte.

"If only Miss Annalisa were among us to play." Abigail gave a subtle wink, and she was upon the bench. "Her playing is far more accomplished than mine."

In the middle of the room, opposite from Annalisa, Peggy giggled. "Do your best, Lady Essex. Play a cotillion."

The first notes of "Corn Rigs are Bonny" erupted from Abigail's capable hands, beginning the dance. As they stepped in time, Annalisa recalled dancing in this same house to this same cotillion with the commander in chief himself, General Washington. *How long ago that now seems!* Quinnapin and Mary laughed and twirled, the same as Peggy. Annalisa's head light and dizzy with port and brandy, she, too, offered a deep guffaw. The opportunity to garner information was ripe—a cherry for the picking.

When the song ended, Abigail started "Flowers of Edinburgh," Annalisa's favorite reel. Peggy threw her head back with laughter, her cheeks rouged with far too much claret. When the song ended, Annalisa collapsed onto the sofa and Peggy onto her lap, giggling.

"That was marvelous, Mr. Cavendish," she cried. "Pray, you dance so very well."

Startled, Annalisa replied, "I've sisters at home who taught me well, Mrs. Arnold."

"How I love to dance. I crave it as the air we breathe and the food we eat," Peggy said. "Would that my husband was not afflicted from the war...that he could dance." She hesitated. "Major André danced famously at my father's dinner parties."

"For you, sir." Quinnapin offered Annalisa another drink, one she knew held the elixir to darken her eyes.

She took it readily from him and drank. "Thank you, Quinn."

From the pianoforte, Abigail played Corelli's *adagio* from his Concerto Grosso No.3 in C Major: III. The slow, languid music filled the room, echoing Peggy's forlorn mood as she balanced upon Annalisa's lap. If the major general had wobbled into the drawing room and saw his wife as she was, Annalisa would be whipped and banished from the Shippen household. Anxious to remove Peggy from her, Annalisa shifted her hips. Peggy rocked but kept her balance.

"Mr. Cavendish, I'll fall!"

Annalisa offered a reserved chuckle. "Perhaps my lap is not so sturdy as the sofa beneath me."

"Major André's lap was quite sturdy, I assure you."

Annalisa tingled at the conjecture. "I'm quite lean, I know—"

"I meant nothing by it, sir," Peggy cried. "Forgive me."

"Nothing to forgive." Annalisa chortled. "Only tell me one thing, if you will. Pray, who is your friend Major André?"

"He's an officer in the British Army."

"Then it makes sense to feel such despondency with regards to your dear husband befriending a man of his enemy."

Peggy fell silent. Slowly, she slid from Annalisa's lap, and paced the room wringing her hands. "I did love him, Mr. Cavendish. I loved André. I only wish to keep his acquaintance. Is that such a crime?"

Mary, who had been idly observing the scene from across the room with Quinnapin, stepped forward. "Mrs. Arnold, there is no crime in having loved a man, no matter the man."

Abigail rose from the pianoforte, and in the absence of music, the room vibrated with quiet stillness. She joined them. "I may be married to Lord Essex, but 'tis in name only.

My child, Louisa, belongs to George Howlett, Mary's eldest brother. Sometimes, the heart wants what it wants, but we must marry for convenience, Mrs. Arnold."

Peggy pursed her lips. "Convenience, yes. Or sacrifice."

36

GEORGE

NEW JERSEY, LATE MAY 1780

GEORGE STOOD OVER A cooking fire waiting for his ashcake to finish baking on hot embers. As much as he missed his daughter and wife, he no longer forfeited his ration of food to them, and hence, the rumble disappeared from his victualing office. In the weeks they'd been gone, he'd slowly regained his strength after the worst winter he'd yet lived, and he prayed Abigail and Louisa, too, recovered in Philadelphia. He'd sent a letter three days ago, but the mail proved unreliable.

The fire snapped and rustled, blackening the edges of the ashcake. He scooped it from the embers and onto his tin plate. Memories of Samuel and their days in New York now felt to be ages ago. George lifted his tin cup filled with wibble.

"So fill to me the parting glass, and drink to health whate'er befalls, old rogue," he muttered. In two bites, he consumed the tasteless ashcake, then finished his cheap rum.

"Major Howlett, the general wishes a word."

George glanced at the aide-de-camp, set down his eating

utensils, and rose to his full height. Without speaking, he followed his superior to Washington's headquarters.

"General Washington, I've Major Howlett, sir."

George stepped inside Washington's office. Hamilton, stationed beside the commander in chief, proved nothing other than a pesky rodent yearning to give commands on a battlefield. George's shadow encased Hamilton's wee form, which tickled George's fancy.

"Sir, you wished to see me."

Washington's jaw set. "I've just received notice of General Benjamin Lincoln's surrender at Charleston on the twelfth instant."

"Surrender, you say?" George nearly lost his breath. *Then my uncle rejoices, that reptile.*

"Yes. I require you and Cogswell's to ride from here as reinforcements. Is that understood, Major?"

George nodded. "Aye, sir."

"Colonel Buford knows to expect you," Washington added.

Hamilton handed George a signed and sealed dispatch. "Good day, Major."

George turned to leave when Washington's voice stopped him. "Godspeed, Major Howlett."

He faced the general. "Same to you, sir. May we meet again."

❧

North Carolina

SINCE CHARLESTON HAD FALLEN TO THE BRITISH, GEORGE presumed Colonel Buford had retreated north from Charleston and likely inland toward Charlotte. At least that would have been his plan were he in charge of a column of soldiers. As they neared Charlotte, George ordered his men to approach the town from the south, hoping to intercept Buford and his men as they marched north. They'd made ample time, having marched hundreds of miles within a span of four days. Now, the hot southern sun boiled George's skin beneath his wool coat, a stark contrast to the frigid winter he'd just survived in New Jersey. If only they marched north. New-England springtime proved far more agreeable than this southern swamp-riddled wasteland.

Ahead, a column of Continental soldiers lined a clearing across the route of the march.

"Halt, men." George advanced toward the column and their superior ranking officer. "I'm Major Howlett, seeking Colonel Buford. I come with reinforcements from General Washington."

A gentleman of middle age wearing the epaulets of a colonel in the Continental Army acknowledged him. "Major Howlett. I'm Colonel Buford. You've come at an opportune time, sir. Tarleton and his dragoons have been pursing us since Charleston and are just beyond that ridge. He sent word ordering me to surrender, but comply we will not."

George offered the colonel his dispatch. "We'll join your line, sir."

The colonel scanned the page with brevity. "We're glad to have you."

George rode back up the road to his exhausted, over-heated regiment. "Gents, fall in and make ready. We're joining Buford and his men."

As they reached Buford's column, a line of British dragoons rode over the ridge and into the clearing. For a moment, an intoxicating surge coursed through George as the impulse to ride into battle against those bastards over-took his sensibility. It wasn't until that one column of British turned into three that George's innards twisted with doubt.

He looked to Colonel Buford for orders to retreat, but the colonel shouted, "Do not fire until the enemy is at ten yards."

"This is suicide," George growled. To his men, he yelled, "Make ready!"

They loaded their firelocks and muskets as the first British column, about sixty legion dragoons and mounted infantry, advanced to the right. At the center, light dragoons charged with near forty more legion dragoons. The men surrounding George clutched their muskets, ready to fire.

"Affix your bayonets," he ordered.

Led by Tarleton himself, the final British column charged to the left. At this, George commanded his men according to von Steuben's manual of orders. He, too, hoisted his firelock, Bixby, to his shoulder, aimed at Tarleton's horse, and cried, "Fire!"

The beast collapsed to the ground, and Colonel Tarleton flew from the animal. Several more shots rang out from Buford's men, but to no avail. In a cloud of sulfuric gunsmoke, British dragoons charged into their line with no mercy.

Blood spattered onto George's face from a soldier nearly decapitated by bayonet. He hoisted his bayonet into the offending dragoon, who collapsed from his horse. The beast galloped from the battlefield and into the surrounding woods.

George ordered his men to make ready and fire, but it proved futile against Tarleton's dragoons. Amidst the gunsmoke and green coats of the dragoons, George wielded his bayonet into a mounted infantryman, who dropped from his horse and clutched his wound. Promptly, George ordered his horse to gallop over the fallen man to end his suffering. Or perhaps enhance it.

"We surrender!" an officer shouted.

Another dragoon on horseback heaved his bayonet into the officer's chest, who crumpled into a bloody heap. George jumped from his horse to retrieve the fallen soldier's carbine and saber, then jumped back atop his horse. With Bixby slung over his shoulder, he loaded the shorter cavalry carbine and fired on an oncoming mounted infantryman.

"Retreat, men," George hollered.

His militia scattered from the field as more surrendering Continentals gagged and drowned in a sanguinous rush of their own lifeblood. Acrid gunpowder clogged George's nose and stung his eyes as he reloaded the carbine and fired on an advancing dragoon. The man lurched from his horse, but another charged. The stinging slice of a bayonet through his shoulder stunned him, and the searing pain that followed surged a wave of anger.

George reloaded as he neared the tree line with his horse. He jumped from the animal and ducked behind a tree, where he removed his neckpiece and tied it under his armpit. Once he had tightly knotted it over his bleeding shoulder, George emerged from behind the tree and bellowed, "For Bunker Hill!"

He fired on an assailing dragoon and the man toppled from his horse. George then scurried farther into the surrounding forest. Ducking beneath a bush, he studied the battlefield. Tarleton, who had survived the fall from his horse, ordered his dragoons to bayonet any fallen Continental soldiers. *A massacre. 'Tis a bloody massacre.*

George scanned the landscape for Colonel Buford, but could not make out the gentleman. Perhaps he, too, had fallen with his men.

The air, muggy and thick, clung to the pungent gunpowder and coppery blood. His breath quick and unfulfilling in such humidity, George heaved. His insides expelled nothing but bitter green bile until his sore, contracted abdomen burned. He rested against a large tree, sweat dripping down his temples, neck, and chest. In a final attempt to preserve his life, George tightened the linen neckpiece about his shoulder and closed his eyes. Only divine Providence knew if he would survive this day, though he prayed to whomever would listen to spare his life for the sake of his daughter and his Abigail.

And in the darkness, he saw the boy he buried at Jockey Hollow, the son he never knew.

37

JACK

TOPSFIELD, MAY 1780

DRIVEN BY A BURNING resolve to locate Benjamin Cavendish, Jack galloped into town with an ailing Mr. Peabody clinging to him. Not knowing the man's residence, Jack took him back to his own family's estate, where Peabody would at least be able to convalesce in comfort. The poor sir hobbled under Jack's sturdy form, a mere shell of his prior being.

Mercy opened the front door before Jack knocked. He hurled inside with Mr. Peabody.

"Have Andrew call on Dr. Brown," Jack said.

The housekeeper flew from her post by the front door, and Jack guided Mr. Peabody up the stairs to Abigail's vacant bed-chamber.

"I know not...how I may thank you...Lord Brunswick." Mr. Peabody's teeth chattered despite the temperate spring day.

"No thanks be needed, sir." Jack pulled the man's boots from him and assisted him into the bedstead.

Mr. Peabody trembled with the coverlet up to his chin.

Jack sat opposite the bed, one leg crossed, awaiting Dr. Brown.

"I'm quite well to lie here," Mr. Peabody said. "You needn't offer me more company than you've already done, sir. I'm grateful to you, my lord."

Jack leaned forward. "'Twas the least I could do—"

"For me?" Mr. Peabody coughed. "I was a stubborn...cow to have gone on such an errand. Surely, you did this...for Miss Annalisa?"

The question caught Jack off guard, and the door flew open. Dr. Brown bustled within, followed by Oliver and Andrew. The doctor set his effects on the foot of the bedstead.

"Allow me to inspect the patient, Lord Brunswick."

Jack rose and followed his brothers from the chamber. The door closed behind them, they convened in the hallway.

"What befell that sorry sir?" Oliver asked.

"Imprisoned at West Point," Jack replied.

Oliver's brow lifted, though he kept his voice low. "On what account? Is he a traitor? I thought him to be Patriot."

"Peabody is no traitor," Jack replied. "'Twas along the road when he associated himself with Benjamin Cavendish. He was detained and taken by the Continental Army. Apparently, Cavendish is wanted for treachery."

Andrew grimaced. "A foul happenstance. Pray, I wonder by what account Cavendish is wanted by the Continental Army?"

"Henry's intercepted letters at the Willow that were written by Cavendish to Lord Essex, and one to Benedict Arnold," Jack replied. "Perhaps since Arnold's marriage into a Loyalist family he's been under scrutiny? I know so little of the inner workings of Washington's army."

The door creaked open behind them, and Dr. Brown stepped into the hall. "He's resting, but the consumption is upon him. I gave him a blood-letting and laudanum for the cough."

Jack nodded. "Thank you, Doctor." When Dr. Brown disappeared down the stairs, Jack addressed his brothers. "Pray, where is Quinnapin? Perhaps he may offer Mr. Peabody some other kind of remedy?"

Oliver's lips pursed. "He left for Jockey Hollow to bring Abbie and Louisa home."

"It should have been me to go," Jack replied. Overridden with guilt, he turned toward the door. "Peabody had no business retrieving Abigail. Stubborn ox that he was..."

"'Tis obvious he did it for Annalisa," Oliver said.

Jack's jaw tightened. "Would you bring Annie here so she may see the state of her betrothed?"

Oliver shook his head. "She and Mary have gone to Philadelphia."

"What for?" Jack whispered. "Please do not say to visit—"

"To visit Peggy Shippen Arnold," Oliver and Andrew said.

Jack fisted his hands and returned to the door. "The world has turned upside down." He unlatched the door and stepped inside the room. Mr. Peabody lay with his eyes closed. Jack sat in the chair and watched his steady breathing.

"Is that you, Lord Brunswick?"

"It is."

Mr. Peabody offered a solemn smile. "I suspect—no, I know—how you care for her. To do what you've done for me was certainly also for her."

Jack held his face. "Sir, I wish I could speak plainly, attest all you say is false, but I cannot lie to you. I've loved Miss Annalisa the better part of my life."

"Then perhaps 'tis you who should marry her, sir."

His breath caught, and he sat upright. "I beg pardon?"

"I cannot stand in your way if you love her, my lord. I will not do it."

"Peabody, you can't mean it."

"I do." Mr. Peabody's thin, cracked lips pursed. "I may not have many more days upon this earth—"

"'Tis folly to suppose the time of one's death," Jack cried.

"Sir, I've seen the face of Death in that prison, and I daresay I know him well. When he takes me will be a tale for another time, but I shan't draw you or Miss Annalisa into a fate of despair."

Jack lifted from the chair and knelt at the man's side. "I've seen the face of Death, too, and I need to tell you that living is far worth the fight, sir."

Mr. Peabody coughed into his handkerchief. Specks of blood dotted the linen. "I've made my peace. And you have my blessing. Will you make yours?"

Jack fell silent, studying the pale, gaunt man shivering in springtime sun. He'd been agreeable, strong, and full of vigor. Now, he lay a broken man because of another. A slow anger bubbled from within, and Jack loosened his neckpiece.

"You have my word, sir, I will find the traitor Cavendish and bring him to justice."

❦

THREE DAYS LATER, JACK RODE TO THE WHISPERING Willow. The old haunt had once been a place for rowdy nights of drinking and song. Now, it remained void of George's boisterous laughter. Jack trudged toward the bar, where Henry and William Howlett convened.

William rounded the bar and greeted him. "How fares Mr. Peabody?"

Jack shook his head and leaned over the bar. "Not well. His cough has worsened these last two days. I fear Annalisa may return too late."

William's face fell. "'Tis that dire?"

"Aye. Dr. Brown says 'tis the consumption."

Henry made a pitcher of rattle-skulls, a concoction of ale, rum, molasses, and a squirt of lime, and carried it to their usual table. William set out three tin cups for each of them.

"The poor sir." William poured from the pitcher. "Never stood a chance being engaged to Annie. That girl is bad luck."

Jack suppressed a grimace. It certainly seemed everything Annalisa touched soured, though he knew this engagement was hardly her doing. What plagued him most was Benjamin Cavendish. Somehow, the rogue had been identified a British spy, landing Mr. Peabody in gaol. The ill fortune was uncanny.

"Any word on Cavendish?" Jack asked. "I need to find the rogue and question him. Nay...I need turn him in to the Continentals for questioning. The man must be court-martialed at once."

Henry sighed. "I've not confiscated a letter in months, I'm afraid."

"Then I'll leave town and scour the colonies until I find the bastard," Jack growled.

"You're daft." William wiped his mouth on his sleeve. "You'll never find him."

"Perhaps write to George and ask if he's saw Cavendish in New Jersey," Henry said. "Maybe he has something to tell of the lad."

Jack slammed his hand upon the wood table. "Mr. Peabody was imprisoned for mentioning the rogue's mere name. Blood shall be on his hands if Peabody dies. I need avenge that poor man."

"Easy, Jack," Henry said.

Near the hearth, Mr. Averill's guitar played "The Parting Glass" while other townsmen gambled and read pamphlets.

Jack finished his rattle-skull. The alcohol burned his throat and he coughed, clearing the liquid. "I mean no harm, gentlemen. I only wish to bring justice."

"There are more players in this charade than I care to worry about," William said. "What of Lord Essex? Has he written to Jane from England?"

Jack shrugged. "I speak with Jane as little as I might. Henry?"

Henry shook his head. "I've not seen any mail from England reach her hands, no. But I do wonder if there's a connection between Jane, Lord Essex, and Benjamin Cavendish. They each were in Philadelphia for Peggy Shippen's wedding."

"Lord Essex is a master manipulator," Jack said. "I've no doubt he used Jane in the way he used Abigail. Though Jane's Loyalist sentimentality proved more conducive. They could plot together, whereas Essex used Abigail as a conduit to Patriot information. 'Tis why he withheld her mail when they were in England. I'm sure of it."

"And?" Henry leaned forward.

"Which leaves me to ponder if there's always been another source here in the colonies," Jack added. "Mayhap that source is Cavendish. He certainly fits the profile, no? Fought at Bunker Hill and Saratoga for the Continentals and is known to George. Perhaps he planted himself among us at the appointment of Lord Essex to garner information."

Henry nodded. "I think that is a possibility. My source at Oyster Bay wrote something similar."

"What could Lord Essex be after?" William asked.

"Power is always a corruptible vice," Henry said. "Or influence."

They maintained an air of silence until Henry added, "I think you should write to George. If he's seen Cavendish, then ride forthwith."

"And leave town before Annalisa returns?" William asked.

"Jack, if you mean to find Benjamin Cavendish and bring him to justice, you must write to George," Henry said. "'Tis probable he's seen Cavendish these several months if the lad is still within the army. Mayhap he wintered in New Jersey."

"Then he may already be dead," William said flatly.

Writing to George meant waiting another several weeks, if not months. Jack tapped his fingers on the table.

"I will find Cavendish," Jack said. "Annalisa may not be my wife, but my heart's wasted on her. Any slight to her and her betrothed is a slight to me."

The tavern door flew open, and Josiah Averill stepped inside. He held aloft a newspaper. "Gents, news from North Carolina. Bloody Ban has massacred hundreds at Waxhaws."

Another British victory in the south. Dejected, Jack rose. "I can stomach no more."

"Where are you going?" William asked.

"To kiss my son. Then I ride for New Jersey."

"But you just returned," William said.

"I'll go mad waiting here to receive a letter of confirmation from George about Benjamin Cavendish." He turned to leave, then addressed the Howlett brothers, "Please, when next you see Annalisa, do give her my regards. Peabody gave me his blessing, and when I return, I will ask your sister to be my wife."

38

ANNALISA

TOPSFIELD, JUNE 1780

ANNALISA, QUINNAPIN, MARY, ABIGAIL, and Louisa reached town a week after the Strawberry Festival. In the privacy of Quinnapin's home, Annalisa removed her Benjamin Cavendish clothing and assumed her stays, linen petticoats, and dress. The journey from Philadelphia had been long with Louisa, but they'd made ample time once they reached Massachusetts.

The familiar lush fields separated by stone walls greeted them as they rode down the narrow lane toward the Howlett farm. Her family's saltbox house piped smoke from its wide central chimney. No matter the season, Liza kept a roaring fire in the sizable kitchen hearth. *Mamma is sure to welcome Mary and me, but will she accept Abigail and Louisa?*

Their horses stabled in the barn, Annalisa led them up the path and knocked on the red-painted front door.

Liza answered quickly. "Miss Annalisa, Miss Mary! Lady Essex..."

Mamma hurried down the hall and into the foyer. "You've returned, thank heaven!" She pulled Mary into an embrace, then Annalisa. "Oh, my dear Lady Essex." Mamma cupped

Abigail's face, then kissed Louisa. "Sweet girl, how you've grown."

Jane, with Robby, peeked out from the parlor. "Annalisa, your visits home are always well-timed. You just missed Jack."

"Jane Howlett," Mamma scolded.

Ignoring Mamma's shriek, Annalisa charged into the parlor after Jane. Her sister had just taken up her needlepoint in a chair by the open window. Annalisa grabbed her sister's canvas and threw it outside.

"This is how you greet me?" Annalisa eyed Robby carefully before continuing in a softer tone, "What of Jack? Where is he?"

Jane smoothed her skirts. "He left town two days ago."

Annalisa bent down and planted a kiss on Robby's rosy cheek.

"Auntie Annie." He wrapped his arms about her. "I miss you."

"I missed you, too, little man." Annalisa returned her gaze to Jane. "Then he returned from New York—"

"It matters little, doesn't it? Don't you care to know if he found your betrothed or not? Or do you only wish to take Jack to your bed at once?"

"How dare you?" Annalisa sneered. "I do wish to know Mr. Peabody's well-being. Did Jack find him?"

Jane reached into her pocket and wagged a note in the air. "Jack wrote you a letter. Foolish of him leave it with Mamma. Would've been in better hands with Lady Perkins."

Annalisa lunged for it. The seal had been cracked. "You opened my letter. How could you?"

"Easily. I care little for your charades. You've damaged enough lives, haven't you?"

"Enough. I'll not endure your wrath for nothing. Have not I done good by bringing Abigail and Louisa home?"

Jane's brow quirked. "I thought you and Mary went to visit Peggy. How have you come by Abigail and Louisa?"

"'Tis none of your business," Annalisa snapped. Her heart in her throat, she unfolded Jack's letter. Before her scrawled his impeccable script:

> 10th June 1780
> Topsfield
> My dearest Annalisa,
> It pains me to Quit town before your Return. You'll be relieved to Know Mr. Peabody is safely Return'd from a Continental Army gaol at West Pointe. I wish I could write he is well from said imprisonment, but 'tis far from the Truth. He is resting at Perkins Estate. Please be with him, care for him until his end, as I believe will be imminent.
>
> Worry not for me. I've gone to New Jersey to find George with the hopes of seeking the perpetrator who hath landed Mr. Peabody imprisoned by the Continental Army. The man shall not be named, but Know my devotion to you remains unchanged, and always shall remain so. May we meet again soon, my darling girl.
> Yours affectionately,
> J

Her breast rattled with her beating heart. Annalisa tucked the note into her pocket with her Bunker Hill musket round and caught a whiff of Jack's amber perfume. Ignoring Jane's stare, she said, "I must see Daniel at once."

Mary and Abigail hurried into the parlor with Mamma and Louisa. Robby ran to them and embraced Louisa.

"What is it, Annie?" Abigail asked. "You look pale."

"Mr. Peabody is unwell, and I must go to him at once." Annalisa kissed Mamma and Abigail and fled the parlor.

"Annie, wait." Mary chased after her into the hallway. "Meet me at the Willow tonight."

"I'll try." Annalisa pecked Mary's cheek, then quit the house.

Annalisa raced to the barn, tacked her horse, mounted the animal, and rode from the farm with haste.

❧

ANNALISA HASTENED UP THE FRONT STEPS OF THE PERKINS Estate and knocked. She hadn't glimpsed herself in a mirror, nor had she washed the grime of travel from her; it hadn't occurred to her to check her appearance until Mercy answered the door.

"Do come in, Miss Annalisa."

She stepped inside, conscious of her disheveled appearance in the foyer looking glass.

Lady Perkins slinked from the parlor and into the foyer. She greeted Annalisa with a disparaging stare, then motioned toward the stairs. "Your betrothed convalesces in Abigail's chamber."

Annalisa brushed past her and scurried up the stairs and down the corridor. She knocked once, then entered the room that had once kept her beloved friend.

"Daniel?"

Her betrothed lay in Abigail's canopied bed, a pale apparition of his former self against the dark bedding and his curling hair. He reached for her.

"Annalisa."

She sat beside him and drew up his chilled, dry hands. Always cold, they were. "You're safe," she whispered, brushing his dark curls from his forehead. "What happened, sir? How were you imprisoned?"

Daniel shook his head. "Let's speak not of it—" A cough escaped his cracking lips, one that returned the color to his face for only a moment until he expectorated blood. *The consumption, for certain.* Annalisa quaked, supposing his prognosis. Everything else mattered little: his imprisonment, the secrecy and lies swirling about her muse, Benjamin Cavendish. The war. Jack Perkins.

A reverberating shudder quaked her. *Salvage it all, Mamma.* That little voice iced her spine, lifting the hairs on her arms. To anyone else, it might have been the chill of the bed chamber or the person within it so very near to death. But for Annalisa, it was her daughter, an omnipresent spirit gently reminding her to live and let live despite the hardships of wartime. Despite the tragedy, death, and despair. In spite of her ill judgment—and Jack's. *I will salvage it all, my darling girl.*

Beyond the canopied bed, life as she knew it dissolved, leaving her with Mr. Peabody. In whatever time he had left on this earth, she would spend it with him. To atone. To forgive herself. To forget the war.

❧ 39 ❧

JACK

NEW JERSEY, JULY 1780

JACK ARRIVED IN NEW Jersey mere days after Washington's army had abandoned their encampment at Jockey Hollow. After a week seeking information throughout Morristown, he collected varying accounts of Major Howlett's regiment having been ordered south to support efforts to recapture Charleston from the British. A younger fellow, introduced to him as Nathaniel, offered what he heard during his time at camp.

"Major Howlett ventured south to support Colonel Buford's retreating men. I heard they encountered Bloody Ban at Waxhaws back in May."

Jack spun his signet ring, his nerves heightened that George may have fallen at the massacre. "Thank you for your information, sir. And in your time at camp, did you meet a man called Benjamin Cavendish?"

Nathaniel furrowed his brows. "No, sir. But I know that name. I fought with a Benjamin Cavendish at Bunker Hill."

"You were at Bunker Hill?" Jack started. "And you know Cavendish?"

"*Knew.* I hardly know him now, sir."

Nathaniel's lady called to him, and he turned to leave.

"Mr. Hitchcock, please, sir, if you can recount Cavendish, may I write to you?" Jack withdrew his pencil and notebook and offered them to Nathaniel, who scribbled his contact information.

Before Nathaniel left, he tipped his hat. "Sir, by your leave."

"Many thanks, sir."

Jack watched the young man follow his wife with a small babe in her arms, then returned to his horse. Unwilling to ride into enemy territory, Jack rode south to North Carolina, hoping to encounter Cavendish along the way or, by the grace of God, his beloved cousin George.

❦

Camden, North Carolina
August 1780

Oppressive humidity coaxed beads of sweat from his temples, curling Jack's hair along the edge of his hat. His horse snorted in the swampy, breezeless air. He couldn't help but ponder how Abigail and George had endured such a torrid and suffocating place for so long.

In the twilight before dawn, Jack arrived at Rugeley's Mill, north of Camden, where Major General Gates had stationed his men. Jack dismounted after entering the camp and approached a subaltern.

"Sir, I'm seeking a Major Howlett or Private Benjamin Cavendish."

The officer, younger than he by at least five years, quirked a brow. "I know not a Private Cavendish, but there's a Major Howlett. Let me take you to him, Mr.....?"

"Lord Brunswick," Jack said.

"Of course, my lord, let me take you to him."

A flood of relief washed over Jack. *My cousin lives.* He followed the subaltern down a row of tents, where they paused outside one.

The subaltern cleared his throat. "Major Howlett, sir, you've a gentleman—"

George appeared from within looking rather disgruntled. Upon seeing Jack, his countenance lifted. "Cousin."

The officer quit the reunion, and George embraced Jack, then stepped back to appraise him. "You dandy," George guffawed. "Even with the arduous course of riding for weeks through this swampy quagmire, you still manage to appear handsome as ever."

"And look at you, Major." Jack admired his cousin's insignia.

"Aye. 'Tis about time."

"To think, you survived Bloody Ban." Jack appreciated his cousin's sturdy build.

"Aye, and 'twas exactly the sort of massacre you might imagine. I'd like to forget it." George clapped his shoulder. "But what brings you here? Are you to enlist? You've come on a most auspicious day. Pray, how fare Abbie and Louisa? Came you from Topsfield? Is Annalisa well?"

The onslaught of questions gave Jack pause. "Annalisa... I've not seen her in months. When last we spoke, she was well. Abigail and Louisa, I've not seen them either—"

"Then where've you been?" George bellowed. "Pray, Abbie and Louisa made it to Topsfield, yes?"

"I was on an expedition of my own seeking Annalisa's betrothed, Mr. Peabody. He was imprisoned by the Continentals—"

"The Continentals?" George roared. "The dilberry is a Loyalist?"

"No." Jack shook his head. "The poor man was imprisoned on false charges. He claimed to have known—"

"Major Howlett!"

George faced the address. A corporal barreled forward.

"What is it, Corporal?" George asked.

"Cornwallis, sir—"

"Is it time?"

"The skirmish last night, sir...General Gates has asked for his officers. He seeks advice, sir."

George regarded Jack, his emerald eyes wild and blazing. "Barricade yourself in my tent, Perkins."

"Not a chance. I'll fight under your command—"

"Gates is a squeeze crab. Far too much hubris. And today, we fight. Unless you wish to infect yourself with dysentery, make haste and leave this place at once." George hurried away with the corporal.

His musket and effects slung over his shoulders, Jack abandoned the row of tents and made his way through the encampment. If he couldn't find Cavendish, he would at least join the lines and fight Cornwallis and his army of Lobsterbacks. And perhaps if he remained within the army long enough, Cavendish may find his way there.

GEORGE

CAMDEN, SOUTH CAROLINA,
AUGUST 1780

GEORGE STOMPED FROM GATES'S headquarters. After uniting his regiment, or what was left of it after Waxhaws, to Gates's army earlier in July, George found himself wondering if the major general had the stamina and wit to prevent British advancement northward. Yes, Gates had aided in their victory at Saratoga, but he was wanting for military genius. And humility.

Now, despite his sought advice, Gates ordered the formation of his men, placing experienced regiments from Maryland and Delaware on the right, a militia from North Carolina at the center, and inexperienced Virginia militiamen to defend the left flank.

George's stomach in knots, he turned to his subordinate. "Gates is a foolish dilberry—"

"But he burgoyned the British at Saratoga—"

"Aye. I was there. But look you..." George paused and drew a diagram in the red dirt with his bayonet. "Cornwallis will have his most experienced men on his right, and our left flank is a Virginia militia that hasn't seen battle. I told Gates he needs to replace the Virginians with either the Maryland or Delaware regiment. That way men who've seen battle would be amidst the green Virginians. We need experience on both the right and left flanks." George sucked in an anxious breath, then released it. "This will not end well." He kicked away his diagram and sheathed his bayonet.

His sergeant looked on nervously. "I...I know not what to say, sir."

"'Tis no matter, now," George grumbled. "Not my orders."

As the hot sun rose over the horizon, Cornwallis's Lobsterbacks marched into view and formed their line across the field.

George peered at his subordinate. "Sergeant, we'll assist the Virginia line, though I fear it will be futile. If the line falls or they flee, we join the center, then the right."

"Is...is that General Gates's order, sir?"

"'Tis *my* order," George barked. "Make ready."

"Aye, Major Howlett."

The familiar voice lifted from behind him. George turned.

Jack stood with musket ready.

An amalgamation of fear and relief flooded him, but he grinned. "You old dandy."

"I'm with you, Cousin." Jack's cheek dimpled. "Like Lexington, Bunker Hill—"

"New York." George reached for his cousin and pulled him to his right, displacing his sergeant. "Brother." To his sergeant, he said, "This is Lieutenant Perkins. You will acknowledge and follow his command. Is that understood?"

"Aye, sir," the sergeant replied.

George's palms moistened around his firelock. Positioned behind the Virginians, he recognized the British regulars to Cornwallis's right, as he'd presumed. On Gates's order to advance, George's men marched behind the Virginia line. The deafening blast of guns shook the ground from both sides, and thick smoke from the artillery clouded the field in a sulfuric haze.

As they approached the British, George appreciated the Bloodybacks had already started to advance with bayonets affixed. Cries of "huzzah" echoed over the rumble of cannonade.

"Make ready," George yelled.

The regulars fired on them. Most of the Virginia militia turned and fled to the rear, leaving George and his men exposed.

"Fire," George shouted.

The crack of musket-fire rang out from his men, but it was hardly enough to stop the advancing Lobsterbacks.

"Make ready," he cried. "Fire!"

To his horror, the North Carolina provincials threw their loaded firelocks and muskets to the ground and abandoned the center.

"Join the right," George ordered. "Join the right!" He found Jack behind him. "This way."

They weaved through fleeing North Carolinians to join with the advancing First Maryland Brigade. Shots rang out, rattling his chest and clouding the battlefield with smoke. The right flank continued to fire on the advancing British. By the time George and Jack, and whoever remained of his regiment, joined with the right flank, the commanding officer, DeKalb, ordered a second attack. Blinded by the haze of gunsmoke, George loaded Bixby and fired.

For another thirty minutes or so, they held off the British until the First Maryland Brigade attempted to fill the hole created by the fleeing North Carolinians at the center, but their attempt proved futile. British infiltrated the center. A volley whizzed past Jack and struck George in the calf. Searing pain radiated up his knee to his thigh, and he collapsed.

"Fie!" George growled.

Jack rushed to his side and tore his soiled neckpiece from his neck. He wound the linen about George's leg. "To your feet, Major."

George snaked his arm about Jack's shoulder and, despite the agonizing pain in his left leg, hoisted to his feet. Together, they hobbled from the battlefield. They ducked between fleeing Continentals and British volleys until they reached the forested perimeter of the field.

Within the confine of shady trees, George leaned against a wide tree as Jack unwound the linen for a moment to assess the wound. Hot blood spilled forth, coating George's filthy breeches. In the distance, musket-fire and cannonade rang out, obscuring the muggy forest with pungent, sulfuric smoke.

"What's the damage?" George asked with a grimace.

"'Tis not good." Jack re-tied and tightened the linen. "I need yours as well."

George unwound his neckpiece and handed it to Jack, who looped it about his calf and over his knee, tying it tighter than the first.

"That should do until we get you back to camp. But you need a surgeon."

"No." George ground his teeth against the pain. "I will not lose this leg."

Jack's eyes glistened, and his lips flattened into a line. He nodded but said nothing as he scooped his arm beneath George's and helped lift him from the ground.

In the sick tent, George gnawed on a piece of leather as the surgeon poked and prodded to remove the round embedded within his left lateral calf muscle. Jack looked on from the foot of the cot with a stern countenance.

"Fie." George spat the leather to the ground. "More wibble."

Jack handed him a bottle of cheap New-England rum, and he gulped the searing fluid. The liquor warmed his innards, and he leaned back on the cot. Memories of removing Annalisa's round from Bunker Hill overtook him. She was lucky to survive such a festering wound. Her later injury at Saratoga—a round to her thigh—had healed far better, having been extracted by Quinnapin. *Would that this injury heals the same.*

"Cousin, 'tis out."

George opened his eyes. A blurry Jack hovered over him holding the bloodied round. George reached for it and examined it. "'Tis remarkable such a small entity causes such harm."

His left leg bandaged, George rolled onto his right side and closed his eyes against the dizzying onslaught of cheap rum. "Write to Abbie," he mumbled. "Tell her I survived Camden. For now."

"And Annalisa?" Jack asked.

"Yes. Write to her as well. Give her..." The world darkened for a moment until Jack's voice brought him back.

"What shall I tell her?"

George opened his eyes, but his heavy lids slid down. "Tell her...give her my regards...that I understand...wounds...we're even now." He drifted to sleep, the scent of gunpowder abound and his cousin beside him.

❈ 41 ❈

ANNALISA

TOPSFIELD, OCTOBER 1780

IN THE EARLY WEEKS of September, news of General Gates's horrific defeat at Camden finally reached Topsfield. By the first week of October, George's letters arrived. Mary rushed into the drawing room for Annalisa as she sat at the spinet with an unopened dispatch addressed to her.

"Annie, a letter for you."

She left the bench and met her sister in the middle of the room. She gasped at the seal. "Jack wrote this." Her finger broke the wax and she unfolded the page. His immaculate pen scrawled over the page.

> August 26th, 1780
> Charlotte, NC
> My dearest Annalisa,
> I write to you for your devoted brother, George, who has incurred an injury to his leg at the recent battle at Camden. I wish I could

write we were victorious, but by the time of your receiving this, you may already know the Unhappy truth of our humiliating loss. George fought gallantly, as you might well suppose of a man of his Stature, but his Injury was not insignificant. We've managed to relocate to Charlotte in North Carolina, where he may convalesce from his wound, as he hopes to keep his leg.

I pray this letter finds you in good health, and that Mr. Peabody has not yet left this world. You are ever in my thoughts, and my heart.

Yours affectionately,

J

Her heart aflutter, Annalisa peered up. "George has been gravely injured at Camden."

"Injured?" Mary's hand flew to her breast. "Where?"

"His leg. Jack writes he hopes George may keep it. Does Abbie know?" Annalisa's face numbed with memories of Saratoga, having witnessed far too many men lose limbs to the bone saw—and their lives to festering stumps. "He cannot lose his leg, Mary. If he does, he shall surely end."

"Shh." Mary embraced her. "George is strong, the strongest of them all. He's endured this war for nearly the entirety of it and has healed from all his wounds."

"Yes, you're quite right." Annalisa pulled from her sister and folded the note. "Would that I could be there to help heal him."

Mary shook her head. "No, Annie."

"I know I can't leave," Annalisa whispered. "Not while Daniel lives. And I pray he does."

"Is he faring better?"

Annalisa frowned. "He lingers between worlds. Some days, he speaks to me as though he could jump from his bed that instant. Other days, he suffocates from cough and burns from fever."

When Mary didn't speak, Annalisa said, "What is it?"

Her sister wrung her hands, then smoothed her skirts. "I know not. 'Tis a feeling of malcontent I can't shake. I fear something terrible must happen soon, be it Daniel or George."

Annalisa cupped her sister's shoulders. "I know the feeling. Let's meet at the Willow. Tonight. I think we could use a strong mugful of flip and the company of our dear brothers."

❧

THE COOL, CRISP AUTUMN AIR REVIVED HER AS ANNALISA galloped hard and fast down the lane toward her brother's tavern. A rejuvenating September breeze blew through her long curling tresses, unbound from her cap. When she finally turned down the narrow road toward the Whispering Willow Tavern, she trotted toward the establishment and jumped from her mare. She tied the beast to the wood fence surrounding the tavern's perimeter, then hurried up the steps and into the familiar building.

Her brothers, Quinnapin, Mary, Abigail, Sarah, and Oliver crowded about George's table near the rear of the main tavern room.

"Annie!" Abigail rose and clutched her. "My dearest friend."

Abigail appeared well, having lost all gauntness from her face, and the color had returned to her freckled cheeks.

"I need to remain with Daniel until he no longer requires me," Annalisa said. "'Tis the least I may do for him in this wretched illness."

"I know," Abigail said.

"Come, we've plenty of pitchers of flip." William lifted an unclaimed tankard and offered it to her as she greeted the others and settled between Mary and Abigail.

Annalisa sat and sipped the frothy beverage. The earthy bitterness agitated her stomach.

"Ollie has some news to share but wished to await your arrival, Annie," Henry said.

Annalisa regarded Jack's brother, who clasped Sarah's velvety, umber hand. He released Sarah's hand, then retrieved a note from his waistcoat pocket. "I've news most interesting." Oliver spoke with such aplomb Annalisa could never have anticipated what next he spoke. "I've information that British Major André has been detained by the Continental Army."

"Peggy's paramour," Annalisa said. "You don't suppose he met with Major General Arnold, do you?"

Oliver nodded. "I do."

"Then Arnold is a turncoat." Annalisa regarded Mary and Abigail. "I knew it. I knew Peggy would facilitate such an acquaintance."

"How did you come by such information?" Henry asked, appearing as shocked as the rest of them. *A marvel, to shock Henry!*

Oliver adjusted himself over the table. "I've an old contact from my time in the British Army who also defected. Henry, your contact at Oyster Bay, is he reliable?"

"Aye, very," Henry replied. "I'll write him at once. It shan't be long before news of Arnold's treason reaches General Washington."

Annalisa reached into her pocket and fiddled with her

musket round. She rolled it between her thumb and forefinger, her nail scraping its grooves. Perhaps it had been their information about Peggy that spread from Henry's letter to Oyster Bay upon their return from Philadelphia. Some small part of her filled with purpose, that she and Mary may have played a role in warning of Arnold's potential treachery, which had, in fact, been true. She wondered if Peggy's entire marriage was for this, if she had sacrificed herself for Arnold's treachery. The thought chilled her, that a woman so devoted would marry a Continental Army officer only to persuade him to defect. *What power! But for what? She fooled everyone, risked everything, and her lover was caught.* It would only be a matter of time before Benedict Arnold would be court-martialed by Washington and the Continentals.

But Annalisa marveled at Peggy's bravery. Only time would tell if she'd be a martyr to the end.

As the war continued to rage in the south, Annalisa considered how George and Jack fared in North Carolina. She studied Abigail, who told not a solitary tale of grief. Perhaps her letter from George had not been written so explicitly. Abigail had endured much at Jockey Hollow; perhaps George wished for Jack to withhold the unfortunate news so to not further disturb her. *Another martyr, my brother.*

But George was the glue that held them all together. With her final sip of the drink, Annalisa decided she would ride south to heal George's leg. It was the absolute least she could do for the brother she cherished most. Yet she still had Mr. Peabody to consider.

42

ANNALISA

TOPSFIELD, NOVEMBER 1780

NEWS OF MAJOR ANDRÉ'S hanging, and Benedict Arnold's treason and escape from West Point spread throughout the Province of Massachusetts Bay. The information had Annalisa wondering if the general had left Peggy behind to answer to General Washington, whilst mourning the hanging of her beloved Major André. *A martyr, dear Peggy.*

In that time, Mr. Peabody's health improved enough for him to leave Perkins Estate for his parents' home in Boxford. Annalisa traipsed to the Peabodys' to read each newspaper article to Daniel on the matter of Arnold's betrayal, but to her chagrin nothing was ever written about Peggy. She tamped away her yearning to write Peggy, to ask how she fared during this horrific charade, as such an act proved far too dangerous.

"What news...today?" Daniel croaked.

Annalisa changed the cloth over his forehead. "Nothing new." She forced a smile for him.

His lips parted to grin, but he coughed. This time, the attack lasted so long the handkerchief soaked with blood. Horrified, Annalisa threw away the rag and replaced it with her own before he noticed. But her fear proved futile; Daniel's gaze noticed little, if anything, of the room or her. He rested against the pillow and closed his eyes.

Her hand upon his forehead, she uttered, "Rest, sir."

"Annalisa," he whispered. "This shall be...my last, I'm afraid."

"Your last what?"

"My last...Christmastide."

"Don't speak thus. You were well yesterday. You need more rest—"

"No." He slowly shook his head. "Promise me."

"Promise you what?"

A tear leaked from the corner of his right eye and landed upon the pillow. "I failed you."

"Why would you think that?" Her throat tight, Annalisa fought back her own tears as she wiped his.

"We cannot marry," he whispered.

"'Tis all right." She blinked until the blurriness disappeared. "Some things are not meant to be."

"I wish for you...to have the children...you deserve. The life...you deserve."

Her heart wrenched with melancholy, but she could not speak.

"Promise me." Daniel's cough returned, this time turning his face from crimson to purple.

Mrs. Peabody opened the door. "Let me call for Dr. Brown."

"No," Daniel wheezed. "No...blood-letting."

His mother rushed toward the bed and tossed Annalisa from his side. "What, no blood-letting? Have you given up, my darling?"

"I...cannot." He licked his bloodied lips. "I will not." Daniel struggled for a lungful of air, but he did not expel it. His face darkened from purple to blue, a kind of suffocation

Annalisa had never witnessed. Not even in her days with the army had she seen such a prolonged, painful demise. It was exactly the worst death for such a kindhearted, selfless man.

Mrs. Peabody's cries turned to shrieks as she hovered over his body. Trapped in the corner, Annalisa cupped her mouth and knelt to the ground.

Mr. Peabody's father rushed into the chamber, and Annalisa covered her face as she wept.

"Annalisa, help me retrieve Mrs. Peabody," he cried.

She opened her eyes to her Daniel's father pulling his wife from Daniel's body. Mustering her strength to stand, Annalisa scrambled to her feet and assisted Daniel's father.

"Take her to the parlor while I call on Dr. Brown," he said.

Annalisa tugged Daniel's mother from the room and ushered her down the stairs and into the parlor, where she proceeded to faint beside the sofa. Thankful for Mrs. Peabody's slight frame, Annalisa hoisted her upper body onto the couch, then her legs, and fanned her face until she came to. Hardly able to grieve herself for Daniel's death, Annalisa forced her attention on Mrs. Peabody until Daniel's father returned with Dr. Brown, who pronounced Daniel's death.

The hour was just before midnight.

Tears flooded her face. She would face this Christmastide with far more to trouble her than she had this past year. If only Mary were there, or Abigail, to grieve with her, to rub her back and offer words of kindness. But until morning, she could do nothing but mask herself and her melancholy.

IT TOOK THREE DAYS: THREE DAYS TO ANNOUNCE DANIEL'S death, host the funeral, and bury him six feet beneath the frozen earth. Henry and William guided Annalisa up the stairs to the room she shared with her sisters. Jane and Mary descended on her in a solitary embrace, and Annalisa's knees buckled.

Jane's lavender perfume clogged her nose as she brushed the hair from Annalisa's forehead; Mary swiped the tears from her cheeks.

"All will be well, Annie," Mary said.

Annalisa sobbed into Jane's bosom. "How can it?"

"Because it must," Jane replied. "You've no other option."

Her sister's soprano, a sound she so long detested, offered comfort, and for that, Annalisa peered at Jane with refreshened eyes.

"This was not supposed to be how our lives progressed," Annalisa said.

"I know." Jane offered a sad smile. "Things are never as they seem, are they?"

Abigail knocked on the open door with Louisa. Annalisa outstretched her arm, pulling them into the embrace.

"How comforting to have us all under this one roof, though," Mary said.

"Almost all of us," Annalisa said. She broke free from them. "George is still gone."

Abigail kissed Louisa's cheek. "But he will return in the spring when he's well. Won't he, Weeza?"

"Papa is getting better," Louisa said. "Then he will teach me how to fire his firelock."

Jane and Mary stared at Annalisa.

"What? It can't only be me he teaches to use a musket." Annalisa smiled through her tears.

They all chuckled, then Abigail said, "Your mamma and Liza have prepared something special for supper, Annie. Come, let's to the dining room."

Mary and Abigail led the way with Louisa, but Jane tugged

Annalisa back into the room a moment. "I want you to know how truly sorry I am for your loss, Annalisa."

"Thank you."

"I know I've not been the best of sisters to you. I'm ashamed by all I've been persuaded by." Jane blinked several times. "You don't deserve any of the losses come by you, and I pray you and Jack find each other. You're both free to marry now."

"If he will still have me after so much time. He's been absent for months. And..." Annalisa hesitated, fearing to reveal to Jane all Lady Perkins had threatened.

Her sister's lips pursed. "I understand it perfectly. But you must know Lady Perkins is not who you think she is."

Annalisa's heartbeat quickened. "She and Mamma accepted Daniel's proposal. I know that much is true."

Jane nodded. "To prevent you from marrying Jack when she believed it impossible for him to divorce me." She licked her lips. "Lord Perkins was the one to block Jack's court petitions—"

"Lord Perkins!" Annalisa cried.

"Shh, Abbie knows not," Jane whispered. "Yes, 'twas Lord Perkins who paid the magistrates at Boston and Salem to burn Jack's petitions, but it was at the behest of Lady Perkins. She coaxed him to do it."

Annalisa's chest rattled. "But why?"

"She promised Mamma I would marry Jack, I suppose for consolation of having lost George's natural father. Mayhap she wished to keep her promise at all cost."

"That seems unnatural," Annalisa replied. "How could she plot something so devious and without regard to the wishes of her son and mine?"

"I know not. But it seems she has more contacts than I imagined. Lady Perkins is well connected."

Annalisa bit her tongue, then said, "Lord Essex?"

"Yes."

"But I thought Lord Essex was Lord Perkins's acquaintance."

Jane nodded. "He was, but 'twas through Lady Perkins they met. That is all I know."

Annalisa reached for Jane's hand. "Where is Lord Essex now? Does he remain in England?"

She frowned. "I've not heard from him in half a year, perhaps longer. As far as I know, he's remained there. Lady Perkins has not said much. As you know, we hardly speak these days unless I'm bringing Robby to see her and Tommy."

Annalisa considered this. Her sister's situation proved nearly as convoluted as hers; with her ex-mother-in-law's charades and two children by different fathers—brothers, no less—Jane's reputation suffered as much as her own. But perhaps in the encroaching new year, Jane could earn back Annalisa's trust. After all these years of quarrels and loathing, nothing would please her more than to move forward with both her sisters by her side. If only she could heal George's leg...

With Daniel now gone, Annalisa could waste no time in riding south for George. Surely, her confidante Quinnapin would accompany her. And with the traitor Arnold now revealed, she feared little donning Benjamin's clothes for one final journey south to bring George home.

❧ III ☙

1781-1782

43

ANNALISA

NORTH CAROLINA, JANUARY 1781

THE FARTHER SOUTH ANNALISA and Quinnapin rode, temperate air gave way to less snow blanketing the roads until, finally, landscapes of leafless tress and dead grass greeted them. By mid-January, they reached Charlotte, North Carolina. Having searched for three days for George and the Continental Army to no avail, they continued into South Carolina. Information that General Nathanael Greene had taken up charge of the Continental Army after Gates abandonment following the loss at Camden led them to an area known as the Cowpens.

By dusk, Annalisa and Quinnapin caught up to Brigadier General Morgan's army encamped near the banks of the Pacolet River. Word of Colonel Tarleton's dragoons looming nearby rose the hairs on Annalisa's arms. *Bloody Ban's massacre. The Butcher, they call him.* George's letters haunted the back of her mind as she dismounted her horse, her body cramped and aching from riding. Campfires danced about as the soldiers settled in on what felt to be the eve of imminent battle.

"Think you we may find George among these tents?" she asked.

Quinnapin studied their surroundings. "The sick tent is that way, but I'm certain George will lie within his own."

"Let's make haste, then."

They quickly erected their dwellings on the outskirts of the encampment, then set to finding George. It wasn't until they commenced down a narrow corridor of tents that the fear of meeting Jack overwhelmed her. She rolled her shoulders against the tightness building within her breast and barreled down the row until an icy irritation edged its way down her spine.

"Major Howlett?" she called.

"The major rests there." A private pointed to a tent positioned at the head one row.

Annalisa held Quinnapin's stare before announcing her presence. "Major Howlett, 'tis Private Cavendish."

Silence, then a deep groan rumbled from his tent. "Enter, Private."

Annalisa and Quinnapin ducked beyond the flap. George lay on blankets, bare-chested and sweating. His left leg, red and seeping purulence, had swollen to nearly twice the size of his right.

"My God." Annalisa knelt and embraced him.

His burley arms wrapped about her. "Little One. I've never been so glad to see you."

"Your leg. 'Tis horrible," she cried. "You must let us treat you—"

"You're here," he said grimly. "This must mean Mr. Peabody has passed."

Startled by the harsh reminder of Daniel's tormented death, Annalisa bit her lip. "Aye. November. Before Christmastide."

George lowered his gaze. "My apologies." He remained silent for many minutes. "I know not if I'll live to see this month's end."

Her breath caught. *I should've come sooner.* "No, you can't speak thus."

"You incurred this injury months ago," Quinnapin said. "Surely, it would've claimed you by now, Brother."

George's frown uplifted into a sardonic grin, and he eyed Quinnapin. "Would that were true, old friend."

Quinnapin knelt and glimpsed his leg. "May I?" His expert fingers removed the bandage from George's left calf.

Annalisa gagged against the sour stench. Beneath the muslin, a half-healed festering wound emerged.

"I believe this to be curable," Quinnapin said. "But we must act. Chances are you already have the poisoning in your blood." He removed several items from his haversack and prepared them. From the flickering lantern, he lit a bundle of herbs and swirled the smoke about the tent.

Determined, Annalisa rummaged through her physick diary and collected all she required to brew one of Addy's teas. They saved Benedict Arnold from losing his leg after Saratoga, and they would save George from losing his.

George chuckled darkly, as though hearing her thoughts. "I'd rather lose the limb than be compared to that traitorous reptile." He spat. "The cock robin."

"Then 'tis well-known of his treachery."

"Aye, of course," George said. "Apparently, his lady remained at West Point to receive Washington and his fart catcher, Hamilton. Put on quite the performance, from what I heard."

Annalisa's bound breast constricted for poor Peggy, who'd sacrificed herself. *When will my own charade end, my own curtain close on my performance as Benjamin?* Her spine pricked at the thought, and she returned to her herbs. It must not be before she could heal her beloved George.

DAWN ARRIVED SOONER THAN SHE WISHED, THOUGH SHE was greeted by Quinnapin's spirited company just beyond her dwelling.

"Cav, wake up. Tarleton and his men have been spotted about five miles from us, marching."

"Have you seen George?" she asked.

"Aye, I changed his bandage again before dawn."

The morning held a chill reminiscent of October. Seated about a small fire Quinnapin had made, Annalisa drank the elixir to darken her eyes. After having only taken two bites of johnnycake, a Continental rider broke news they were to march into formation.

She downed the remainder of her tea. "I need to bring George his." Quickly, she returned to her dwelling to retrieve the physick when she felt a trickle between her legs.

The morbid flux! The flux had not plagued her in months, as her menses had always proved rather irregular. *Of course it should come now.* Annalisa unbuttoned her breeches and quickly searched for her menses apron, of which she hadn't packed. In her haste to leave home, she'd packed a regular linen apron instead.

"Damn it! Fie!" She grabbed the apron and tied it about her waist and pulled it up between her legs. "Please let this suffice." Annalisa buttoned her breeches and adjusted them over the apron. It would have to do. She held no other option.

Annalisa quickly made her way to George's tent. "Major Howlett, a tea for you, sir," she called from outside.

"Come in."

She entered and handed him the mug. "Drink it now. But I must go. Bloody Ban's been sighted not five miles from here. We march now." Annalisa turned to leave, but George grabbed her arm.

"Cav, wait."

She faced him.

"Don't hesitate to cry out in battle, 'For Bunker Hill,' or, 'Tarleton's Quarter.'"

She nodded. "I shall." Annalisa lunged forward, wrapping him in a tight embrace. "I fight for you, Major Howlett. May you heal enough to fight beside me again."

George kissed her cheek and adjusted her hat so it angled over her right eye. "I swear I will. Now go. 'Tis an order, Private."

Annalisa pulled from him. "Aye, Major." She slipped from his tent and hurried to join the line forming, where she slide beside Quinnapin.

With the river to their rear, there was nowhere for them to retreat. Her heart in her throat, Annalisa gripped her musket. Her knuckles whitened, when from up ahead, a steady drumming preceded the enemy. Through a pearly-white fog, as if from another world, the British materialized at a steady pace. From across the meadow, a fife played "British Grenadier," filling her with dread. As they pressed onward, the black crested hats of fusiliers stretched upward, piercing the fog. Memories of Bunker Hill's bloodshed and terror consumed her, but she held steady the image of victory against the fallen fusiliers with General Stark and his First New Hampshire regiment. With a purposeful exhale, Annalisa expelled all dread from her body.

Their commander, a man she quickly learned as Andrew Pickens, shouted, "Make ready!"

As the British marched within range, the front line made ready with their muskets. A clicking of the cock cascaded down the line.

"Fire!"

Several oncoming regulars and fusiliers fell. The rest marched on, stepping over the wounded as the second line lifted their muskets, aimed, and fired.

Beside Quinnapin, Annalisa discharged her musket. The spark of battle overwhelmed her, as though she'd never left the army. Sulfuric smoke filled her nostrils and clouded the field from view as a *boom* of artillery rattled the earth.

Minutes into battle, their line held strong, firing upon the British. Dozens fell, and Annalisa quickly reloaded and fired when Colonel Tarleton's dragoons in their green coats rode into view. The cavalry charged. Tarleton appeared on horseback. A young, handsome man with an agreeable figure, he was not at all the hideous fiend she'd conjured in her mind. *Bloody Ban. But he is still a monster, no matter his appearance.*

Quinnapin shouted, "Cav, look out."

Annalisa dove into the grass.

Her line fired as the British started to break. At this, her regiment retreated behind the hill as American cavalry rode from behind it. She scrambled to her feet and sprinted with Quinnapin through the field to keep up with the loose formation of their regiment. *Are we in retreat?*

Amidst the confusion, she reloaded her musket and discharged at oncoming fusiliers. By the time she reached the rear of the hill, most of Morgan's army hid behind the slope. Her energy surged as she realized the strategy, and her breath quickened with each anticipating moment. *If only George was beside us.*

As the Redcoats descended over the hill, Pickens shouted, "Make ready, fire!"

Annalisa fired on the advancing enemy, then reloaded. Beside her, Quinnapin did the same. *Three volleys a minute, Little One.* George's instruction overtook her, and she fired and reloaded. *Three volleys a minute.* Her hands no longer trembled. She reloaded and fired again.

The American cavalry rode from behind a second hill, attacking the British on their flank.

"Charge," Pickens ordered.

Annalisa and Quinnapin advanced with their line behind the American cavalry and infantry.

"For Bunker Hill," Annalisa bellowed. "Tarleton's Quarter!"

Swirls of smoke obfuscated the field, veils of grey to distract from the symphony of musket-fire. Balls whizzed past. She glimpsed Quinnapin, who reloaded and discharged his firelock with cool reserve. His countenance stiff and focused, he aimed and fired.

Her teeth ripped into another cartridge, and she spat the litter to the ground. A round followed by another fired. What felt like an eternity surely endured for minutes when, to her shock, the British started to flee the field. *A victory at long last?* Or perhaps an ambush in the making.

Annalisa held her breath and reloaded.

❦ 44 ❦

JACK

NORTH CAROLINA, LATE JANUARY 1781

JACK HASTENED FROM THE battlefield, eager to report to George news of their victory. While the fight had proved advantageous for the American cause, he suspected Morgan would be swift in evacuating South Carolina, lest he wish to provoke a reaction from Cornwallis.

As nightfall blanketed the encampment, Jack weaved through soldiers gathered and hurried toward the countless rows of tents. In the dark, he glimpsed a tall, lanky fellow at the end of a row. The young man could be no older than seventeen, yet boasted a countenance Jack recognized. His breath quickened as he hastened after him.

Yes, 'tis he, Cavendish. "Cavendish," Jack called.

The boy stiffened, then slowly turned. In the dark, Jack could hardly make out the man's face, but his dark eyes echoed of the duel they'd fought years ago at Saratoga.

"Sir, I'm your most obedient servant." Benjamin bowed.

Jack's heart raced as he lurched after Benjamin and bent his arm behind him. "You're under arrest, *traitor*."

"Traitor?" Benjamin asked. "What for?"

"You've been named as such to the Continental Army in

the north. I'm astounded you'd show your face here in the south. I've hunted you from New York to South Carolina. Come with me, rogue." Jack hauled the young man through the camp until he reached General Morgan's dwelling. To the officer stationed beyond the tent, Jack said, "I've a prisoner here. A traitor to the Continental Army, a spy for the British."

"Please enter, sir," the aide-de-camp said.

Jack threw Benjamin before General Morgan. "This traitor is a British spy, sir," he said. "He's wanted in New York for treason."

Morgan peered up from his diary. "Name?"

"I'm Lieutenant Perkins, and this is Private Benjamin Cavendish."

General Morgan's brow twitched. "Cavendish." He flipped through the pages of a ledger, then, using his forefinger, scrolled the page. "Cavendish? You're accused of being an accomplice to the turncoat Benedict Arnold. You're wanted in New York—"

"N-No, sir," Benjamin cried. "No, I'm n-no traitor, I assure you. I...I'm n-no accomplice t-to M-Major Arnold, sir."

Morgan closed his book and peered up at Jack. "Thank you, Lieutenant." The general regarded his aide-de-camp. "Clap Cavendish in irons and take him away."

Without looking back, Jack ducked from the tent. *Why do I feel such consternation?* On his honor, he'd sworn to avenge poor Daniel Peabody, and he had; yet a rock of dread impounded him. *'Tis only because the lad never saw it coming.* Jack hastened to George's tent, eager to tamp away the foreboding with news of the victory.

OVER THE NEXT SEVERAL DAYS, THE ARMY MARCHED NORTH and across the Catawba River to a location called Sherrill's Ford in North Carolina, where they set up camp.

Jack slipped inside George's tent to find Quinnapin seated within. Startled, Jack greeted his old friend. "Quinn! Whatever brings you to North Carolina, old friend?"

Quinnapin returned Jack's greeting with a hesitant smile. "I've been with the army since the Cowpens. I knew not you were here, either, Brother."

Jack clapped Quinnapin's shoulder. "'Tis madness, is it not? Pray, were you at the battle, then?"

Quinnapin nodded. "Aye. But I've more pressing matters, presently. I traveled here with my old friend, Ben Cavendish. Have you seen the lad? I've been unable to locate him since we left South Carolina."

George's countenance sagged. "I wonder where he could be."

"No bother, gentlemen," Jack said. "I intercepted the lad the night of the battle. He's a traitor to the Continental Army and was wanted in New York. I happened upon him and brought him to General Morgan—"

"You what!" George roared.

Jack started at his cousin's overreaction. "Aye, the man's a British spy. Even Morgan had him upon the list within his ledger. I know 'tis a harsh blow. You had befriended him, but he's a danger to us. I did what is right by the Continental Ar—"

"Benjamin Cavendish is Annalisa!" George bellowed.

Jack's face numbed. "I beg pardon?"

He looked to Quinnapin, who held his face in his hands. "Cav is Miss Anna."

Jack's heart galloped. "I'm not sure I understand..." Though he spoke the words, his conscience suspected the impossible, the unlikely, to be true.

"Benjamin Cavendish is Annalisa...dressed as a man," George grumbled.

Jack shook his head as he rotated the signet ring about his little finger. He focused on his cousin and friend, the tent, their encampment, and all that was visibly true before him, anything and everything deemed rational. Real.

He chuckled. "You jest."

When neither Quinnapin nor George joined his laughter, Jack reached for his chest. A blackness encroached from his periphery, and his innards roiled like a rope about a capstan. Memories of dueling Benjamin Cavendish and maiming his leg at Saratoga pummeled forth. A wash of light-headedness dizzied him, and in one forceful heave, Jack doubled over. He choked and gagged until Quinnapin's gentle hand rested upon his shoulder.

"It cannot be true," Jack croaked. "It can't be her..." He held his face in his hands. "You are mistaken."

"I wish 'twas a jest, Cousin." George's bass surrounded him in a deep, familiar void.

"I...shot her at Saratoga," Jack moaned.

"You didn't know 'twas her," Quinnapin replied.

"No. And now she's being carted north, a prisoner." A burning fury rose from within, and Jack unwound his neckpiece and tossed it to the ground.

"Cousin, we'll locate her," George said. "You didn't know—"

"And *you* did," Jack cried. "Both of you knew and withheld it from me." The burning eroded his insides. "You allowed me to duel her!" He threw up him arms, unable to contain himself. "This is some hideous charade, a lark of the cruelest sort."

He gathered his neckpiece from the ground and launched from the tent before either of them could contain him. The world a blur, Jack rushed through the encampment, shrugging off his coat and unbuttoning the shirt collar about his neck. His lungs begged for air, and he needed to oblige.

On the outskirts of camp, Jack threw his coat and neck-piece to the ground. His hands on his thighs, he bent over and heaved, his chest tight with each gasp. *If only I had the laudanum to help me breathe...*

"No." Jack slapped his cheek. "'Tis a weakness."

His smarting face burned but proved enough to snap him from his stupor. Slowly, he wordlessly counted and inhaled through his nose, then exhaled. This he did for at least a minute until his lungs filled with life-giving air.

Engulfed by rage, he trembled with teeth chattering. Jack gathered his coat from the ground and pulled the garment about his shoulders. He sat, his head dipped between his knees. *It can't be true. They allow me to wallow for sport. Annalisa would never do this...*

He couldn't finish the thought.

Annalisa *would* do this, and the fact he hadn't seen it, observed it, *known* it, proved worse than her having committed such crimes. *Do I even know her at all?* The thought constricted his chest against the bile rising from his stomach. Despair mixed with anger, and he remained seated beyond the encampment, wondering how he could love someone so much, offer himself in every way, only to now question it all and doubt every bit.

❧ 45 ❧

ANNALISA

VIRGINIA, LATE JANUARY 1781

HER WRISTS IN IRONS, Annalisa sat within the prisoner tent. Rather than struggle, she studied her surroundings. Others, presumably real British spies or prisoners of war, hunched over. *Accused as a British spy.* That, she could deny. George could attest to her conduct.

But her other secret, not so much.

Annalisa said nothing, fearing her true identity might be uncovered. If the Continentals discovered her as a woman masquerading as a man, she, George, and Quinnapin would all hang, especially if they still believed her an informant of the enemy. Washington's army would show little, if any, mercy to her brother and friend.

Yet what vexed her most was Jack. He believed Benjamin Cavendish an enemy. *A cruel twist of fate that my beloved should capture me, unbeknownst to himself.* She blinked away the tears and turned her head from the others within the tent. They needn't see her cry as a woman would do.

Would that George learns of my capture...that he may write to Mary and Henry to warn them. Her throat clogged. *Jack will tell*

George and Quinnapin of my capture...and they will tell him 'tis me and not Benjamin. He will learn 'tis me, that 'tis been me all along.

She suppressed a shudder. Mayhap, he would rescue her when he learned the truth, but for concealing such information from him for so long, she questioned his reaction. If only they hadn't dueled at Saratoga. Jack would never forgive himself for injuring her, and for that alone, he may never forgive her for leading him to believe her to be Benjamin.

The gravity of her lies and the years she lived them weighed upon her like the great Common Rock at the edge of Topsfield's common. If only she could atone for her hubris, that she could live so recklessly and without abandon for so long without consequence. Strangely, despite this, her breathing did not catch, nor did she tremble. Perhaps she'd supposed this would happen all along. The fear had certainly been with her since the days of drilling with Captain Foster and the Danvers militia. But it had always been veiled by the thrill of donning her brothers' clothes, riding to Danvers before dawn, and firing Bixby with Nathaniel and Ebenezer— God rest his soul.

Rescuing Nathaniel at Bunker Hill still proved her proudest memory.

"You will be charged with impersonation—and jailed. At worst, hanged, if you're found by the enemy. And I along with you, for knowing." She carried George's words since the day he said them, but not for any fear of her own safety, only to protect him. He hardly deserved to be imprisoned for keeping her secret. None of it felt real until she faced her captors: the Continental Army.

At least 'tis not the British who hold me.

"Get up, you slog."

An officer hollered from the entry of the tent. "On your feet."

Her arms still clasped behind her, Annalisa struggled to rise. The cold, unforgiving iron dug into her skin, but she masked her grimace with a grunt as she stood. The other prisoners slowly rose, one by one, until a second soldier entered the tent.

"This way."

"Where are we going?" one of the prisoners asked.

"Shut your potato trap and give your tongue a holiday, Lobsterback bastard," the first sneered.

The second soldier pointed to two prisoners of war. "Come with me. You're being traded."

"Cavendish, with me." The first soldier grabbed her and tossed her toward the tent opening. When she exited, the sky at the horizon lightened. "Into the cart, reptile."

Her heart skipped, fearing an imminent date with the gallows. "Where are you taking me, sir?"

"Silence, whelp." He kicked her.

The force of his foot emptied the air from her, and Annalisa lurched forward. Rather than fall to her face, the man pulled her back by her cuffed arms. The irons ground into her wrists, and she gritted her teeth to suppress her scream.

He hurled her into the back of a wooden cart drawn by two horses. *To the gallows, then.*

Annalisa closed her eyes against the sting of tears as she rolled with the pitch of the cart. Her nose to the wooden planking, she breathed in the rancid scent of rotted hay and disease. Perhaps others had been transported to their deaths in that same cart. Just but a number, she swallowed her pride and focused on all she had accomplished in her four-and-twenty years. She saved a man; earned the love of another; befriended the Duchess of Devonshire; fought in a war for all she believed despite her place in Society as a woman. She defied it all but would now pay the price of her actions, a consequence she could no longer evade. As the cart juddered and jolted along the craggy road, she vowed to meet her death with honor and her head held high. Not as a traitor to the Continental Army, but as a martyr to the cause.

❧ 46 ❧

JACK

SHERRILL'S FORD, NORTH CAROLINA,
LATE JANUARY 1781

AFTER A SLEEPLESS NIGHT upon the cold, hard ground at the edge of camp, Jack jolted awake. His neck and body stiff, he rolled onto his side. *Was it all a nightmare? Did I consume too much wibble last night?* Head throbbing, he shifted to his knees, then stood. Dazed, he rubbed his stubbled face and returned to the rows of tents behind him. Rather than find his cousin and Quinnapin, Jack sought the prison tent on the other side of camp. A futile hope, knowing she was no longer with the army, but one he grasped.

The guard, appearing quite sleepy, regarded him with reserve.

"I'm seeking a prisoner, Benjamin Cavendish, for questioning." Jack spun his signet ring, anticipating the guard's response. Without a word, the guard opened the tent and allowed Jack entry.

Four men sat slumped over, none of whom were Benjamin Cavendish...or rather, Annalisa.

Jack turned to the guard. "I don't see him, sir. Thank you." He dipped from the tent and made his way back to the rows of tents, eager to find Quinnapin and George.

"George? Quinn? 'Tis me."

Quinnapin pulled him inside George's tent. "She's gone, Jack."

"Aye. There is no such Benjamin Cavendish...nor Annalisa. Pray, 'twas all a nightmare, no?"

"They've carted her to Philadelphia," Quinnapin said, his voice hushed though urgent. He peered at George, who tossed upon the ground.

"Then 'tis true..."

Quinnapin's amiable stare held his as he cupped Jack's shoulders. "Aye, Brother. And I'm so very sorry for you to discover it this way. But it is true. All of it."

"I...I can't understand it," Jack replied. The torments of the previous night returned and he quaked with anger and despair. "They'll hang her for treachery in Philadelphia. We must ride north."

Quinnapin glanced at George. "His fever returned this morning. I need to remain here to heal him." His candid gaze shifted to Jack. "But you must go. Pursue them. And when George is well enough, I'll join you. Of that, I promise."

Jack nodded. "I'll leave straightaway."

February 1781

JACK RODE NORTH, AND BY THE FIRST FEW DAYS OF February, he galloped into American-held Philadelphia. Exhausted and battered by inclement northern weather and the heady emotion driving his journey, he rented a room at the local inn, where he rested his aching body a mere hour before continuing his search, which led him to the town gaol.

Jack ambled up the icy steps of the brick building, a task

reminiscent of his time in London at the Old Bailey. How long ago that seemed, and the plight for his divorce. If only he'd returned to an unattached Annalisa. A simple complication compared to the one he now faced.

His nose wrinkled against the rancid stench as the gaoler led him down a cold, dank, narrow corridor. Moans and groans echoed through the cavernous hall. A large rat scampered past, and his hair stood on end. The dread and anticipation of seeing his Annalisa contained between these miserable walls quaked his very being.

The gaoler gestured to a tiny cell with a wrought-iron door, then returned from where they'd come. When he'd gone, Jack forced himself to peer inside.

A lanky young man rested against the stone wall, his arms bloodied and wrenched overhead in iron fetters. Matted tresses of honey-brown hair hung over the man's bowed head. Jack knelt to peer at the face, caked and smeared with dirt.

"Annalisa?" Jack's voice rasped, though he meant to whisper.

The young man lifted his pitiful head and peered at him. Through the darkness, Jack recognized the green of her eyes, and his heart plummeted.

Tears curled over the bottom rim of her eyelids and carved through the grime upon her cheeks. "Jack, I'm...I'm s-so s-sorry."

The utter agony of seeing her like this, in tandem with her deceit, corroded what was left of his sensibility. Jack gripped the cell, his knuckles whitening. "Why, Annalisa? Why?"

"I—"

"You lied to me," he growled. "All these years, you kept this from me, with not a thought of remorse or consequence."

"Jack—"

"No," he hissed. "Do you understand what you've done? What you're accused of and the danger you're in? That your brother and Quinnapin, too, will be questioned? How could you be so careless, so reckless?"

"I kn-know it all!" she cried.

This stilled him, icing the blood in his veins. "Then you're more heartless than ever I imagined."

"N-No, p-please, you m-must understand—"

"I dueled you," he hissed. "I will never forgive myself for injuring you that day...but neither can I forgive this." He rose. "How could you do this, Annalisa? To me? To *us*?" The last word caught in his throat, and he turned. His back to her, he muttered, "You've broken me for the final time, Annalisa Howlett."

Jack fled the corridor before the sound of her voice could stop him, because he knew it would. One word from her and he'd return to her cell and die with her. He loved her with every bit of his being and seeing her wretched, bloody, and covered in filth shook every pillar of his devotion. If he could release her at once, he would, and ride away with her from this cesspool of disease and mire. But her hideous, unpardonable deceit gnawed at him like the vermin infesting the gaol. The woman he loved, the woman to whom he devoted himself, withheld such a secret from him. Would that she had killed him than face the ugly truth of her lies.

As he exited the gaol, the blinding light of a February winter shocked his vision, and his lungs filled with cold, dry air. He coughed and wiped his mouth. A broken heart could only propel a man to do one of two things: surrender or fight. He'd he fought long and hard for Annalisa Howlett. *When is enough, enough?* The thought tortured him as he trudged through the wintry streets of Philadelphia and back to his inn. He needed to write to Mary and Henry, Abigail, and George and Quinnapin. They needed to learn what had transpired for Annalisa Howlett and the unfavorable fate that would soon befall her.

❧ 47 ❧

JACK

PHILADELPHIA, MID-FEBRUARY 1781

A LARGE, ROARING HEARTH warmed the inn's tavern to sweltering temperatures, though Jack welcomed such luxury compared to the gaol in which Annalisa resided. Before him, he sprawled open books and letters over the rickety wooden table. He sipped his ale, then bit into a mince pie. He'd not much of an appetite since seeing Annalisa imprisoned, but he forced himself to eat.

"A letter for you, Lord Brunswick." The potboy handed him a sealed noted.

Jack thanked the young fellow, then cracked the seal.

> February 11th 1781
>
> Dear sir,
>
> I am most obliged by your letter, and made mention to Henry of the imperrative Nature with which you wryte. He and I are fast to pack and leave for Philadelphia at once. We Hope to be at Your inn presently.

Your most obeedient Sarvent,
M. Howlett

Jack folded Mary's letter. She and Henry should be nearing Philadelphia as of this week instant. He returned to the law books and pored through the pages for anything and everything he could glean from the charges Annalisa faced as a spy and if they uncovered her, an impersonator.

At least 'tis the Continental Army who imprisons her, and not the British. A tiny glimmer of solace amidst a quagmire of hopelessness. If only his mentor and law partner, John Adams, weren't abroad in Europe. Jack certainly would welcome his wisdom and sage advice on these legal matters. But it was no matter. The gentleman resided across the Atlantic, too far to post a letter and hope for a return before Annalisa's court-martial.

Jack stiffened in his chair. He rose, left his things across the table, and made for the door. To the potboy, he said, "Mind this table. I'll return in a half hour or so." Without donning his winter cloak, he fled the inn and hastened through Philadelphia's streets until he reached the gaol.

Ushered before the gaoler, Jack hurried down the dimly lit corridor until he reached Annalisa's cell. He'd not visited her since the first day he arrived in town. Jack lingered outside the cell, waiting for the gaoler to leave them be.

"Have you a court-martial date yet?" he asked.

Annalisa peered up at him with hazy eyes. "Jack?"

His chest constricted and he knelt. "Have they given you a date?"

"I...d-don't b-believe so," she wheezed.

Jack reached for her through the iron bars but stopped when he remembered her arms remained bound in iron fetters above her head. "Annalisa...I'll represent you and your case. I'll secure you a date." He sucked in a breath. "God be my witness, you will not hang."

She blinked several times, perhaps to conceal the flood of tears. They fell from her eyes and moistened her dry, cracked cheeks. "You...you'd d-do that...for m-me? After...all...this?"

His heart twisted. "I'd do anything for you." Jack stood, hardening his voice. "But this shall be the last of it."

He fled the gaol as quickly as his legs could carry him without running. There was much to gather as evidence to free her from a destiny at the gallows.

When he reached the gaoler, he said, "Sir, pen a letter for me to the Continental Army in charge of prisoners. I wish to represent Benjamin Cavendish. Has he yet been assigned a court-martial date?" He hesitated. "Or a date of hanging?"

The gaoler rummaged through a pile of pages upon a small, wooden desk. "I've not heard of a trial or hanging, only that the prisoner may be transferred to New York. Since the mutiny in January, there's—"

"Mutiny? What mutiny?"

"Aye, fifteen hundred men of the Pennsylvania line. The mutiny led British General Clinton to send men to coerce the mutineers to fight for the Redcoats in exchange for pay owed them by Congress." The man licked his lips. "Rather, the mutineers captured Clinton's men and handed them over to their former general for execution. Only then did they meet with Congress on the seventh of January to come to reasonable agreements."

"I see." *Perhaps Annalisa might meet a similar pardon.* "Then I shall write directly to the commander in chief. Good day to you."

Jack hurried from the gaol and returned to the inn, barely taking note of the bitter wind blowing into his coat. Sat at his table, he penned a letter to General Washington in New York requesting to be Benjamin Cavendish's counsel. It was the most he could do and the least he owed Annalisa, no matter her duplicities. He loved her, and he would until the end.

48

ANNALISA

JACK CAME TO HER a week after his previous
visitation. What prevented him from being there with
her day and night, she knew not, but she suspected he
wished to see her as little as possible in such a condition.
She'd severed any last shred of hope lingering between them
and certainly held no wish to continue in this life without
him, court-martial or no, hanging or no.

He stood before her now, his baritone a mere whisper
amidst the squeaky rats scurrying about her cell. "And they
continue to acknowledge you as Cavendish?" he asked.

"Aye."

"Then at least they know not of your other crime," he
whispered. "Tell me of that Nathaniel you fought with at
Bunker Hill. I may use his testimony as evidence of your
devotion to the cause and your good character."

"Nathaniel Hitchcock. He fought w-with m-me. I s-saved
him."

Jack frowned. "Your saving Benedict Arnold's leg is one of
the pieces of evidence they have against you, given his defection." He turned and scratched his cheek.

"Quinn and I...helped Arnold. We are b-both g-guilty of... th-that."

"I know," he replied. "But you're being charged with treason. Your presence at Peggy Shippen's wedding is under scrutiny and is being used as evidence."

"P-Peggy Sh-Shippen!" Annalisa cried.

Jack knelt and clutched the cell bar. "You've consorted with Loyalists in this town, and now 'tis being used against you, whether it be true or not. I need to present evidence 'tis all presumptions made in error."

"M-My g-good character," she stuttered. No matter how many times she recited Mad Madge's poetry, day and night within her lonesome cell, the stutter returned with a vengeance.

"Yes, of course." Jack rose.

"Has M-Mary c-come?"

"No, not yet."

"And how is G-George?"

"Not well." Jack procured a letter from his pocket. "I don't wish to burden you with more foul news, but Quinn wrote." He proceeded to read aloud to her: "'I regret his leg has not healed in the way I hoped it would...'" Jack paused, glimpsing her from behind the page. "Cav?"

She winced at the way he spoke her other name, knowing he loathed the feeling of it rolling off his tongue. "You n-needn't c-call m-me that."

"I must, lest you're discovered. Then we've an entirely new accusation from which to acquit you..." He trailed off, and Annalisa recognized the gears of his mind turning. "I'll devise something. Someone's scurrilous remarks against you will come to justice. I swear it." As though catching himself in a moment of passion, Jack's face hardened. "What I truly came to say is...your court-martial date has been set for March the tenth—"

"Your birthday," she wheezed.

"Aye."His lips pursed. "In New York. You'll be transferred in the coming days. I'll return before then. I promise."

He quit the cell with an expediency she'd not seen of him these few weeks.

In New York? Whatever for? Any gaol would be as miserable as this one. What difference did it make? Surely, a court-martial could be held anywhere. Curling her legs beneath her, she lifted from the dank stone floor. The shackles offered just enough length to lower her arms, which returned the blood and feeling to her hands. Her wrists, bruised and scabbed and speckled with fresh and dried blood, ached. *If only Jack didn't see me like this.* The thought lingered, not because she believed herself unpretty, but because she deserved it.

Tears returned to her eyes. Unable to wipe them away, she craned her stiff neck and brushed her cheek against her shoulder, itching her ear in the process. She only guessed how infested she was with mites and fleas, let alone lice. In the weeks since her imprisonment, she longed to forget the constant itch within her scalp. *Dearest daughter mine, where are you? Are you at rest?* Strange, thoughts of Eliza should comfort her now when they used to only cause her grief and pain.

Mamma, Papa still loves you.

A tiny voice echoed from the corridor, as though a small girl lingered within this hellish space.

"How can he?" Annalisa sobbed. "I hardly love myself for what I've done."

She closed her eyes and wept, drenching her cheeks in salty tears reminiscent of the ocean. When she opened her eyes, the apparition hovered into her cell.

"Mamma, salvage all you can. Salvage it all, because you need your strength, you need your courage." Eliza looked upon her with those dark, Atlantic-blue eyes, the same as her father's. "Molly needs you to. Her life depends upon it."

Before she could reply, Eliza vanished, leaving Annalisa alone and trembling.

❦ 49 ❦

ANNALISA

WEST POINT, NEW YORK, MARCH 1781

"ON YOUR FEET CAVENDISH." A Continental Army soldier kicked her ribs. "With me."

Curled into a ball on the cell floor, she gasped and a sharp pain bolted through her side with each inhalation. *Where is Jack?* "Where...is...m-my c-counsel?"

"Enough of that." The soldier hoisted her up and shoved her from the cell and down a hall similar to the one at the Philadelphia gaol.

"Sir, hold the prisoner," Jack called.

Annalisa stepped with the soldier into daylight for the first time since her transfer to New York. She squinted and turned her head in the direction of Jack's voice.

He ran toward them. "My apologies, sir, for my tardiness." To Annalisa, he said, "Mr. Cavendish, speak nothing unless spoken to. Is that clear?"

She nodded.

"Good. Let's commence."

Jack walked with them to a permanent building within the fortification. Overlooking what seemed to be a river, Annalisa supposed the place to be West Point. Though she'd never been there, it made sense the court-martial would take place in the last Patriot stronghold of the north since the war raged in the southern colonies. *I wonder how George fares with his leg.* She suppressed a shiver at the thought of her brother, hundreds of miles away, who may lose his leg.

Weakened from a month in gaol, her knees buckled and she dipped in her stride, but held her head high. Jack caught her for only a moment, then instructed the soldier to guide his prisoner more properly.

They entered the modest building for her court-martial. To her shock, General Washington sat behind thirteen Continental Army officers from varying regiments who would serve as the jury. Though her heart rattled within her bound breast as she sat before the high-ranking assembled gentlemen, her nerves heightened for the unknown witnesses now sequestered beyond the room in which they sat.

The officer presiding as the prosecutor introduced himself as Captain Hastings. "Good day and welcome to our regimental court-martial of Private Benjamin Cavendish. We are gathered here today under the jurisdiction of treason, which, by militia law, Private Cavendish stands accused."

Captain Hastings proceeded to instruct the court of military law, then swore in the court and Annalisa as Benjamin Cavendish. "Pray, stand and plead your case, Private Cavendish."

Annalisa stood. Deepening her voice, she said, "I plead not guilty, sir."

Captain Hastings called forth his first witness. "Mr. Wentworth, will you please speak your troth."

Annalisa tensed at the mention of Wentworth, and she held her breath. *That reptile!*

Mr. Wentworth stood before the assembled officers. "Sirs, I met Private Cavendish in the Shippens' grand home at Philadelphia. He made no mention of treason, of course, but he easily befriended the former Miss Shippen, now Mrs. Arnold, who we all know to be married to the turncoat Major General Benedict Arnold. Cavendish was also present at their wedding at the behest of Arnold himself for having saved his leg at Saratoga."

Annalisa's face burned.

"And is it reasonable to believe a man if guilty of treason for having had a mere connection with Major General Arnold who has been found guilty of treason?" one of the assembled officers asked.

"I believe it is fair to recognize such a connection," Mr. Wentworth replied.

"You yourself were also present at this wedding, were you not, sir?" Jack asked.

"Yes, I was," he replied.

"And so were several officers of the Continental Army, were they not, sir?" Jack asked.

"Yes, I believe so," Wentworth replied.

"As far as we know, the major general had not defected at the time of his wedding," Jack said. "Your conjecture of Private Cavendish's attendance at said wedding would insinuate that all associated with the Continental Army who were present at the Arnold-Shippen wedding should also stand to be court-martialed and accused of treason."

Mr. Wentworth said nothing.

"I have no further questions," Jack said.

Captain Hastings dismissed Mr. Wentworth and called his next witness.

Lord Essex sauntered into the room, and Annalisa dug her jagged nails into her breeches. *When did he return from England? How could he possibly be included in this?* And yet a part of her always had suspected him.

"Good sirs, I'm Lord Essex, brother-in-law to Lord Brunswick. Unfortunately, I, too, was present at the Shippen-

Arnold wedding and saw much to distress me. Private Cavendish is not who you believe him to be. His acquaintance with Major General Arnold is problematic enough, yes, but I must inform you of a matter perhaps as troubling to this man's treachery—"

"I object," Jack said. "Lord Essex, you must speak to matters of what the defendant is being accused—that being accounts of treason—and nothing more."

Lord Essex smirked. "Of course, my lord." He faced the jury of officers. "But deception is deception is it not, gentlemen? Most esteemed officers, this man, Private Cavendish...is no man."

Lord Essex approached her and ripped open her tattered shirt to reveal the linen bound about her breasts. "This man is a woman masquerading as a man. And has been so all along, which only further incriminates her."

No longer able to feel her face and hands, Annalisa focused on the pounding of her heart and wondered how Jack would rescue her from both treason and impersonation.

ANNALISA

WEST POINT, NEW YORK, MARCH 1781

A RUMBLE OF MURMURS erupted from the assembled jury of officers. Jack stood, his neck and face red. "Peace, gentlemen."

"Counsel, what have you to say of this accusation?" one of the officers asked.

Jack's fingertips lingered over his signet ring as he faced the jury and General Washington. He bowed. "Lord Essex's chicanery is ripe. Aye, I cannot deny this is a woman, gentlemen of the jury, but she is no spy, which is why this court-martial is here assembled. Allow me, if you would, to share something of my character with you at this time.

"To our commander in chief, General Washington, and our assembled officers of the jury, I'm Lord Brunswick. I've served under Major Howlett in Cogswell's regiment while in New York and am a veteran of both Bunker Hill and Lexington and Concord, as well as Saratoga and the Cowpens. My father is Lord Perkins and has served alongside Mr. Jefferson, Mr. Hancock, and Mr. Adams in Congress since 1775. As a graduate of Harvard College, I studied law under Mr. Adams himself and stand before you today not only as a devout Patriot of this war, but as the defense counsel for the accused, Private Benjamin Cavendish. I should like to call on my first witness to please speak his troth."

Lord Essex cried, "This is an abomination."

"I'll allow it," General Washington said. "Please take you seat, Lord Essex. I should first like to hear what is to be said of Private Cavendish's alleged treachery."

Annalisa resisted the urge to slouch in her chair. Rather, she sat upright and awaited Jack's first witness: a young man, no older than she, who entered the room and was sworn in by Captain Hastings. She held her breath, recognizing the man, though he'd been a boy of seventeen when she first met him upon the Danvers common. His gaze locked with hers.

"My name is Nathaniel Hitchcock. I knew the defendant when we were both in the Danvers militia serving under Captain Foster. Cav was reliable and quite a marksman. We fought, by chance, together at Bunker Hill with Stark's First New Hampshire regiment and decimated fusiliers by the Mystick River. On our retreat, I was shot in the leg. Cav carried me across Charlestown Neck to safety, even after he'd been maimed in the shoulder. I believe I would not be here today, sirs, if not for the selfless bravery and courage of Private Cavendish."

"And at any time did you ever suspect the defendant was anything other than who he—she—stated she was?" asked Captain Hastings.

"No sir, never," Nathaniel replied. "But I also did not know Private Cavendish to be a woman..."

"That is neither the reason for the court-martial, nor the pretense as to why we've been assembled here today, sir," Jack said.

"Aye, sir. Then I've nothing more to say of the matter."

Nathaniel left the room and Jack addressed the room. "I call the next witness, Major George Howlett."

Annalisa dared not breathe as she fought the onslaught of tears. *My brother, my most beloved George.* She clenched her jaw to stave off the wave of emotion upon seeing him hobble into the room with a cane and Quinnapin at his side. George held her gaze for only a moment, then sat in a Windsor chair provided him; he propped his injured leg on another chair.

"Please state your name to the court," Jack said.

"Major Howlett, formerly Captain Howlett of Cogswell's regiment," George said, his bass voice strained. "I've known Private Cavendish since Bunker Hill, informally. I've known him as a private of the Continental Army since Saratoga. He fought gallantly and without reserve. Echoing the sentiment of Mr. Hitchcock, his marksmanship should not only be admired, but revered amongst his superiors. It was an honor for him to serve under my command, sirs. Truly, he is no threat to the cause and certainly is no traitor."

"But you knew Private Cavendish as a man, did you not?" one of the officers asked.

"I did," George replied.

"And did you never once question Private Cavendish's dedication to the cause?" Captain Hastings asked.

"Never."

Annalisa bit her cheeks to keep her tears at bay. How many miles had he ridden to get to her? How much pain and hardship had he endured to now give testimony of her character? A considerable feat for a man about to lose his leg. Selfless acts of brotherly affection for which she could never atone. Her throat clogged, and she averted her gaze from his.

Another officer asked, "Major Howlett, this woman's identity is now in question—"

"Sir, the woman's identity is not the reason we've been assembled here," Jack said. "Nor is it why the defendant is being court-martialed—"

"Enough." George struggled to ride from his chair. "Private Cavendish is my sister."

Jack glared at George. "Major Howlett—"

"Gentlemen, I've been awaiting this day for many years, and today has not disappointed." George chuckled darkly. "I've known of her guise since Bunker Hill. Any respectable brother would've done otherwise, but I encouraged her when I should've disciplined her. I'll not regret it in the least. She's killed as many Bloodybacks as myself, Quinn, and Lord Brunswick combined, and I'll be damned for her to hang for unfounded slander of treason. If you mean to hang her, then you must hang me also. I'll not see her go without me."

"And me." Quinnapin stood and supported George.

His entire defense gone to hell, Jack sucked in a breath. "I'll join them as well, sirs."

"I've heard enough." General Washington rose from his seat and approached, bypassing the jury. He addressed Annalisa directly. "Miss Annalisa Howlett?" His glance flickered to George, then returned to her. "I do see the resemblance. Remarkable, your guise. If I'm not mistaken, I believe we shared a dance at the Shippens'."

Her heart pounding, Annalisa nodded. "Yes, sir, we danced to 'Corn Rigs are Bonny.'"

"My favorite cotillion."

"Aye, sir."

"I remember well our intercourse. You suffered much from this war, as countless others have." General Washington turned to address the room. "I've heard enough. The court, having duly considered the evidence against the prisoner, Private Benjamin Cavendish, together with what was provided for the prisoner, is of the opinion that he is not guilty on charges of treason." Washington paused. "I do, however, find you, Miss Annalisa Howlett, guilty of impersonating a man in the military. That is, however, as your counsel stated, not the purpose of today's regimental court."

She bowed her head, "Sir, I do not deny it."

"Since that is not the reason we've assembled here today, Miss Annalisa Howlett, you shall receive no sentence of said conviction at this time. You are free to go."

The commander in chief exited the room, and the other assembled officers of the jury rose. Annalisa's hands unbound and wobbly on her feet, she made her way to where George sat with Quinnapin. She collapsed into his arms and wept.

"Oh, George." Annalisa held him close. "I'm s-so sorry," she heaved, "So s-sorry."

George held her. "I know, Little One. I know. But we'd do anything for you." He removed her and held her at arm's length. "Yes? We'd do anything for you."

She nodded. "I w-want to g-go home."

"Aye," Jack said. "Let's go home."

Lord Essex strolled to their party and dipped a formal bow. "A wonderful trial, gentlemen. Miss Annalisa, you were most convincing as Cavendish. I applaud you. You nearly had me fooled at the Shippens', but your sister Jane, bless her, was quick to inform me otherwise."

"Jane?" Jack asked.

Lord Essex nodded. "She's a beauty, is she not? And quite the informant."

"How did she know about Benjamin?" Annalisa asked.

"You reptile." George attempted to lunge from his chair for Lord Essex, but Jack and Quinnapin held him back. "You reptile, I'll have you hanged!"

Lord Essex continued, unaffected, "Supposedly, she overheard you speaking to Major Howlett the night after Bunker Hill. But that is merely what she told me. Could've been a lucky guess." He chuckled. "In any event, congratulations on having escaped the noose. Your poor sister, Mary, may not prove so lucky."

Jack wrapped Annalisa in his arms and held her head to his chest. "Hush, be still."

"What have you done to Miss Mary?" Quinnapin asked.

Lord Essex smirked. "She has a date with the gallows for a similar offense."

Quinnapin lunged after Lord Essex as he turned to leave. "Miss Mary is innocent in all this." He gripped the earl's shoulder and with his other fist, struck Lord Essex's jaw.

"Zounds!" The earl stumbled back from the blow. Rubbing his face, he said, "She's with the British, I'm afraid."

"I'll challenge you, you reptile," George bellowed. The chair creaked and groaned while he struggled to rise from his seat. "For all you've done to Abigail."

"Enough," Jack cried. "Abbie and Weeza are safe—"

"I'll kill him for you." Quinnapin struck Lord Essex again. "For this slander upon Miss Anna and for your accusation of Miss Mary."

Two officers from the jury reappeared through the door. They quickly seized Lord Essex from Quinnapin's pummeling fists.

"You're under arrest, Lord Essex. You shall have all the courtesies offered a gentleman but will be taken henceforth under suspicion of espionage."

"Espionage?" Lord Essex strained against their containment. "You've no reason to imprison me. I—"

"Does the name Admiral Bixby of the Royal Navy ring a bell, my lord?" one of the officers asked.

"You've no proof," Lord Essex sneered. "I'm an old friend of Lord and Lady Perkins, honorable and devoted Patriots to the cause."

"Admiral Bixby?" George's face turned from red to purple.

The officers hauled Lord Essex from the room, leaving Annalisa to look on with Jack, George, and Quinnapin.

"If he's been in correspondence with my uncle, they need hang that dilberry at dawn," George grumbled. "Would that I could challenge him—"

"George, you can barely stand," Jack said. "Justice will be done, I swear it."

A man cleared his throat behind them. "Miss Annalisa Howlett."

They all turned.

Annalisa approached Nathaniel. "Mr. Hitchcock, a pleasure to meet you as myself."

"I can't believe you fooled me." He shook his head, though he returned her smile. "I'm astounded, truly, by your courage. 'Twas an honor to fight beside you at Bunker Hill, and 'tis an honor to know the real you."

"Thank you for your testimony." She clasped his hands. "And you'll never know how much you and Captain Foster's militia saved me. 'Twas equally an honor serving beside you and Ebenezer."

Nathaniel bowed to her. "Cav."

She bowed to him and watched as he left the room. When he'd gone, she turned to Jack. "How ever did you find him?"

Jack bit his lip to conceal his smile. "I reached out to many who fought at Bunker Hill, including Captain Foster's militia, but as it happened, I met Nathaniel by chance on my way south."

"I have little to explain such an occurrence." Annalisa held Jack's gaze, and she knew he, too, felt Eliza's inexplicable presence.

"Let's quit this place," George said. "We've endured quite enough for one day."

Quinnapin closed and opened his fist, the knuckles bloodied from Lord Essex's face. "Aye."

Annalisa gripped Quinnapin's hand. "I would've never survived being Benjamin were it not for you, dear friend. Thank you for risking yourself for the sake of my insensible endeavor."

"You were meant to accomplish all you did, Miss Anna. Never forget that," Quinnapin replied. "I played my part in your journey as much as you."

With Jack's aid, George struggled to his feet and leaned heavily on his cane. "I'm about ready to find Mary and Henry. That dog, Essex, has my victualing office in knots."

"They never came to Philadelphia after they wrote," Jack said. "I'll start on ahead of our party to see if I may gather information."

"I'm going with you," Annalisa replied.

Jack's face hardened for only a moment before he answered her. "Quite. We leave at once." He collected his belongings from the trial, then led the way from the building.

❦ 51 ❦

ANNALISA

NEW YORK, MARCH 1781

WEST POINT BEHIND THEM, Annalisa trotted after Jack through thick woods of the Hudson Highlands. Following the river south and nearing British territory, Jack appeared heightened in observing their surroundings, lest they befall Redcoats lurking for passersby. Annalisa followed suit, eager to spot one of their crimson coats tucked up the road behind a bush or tree. A few miles or so behind them, Quinnapin rode with George at a slower pace to accommodate his injured leg. *I pray that leg heals. I pray Quinn's physick is magick for George's leg.*

"You've not spoken a word since leaving West Point," Jack said. His soft baritone severed her thoughts and filled the eerie woods with pleasantness.

"I've been lost to m-my thoughts, sir."

"Quite like myself."

She dared not mention their friendship, nor the romance which had bound them these last six years. Her secret, the worst of what she could have withheld from him, had finally been exposed, and she accepted the consequence.

Annalisa glimpsed her swollen wrists colored in purple

and yellow bruises of all stages of healing. Gripping the reins in one hand, she rotated one wrist at a time to loosen the ache.

"They must plague you with much pain." Jack slowed his horse to ride beside her.

"'Tis a c-corollary I'm willing t-to suffer. I'm far luckier than G-George in acquiring injury."

Jack's fine lips pursed. "I hope you understand my feelings on the matter."

Annalisa sucked in a breath, hoping to ease the stutter. Slowly, she spoke, "You certainly have every r-right to loathe m-me. I'll...not...object to it after what I've k-kept from you."

"I certainly don't loathe you. Far from it, I'm afraid." He glanced at her from his periphery, then returned his gaze to the road. "My loathing would've left you to rot in that godfor-saken gaol in Philadelphia."

She released a breath, one perhaps full of relief to hear him speak so, yet she suspected he wished to say far more unfavorable things. An addendum, of sorts. She clutched the reins, waiting.

Many minutes passed in silence as they cantered down the road. Overhead, early spring birds chirped and chattered as the sun lingered on the horizon. They would have to stop and set up camp soon. Jack must have heard her unspoken thoughts, because he stalled his horse and gestured to a clearing up the road.

"We'll set up for the night."

They trotted a meager distance and dismounted. Without any aid from Jack, though he loitered by, watching, Annalisa retrieved the effects given her by the Continental Army on their departure from West Point. She tied the canvas to a low-hanging branch of a tree, in the way she'd learned during her time in the war, and staked the opposite end to the ground. After feeding and watering her horse, she roped the beast to a tree, rolled out her blanket, and sprawled it beneath her modest shelter.

Jack studied her setup and pressed his lips as though to conceal a satisfied smirk. "Your site looks quite good."

"'Tis not m-my first." She offered a wink.

Her gesture, meant to bring out his smile, only caused him to frown. "I'm well aware. Now." Jack returned to starting their campfire. Once the flames caught, Jack rolled out his blanket, crawled atop, removed his hat, and rested on his back, eyes closed.

The fire rustled and snapped, illuminating the day's waning light. Annalisa waited near ten minutes before turning to her side. Propped on one arm, she studied Jack as he slept. The shape of his straight nose, the gentle cupid's bow of his upper lip; his smooth cheeks, freshly shaven, greedily with-held from her the dimples she so adored of his smile. *A smile I've not seen in months. How can he when he's learned of all I've done?*

❧

THE FOLLOWING MORNING, GEORGE AND QUINNAPIN, WHO joined their campsite after dusk, met Annalisa by the camp-fire. As Quinnapin rolled his and George's blankets, her brother hobbled beside her and sat. His arm wound about her, and he kissed her forehead.

"Little One, I've never been prouder of you."

Her throat tightened at the admission. She didn't believe any of them should be proud of her for such tomfoolery, having nearly landed all of them at the gallows. "Hearing you speak so astounds me."

George chuckled. "I'm not proud of you having been gaoled. I'm more bewildered that you danced with General Washington at the Shippens'."

"Aye, we danced his favorite cotillion. He was quite kind."

"You loathe dancing, and 'twas probably the occasion that saved us." He shook his head. "The irony is not lost on me."

Annalisa laughed. "Had it been a minuet, we would've been sentenced to the gallows for certain." She sobered as Jack stirred behind them. "But in all truthfulness, I think your reputation saved us. The general holds you with high esteem."

George nodded but said nothing, and she suspected he wished to be back with the army.

She peered behind her at Jack, who, though he'd stirred, still slept. Her voice low, she uttered, "Would that he forgives me."

"Give him time. Your secret injured him deeply, as I knew it would."

With a stick, Annalisa retrieved the ashcakes baking on embers. Steaming, she tossed one at her brother. He gnashed into the cake, consuming it in two bites. Annalisa nibbled on a charred corner.

"I fear I've wounded us beyond repair."

"If that be so, you must learn to live with it. Life is—"

"Rarely what we think it should be," they said in unison.

She smiled up at him until the sound of horses and a cart echoed from up the road. Quinnapin bolted to Jack's side, waking him.

"Riders at this hour?" she asked.

"Load your musket and make ready." George hoisted himself up with his cane. "Quinn, Jack, make ready and disappear from the road."

Jack rolled his blanket and Annalisa's while she threw dirt, rocks, and sand over the fire. In less than five minutes, they absconded into the surrounding woods.

Tucked behind a tree with Jack, Annalisa loaded her musket. Her heart rattled within her breast, bound in filthy linen. Her breeches and stockings, torn and smeared with grime from the gaol, allowed cold bits of waking earth to assault her legs. She clamped her jaw to suppress her chattering teeth.

"Not all wounds are beyond repair," Jack whispered, his gaze fixed on the road. "Others require amputation."

He means to remove me, as though a wounded limb, from his life.

Before she could respond, riders trotted into view. Redcoats, officers, perhaps, led the way for a cart toting two prisoners.

Annalisa peered at Jack. To her left, George and Quinnapin hid behind a large bush.

Her brother's frown deepened, and he mouthed, "On my command."

They watched in stillness as the British—two officers and two privates—stopped in the clearing. A private tossed a tied rope over a thick tree limb and tightened it. The looped end of the rope dangled over the prisoners in the cart.

Annalisa squinted at the souls to be hanged and gasped. The lifeblood drained from her face and numbed her cheeks. "'Tis Mary and Henry."

"Shh." Jack reached for her. He craned his head toward George and Quinnapin and mouthed, "Mary and Henry."

George's face greyed for only a moment before the menacing green of his eyes returned to the assembled scene before them. He gripped Bixby until his knuckles whitened, and he inched toward Annalisa.

"We must wait until they place the noose. You will, on my command, aim and fire at the rope. Is that understood?"

Annalisa nodded, though she quaked. *Will they choose Mary first to hang or Henry?* She peered at the branch from which the noose dangled—certainly not strong enough to withstand the hanging of two people, no matter the slight frame of her dear sister.

Her musket loaded, Annalisa fully cocked it and aimed. Everything she learned from George of shooting, each practice in the clearing beyond the ancient oak, every drill with the Danvers militia, had been for this very moment. She could not fail now.

Jack's hand rested on hers. "Steady, my darling girl."

His voice, so calm and smooth, mollified her enough to cease the shaking. She adjusted her aim and waited.

In the clearing, a Redcoat pulled the loop over Mary's head and tightened it about her neck.

The presiding officer announced loud enough for them to hear: "Mary Howlett, you were found guilty of espionage for the enemy and sentenced to be taken hence to this place of execution, where you shall be hanged by the neck until dead. May the Lord have mercy upon your soul."

"Make ready," George whispered.

Her heart pounding, Annalisa tightened her grip about her musket and held aim.

"Eeyah!" The officer shouted, and the horses rode forward. The cart lurched.

George shouted, "fire!"

Snap-crack!

Crack-boom!

The discharge of their musket-fire rang through the clearing, and the noose containing her sister's body snapped. Mary dropped to the ground with a thud. Henry, bound, shuffled toward the commotion as two officers and a private collapsed. Quinnapin leapt from behind the bush and scooped Mary's limp body into his arms.

Annalisa scrambled from behind the tree and past the deceased officers. "Mary," she cried. "Mary!" She knelt beside Quinnapin and removed the rope from her sister's bruised neck. "You mustn't die, you foolish girl." Thick tears toppled from her eyes onto Mary's placid face.

Jack unbound Henry's wrists, and Quinnapin felt for Mary's pulse. A serenity returned to his face.

"She lives."

George hobbled upon his cane, pistol cocked and aimed at the injured private who scampered away. "Return to your loathsome barracks, you Bloodyback reptile," he shouted.

Jack jumped up, snatched George's pistol, and fired on the retreating private. The man staggered several feet before crumpling to the ground in a bloody heap. When Jack returned the smoking pistol to George, he muttered, "'Twas a risk I'm not unwilling to take."

"She has a pulse," Quinnapin said again. "Let's get her into the cart and make haste. Miss Anna, will you ride with her?"

"Of course."

"Henry, are you harmed?" Jack asked.

"No." Henry shook his head. "I will ride, if you've a horse."

"How came you to be imprisoned by the British?" George barked.

"'Twas on accusations made by Lord Essex," Henry replied. "He claimed we spied for the Continentals—"

"Which is true," Jack said.

"'Tis neither here nor there," Henry replied. "Lord Essex corroborated Mr. Wentworth's accusation."

"Mr. Wentworth meant to court Mary," Annalisa cried.

"Court her or spy on her himself?" Quinnapin hoisted Mary into his arms, lifted her delicate form from the ground, and carried her to the British cart affixed with two horses.

Annalisa hopped in and helped pull Mary inside. Jack handed her their effects from West Point and mounted his horse. Quinnapin aided George onto his horse, then mounted one of the cart horses. Once Henry lifted onto Annalisa's horse, they galloped from the clearing.

Seated within the juddering cart, Annalisa placed Mary's

head on her lap and smoothed her sister's light brown tresses from her forehead. Tucked behind those pallid eyelids crowned with thick lashes, she pictured Mary's inquisitive hazel eyes.

"Shall I recite M-Mad Madge for you, dear sister?"

From memory, Annalisa delivered the words of their favorite poem written by Margaret Cavendish. Those familiar verses, so often shared between them beneath the shade of the venerable oak, proved physick to quell her stutter. Surely, their power could rouse Mary.

An unsettling despondence settled into her bones at Mary's unresponsiveness. *I may have honed my shot well enough to sever the rope, but I was not quick enough.* The thought closed her throat and paused her recitation.

As though he'd heard her thought, Quinnapin glanced back. "You were quick enough, Miss Anna. 'Twas the fall, not the rope, that injured her. She will survive this."

Annalisa's breathing slowed and she returned her gaze to Mary, the only sister she trusted and loved. Would that she be saved from this nightmare.

52

JACK

TOPSFIELD, APRIL 1781

THEIR RETURN FROM NEW York had been a slow, grueling journey across terrain mixed with melting snow, lending much of the road to thick patches of mud. Their cart wheels, having stuck several times, delayed their arrival, but in the second week of April, Jack appreciated the rolling hills of Topsfield.

"We've made it," Annalisa said to Mary. "We're in home."

Mary, suffering from a large bruise to her head, said nothing, though she smiled. Annalisa returned her grin, and Jack's heart pained for the girl's involuntary silence; a consequence of the fall, he presumed.

The cart juddered and wobbled down the narrow lane. As the Howlett homestead came into view, Annalisa pointed. "We're home, dear sister."

They rode up the drive, and Quinnapin dismounted. He wasted little time in removing Mary from the cart and carried her to the front door before Annalisa crawled from the cart. Jack dismounted and assisted George from his horse. His cousin grimaced with the motion. Though he wouldn't admit it, Jack knew the ride caused him great suffering. His affected leg had swollen to twice the size of his good leg. Henry hobbled behind them all, perhaps unsure of what to tell their parents.

When Mr. and Mrs. Howlett and Liza received them at the house, they allowed Quinnapin to transfer Mary to the room she shared with Jane and Annalisa. Mrs. Howlett followed them into the room.

"Papa!" Robby's rosy face greeted Jack from beside Jane.

Jack bent down and tousled Robby's chestnut hair. "You took good care of your mamma, young master. Well done." He kissed his forehead. "Now, I need to attend to Uncle George." He continued up the stairs with his cousin and down the hall to the bed-chamber Abigail and Louisa had made their own.

"My God, Jack. George!" Abigail wailed and threw herself at them. "Thank God, you've returned."

Jack pecked his niece's cheek. "Weeza, how you've grown. You must take extra good care of your papa."

George sat on the bed and chuckled, though his face twisted. "Come here, little mite."

"Papa, I missed you." Louisa wrapped her arms about George's neck.

"Your leg is ghastly. Come, lie down." Abigail removed Louisa from his lap and helped him recline.

"Mary suffered at the hands of the British as well," Jack said. "Quinn's been rather attentive to her healing—"

"Oh, poor thing," Abigail cried. "We all told the twins not to go thither. And what of Annie? Where is my dearest friend?"

Jack's jaw twitched. "Downstairs." He withdrew from the chamber, ambled down the stairs and into the parlor, where Annalisa sprawled over the sofa. Her face pale and still covered in filth, he inched toward her.

"Annalisa?" His baritone filled the room, rousing her. "My God, you look affright."

"I f-feel it, sir." She threw an arm over her face and sobbed.

Jack drew her into his arms, and she trembled against his chest. "Liza, quickly!"

The indentured Irish girl stepped into the parlor. "What be it, Lord Brunswick?"

"Have Dane or Zeke ready the chaise. I'm bringing Miss Annalisa to my parents' house at once."

"Aye, my lord." Liza dipped a curtsy and fled the house.

"N-No. I w-want to stay with m-my family. M-Mary and George n-need me..."

"There is no room for you to convalesce here. Quinn is caring for Mary, and Abbie is with George. They will both be well cared for."

"And Henry?"

"Your brother appears unharmed, though has much to say of their abduction."

"Your mamma...loathes m-me."

Jack scooped her into his arms. "To hell with my mother."

ॐ

JACK CARRIED ANNALISA THROUGH THE FRONT DOOR OF HIS parents' large yellow house and past Mercy, their house-keeper. Without so much as greeting his parents seated about the parlor with his brothers and sisters, he hoisted Annalisa up the stairs to his bed-chamber, where he lay her across his canopied bedstead.

"Mercy!" he cried.

The housekeeper appeared at his open door. "Yes, sir?"

"Draw a bath for Miss Annalisa at once, and have some

fresh clothes for her at the ready. When you've done that, please bring her something to eat and drink."

"Yes, my lord." Mercy curtsied and dipped from the room.

Beyond the casement, a periwinkle twilight had faded to night by the time enough hot water filled the metal tub that had been placed inside his chamber. A rap at the door turned his attention from the window.

"Lord Brunswick, may I be of assistance?"

Sarah.

Jack hesitated. "No, thank you, Miss Devonshire. I'll call for you if I require your assistance." He returned to Annalisa, who lay upon his bed. "Come now, you need to remove your clothes."

"Whatever for?"

"A bath."

"Let Sarah help me, p-please."

"I wish to help you." His chest constricted. He hadn't aided her once on their journey from New York, and the guilt crawled over him like the lice littering her matted tresses. "Come now. Breeches off."

Her hands fumbled with the buttons, and he assisted her.

"Of all the times I'd imagined undressing you, 'twas never akin to this." He guided her into the tub, and her quaking body eased as she craned her neck back. Jack removed his coat and hung it over his desk chair, then rolled his sleeves to his elbows.

She sighed. "I can't remember the last b-bath I've had."

Jack reached into the hot water for her arm and sponged away the grime. The water and soap, scented with orange blossom oil, proved the first pleasant aroma he'd smelled in months. Gently, he washed away the dried blood from her wrists. Annalisa opened her eyes and peered at him.

"Thank you. I know how little I deserve your kindness."

He said nothing as he washed her back. Yellow and purple

bruises dotted the bony prominences of her ribs and spine. His heart panged at the sight, and he ran a gentle hand over her skin. "Dip your head."

She did as she was told and submerged her head in water. When she reemerged, her matted locks clung to her face and skull like a fishing net. Carefully, Jack combed through the tangles until her curls hung about her shoulders, unadulterated. He rubbed the soap between his hands, then ran his fingers through her wet locks until the hair smelled of orange blossoms.

"Rinse."

Annalisa slipped beneath the water once more, then emerged.

"'Twill be a while before we rid you of these vermin." Flecks of lice and dead fleas speckled the filthy bathwater. "Come." He helped her from the bath, then wrapped her naked form in his banyan.

Jack retrieved the clean linen shift Mercy had laid out and handed Annalisa the garment. He turned from her as she dropped the banyan to the floor.

"'Tis nothing you haven't seen."

"As a gentleman, I owe you the respect of some privacy." His lie sounded harsher than the truth: he couldn't bear the sight of her tortured figure.

When he faced her, Annalisa's sunken countenance bore the remnants of disappointment and humiliation. Perhaps she considered him repulsed by her. How could he possibly verbalize he did wish to lie beside her, to stroke her orange-scented hair and kiss her forehead, to tell her he loved her and always would, despite the incessant gnaw of her dishonesty? *How can I marry such a woman?* The thought left him reeling with anguish. He never conjured that something so dire, so irrevocable as this, would stand between them.

"Come, lie in my bed and rest. I'll not leave until you're sleeping."

"Will you rest beside me?"

"I may sit with you, but nothing more."

And this he did as she sank beneath the coverlet and closed her eyes. Seated on the edge of his own bedstead, he smoothed her damp curls from her face and traced the curve of her gaunt cheek with his forefinger. His thumb lingered over the healed scar beneath her right eye. He couldn't help but marvel at the honed skill of his brave, darling girl. She'd saved Nathaniel Hitchcock at Bunker Hill and rescued Mary from certain death. He could hardly love her more. And while his heart urged him to recline beside her, his sensibility pleaded with him to remain upright upon the bed.

53

JACK

TOPSFIELD, MAY 1781

AS MAY BLEW AWAY the final remnants of April, open windows offered spring breezes, rest, nourishment, and visits from Sarah, all of which returned the color to Annalisa's cheeks. Throughout her convalescence, Jack conjured fantasies where he would always return to Annalisa at the end of each day, but for countless sleepless nights upon the floor of his room, better judgment combated the yearning of his heart. *Yes, I still love her more than I should.*

And as Annalisa sat at his desk by the open window, her hair unfurled down her back, Jack turned from her and forced himself to venture on his daily visit to the Howlett farm.

When he arrived at the homestead, he dismounted and stabled his horse, and met Quinnapin, crouched within Annalisa's herb garden.

"How fares George today?" Jack asked.

Quinnapin frowned. "Not well. I fear he may lose the leg, after all."

"Will he survive an amputation?" Jack grimaced, pondering how to break such terrible news to Annalisa, who had so recently regained strength.

"I will do everything in my power, Brother. Fortunately, Miss Mary's speech is slow to recover."

"Some good news, then." Jack smiled and followed Quinnapin from the barn and up the path to the house.

Peering back at him, Quinnapin asked, "How does Miss Anna?"

"She's better. I've combed nearly all the vermin from her hair, and she's gained some weight. I'm remiss to let her return home. I daresay I'll miss seeing her each morning and every night."

A small grin danced on Quinnapin's lips. "Perhaps you needn't let her come home."

They stepped inside the house, and Jack hastened up the stairs with his friend. Quinnapin entered George's bedchamber and knelt at his bedside.

"Jack's here, old friend."

Abigail, who sat beside George, rose and hurried to Jack. She threw her arms about his neck. "Oh, Jack. He is going to lose his leg. I know not what to do."

Jack pulled from his sister's embrace. "He will recover. He's strong-willed. That much is certain."

Abigail swiped the tears from her freckled cheeks. "I just wish for him to return to health. I miss those days where he had strength enough for ten men."

"Aye. I know," he replied. "Pray, how is Louisa?"

"Well. She's playing with Robby. He is a good distraction for her."

Jack forced a pained smile for having missed his son's fourth birthday in March. *I've been an absent father.* In a desperate moment, he silently thanked Jane for her ever-present care of their son in his time away. With as much fault as she possessed, she truly loved her sons.

As quickly as his gratitude flooded him, it vanished with the recollection of Lord Essex's exposure of Jane at the trial. She had been the one to tell Lord Essex of Annalisa's secret.

Burning to address Jane, Jack regarded Abigail. "Where is Jane? Is she with the children?"

Abigail nodded. "Why?"

"I have a need to speak with her." He quit the room and made his way outside the Howlett house.

The verdant fields blossomed with flowering plants and chartreuse leaves. The scent of life returning to the earth led him across the farm to the ancient oak. Beneath its hefty boughs, the children played whilst Jane sat upon the lowest limb with a book.

She peered up at him, closed her book, and smiled. "Jack."

He tipped his hat to her. "Miss Howlett."

Jane frowned. "How far I've fallen in your graces for you to call me that."

"You haven't been my wife for over a twelvemonth. Why should I continue to honor you with the title of Lady Brunswick?"

Jane opened her book and returned to reading. "Have you come to chastise me, then?"

"No. Only to interrogate you on matters most serious." He sat beside her, and together they watched Louisa chase Robby about the wide trunk until she caught him. They collapsed to the ground in a fit of giggles mere feet from Eliza's resting place. Jack yearned for the daughter he never knew, yet whose voice came to him. A shiver inched down his spine.

"Speak, sir." Jane's delicate soprano him broke from the shudder.

He gathered his thoughts and delivered them as though at a court proceeding. "At Annalisa's trial, Lord Essex was witness for the prosecution. He mentioned having learned of Benjamin Cavendish from you, madam."

Jane's rosy cheeks paled. "Lord Essex returned from England?"

"Aye, but 'tis no matter. He's been arrested by the Continental Army and awaits sentencing of his own. For espionage."

Jane fell silent for several minutes as her soft, pale hands smoothed the wrinkles from her skirts.

"Yes, I spoke of Benjamin Cavendish to him. I overheard Annalisa speaking to George that night after Bunker Hill. I remember he asked what she called herself, and that was the name she offered. At the time, I thought little of it and never again thought she'd pursue the endeavor. Save for my own jealousy. Annie only ever sought George's approval, never mine. I used to wish she would confide in me, Jack. I'm her older sister...the one she should've idolized...the one to have shown her how to be a lady." Jane wiped her cheeks. "And yes, in my horrible misjudgment in befriending the earl, I told Essex about her ridiculous stunt at Bunker Hill and that she'd called herself Benjamin Cavendish. We laughed about it, Jack. I never suspected he would remember it, let alone use it against her."

"Then you knew at Peggy Shippen's wedding 'twas Annalisa and not some other fellow?"

"I've always known. I said nothing because I knew someday it would be exposed, and she would reap the consequences of such foolish actions."

Jack's jaw hardened. "How could you be so heartless as to entrust that man with something as scandalous as Annalisa's masquerading as a man?"

"I honestly thought it a one-time affair. A bit of gossip, really, perhaps to elevate myself in his eyes...I know not what I thought at the time. But I never anticipated Annalisa would don those clothes time and again to fight in this heinous war —or befriend Peggy Shippen!"

"Then who used her name to slander her in those letters Henry uncovered? Was it you?"

Jane bit her bottom lip.

"Come, Jane. Lord Essex cares little for you. His chicanery is proof enough he inveigled you."

Her lip quivered. "Yes, he did use me for information. I'll not deny it. But I never wished to harm anyone—"

"Yet you poisoned Annalisa," Jack growled. "You caused her to stillbirth our daughter."

"'Twas your mother!" cried Jane. She jumped from the branch and faced him. "I've denied it every day since it happened, and I shall continue to deny these accusations. 'Twas your mother who added the pennyroyal to the tea. And 'twas your mother who penned the letters at Lord Essex's instruction to use the name Benjamin Cavendish. Everything was by her design and his. She's a witch who cajoled me, for the sake of Society and preserving my reputation, into partaking in things I never wished to be a part of. That is the truth of it, sir. I swear it upon my life and Annalisa's."

Jack slid from the branch, his entire body icy and numb. "My mother?"

"Yes." Jane paced about, wringing her hands. "She's wicked and plays the part of your father's wife so well—"

"She and my father have been married nearly as long as I've been alive. They've always been happy—"

"She's weary of this war and his constant leaving for Congress. I'd know. I've been her closest companion these few years."

He rubbed his throbbing temples.

Jane continued, "She and my mamma planned much in our betrothal, but your mother has spoken of Annalisa and my family with such vitriol, such scurrilous invectiveness, it surprises me little she now wishes to abscond to Halifax with other Loyalists."

"Other Loyalists?" His heart galloped. "Then my parents have defected?"

Jane shook her head. "Your mother wishes to leave, but your father does not. Andrew has been most cautious in observing them. He relayed much to Henry and Mary... before they left to find you in Philadelphia."

"Henry and Mary's capture...my mother couldn't possibly have anything to do with it?"

"I know not, but I've seen her pen letters to her younger brother. I believe you are aware of your uncle, Admiral Bixby?"

His heart skipped. "She writes to him?"

"Yes. He's commander of a British fleet and also friend to Lord Essex."

"That is Essex's contact," Jack cried. "Essex's espionage charge is on his correspondence with Admiral Bixby. Then 'tis they three—Bixby, Essex, and my mother." It nauseated him to speak of her with such loathing, but with all that had befallen them, only mere threads of his affection remained. "I must go to my father at once."

He turned to leave but returned, taking up Jane's hands. "I know terrible things have passed between us, but I pray you speak nothing but truth to me."

"I have little reason to defend Lord Essex or your mother after all they've done. I've seen firsthand their cruelty and all I would be had I continued to follow suit. Yet I fear the damage is done, sir." She returned to the tree bough. "I, too, am weary of it all. Tired of this war and living like this... seeing my family and others suffer so. Truthfully, I care little for whichever side claims victory...only that it may happen soon."

Jack softened at her sentiment. He, too, wished for this war to end, but after all they'd endured, he could hardly stomach the idea of living within the colony should the British claim victory.

He kissed Robby and fled the Howlett farm, eager to collect Annalisa and return her to the safety of her family's house. He'd never anticipated she'd be in any danger in the care of his family; quite the opposite, in fact.

When he returned home, he burst inside and ran up the stairs to his room, where Annalisa still sat at his desk, writing.

"Collect your things and take my horse."

She turned. "Whatever for?"

"You need to leave this instant."

Sensing the danger in his voice, her face fell. "Jack, what is it?"

"You're not safe to remain here, my darling girl. You're quite well enough to ride two miles down the lane, yes? Your parents will be expecting you...and George and Mary need you."

"Of course. I'll leave this moment. But pray, what did you learn?"

Jack locked his door and drew up her hands. "Jane revealed the most odious of accusations."

Her brow arched. "But can she be believed?"

"I do believe her. Her actions, previously thought to be of her own devices, were nothing more than my own mother's arrangements in tandem with Lord Essex."

"Your mother?" Annalisa's face paled. "The miscarriage?"

"Aye." Jack nodded. "'Twas my mother who brewed the tea with pennyroyal. Not Jane."

"She always denied it..." Annalisa fell silent. "And we are to believe this?"

"Aye." He swallowed over the lump in his throat. "She also penned the letters Henry uncovered damning Benjamin Cavendish."

Annalisa turned from him, her hands shaking. "Your mamma threatened to burn my family's farm if I did not marry Mr. Peabody. I'm certain she is capable of terrible things."

"None of that will happen, I swear it." Jack gritted his teeth. "Return to your house, and I will join you by the end of this day." He kissed her forehead and pulled her to her feet.

Not satisfied until he'd saddled her upon his own mare, Jack watched her ride down the narrow lane wearing nothing but his breeches, shirt, and coat. It would do until she reached her farm and the safety of her family.

Jack returned to his house and the parlor in which his mother and father sat. Oliver and Sarah played a game of cribbage with Andrew while his sisters Charlotte and Susan, practiced needlepoint. The scene was much as he'd left it, innocent enough and without much to fear. But the time had come to tear it apart.

54

JACK

TOPSFIELD, MAY 1781

"SIR, MADAM, I HAVE much to speak with you about."

Father glanced up from his newspaper, then set down his pipe.

"Of course." He folded the paper, rested it over the side table, and gestured to the seat across from him.

Jack spun his signet ring for only a moment before meeting Oliver's steady gaze. His brother nodded for him to proceed, and Jack tucked his arms behind him. "I'll stand, thank you." He paced before his mother, who set aside her needlepoint canvas.

"It has come to light that our involvement with a certain gentleman by the name of Lord Essex has grown toxic and has hence lent itself to another relationship with a certain estranged family member: Admiral Bixby, your younger brother, madam."

Father peered over his spectacles. "Your brother, Bette? 'Tis been decades since last you corresponded with the lout." He stared at Jack. "How came you by such information, Jack?

Bixby has not written us since he left England for the West Indies...oh, twenty-five years ago?"

Jack studied his mother. "Madam, do you not deny writing Admiral Bixby?"

"My brother, Richard?" His mother held his stare. "I'll not deny it."

"I beg pardon, madam?" Father sat forward in his chair. "You wrote to Richard?"

Mother sighed. "Oh please, John. How else do you think I was able to convince Lord Essex to marry Abigail? He and Richard were friends since before Edward died at sea. Of course I wrote to him."

Father's forehead vein bulged, and Jack glanced at Oliver, who poised on the edge of his seat. Andrew, having set down his cards, straightened.

"Bette, you know I've never trusted your younger brother. And I knew not of his friendship with Essex. How came this about, Jack?" Father asked.

"Jane Howlett."

"That wench." Mother's face reddened. "How dare she slander me after all I've done for her and the Howlett family?"

"Is it true?" Jack asked.

"Is what true?" his mother snapped.

"That 'twas you who brewed the tea with pennyroyal. That it was you who corresponded with Admiral Bixby and Lord Essex."

His mother folded her hands and stared hard at him. "I'm sorry, Jack, but I did what I must to prevent another scandal. So yes. I admit it. I added the pennyroyal. But you were married to Jane, and that twat Annalisa carried your child. I could hardly allow her to further destroy our family's reputation. She'd done enough already. I know not how that girl came from Mrs. Howlett. It must be her father's Pawtucket blood—"

"That *twat* happens to be the love of my life and the best thing that ever happened to me," Jack shouted.

"'Tis no matter now." Mother shrugged. "You're free to marry her now that poor Mr. Peabody is dead. But I shan't be there to witness it."

"You shan't be invited," Jack replied. "Word is you'll be in Halifax with other Loyalists who've escaped Boston."

"What is this?" Father glared at her. "I beg pardon, madam?"

Mother threw up her hands and stood from her chair. "I can't live like this, John. Your presence is absent from this house more than I care to recount. I curse your Congress and this war and all 'tis done to our family and our life in this country."

"Peace, Mother." Andrew rose from the gaming table and approached her. "All will be well. This war will end soon."

Mother shrugged his hands from her. "What we've suffered is irreversible. I only wish to rebuild our lives elsewhere. If Halifax is safe, then so be it. We shall relocate."

Father shook his head. "I'm going nowhere, Lady Perkins. This is our home, where our children and grandchildren reside. That is final." He removed his spectacles and rubbed his face. "I am utterly sickened by all I've heard. Jack, are you quite satisfied?"

"Aye, sir."

"What, Jack?" Mother cried. "And no word of reproach for the gentleman who willingly blocked your divorce petitions at Salem?"

Jack bristled. "Father and I have reconciled while we were in London. Though I admit my discouragement on the matter, I've chosen to move beyond it, as a resolution came to fruition. He's my father. But you, madam, my own mother, murdered my child...*your grandchild*. What sort of mother does such a thing? For that, I can't, and never shall, forgive you."

He turned to leave the parlor, but his mother grabbed his wrist. "Everything I've done was to secure your happiness, Jack, and preserve the good reputation of our family. You might not understand it, but my love for you is boundless, and you shall always remain in my heart."

Jack ripped his arm from her grip. "You've a strange notion of love, madam, one I'm not sure I'll comprehend in this lifetime." He turned to leave the parlor but hesitated. "I regret to inform you I'll not return to this house so long as its mistress resides here."

"Be reasonable." Father gestured to Jack's stunned younger sisters, who sat silenced upon the settee. "You've sisters who will continue to miss their eldest brother."

"Is it unreasonable, sir, after all you've learned this afternoon?"

Father's lips pursed. "Your accusations and feelings are not unfounded. Know that I'll accept you into this house any hour of any day, my darling boy."

Jack reached for his father and held him. "Sir." The scent of tobacco fresh in his nose, he pulled from Father. "I welcome you any time to my own house, wherever it may be." He shook Andrew's and Oliver's hands, whispering to meet him at the Willow that night, kissed his sisters, and quit the parlor.

Before leaving the house, Jack shouted from the foyer, "Lord Essex was detained at West Point after Annalisa's trial for espionage. It shan't be long before he has a date with the gallows."

❈ 55 ❈

ANNALISA

TOPSFIELD, MAY 1781

A S ANNALISA RODE DOWN the drive, so did Dr. Brown and his apprentice. She swung from Jack's mare, stabled the beast, and ran after the doctor.

"Dr. Brown!"

She stepped inside her house behind them, and Abigail and Mamma met the doctor in the foyer.

"He's in the basement pantry, sirs," Mamma said.

"Oh, Annie." Abigail clutched her, flooding Annalisa with an amalgamation of rose perfume and the mawkish putrescence of George's ailing leg. "I can't stand it. They're going to take his leg."

"You speak truth?" Annalisa tore from her friend. "There's nothing can be done by Quinn or Addy?"

Abigail shook her head. "The skin below his knee has turned purple. Quinn says the limb must go if he wishes to preserve his life."

Before Abigail finished speaking, Annalisa hurled past her friend and down the hall, into the kitchen, and down the steep basement stairs. She burst inside the basement pantry and gagged. The sweet scent of dried herbs succumbed to

George's festering leg wound. With a shudder, she returned to the day in that same basement with Liza and Addy, weeks after her injury at Bunker Hill. George had thrown her upon the very table upon where he now lay for Quinnapin to remove the round from her shoulder.

Mamma hovered over George. Her hand in his, she peered at Annalisa, her icy-blue eyes rimmed in red. "Annie, how good of you to be here. You will stay with Georgie, won't you?" Mamma kissed her eldest son's forehead, beaded with perspiration, then met Annalisa at the doorway. "You were always his favorite, you know." She squeezed Annalisa's hand and passed by without peering back.

Her heart in her throat, Annalisa inched toward the table as Dr. Brown and his assistant removed a bone saw, crooked needles, a leather protractor, and a tourniquet from his bag.

Dr. Brown glanced up at her. "You might wish to find your brothers and father for assistance, Miss Annalisa."

"I'll not leave his side, sir." She set her jaw and lowered onto the bench by the table where her hulking brother lay.

Dr. Brown said nothing, then handed his assistant a bottle of rum, followed by a small vial of opium. "He must drink."

George, half-asleep, stirred. "What is this wibble?" He leaned on his elbows to sit up and grimaced. "Annie. You've come for the show. Pray, where's Quinn? He tried to save it, Little One…"

"Shh. Drink the rum." Annalisa took the bottle from Dr. Brown's apprentice and held it to his lips.

The basement stairs creaked, and Quinnapin poked his head inside the cool, crisp room. "Miss Anna, you came."

Behind him, William followed.

Annalisa rose from the bench and embraced William. "Oh, Will." She sniffled against his coat but blinked back her tears. *Not today. I cannot weep when I must be strong for George.*

She returned to the bench, where Quinnapin sidled beside her.

"I did everything I could," he said.

"Blame not yourself." She cupped his shoulder. "You've done more than I could have to help him."

William shook his head. "I always feared this day."

"*Wilhelmina!*" George guffawed between gulps of rum, then glugged the laudanum. "Thank God, you've come." He tossed the empty vial to the stone floor, then flopped back against a pillow. "'Tis enough, Doc. Have at it." To William, added, "Hold my arm tightly."

Dr. Brown's assistant tied the tourniquet just below George's left knee, about four fingers above the unhealthy section of shin. Before Dr. Brown started to cut, Annalisa locked her hand with George's. "You will survive this. Swear to me, George Howlett. Promise me you won't let this take you."

He held her stare, his green eyes glassy. "Little One, I swear it shan't take me."

Quinnapin placed a piece of leather between his teeth, then circled the table to hold George's leg as Dr. Brown started to cut.

George growled against the leather, his face bursting beet red. The force of his grip tugged Annalisa forward. She focused on William's face across from her as he strained against George's other grasp. She glimpsed his crimson face and the sweat beading at his temples and across his dark, heavy brow.

Annalisa's lips twisted against the onslaught tears prickling her eyes. But she swallowed through the lump building in her throat, grasping at anything at all pleasant. "Louisa is growing into such a good girl, George. You and Abbie have done well by her. She needs her papa."

William peered at her. "Aye, and when Fanny is old enough to keep up, she'll learn much from Weeza."

"Louisa gets along quite well with Tommy and Robby," Quinnapin added. "She's lucky to have such wonderful cousins."

"Aye. And Lord Essex will surely hang. George, then you and Abbie may officially be married here in town."

George's hand slid from hers.

Her breast tight beneath Jack's shirt, Annalisa glanced to her left, between George's legs where Dr. Brown stood. Already, the lower leg lay upon the cold stone floor in a pile of hay, and Dr. Brown's assistant worked on suturing the arteries.

Her attention returned to George, who lay unconscious, though still breathed. Quinnapin released his grip on George's healthy leg and closed his eyes. Muttering something in Wampanoag, he paced the room.

The basement stairs creaked, and Jack tore into the cellar. He hastened toward the table and stood at George's head. "I'm too late." His hands cupping George's face, he lowered to kiss his cousin's forehead. "Brother, 'tis Jack. I'm here." His soft baritone replaced the overwhelming dread with a semblance of calm. When Jack lifted his head, he met Annalisa's gaze and whispered something into George's ear. He removed his left hand from George's face and reached for her. "He will survive this."

She wanted to believe him, to know with certainty her most beloved brother wouldn't succumb to a festering stump. But nothing was certain. As she'd learned from George, nothing about life was as it seemed. Since 1775, they each, at least once, had danced and flirted with death; it was a matter of time before this war claimed at least one of them.

❧ *56* ❧

ANNALISA

TOPSFIELD, MAY 1781

A DEEP GROAN ECHOED from down the hall. *George survived the night.*

Annalisa rolled onto her side and exhaled a relief she never knew when caring for poor Mr. Peabody. *May his soul be at peace.* She wiped a rogue tear from her eye and peered beyond the casement. Birds chirped and chattered in the early morning grey. Beside her, dear Mary's figure rose and fell with each breath. At the foot of the canopied bedstead, Robby snuggled upon a small bed not far from Jane, who lay on the other side of Mary.

Annalisa slid from the coverlet and donned her front-lacing stays and blue dress. She marveled at the act with ironic bitterness; a decade ago, she'd slipped from this very room to don men's clothes and ride to Danvers for practice with the militia. Now, she crept down the hall to care for the brother who had prepared her to fight.

"Abbie?" She pushed open the door. Louisa sprawled beside George in the bed, and Abigail slumped in a chair. Her friend peered up as she entered the room.

"He's just fallen asleep," Abigail whispered. "I've not slept a minute."

"Go to my room. Jane and Mary are still sleeping. I'll watch him."

"Thank you." Abigail rose. "I'll only get a couple hours—"

"Sleep all day if you require it. I'll be here until you wake."

"Bless you, beloved friend." Abigail kissed her cheek, then left the room, glancing at George once more before disappearing down the hall.

Annalisa replaced her friend upon the wooden Windsor chair. George's chest rose and fell in steady rhythm beneath the coverlet. The clean linen about his stump, propped on a pillow, appeared to have recently been changed. *Poor Abbie. I'm certain she thought she was through changing bandages since leaving Washington's camp.*

A knock upon the chamber door stiffened her in her seat. "Come in."

Addy balanced a tray with a bowl of steamy broth and cup of tea. "Miss Annie, Quinn asked me to come aid Mr. George this morning."

"Oh, Addy, thank goodness for you." Annalisa stood and took the tray from her. "I know you and Quinn have done everything you could."

"He's unwell, Miss Annie, but he'll heal. Just like you did." Addy winked. "My magick, remember?"

Annalisa smiled. "Thank you." She placed the tray on a side table and hovered over the bed. Her brother's face, relaxed in gentle repose, hinted at neither pain nor anguish. Mayhap, in the healthy air of their parents' home, far from the sick tents of Washington's camps, he could heal.

"Pray, how is Sarah?" Annalisa asked. "Are you well situated at the Perkins'?"

"I've been staying at Mr. Quinn's with Mr. Perkins."

Annalisa perked at this. "Jack is at Quinn's?"

Addy nodded. "Yes'm. Since yesterday. He brought all his belongings from Perkins Estate. Says he won't return there so long as Lady Perkins is there."

Annalisa bit her lip. "He means to remain with Quinn until..."

"His house in New Castle is built, which should be by July, says he."

She pursed her lips to hide her frown. That house was supposed to have been their summer home. Now, he meant it to be his permanent residence. *Jack will move from town, away from his family...away from me.* Annalisa could hardly blame him; her dishonesty had been the root of it all, and she no longer wished to cause him pain. They'd both suffered plenty at the behest of those lies.

She focused on George. *It will not be long before he's again awake and in agony. Such was with Daniel Peabody.* With George recovering from his amputation and Mary's speech slow to return, she now had two siblings who required her attention. Even Henry had little energy to speak of all that had befallen them prior to and during their capture by the British. Her poor brother had been as mute as Mary since their return.

They were, each of them, broken.

Even William had endured capture and imprisonment at Ticonderoga. *This war has changed and ruined us all. We are, each of us, a martyr to the cause.*

Except Jane. Her thoughts turned to her older sister and what Lord Essex had said after her court-martial about Benjamin Cavendish. Jane had remained mostly unscathed by the war, or so it seemed. A knot returned to her stomach for the unknown she set aside, a truth perhaps more hideous than anything she had yet unveiled. Annalisa held her head. *Would that we defeat the British. Only then shall it all have been worth it.*

THAT EVENING, ADDY REPLACED HER AND ABIGAIL AT George's bedside so they could take Mary to George's tavern. Relieved to quit the somber homestead, Annalisa drew in the pleasant May evening air, lingering a moment longer outside the Whispering Willow before stepping indoors.

Henry and William sat with heads bent over tankards while Mr. Averill and Josiah, ever at the tavern, harmonized guitar with fiddle. Annalisa yearned for the sound of Jack's violin as she joined her brothers at their table. Only then did she contemplate her own lack of playing. Months had passed since she last touched a spinet.

Mary slid a chair beside Henry and rested her head on his shoulder. William poured Abigail and Annalisa a tankard of what she presumed to be a stock brown ale. She lifted the pewter and sipped the tangy, mildly sweet drink. *A rattle-skull.* Grateful for the strong concoction of ale and rum, she drank again, this time heartily for George.

"Sluice your gob," she said.

Her brothers and Abigail toasted.

The tavern door opened, and Oliver and Sarah entered with Jack and Quinnapin. Her heart fluttered at the sight of Jack, and she gulped the remainder of her rattle-skull. Mary sat upright and ran to Quinnapin, who scooped her into an affectionate embrace. Annalisa glanced at Abigail, who returned her smirk with a giggle.

"I've known it all along, dear friend."

Annalisa's spirits lifted at the sound of Abigail's girlish laughter, a sound she'd not heard in months. She could hardly prevent her own lips from curling with joy.

Mary returned to the table, her fingers laced with Quinnapin's. She met Annalisa's gaze and grinned. "He... loves me."

Annalisa melted at the sound of her sister's voice, no matter the delay, and caught Quinnapin's stare. He returned her regard with a similarly affectionate beam.

"It is true, Miss Anna. I have for quite some time."

"You certainly have our blessing, old friend," William said.

"My love for you both is without bounds," Annalisa replied. "I couldn't envisage a more perfect match."

Jack studied her for no more than a second or two before excusing himself to the hearth, where Mr. Averill and Josiah played. As Annalisa poured herself another rattle-skull, the sound of Jack's fiddle filled the tavern. She sipped her drink, and rested her head against the wall. Eyes closed, the notes and trills borne of his fingers washed over her, covering her forearms in goosebumps. A kindly hand rested over hers, and Annalisa opened her eyes.

Sarah beamed down at her. "We've news, too, Calais."

"What is it?" Annalisa straightened.

Sarah looked to Oliver, who grinned. "Mr. Oliver asked me to be his wife."

Annalisa gasped. "Oh, Sarah, congratulations."

"Zounds," Abigail cried. "Ollie, you said nothing to me."

Annalisa and Abigail jumped from the bench and crowded them. Sarah showed Abigail her ring, a lovely ruby set in gold.

"That is my papa's mother's ring," Abigail crooned. "How lucky! I know Jack gave Annie the sapphire—" She cupped her mouth. "I'm sorry. I mean not to bring it up...I only wonder if Jack still has the ring. 'Twas my mamma's mother's ring, my grandmama Bixby."

Annalisa shook her head. "I'm quite over him, I assure you. And I'm certain Jack still has the ring should he one day require it." She gathered Sarah's umber hand in hers and studied the jewelry. "'Tis beautiful. And you, Oliver, well done, indeed. I hope you know you've ensnared the heart of a most devoted and courageous young lady."

"Don't I know it." Oliver kissed Sarah. "She's made me become the man I always wished to be, and for that, I haven't the words to express…except that I knew I couldn't endure this life without her by my side."

"Then perhaps we'll have a double wedding come harvest." William gestured toward Mary and Quinnapin. "Or perhaps Christmastide."

Annalisa vibrated with elation. *My younger sister to marry Quinn, and Sarah to wed Ollie! What good fortune. Divine matches amidst such devastation.* She looked to Jack, who continued to play "The Parting Glass," and thought of George, who's oldest friend, Samuel, had succumbed to his own amputation in New York.

Her glass above her head, she said, "To the happy couples."

"Sluice your gob, rogues," Abigail shouted. To Annalisa, she whispered, "And to George. May he recover."

"Hear, hear!"

"Huzzah!"

Singing commenced as they fled the table to dance, but Annalisa remained behind with Abigail. A silent darkness settled over them despite the jovial news and cause for celebration; the war still raged on, and those they loved continued to suffer the consequences.

When Jack finished playing, he passed the fiddle to Josiah, who started "Dribbles of Brandy," and made his way to the table. He sat across from Annalisa and Abigail and poured himself a rattle-skull from the pitcher.

"Ladies." He toasted to them, then drank. "How fares my cousin?"

"He's as well as can be," Abigail replied.

Jack held Annalisa's gaze. "And how are you, Miss Annalisa?"

"As well as can be, sir."

With her forefinger, Abigail drew a circle about the rim of her tankard. "Jack, any news of Lord Essex?"

He shrugged. "I know not. The man's imprisoned with the Continentals."

"May he hang." Abigail finished her rattle-skull.

The ice behind her words chilled Annalisa, but she felt the weight of Abigail's curse. She, too, wished for him to hang.

"And Admiral Bixby?" Annalisa asked.

Abigail cocked her head. "What of my uncle?"

Jack relayed all he'd learned of their mother's letters to the admiral. "Should Mother receive another dispatch from him, Andrew said he will confiscate it."

Abigail shuddered. "To think her capable of such deceit."

Jack held Annalisa's unbridled stare. "Sometimes, those we most cherish are the ones who wholly damage us."

Annalisa stood. "Jack Perkins, I will live with my errors the rest of my days—a sentence far worse than hanging, I assure you—but I'll not remain here and listen to you compare me to the woman who murdered my—*our*—daughter. Good night, sir." She hastened from the table, past the keg vestibule, and out the rear door.

"Annie, wait!" Abigail shouted.

Jack followed, shoving the door as he passed. "Annalisa Howlett, stop where you are."

Unsure of why she obeyed his command, she froze until he clambered down the steps and stood before her.

"Let me be clear on one thing: I will never compare you to my mother. Is that understood?"

She nodded, hoping he might, perhaps, take her in his arms.

"That being said, you have utterly wrecked me, Annalisa Howlett. Damaged me beyond recognition. I have done everything for you. Everything within my power. Is it not clear how unbelievably, completely, fantastically in love with you I am? That I would cross the ocean to obtain a divorce petition issued by Lord Mansfield himself; that I would risk my life to find your betrothed to bring him home to you; and that I would, against my better judgment, choose to represent you at your court-martial after learning of your betrayal?

"No, I can't even consider your engagement to poor Mr. Peabody as a betrayal. That man was a saint, an innocent godsend whom neither of us deserved, and now he's gone because of us. But you betrayed me, Annalisa. You kept your secret of Benjamin Cavendish, hid it as though I were some sordid knave, unworthy of such information, or couldn't be trusted to learn it—then dueled me at Saratoga. I injured you, Annalisa, believing you some rogue! Do you even consider the guilt that eats at my conscience each time I revisit that horrid memory, made more diabolical knowing 'twas you? Why keep it from me when others were privy?" He counted upon his fingers, "Quinn. George. Abbie. Sarah. Ollie. Mary. Who else, *Cav*? Pray, who else!"

"N-No one."

His face reddened. "Oh, brilliant. Just marvelous. Nearly half the friends and family of our circle. I hope you realize I feel as betrayed by them as I do you, Annalisa. There is little, if any reason, for this to have been kept from me—"

"I—"

"I was your husband!" he cried. "Who else has been closer to you, than I? I implanted you with my seed. We created a child together, and yet you could not trust me?" Jack shook his head, then wiped his eyes. "Have I not offered myself to you in every way possible? Have I not shown you I worship the ground you walk upon? That I've longed for nothing but for you to stand beside me always as my partner *and* my equal?"

Annalisa trembled at his onslaught of words. "Y-Yes."

"That dream is dead."

She froze, as though plunged beneath the crackling ice of a half-frozen pond and left to sink into a black, brumal abyss. His kindness upon their return to town had been nothing but a pitiable display of degradation for her situation, an atonement, perhaps, for her dead betrothed, and disappointment for the time he wasted devoted to her all these years.

"It shall never happen." Jack turned from her. "I can hardly look at you. 'Tis as though I know you not at all. Forgive me, I lose myself. But this...whatever this is between us, is ended. I'm sorry." He disappeared around the tavern, and the breadth of all he'd said weighed upon her with the gravity of ten howitzer guns.

Annalisa crumbled to the ground, her face in her hands. The rear tavern door creaked open, then closed, and a convivial body scented in rose enfolded her in a silken embrace.

"Shh." Abigail clutched her to her breast. "I heard the whole of it. I'm so very sorry."

"He's right." Annalisa sobbed. "I deserve this. I never should've kept it from him."

"Fie. You did it to protect him. He doesn't know that—at least he hasn't understood it yet. Give him time. He'll realize it soon enough."

"I thought mayhap he did, after he cared for me when we returned home. But 'twas nothing but pity."

Silence settled over Annalisa with discomfiting gall, as Abigail's failure for words proved as common as snow in July. If her best friend and confidante could muster nothing to say on the matter, perhaps Annalisa had truly wounded Jack beyond repair. She disappointed not only herself, but the child they'd created who now rested eternally at Keihtánit's house. And for that, she could never forgive herself.

❧ *57* ❧

JACK

NEW CASTLE, THE PROVINCE OF NEW
HAMPSHIRE, AUGUST 1781

TWO MONTHS AFTER GEORGE'S leg amputation, Jack left Topsfield quite convinced of his cousin's recovery and eager to settle his new home at New Castle. Nothing could be more pleasant than summer by the sea—except for having Annalisa by his side.

Jack lingered by the kitchen hearth within his large, blue clapboarded home, his gaze fixed on the empty securement built for Annalisa's musket. The latest print of *The New Hampshire Gazette* collapsed in his fist, which referred to him as Portsmouth's most eligible bachelor. Wishing to toss the pages into a roaring fire, Jack turned from the cold, unlit bricks and made his way outside.

The Atlantic, a duplicitous lover, sparkled and swelled beneath a late-setting summer sun, as though the ocean had never caused him harm. A taunting view, like the house, for he could neither enjoy the sight nor the dwelling as he'd intended. But he could hardly have imposed upon Quinnapin much longer; the further he delayed, the harder it proved to leave Topsfield.

And Annalisa.

Even here, at the perceived end of the world, he could hardly escape her. "The sentence for my blind devotion." He removed his grandmother's gold ring from his pocket. The sapphire glimmered like the ocean below. Overcome with an urge to toss it into the waves, he willed himself to return it to his waistcoat pocket. Perhaps it might one day find its place upon another lady's hand. The thought, entirely reasonable, somehow felt impossible. *Portsmouth's most eligible bachelor.* He suppressed a derisive chuckle and tossed the newspaper into the breeze. It sailed on the wind until finally spiraling to the waves below. *Who, other than Annalisa, could ever wear this ring?* Jack turned his back on the sea, ready to return to the house for the evening.

Papa...

A small voice carried on the sea breeze, and he faced the fading Atlantic once more.

Papa, Mamma needs you. Please come home...

"Eliza, my darling?" He scoured the yard for his daughter and her tiny voice.

Come home, Papa.

"I can't, darling girl. What is it you wish of me?"

Come home, Papa. Mamma needs you.

The hair on his arms raised, and he hastened inside the house. His housekeeper, an older woman called Eloise, had already lit candles in the foyer and kitchen for the encroaching evening.

"Would you like a brandy, Lord Brunswick?" she asked.

"No—no, I don't drink brandy, ma'am." He hurried toward the staircase. "A glass of Bordeaux, please. And my pipe." Jack ran upstairs to his bedchamber and threw open the trunk at the foot of his canopied bed. He withdrew Annalisa's poetry book written by Margaret Cavendish. He flipped several pages to read her penciled script about Benjamin Cavendish.

Jack carried the small, tattered book from his chamber, down the stairs, and into the newly furnished parlor. He sat beside the cherry table where Eloise had neatly placed a glass of Bordeaux beside his pipe. The book in his lap, Jack settled in the chair and took up his wine. He flipped to the final page, a blank space without printed material, and re-read her scrawling pencil with fresh eyes:

> *Benjamin Cavendish knows me Better than Anyone in this Worlde.*
>
> *He is my Muse, my sence for living, my Sun in daytime and my Moon at night.*
>
> *He shall be Me, as I shall be him. One day, we shall live as One.*

"My Annalisa is Benjamin Cavendish." He closed the book. "She was all along."

Jack set down his glass of wine, then lit his pipe using the banked fireplace embers and a paper spill. He drew in several sips of the pipe, then expelled a long swirl of smoke. His head rested against the blue damask wingback chair, Jack closed his eyes.

How foolish I was. How blind, to believe Benjamin was Annalisa's lover and not she herself. Yet such an occurrence proved so aberrant, so uncommon a charade, he could hardly have supposed his Annalisa lived a second life as Benjamin Cavendish. *A fool I am, indeed.* As such an onerous consequence, he remained in his parlor alone, wishing his lady sat across from him to pass the evening. To dine each night in her absence proved trying, indeed, yet he would do so again tonight and each night thereafter. Such was the fate he had chosen for himself in rebuking Annalisa and her lies.

"My lord, dinner is served in the dining room."

Jack jerked from the chair, startled. The sun had set beyond the windows and purple twilight spilled into the room. "Yes, yes, of course. Thank you, Eloise." He tucked the small book into his waistcoat pocket, retrieved his half-finished glass of Bordeaux, and meandered from the light-blue-papered parlor into the ocean-blue-painted dining room. The scent of buttery baked cod reminded him of Annalisa's favorite dish: fish-and-cheese pudding.

His stomach soured. *Must everything remind me of her?*

A setting for one beckoned at the head of a long mahogany table meant for twelve. There, he sat and chewed his baked cod in silence, unable to contain his thoughts, nor his daughter's voice.

His meal half-eaten, Jack pushed aside the plate and beckoned for Eloise. "Please have my belongings packed for a week—no, a fortnight. And ready my horse."

"My lord, mean you to ride at this hour? Shall I not have your carriage prepared, sir?"

"No." Jack shook his head. "I ride at dawn."

❦

Jack arrived in Topsfield before nine o'clock. He trotted down the familiar lane. A fair day, though more humid than was favorable, he rode toward the Howlett farm. As he neared the twenty-acre property, the scent of woodsmoke permeated the air and large plumes of grey penetrated the azure sky. *Strange the Howletts should be burning a pyre this time of year...and so near their woodlot.* His heartbeat quickened to match the pace of his mare until thick smog and flames ebbed and swirled, obscuring his view of the late-summer farmland.

His stomach knotted, he galloped down the drive and

dismounted. The house, a large saltbox with central chimney, stood unaffected amidst billowing smoke. Jack hurried up the path as Annalisa, the Howletts, and her siblings evacuated the house.

Bright flames danced across the fields.

Jack tore from his coat, rolled his sleeves, and ran toward the barn. At the water pump, he met Henry, who sprinted from inside the barn with several wooden buckets.

"Let me." Jack grabbed two pails from him and pumped water. He handed the buckets to the Howletts' hired farmhands, Dane and Zeke, who scattered into the fields.

A third bucket filled, Jack hoisted it into the arms of the tallest member of the Howlett family. George, despite his left leg amputated below the knee two months prior, hobbled upon a wooden leg with one arm outstretched; the other leaned upon a wooden crutch.

"Give it to me, quickly," George roared.

"What's happened?" Jack handed another pail to Mr. Howlett.

"Henry, make haste to William's and have them sound the alarm," Mr. Howlett shouted over the roar of flames and disappeared into the smolder.

"I know not," George said, "but we woke to the sound of riders, followed by the scent of smoke."

Annalisa dashed toward them, her petticoats gathered between her legs.

"Quickly!" She reached for the pail Jack handed to George. "'Tis nearing the oak."

"Well, I'll be damned," George said.

Jack's chest tightened. "I'll go with you." He filled the remaining bucket as Dane and Zeke returned with theirs and sprinted into the smoke-filled fields.

58

ANNALISA
TOPSFIELD, AUGUST 1781

TWO LEAPS IN FRONT of Jack, Annalisa weaved with her bucket of water through the smoldering fields toward her sacred oak. Her heart pounded with each catapult of her legs, splashing cool water onto her arms and apron.

Not my tree. Not my Eliza. Not my tree. Not my Eliza...

Her lungs burned as she neared the edge of the property. Already, hot blazes and smoke engulfed the oak's low-hanging boughs. She tossed the water onto the branch upon which she so frequently sat. Behind her, Jack discharged his pail on the same limb.

"Robby, no!" Jane's shrill cry puckered Annalisa's skin despite the desperately hot, hazy air.

"Jane, where are you?" Annalisa flung her bucket and coughed. "I can't see you in this smoke."

"Mamma!" Robby's shriek lifted from somewhere near the oak's massive trunk.

Smoke ebbed and twirled about the tree, reminding her of Bunker Hill and Saratoga, lands imbued in sulfuric wartime fog. But this was no battlefield; this was her home.

Jack flew toward the sound of Robby's cries.

"Jack, no!" Annalisa reached for him as he ran past and disappeared between murky branches.

"Robby?" Jack's strained baritone rose from the smog, followed by a fit of coughing. "Robby!"

Annalisa retreated toward the tree's perimeter, where she, Mary, and Quinnapin hurled through the smoldering branches with three more buckets of water. They dumped them across a series of flames near the base of the tree.

Frozen amidst the opacity, Annalisa's chest stung with inhalation. Unable to speak, cry, or scream for her world, her tree, the hallowed place where her daughter rested and her niece and nephew played. Trembling, her fingers grazed the busk nestled within her stays, the relic Jack had carved for her from this very oak. *Our burning oak...*

William ran forth with his father-in-law, Mr. Perley, and his brother-in-law, Isaac. They each tossed water onto the burning tree. Shortly thereafter, Josiah and Mr. Averill joined, followed by Ezra Kimball, Mr. Andrews, Captain Gould, Elisha Porter, and others from town. They all heaved great buckets of water over the burning fields and the oak.

"Annie...come," Mary cried. "Now!" Her sister tugged her from the space by her favorite bough.

Mary's tortured voice severed whatever spell kept her. Annalisa gasped, as though returned to her body. No longer a passive observer of her farm's destruction, she turned in all directions and shouted, "Jack! Jane! Robby!"

"Salvage all you can. Salvage it all, dearest Mamma."

The little voice answered her from the base of the tree, which remained in obscurity beneath the oak's burning leaves. Her feet no longer planted to the earth, Annalisa hurled toward the mass of smoke when burly arms restrained her.

"Let me go." Annalisa writhed, but the arms gripped her tighter.

"I will not let you endanger yourself, Little One." George's bass surrounded her as he clutched her to his chest.

"Robby? Jane? Jack!" Annalisa screamed. Plumes of white filled the space beneath the oak's great canopy, a mixture of mist and smoke impeding her view of the trunk. "Jack, answer me, please!"

"Robby!" Jane's voice rasped.

"I'll retrieve them," George said.

"Not with that wooden leg." Quinnapin flung another bucket of water into the tree, but the act proved as futile as preserving a grain of sand upon a stormy beach. "I'll find them." He lunged into the smoking abyss.

Beyond the smoldering branches, Annalisa lingered for what felt to be an eternity but had been no more than two, perhaps three minutes, until Quinnapin emerged from the smog carrying Jane. As gently as he could, while maintaining haste, he laid her on the ground.

Mary wept. "Janey?" She knelt beside their older sister's unmoving form.

George released Annalisa and pursued Quinnapin inside the murky quagmire that had become the ancient oak.

Annalisa's conscience screamed to follow them, to help retrieve her nephew and Jack, but her attention wavered from the smoldering tree to her sister's motionless body upon the ground. *Janey...*

In a moment of clarity, Annalisa turned to Mary, who sobbed over Jane's body. "Mary, retrieve Will and Henry to help bring Jane inside. She needs a doctor."

Her sister's red face, streaked with tears, met her anxious stare. "She...she's dead."

Annalisa placed her ear to Jane's breast. Within, a rhythmic heartbeat sounded. "No, her heart still beats. Go, quickly!"

Mary rose from the ground and scurried away.

Her sister gone for help, Annalisa returned her attention to the tree, ready to bolt within for her brother and Quinnapin, when from the smog they emerged. Quinnapin hoisted Jack over his shoulder, and George hobbled with Robby, limp, in one arm.

"Robby." Annalisa sprinted toward them. Her nephew coughed into George's chest as he adjusted the boy in his arms. "Jack." Annalisa placed a hand on his sooty cheek. "You can't leave me like this, Jack Perkins."

Quinnapin hauled Jack to the ground where Jane had been. In the distance, Henry and William carried her back to the house, the last structure of their homestead unaffected by raging fires.

Annalisa crouched over Jack, her face to his chest. The faint scent of amber barely tickled her nose over the acrid smoke. Her cheek rose and fell against his chest in a slow, steady rhythm.

"Take Robby." George handed her the boy. "I need to help get Jack inside with Quinn."

"They were trapped in the tree." Quinnapin wiped his face of sweat and ash. Together with George, they lifted Jack from the ground and hauled him toward her house.

She peered down at her nephew. "Sweet Robby. I would do anything to preserve your life, darling boy." Tears dripped onto his little face and coursed through the soot coating his cheeks.

"Annie, give me him." Abigail huffed, clutching her skirts. "The doctor is here." She scooped Robby from her lap and rushed back toward the house, leaving Annalisa alone.

She faced her house. The burning tree behind her, Annalisa wrapped her arms about her torso and sobbed. Overhead, dark storm clouds consumed the red sun. A crack of summer thunder followed a flash of lightning, and cooling rain pelted the farm.

The commotion faded, and Annalisa held her face in her hands. *I should die here. Let me join you, Eliza.*

"Divine Providence graces us with rain. The farm may yet be saved." Her father's hands pulled her to her feet.

"Oh, Papa." Annalisa wept into his chest. "How has this happened? Have not you seen Jane and Robby?" *And Jack.*

Papa hugged her. "Let's inside. There's nothing more we can do. What damage is done, is done." He held her at arm's length. "Let me tell you here and now, if ever a traitor I shunned, I have become one today. Damn him, King George."

"Redcoats?"

"Aye, moppet. I saw them through the woodlot as they rode toward town."

He's not called me that since I was a little girl. Annalisa frowned, knowing it wasn't Redcoats who burned their homestead, but far more likely, culprits hired by Lady Perkins.

Papa placed his arm about her and led her toward the house. If ever there could be a silver lining to such devastation, Papa's allegiance to the cause rang across the farm with such bitterness that not even General Washington, nor his army, could contain it. *A hefty sacrifice, in the name of war. But we must be victorious now.*

59

ANNALISA

TOPSFIELD, AUGUST 1781

ANNALISA AND PAPA MET George at the front door. He leaned heavily on his cane, his green-eyed gaze flickering between them in earnest. "Pa, Robby's awake, but Jane is slow to rouse."

Papa kissed Annalisa's temple. "Stay strong, though I fear I needn't remind you." He winked and lumbered up the stairs.

A small wave of relief lightened the boulder of torment within her. *Is Papa proud of me, at long last?* When he disappeared upstairs, Annalisa faced George. "Where's Jack?"

"The drawing room."

Her breath caught. "And?"

"He's awake—"

"Thank God." She flew past George, but he grabbed her wrist.

"He can't see, Annie. The heat and smoke burned his eyes." George's frown deepened. "I wished to warn you." He released her arm, and she fled down the hall to the drawing room.

Jack lay on the sofa.

Quinnapin placed a wet muslin cloth over the upper half

of his face. Only the tip of his nose and shapely lips remained visible of the handsome face she so adored. Jack swallowed, bobbing the Adam's apple beneath his sculpted chin.

"Is it Robby?" he croaked. "Where's the boy?"

"'Tis Miss Anna." Quinnapin motioned for her to approach, then stood. "He needs rest," he murmured, then slipped from the drawing room.

Jack's mouth twisted. "Annie?"

She drew near him and knelt. "George said Robby's awake. He's upstairs."

Beyond the casement, a flash of lightning brightened the room, followed by a roll of thunder as rain pattered the windowpanes. Jack's hand reached out, and she clasped it.

"Darling girl, will you play for me?" Jack wheezed.

"Of course." Another clap of thunder rattled the house. "What shall I play?"

He hesitated. "Whatever pleases you."

Annalisa moved to the spinet and started the *adagio* from Mozart's Second Piano Sonata. The smoky room filled with somber cadences and trills, and she recollected the day when, in that very space, she first played this piece for him. He'd been as entranced by it as she. Now, she prayed this music be the only physick he required.

She played the final notes and glanced outside at the raging storm. The flames had long since extinguished, leaving white squalls of mist over the farm. *At least nothing burns.*

"Make your peace," Jack rasped. "Go to Jane."

A lump returned to her throat. "Surely, you can't mean..."

"She will not...survive this. Go to her. Else you will regret it."

"I—"

"Your music fills me with ease." He coughed. "You've done enough for me. Please go to Jane."

Annalisa rose from the bench and quit the room.

Quinnapin lingered near the longcase clock with Mary, whose red-rimmed eyes flooded with tears.

"Oh, Annie." Mary sobbed into Quinnapin's chest. "Jane..."

Her heart rattling, Annalisa scrambled upstairs. She hesitated before opening the door to the room they shared. A quick breath, and she unlatched the door. Upon their bed canopied in toile-patterned fabric, Jane rested with Mamma perched beside her.

"Come in, Annalisa, darling."

Rain clattered against the casement. Beyond the glass, white plumes drifted across the fields. As Annalisa neared the bed, she appreciated Jane's delicate form. Red burns scalded her perfectly porcelain cheeks, neck, and hands; blisters erupted upon her rosebud lips, poised and parted to inhale, but rather a high-pitched wheeze escaped.

"Oh, Janey." Annalisa blinked away the tears as she joined her mother and sister on the bed. "Jane Howlett, you can't leave us so soon."

Her sister's soft tongue moistened her bottom lip, and she opened her crusted eyes. Always icy blue as their mother's, they shimmered like the Ipswich River in springtime, a broken dam from which her entire self flooded and drowned.

"You flatter me..." Her lilting soprano croaked like a frog's. "When I deserve nothing but shame and misery."

Annalisa cupped her sister's burnt hand as if rescuing a small bird. "Jack told me everything. 'Twas by Lady Perkins's hand, not yours, I lost my Eliza." She sucked in a breath and exhaled, as though to bequeath new life into her sister. "I forgive you."

"I deserve it not, but I shall accept it." Jane grimaced and tightened her hand about Annalisa's. "You must have Robby. Please."

"Oh, Janey." Mamma sniffled and wiped her eyes.

"Don't speak like that," Annalisa said. "You will survive this—"

"I don't wish to survive."

"Janey." Mamma's hand smoothed Jane's black tresses.

"I...apologize, Annie. For everything. Had I never been... so consumed, so...blind..."

"We know things now we knew not before," Annalisa replied. "Lady Perkins is not who we believed her to be."

"But I should never...have followed her," Jane whispered.

Teardrops dripped from Mamma's face onto the pillow supporting Jane's head. "Bette was my closest friend. You had no reason to mistrust her." Mamma swiped her handkerchief across her cheeks. "'Twas I who was blinded, my darling girls. 'Tis I."

Annalisa reached for Mamma's free hand. "Let us be at peace with it."

"This is...Lady Perkins's doing," Jane wheezed. "She did this...to the farm."

A frigid coil curled its way down Annalisa's spine despite the August heat. "Yes, she'd threatened me with as much if I married Jack."

Mamma gasped. "She did?"

Annalisa nodded, unsure if Mamma could handle the truth of Lady Perkins's threat to burn the farm if she refused to marry Mr. Peabody. And yet she'd done it regardless. *But what, if any reason, spawned such a torrent of misdirected actions upon us now?*

"She...meant to...punish us, for what I did."

"Janey, hush. You must rest." Mamma continued smoothing Jane's hair. "Think not of why such tremendous misfortune befell us today."

"'Twas her," Jane croaked. "The truth about her...was revealed. This...was her way." Jane's grip tightened upon Annalisa's hand. "I did, Annie. I told Lord...Essex, about

Benjamin Cav...Cavendish. I was awake...that night. After Bunker Hill. At Lord Brunswick's on...Tory Row. I overheard you...speaking with George. 'Twas when I learned that name. But I never...I never thought he would...remember it. Use it against us. He told...Lady Perkins. He told...his friend Admiral...Bixby. 'Tis the admiral...the admiral's hand. His... orders." Jane coughed and hacked, expelling droplets of blood across her lower lip.

Mamma crooned, "Peace, Janey—"

"Admiral Bixby...is Lady Perkins's...confidante. Her collaborator." Jane rested her head back and closed her eyes. "She told him to find...a captain. Admiral Bixby found... Captain Fleming. Lord Essex paid Captain Fleming...to turn coat...to sail you and Jack...to Halifax. Lady Perkins asked Lord Perkins...to block the courts with Jack's...divorce petitions. She arranged your...engagement to Mr. Peabody."

"Janey, please," Mamma wailed.

"To be rid of Annie. It has all been...her. And now...she burned our farm. Our home."

Mamma's head bowed as she heaved. "I'm so ashamed. I never saw any of this. I never protected you, my Janey. Either of you."

Dizzy and sickened, Annalisa squeezed Mamma's hand. "I forgive you, too, Mamma. You knew not of what she was capable."

"You grant me mercy where I deserve none, my Annalisa."

"It causes me far more pain to cling to grievances than to release them in the name of compassion. Creator knows I've been punished enough for my sins, and I pray today's disaster be the last atonement for all our family's hubris throughout this war. I can endure little more."

Jane's countenance, despite her gruesome, blistering burns, softened. "My conscience is light. May you keep

Robby, Annie. Love and protect him...as I would. Promise me."

"I promise. I swear it," Annalisa whispered.

Jane's eyes closed, and she drifted into blissful repose with little breath to lift her chest.

Mamma wailed, and Annalisa crumpled over her body and wept for the sister she'd not had until her final breath; for the sisterly affection of a repaired relation gone too soon; for the son Jane left behind; and for the wasted opportunity to redeem herself of her sins.

At least Robby lives. Her death is not in vain. I swear to you, Janey, I'll love him as my own. For you and for Jack, if he should have me.

60

ANNALISA

TOPSFIELD, AUGUST 1781

T HE LATE-SUMMER HEAT AND buzz of cicadas surrounded Annalisa as she gathered with her family at the town churchyard. Perched between George and Abigail—who clutched her hand—and Louisa, Annalisa studied the six-foot-deep hole keeping her sister. Spellbound by the uncanny horror of laying Mr. Peabody to rest, she quaked to know that, somehow, Jane's death pinched harder. *I never truly learned to understand you, Janey. I, too, was blind.* She blinked several times.

At the bottom of the hole, Jane lay hidden within the wooden casket, obscuring all from her heinous wounds. For that, Annalisa sighed, relieved Jane could be remembered for her beauty in life, not the damage she'd found in death.

At the foot of the site, Mary, tucked between Henry, William, and Martha, wiped her tears. Across the grave, Oliver and Tommy stood with Jack. His eyes bandaged, he clung to Robby, who miraculously bore little suffering from the event, save for a productive cough that filled the church-yard throughout the sermon. Annalisa couldn't help but wonder if Eliza had somehow shielded the boy as he barricaded himself high in the oak's branches. *Tommy and Robby, poor boys, now motherless.* And yet the promise she'd made Jane quaked her breast. Of course she could love Robby as her own. But she never would replace the boy's natural mother.

Behind Jack and Robby, Lord Perkins and Andrew gathered without Lady Perkins and the two younger Perkins girls, Charlotte and Susan—a curious absence, one that Mamma would certainly notice.

Reverend Cleaveland adjusted his frizzed periwig and droned on with the final words of his funeral sermon from the Book of Common Prayer: "We therefore commit this body to the ground, earth to earth, ashes to ashes, dust to dust; in sure and certain hope of the Resurrection to eternal life."

George leaned on his cane, shifting his weight. "Will you grab me some dirt, Little One?"

Annalisa bent and grasped two fistfuls of soil, pouring one into her brother's giant hand. One by one, they each tossed earth upon the coffin, planting Jane within the ground, a gesture reminding her of the day she and Quinnapin had rooted Eliza beneath the oak.

Tommy held Oliver's hand, studying the scene with apparent thoughtfulness. He and Oliver knelt and tossed their dirt upon Jane's coffin. Robby wailed into Jack's chest after their earth missed the coffin, and together they turned from the gravesite.

"Wait for me," Annalisa whispered to Abigail. Her conscience thick with her promise to Jane, she sneaked over to them.

"Robby." Annalisa knelt and wiped the tears from his cheeks.

"Aunee Annie." Robby howled into her breast.

"Robby, your mamma is resting with God. She will live in eternal bliss in heaven."

Having abandoned her Christian God years ago, the words saddened her as she said them, wishing for Jane to join Eliza and baby Edward at Keihtánit's house. But Jane's unwavering faith in God and Christ had served her well in life; it must be so for her in death. In this, Annalisa took comfort, no matter where Jane's soul took her.

"I can stomach little more of this," Jack said. "Might you guide us back to the carriage?"

"Of course." A whiff of his amber perfume caught her by surprise as she held his elbow. Her heart aflutter, she took Robby's hand and walked them to Lord Perkins's carriage. A quick lift, and she settled her nephew inside.

"I'm quite well from here," Jack said. "Thank you."

"Will you take Robby back to New Castle with you?" she asked.

He grimaced. "I can hardly care for myself in my present condition. I will return to my parents'."

Annalisa shivered at his icy tone, though she despaired he must stay with his insufferable mother whilst he recovered. "I might go to New Castle with you. To help."

Jack pursed his shapely lips. "I appreciate your offer, Miss Annalisa, but I must decline it."

She bristled. "You've little reason, *Lord Brunswick*." Incensed by his stubbornness, she added, "I merely offer aid, not myself, sir. We shan't make that mistake. Again."

The color rose in Jack's cheeks, but he said nothing. With one hand, he felt for the carriage, then stepped within.

Annalisa retreated from the vehicle as Lord Perkins and Andrew approached.

Jack's father tipped his hat. "Miss Annalisa, I have no words to adequately express my sorrow and condolences. I'd say these are trying times, but the situation is extraordinary and beyond measure."

"Thank you, sir. Your kindness is most appreciated, as always."

Lord Perkins kissed her hand, then stepped into his carriage, followed by Andrew, who offered a heartfelt embrace before disappearing inside. Wheaton, the Perkinses coachman, closed the door. The horses snorted, and the vehicle jolted away from the churchyard.

Annalisa watched them disappear down the road, her insides quivering with remorse. She suspected her use of the formal address had bruised Jack, but not nearly as much as the callous way she'd spoken of their love story. Her heart in her throat, she wished to retract it, to cup his face and lift the fabric keeping his precious eyes from her. If only a kiss upon those eyelids could restore his sight, she would never leave his side. And on this vulnerable day, she so hoped he would reveal why he had come to the farm that day—why, when he'd been removed from Topsfield more than a fortnight, he'd arrived to her family's farm at so auspicious a time. His appearance that day was as though summoned by an unknown entity.

Or Eliza. Oh, please let his sight return to him. It must.

Oliver and Tommy met her in the lane as they awaited his family's second carriage. "'Tis a most abominable day," he said. "Truly diabolical."

"Aye." She peered at him. "Losing my sister has elicited all manner of convoluted feelings. I'm sure you feel such, too, sir."

Oliver kept his gaze on the road. "Jane was a good mother to our son. I only regret that which I could not give her in our marriage."

"A title?" Annalisa smirked.

"Aye." Oliver chuckled. "And land." He ran a hand over Tommy's blond head. "Perhaps the marriage would've ended differently had I not been presumed dead."

"It would've never ended at all," Annalisa replied. "Jane

never would've been wed to Jack had I not been presumed dead as well."

"Such charades are now behind us." Oliver straightened his coat. "I'm well rid of old memories and keen to build new ones. But Tommy here shall remember his dear mamma well, won't you?"

Tommy nodded but said nothing. Too young, perhaps, to grasp the finality of losing his mother. Though Annalisa hoped the five-year-old would remember Jane well. If not, she vowed to recount only good memories for her nephew. It was the least she could do to keep her sister's memory alive. *And for Robby.*

61

ANNALISA

TOPSFIELD, AUGUST 1781

THAT EVENING, ANNALISA RODE to George's tavern to mourn and celebrate Jane's short life. Her older brother sat at his table with wooden leg propped on a chair to ease the swelling, his rescue efforts at the farm having exacerbated all that had healed. Now, he leaned his head against the wall while Abigail pressed her cheek to his shoulder and closed her eyes. Mary, Quinnapin, and Henry silently drank cider with William and Martha. Annalisa marveled at her sister-in-law's round belly. *Little Fanny will be a big sister. When one life is taken, another begins. If 'tis a girl, mayhap they'll call her Jane.*

"I'm sickened to think my mamma played such a role in the destruction of your farm," Abigail muttered. "Think you Jane can be believed? Even upon her deathbed?"

Annalisa frowned. "I mean to trust her. She had little reason to lie."

"Fie." George slammed his mug, and a spattering of cider covered the table. "I need to find my uncle. If his men did this, *he* shall pay. And it will be by my challenge."

"George Howlett, no." Abigail smacked his shoulder.

"Have not you danced enough with death? We've a child to care for, and I nearly lost you from that leg. I shan't worry for you again."

"Abbie's right," William said. "You need rest, George. Recover fully and allow your leg to heal."

George chuckled. "*Wilhelmina,* worry not for me. If I survived this leg, I will endure anything. But upon Jane's death, I'll locate Admiral Bixby and challenge him."

"But what of my mother?" Abigail cried. "According to Jane, 'twas by her hand she wrote the admiral. 'Twas she who orchestrated the destruction of your farm. Can we not hold my mamma accountable and keep you from another ill-fated venture?"

"But...she's your...mamma." Mary's chin quivered. "What can be...done?"

Annalisa reached for Mary and rubbed her arm. "'Tis nothing you must worry about."

Henry set down his mug and licked his parted lips. "George, your admiral is somewhere in the southern colonies. As is Cornwallis." Her youngest brother's gentle voice rose above the group, only to continue as though he'd not withheld his voice from them these several months. "Last I heard, his army marched north, toward Virginia, in pursuit of General Greene."

"Henry," William cried. "How came you by such knowledge?"

Henry shook his head. "I will speak no more of my contact at Oyster Bay. 'Twas by one wanton tongue Mary and I were seized on our journey to Philadelphia."

"Zounds." Abigail held her face. "When shall this war be ended? I can handle little more."

The front door opened and closed, and Oliver guided Jack inside the tavern. Sarah led them to the table about which they gathered and pulled a chair for Jack.

"Where's Abbie?" Jack sat. "Is she here?"

Abigail reached for him. "I'm here, Brother."

"Mother's left town."

Abigail gasped. "Left? Whither did she go?"

"Halifax," Oliver said. "I know 'tis where she went, though we've little proof."

"How? And with Papa?" Abigail asked.

"He's home with Andy," Jack replied. "But Mother took Susie and Charlotte, no doubt to shield them from all this horror. I fear 'tis too little, too late. They've seen and heard too much."

"With whom do they travel?" Abigail asked. "Our uncle?" She caught George's harried glare. "Is Admiral Bixby sailing up the coast to meet her?"

"I know not." Jack leaned back in his chair. "Father and I returned home from the funeral to his house empty of the women. 'Tis all we know."

"Well, I'll be damned," George groaned. "Cousin, I'm locating our uncle and challenging him. There's little any of you may say to stop me."

"Zounds." Jack offered a sinister chuckle. "Then I'm going with you."

"You're mad, both of you," Quinnapin chimed from beside Mary.

"Fie!" George roared. "A blind man!"

"And you, a cripple!" Jack slammed the table and stood. "Be damned, George Howlett. My sight may have been taken from me, but I'll not remain here, feeble. Not when 'twas my relation who ordered your family's farm burned and your sister—my former wife and mother of my son—slain."

"'Tis *our* relation," George muttered. "And by my hand, I'll avenge Jane and my family."

Henry, William, Oliver, and Quinnapin shouted over Jack and George, who resounded louder than the other. When the tavern bellowed with jeers and insults flown from the mouths of the men she loved most, Annalisa slammed the table, silencing them all.

"Fie, enough," she cried. "Both of you, be damned! Jack, your sight is marred; George, you've one leg. Buffoons, both of you, to travel alone. If you insist on ending yourselves on a fool's errand, I will accompany you, and there's little you may say to assuage me otherwise."

"You dare threaten us with Benjamin Cavendish?" George bellowed. "After your imprisonment and court-martial, no less."

"'Tis more than what either of you may offer," she cried.

"Annie, no." Abigail brushed her arm. "Please. Louisa needs her auntie. As do Tommy and Robby."

"The three of you are mad," William said. "Is your blood-lust so great you've not learned a thing since this war's inception? Please, for all that is still good in this world," he gestured to his pregnant wife, Martha, who sat silent among them, "have some reason, some semblance of common decency. How will Mother and Father be if you, Annie, or you, George, should come to meet your end so quickly after they just buried Jane?" He held his face to ward off the timorous motion of his body. "I...can't..."

Mary's gentle hand rested on William's shoulder. "Peace, Will."

"And what of Lord Essex?" Abigail shuddered. "What if you encounter him on your travels?"

George growled, "He's imprisoned, Abbie. That dilberry will hang if he hasn't already."

"That may be so," Henry uttered. "But 'tis unlikely you'll locate Admiral Bixby. He may well be stationed off the coast of one of the southern colonies, either North Carolina or Virginia. But Annie's right. 'Tis a fool's errand. We've just lost one sister. Must you risk yourselves as well, in the name of vengeance?"

William lifted his face to the table, his pale blue eyes rimmed in red—eyes he shared with both Mamma and Jane. Martha handed him her handkerchief, and he wiped his tears. "I think you seek glory in dying like a martyr, George. Lord knows your penchant for battle and justice. I've admired it my entire life...admired *you* my entire life. But dying is easy, Brother. Being spared to live is harder. But I do believe it worth it."

Silence spilled across the table, filling the space with an overwhelming deluge of despair for the ruin of her beloved farm and death of her sister. Jane had died for no cause at all, leaving two boys motherless.

As though hearing her despondent thoughts, Jack said, "My son and Ollie's are now without a mother. Jane had her flaws, but neither did she deserve to perish the way she did. I'm tormented by the event. I meant to save her and I failed. I made it to Robby first; he was tucked in the tree. But Jane could not climb up it to retrieve him. She clung to the lowest branch, clutched it so tightly I could hardly remove her. In that moment, I wished she had your tenacity, Annalisa. She would've flown up those branches the way I've seen you climb these ten years. Had she not been so preoccupied by Society and her reputation—at the behest of my own mother and yours, mind—had she climbed the oak with you, Annalisa, and not stayed inside your parlor perfecting needlepoint, I ponder—no, I know she would've survived this. We failed her...our great Society failed her. She trusted my own mother, who failed her...and yours."

Annalisa shook her head. "And to think, all these years I disappointed Mamma with my charades in the clearing. No thanks to you, George. Would that I had gone after Janey.

Had I known Robby was tucked within our oak's branches, I would have climbed them myself."

"We can't alter the past, but we may carve our future, Miss Anna," Quinnapin said.

Annalisa studied George. His square jaw was set, and his arms crossed his broad chest. She knew he would hunt his uncle, with or without her. Across the table, beside Oliver, Jack chewed his bottom lip, perhaps contemplating all William and Henry and Abigail had said; perhaps he re-lived his failures as both husband and father. Her family's concerns weighed heavily on her, but there was little she could do to stop George. Allowing him to leave was entirely worse than not going with him, though she neither wished to ride nor travel again so soon.

She licked her dry lips. "George, Jack, I've a more honed eye than either of you." She rose from the bench. "Gentlemen, we ride at dawn."

62

ANNALISA

VIRGINIA, LATE SEPTEMBER 1781

HER HEART ACHING FOR the loss of both her sister and farm, Annalisa heralded their expedition south cloaked as Benjamin Cavendish. The journey spanned several weeks as George relearned to ride with his wooden leg, and Jack, with vision spoiled by blur and shadows, required much guidance. *How foolish they were to believe they could complete such a venture in my absence.*

Through Delaware and Maryland, reports of Washington's army marching south with Rochambeau spread through various inns and taverns at which they rested. By the time they reached Virginia, George insisted they camp along the outskirts of towns to save money for their return north. Jack, who possessed both rank and a title, kept more money than either of them knew, but said little to alter George's mind. Perhaps he, too, enjoyed the freedom and privacy his own dwelling afforded him. After sharing a bed with four strangers at each inn they stayed, Annalisa, too, welcomed camping.

Evening fell. Rapt by the dancing flames of their campfire, Annalisa startled at the canteen George handed her. She drank. The cheap rum burned her throat into her stomach, and she coughed.

"Wibble, indeed."

Jack and George laughed.

"We'll have you wrapped in warm flannel in no time, Little One," George guffawed.

"I'd rather a nice mugful of flip," she replied. "That rum is vile."

Jack, flush with liquor, sang:

> *"There once was a ship that put to sea*
> *The name of the ship was the Billy O' Tea*
> *The winds blew up, her bow dipped down*
> *Oh blow, my bully boys, blow."*

George bellowed a deep belly laugh and joined, his bass voice rumbling.

Annalisa laughed and added her contralto. When they finished singing, George handed her the canteen.

"To the spirit of Samuel. Would that he could teach us more shanties. Fill to me the parting glass, old rogue."

"Hear, hear." They saluted their fallen friend.

George finished the rum and extended his wooden leg away from the fire. "We need to seek Washington's camp and join them. Should the commander in chief hold my audience and grant me what I ask, Cav and Jack, you will fall under my command. Then at least we'll have the protection of the army when finally we meet Admiral Bixby."

Annalisa shook her head. "How can you be certain Washington will grant you anything with your leg? I think it best we continue on our own. I'm hardly at leisure to be uncovered again within an army encampment."

"Washington offered plenty to that turncoat traitor Arnold after his wound at Saratoga," George barked. "And

I've done nothing but offer myself to this cause since the siege at Boston. Nay, Lexington and Concord."

Annalisa bit her lip. Her brother was right. He deserved far more than had been offered him for his service throughout the war, but so had many others similarly griped. *Such was the downfall of Peggy Shippen and her husband.* She shifted her gaze across the fire to Jack, who sat in contemplative silence.

"If *Cav* is discovered, she will end gaoled again," Jack said. "I can't allow that to happen."

"We won't allow it to happen," George replied. "We'll merely march with the army until we reach whatever destination they've chosen, which will undoubtedly lead us to the British. 'Tis the safest way for us to continue as we near the admiral and his fleet of dilberries."

With a shake of his head, Jack sighed. "I can hardly refute you, but I shall never forgive myself if she is uncovered for all that she is."

"And what is that, sir?" Annalisa asked.

"A woman I deeply cherish." Jack rose from the fire. "I'm retiring. Good night." He fumbled his way to his dwelling, a sign his sight improved.

She followed him. "Jack Perkins."

"Please leave me be."

Annalisa frowned. Small glimmers of his affection shone through when she least expected it, but still he refused her.

"Cav, leave him be," George said.

She returned to the campfire and settled beside her brother.

"Give him time," he murmured.

"I don't expect him to ever forgive this lie. Though I'm relieved he finally accepts this—" She gestured to her breeches.

George laughed. "'Tis no easy challenge, Little One. But your journey has just begun."

63

GEORGE

YORKTOWN, VIRGINIA, OCTOBER 1781

THE SECOND WEEK OF October, they arrived outside Yorktown, Virginia, exhausted but riveted. Or at least George remained so. The nearer they drew to Washington's camp, his spirit vibrated with the bloodlust of war. Overcome by the potential for imminent battle, even thoughts of Admiral Bixby flew from his mind. He ordered Jack and Annalisa to remain at least a mile outside the encampment while he rode forth, a plan to rejoin Washington driving him forward.

And as though by some design of divine Providence, a familiar voice called out to him.

"Captain Howlett!" Bartlett, his rotund friend from the New York campaign, waved.

George galloped toward the fellow and dismounted. "'Tis Major Howlett now, you old dandy." He embraced Bartlett.

Bartlett's round face flushed. "Major, it does me well to see you." He glanced down, frowning. "Your leg! What's befallen you since last we met?"

"Far too much, but I found myself at Charleston. Then,

making my way north, I endured the wrath of Bloody Ban at the Waxhaws. After that, the Cowpens."

"My God." Bartlett shook his head. "I pray this all ends here. In fact, I daresay it must. Else this war is doomed."

"There's been a battle, no?"

"Aye, since September the twenty-eighth," Bartlett replied. "Are you seeking to join? I'm certain the commander in chief will have you. He always did favor you."

"Will you take me to his headquarters?"

"I'll try to find someone who might admit you." Bartlett led him within the camp.

After about an hour of lingering outside Washington's headquarters awaiting Barlett to return, George spotted that squeeze crab Alexander Hamilton as he stepped from Washington's marquee tent.

"Sir," George called after him. "Mr. Hamilton."

The dandy turned and quirked a brow. "Major Howlett?"

"Aye, sir. Pray, might you take me to the commander in chief?"

Hamilton wavered, his gaze lingering a moment too long upon George's leg. "This way." He admitted George into the marquee tent.

General Washington sat at a desk, his countenance long. He peered up from his dispatches and met George's audience with stern disposition. "Major Howlett. Do sit."

"Sir, I am your most obedient servant." George bowed, then hobbled to a chair.

"It seems you recovered well from the trial at West Point, Major Howlett. This does me good to see. What brings you to Yorktown? Yet I suppose I'm unsurprised to see you here."

"Sir, 'tis my hope to join." He glanced at the obvious hindrance, which Hamilton still perseverated upon from behind the general. "I realize I may prove less than formidable in commanding a militia with my leg. However, I believe the artillery, under Knox's command, would suit me well, sir."

General Washington remained silent as he considered George's proposition. "We mean to overtake British redoubts nine and ten. I've ordered a second parallel to be dug tonight. Such will bring us four hundred yards closer to their line. They've scuttled their ships, at least a dozen, I've been informed, including HMS *Guadelupe*. Across the York River, de Choisy is at Gloucester Point, positioned behind Tarleton, blocking his retreat—"

"Lest he swims the river," Hamilton quipped.

"They're quite surrounded," Washington said. "Think you'd like to witness British surrender?"

George vibrated with a hope he'd not felt since the siege at Boston. "Aye, sir. More than anything. I've been healing since my amputation in springtime. I daresay I'm well enough to serve you at my best. One final time."

"Your best, Major?" Hamilton chuckled. "Your best had four limbs."

Washington ignored the remark and replied, "Very well. Major Howlett, you may join the artillery under Brigadier General Knox."

The general wrote upon a fresh page and signed. "The ledger, if you please." General Washington motioned for him to sign. George scribbled, though a tightness beset him; this would be the final time he signed anything for General Washington, save for perhaps an honorable discharge from the military.

"Thank you kindly, sir."

Washington nodded. "It does me well to see you, Major Howlett. Dare I admit to be...cautiously optimistic?

"'Tis well-earned optimism, sir, but Cornwallis persists," George replied.

"Indeed, he does. Good day, Major." Washington returned

to his writing, but before George quit the tent, his commander in chief looked up. "Major, do give my regards to your sister Miss Annalisa and Lord Brunswick."

George returned to Jack and Annalisa by nightfall. They'd set up camp and a small, crackling cookfire a half mile southwest of Washington's camp. Annalisa sat between Jack's legs as he plaited her long, curling hair.

"Lord Brunswick, have you become a doxy?"

Jack straightened and laughed. "'Tis quite the task with modest sight, but I've been able to differentiate between her hair's color and mine." He finished the braid and tied the ends.

"Ah, then there's a purpose." George guffawed. He settled across from them and stretched his unadulterated leg. "I've been admitted to the artillery under Knox. They've been engaging in battle since the twenty-eighth and mean to overtake redoubts nine and ten. They're surrounded, Jack. The Lobsterbacks cannot win."

"And the ships?" Jack asked.

"Scuttled."

"Then perhaps your uncle is nearer than we thought," Annalisa said.

"Aye, 'tis my guess as well," George replied.

"Shall we seek him out on the morrow?" Jack asked. "I don't wish to engage in battle with my sight as it is."

George tamped away his desire to fight one last battle against the Lobsterbacks. *My last will be against that bastard Admiral Bixby.*

Since Concord in April of 1775, he'd fought the British, witnessed hundreds of men fall, including his oldest friend, Samuel. Now, Washington and Rochambeau sat poised for what George felt certain must be the battle to end it all. After six years of cannonade and musket-fire, hunger and disease, injury and loss, with some victories peppered in for morale, it had all landed him upon this bit of land overlooking the York River. And his uncle's fleet, most certainly bobbing offshore.

"Aye. We seek him on the morrow."

As fate would have it, the following day dawned with booming cannonade in the distance. George sat upright and gathered his blankets as his leg would allow, then roused his sister and Jack from their slumber. "Come, ready yourselves at once."

George gathered his effects and slung Bixby over his shoulder. Had he two sturdy legs to walk upon, he would have marched directly to where the artillery made their stand before Jack and Annalisa even packed their belongings. But his sister, spry upon two slender limbs, burst forth with as much energy as she had the afternoon he'd first taught her to fire Bixby.

"Private Cavendish." George suppressed a grin.

Jack reached for Annalisa. "I believe I can make the march to camp without much assistance."

When they arrived, men from across the colonies mingled alongside the French. An array of accents and clothing colored the encampment like he'd never before experienced. His body tingling with anticipation, George scoured the artillery camp for his old friend from Boston, Henry Knox.

Rather portly, Knox's rosy cheeks brightened at the sight of him.

"Howlett."

"Sir."

"I was made aware of your arrival. Are these your men?" His countenance lifted as he recognized Jack. "Perkins. 'Tis pleasant seeing us Massachusetts men together after Bunker

Hill and Dorchester Heights. Come, Major Howlett, you'll oversee one of the howitzers. Their gun commander was injured last night."

George glanced at Annalisa, then returned a gracious nod to Knox. "Thank you, sir."

❦

OVER THE NEXT THREE DAYS, THE CONTINENTAL trenches extended to within one hundred fifty yards of British redoubts nine and ten. Per Washington's orders, Knox commanded his artillery within range to barrage the British lines to weaken them, in preparation for an evening attack.

In the *boom* of an eighteen-pounder discharging, George assumed his position a small distance away from his crew so he could appreciate them and the field. His voice rose above the deafening roar of the twenty-four-pounder that had just fired, shaking the earth.

"Tend the vent."

An artilleryman to the rear right of the cannon, placed a gloved thumb over the vent hole.

"Advance the worm and out the piece."

Another at the front left of the cannon, inserted a coiled metal rod inside the barrel, swirled it about, then removed it.

"Sponge."

Jack, at the front right, swabbed the interior of the gun with a wet sheepskin-covered sponge to extinguish remaining embers from previous fire.

"Advance cartridge."

A boy, perhaps no older than sixteen, advanced from behind the howitzer with powder sewn into fabric. He handed it to the artilleryman on the gun's front left who loaded it into the muzzle.

"Ram down the charge."

Jack used the opposite end of the sponge rod to ram the gunpowder charge down the barrel.

"Charge ammunition."

An eight-pound ball advanced and was loaded within the muzzle.

"Ram the piece."

Jack rammed the ball down the barrel.

"Prick and prime."

At the vent, another artilleryman inserted a small wrought-iron bar into the vent hole to prick the rammed gunpowder charge. The man then poured gunpowder inside the touch hole by means of a quill tube and left it within the vent opening to maintain contact with the loaded charge.

George's spirit quivered with anticipation as he ordered, "Make ready!"

Their ears blocked, the gun crew leaned away from the gun, save Annalisa, who poised at the cannon's left rear with her portfire.

"Fire!"

His sister, guised as Benjamin Cavendish, lit the charge with her smoldering portfire.

Boom!

Gunsmoke, sulfuric and pungent, wafted back at them.

"Tend the vent," George ordered.

His crew followed command, firing on the British without relent well into the evening until, at sunset, orders arrived from General Washington to hold all fire. The gun crew dispersed, and George, Jack, and Annalisa returned to the encampment and waited.

Beneath a moonless sky, quiet enveloped camp for the first time all day. At this, Annalisa lowered her voice and said, "George, I fear 'tis impossible to locate your uncle in this place."

"Aye," Jack said. "His ship may've been scuttled—"

"Or he's absconded to Halifax," Annalisa said.

"I vowed to find him." George rubbed his stubbled chin in silence. "For Jane. For the farm."

"I know, but I fear 'tis futile," Annalisa whispered. "And far too perilous to sneak away on our own."

"Fie." George fisted his hands until the knuckles whitened.

"Cousin, there's a chance we may be victorious here," Jack said. "Let that be vengeance enough."

When they'd ridden south in pursuit of Admiral Bixby, George never anticipated fighting of this magnitude, with this many men, artillery, militia, and soldiers. It felt to be the end of the world, the end of the war, the final stand. Even if Admiral Bixby somehow managed to survive and keep his ship, he most likely maintained position in the York River, entrapped on the water by the French fleet offshore. If he somehow made it ashore, Admiral Bixby could be one of two impossible places: British-barricaded Yorktown or a world away at Gloucester Point with Tarleton, on the other side of the river.

George chewed his lower lip. He'd made it this far and didn't wish to further endanger his beloved sister or cousin. Meeting his uncle would come by chance when the time allowed. For now, he would have to be satisfied to pummel the British into oblivion and win the war.

64

JACK
YORKTOWN, VIRGINIA, OCTOBER 1781

B Y THE MORNING OF the sixteenth of October, British redoubts nine and ten had been overtaken, and Continental artillery lines fired upon Yorktown with such unrelenting devastation, the British attempted to flee across the York River to Gloucester Point. His own artillery partook in this brigade under George's command and orders from Henry Knox.

Yet amidst this, by the grace of God, or whomever had chosen to hear his prayers, Jack's sight improved enough for him to detect the green of Annalisa's eyes as she peered at him from her position at the howitzer. She was right, of course, his darling girl. They had much to live for when this battle was won. And they would be victorious. The only thing to deter his yearning for Topsfield was George and his need to uncover Admiral Bixby amidst the British foil. Perhaps, and it was indeed likely, their uncle had fled for Halifax in pursuit of Mother, Susan, and Charlotte.

Annalisa fired the cannon, and another discharge of the gun screamed through the air toward Yorktown. George hollered orders from behind, and the ritual began anew. With the addition of new artillery pieces to the line, the bombard-ment lasted hours. *Cornwallis must surrender. He can't hold out much longer.*

That evening, Jack returned with Annalisa to camp while George remained behind to receive orders from Knox. Perhaps the following day would be much of the same, but as weariness beset him, Jack prayed the end was near. He could hardly contain his yearning to return home.

"I'm retiring. Good night." He slipped into his tent, leaving Annalisa by the campfire. Inside his small tent, he removed his coat and set it at the foot of his blankets. As he unwound his cravat, Annalisa's hushed voice lingered from outside.

"Jack?"

His interest piqued at her presence, and he smirked. "'Tis Lord Brunswick, sir."

Annalisa chuckled. "May I enter, my lord?"

Titillating from so near a victory, he softened at the thought of holding her. "You may." Jack knelt upon his blan-kets and awaited her. The bandage removed from his head, his eyes remained closed, though he sensed her inch toward him.

"I will help you with the ointment."

His brows lifted, knowing it left a slight pout upon his lips. "Do as you please."

She retrieved the vial Addy had prepared for their journey and dabbed a small amount to a clean towel that had been soaked in boiling water. With a delicate finger, Annalisa lifted his eyelids and wiped away the crusted discharge.

"What is it? Your face..." Jack reached for her. "You frown. Am I so hideous?"

"No," she whispered. "I only grieve the loss of color in your eyes."

His lips twisted. "Would that I could see you in this dim

light as clearly as you see me. That I could appreciate the curve of your mouth, your eyes, so full of green life...I noticed their color today in the sunlight."

"That is favorable to hear," she replied. "As my eyes are earth, yours were the sea, but no more. I'm loath to be without ocean waves."

Jack drew her to him. "At least I may hold you, and you may overwhelm my other senses. In my blindness, 'tis as though I never truly saw you before now. Your courage, your strength. I always knew they were there, but I only recognized what I allowed myself to see." He traced his thumb across the edges of her face, down her nose, across her lips, and landed upon the space beneath her right eye. "I've seen this scar since the day we met, yet I never truly contemplated it. Your firing George's fowler." He smiled. "And I somehow never noticed it upon Benjamin's face. 'Tis always been obvious, your other self, but I never chose to see it."

Jack reached for his knapsack and withdrew her small, tattered poetry book.

Annalisa gasped. "I thought I'd lost this. How have you come to keep it?"

"Your mother gave it to me when we believed you drowned." He thumbed through the pages, glancing at her penciled script upon the margins. "I feared Benjamin Cavendish when I read about him here. I never suspected 'twas you as you sit before me. But now I appreciate you in your men's clothing. I see you at long last, my darling girl. I see you, and I love you even more than I ever knew myself capable." He set down the book and swiped the tears from her face.

"I deserve you not, Jack."

"Annalisa, you've been nothing if not consistent in who you are from the day we met. When George and I uncovered you the day of the massacre from the Green Dragon, dressed in William's clothes, I should've known to expect more and not less from all I witnessed that night." He smiled wistfully. "Would that I'd been mad enough to chuck oysters and ice at those Bloodybacks as you were. My God, from that moment, I've not been able to rid you from my mind, Annalisa, no matter how I tried. I'm only grieved I could not give you all you asked of me when we eloped. That was my failure to you as a husband."

"Nonsense." Her fingertips brushed his lips, and he vibrated at her touch. "You gifted me our daughter. And in this moment, your forgiveness is more than I could've hoped for."

His chest swelled with conviction. "How could I not? You've burrowed yourself within my heart, my spirit, and have blossomed into the most beautiful, most cherished part of my life. And I love you...I adore you."

Annalisa blended her lips with his.

"'Tis as though I've not tasted you until now," he said between kisses.

She freed the edges of his shirt from his breeches and ran her cool hands over the skin of his back, then pulled the shirt over his head. A brisk October breeze rustled the flap of his tent, puckering the skin on his bare torso.

Jack leaned back. As he did, Annalisa traced the ridges of his abdomen that flexed with his recline. Her touch roused him, and he tugged her over his lap, wrapping his arms about her. As his lips found hers, he unbuttoned her waistcoat, and she slid the garment from her arms. He searched for her neckpiece and untied it, tossing it away. When only her shirt remained, he slipped it over her head. He hesitated at the linen bound about her breasts. She guided his hands to a knot beneath her armpit.

A binding far different from the stays he'd unlaced from her, the linen loosened with each circle about her breast until nothing remained. With a gentle hand, he flipped over her and guided her down upon the blankets. She wrapped her legs, encased in breeches, about him. Jack unbuttoned the garment and tugged them from her hips.

He laughed. "Of all the times I've envisioned myself undressing you, 'twas never akin to this."

"You said that the day you bathed me. I suppose I'm full of shocking surprises." Annalisa chuckled and drew him over her. With one hand, she unbuttoned the front flap of his breeches, exposing his turgid member, and directed him into her.

Their bodies entwined in a rapture of overspent emotion and hunger. Annalisa clung to him as though she wished to never release him from her hold, and he was glad to oblige. The pleasure unmitigated and untarnished by the hold to create life, he sought to delight her in every way he could. She deserved nothing if not for his whole self to cherish and worship her for the remainder of his days—a promise he made her years ago. *This night is the one scrap of joy in our lives this last twelvemonth. Let these delights last an eternity...*

Not even the gods could conjure a more perfect union, a tantalizing reminder of all he'd missed in their time apart. Yet something deep within him stirred, and he knew they would never again be parted from this moment forward. The thrill of such a feeling overwhelmed as they each reached gratification, a delight that spanned beyond the sensory and into a realm unseen.

Annalisa curled against his body, legs entwined, and rested her head upon his chest.

"If I were to die tomorrow, I could do so happily," he muttered.

She reached for his hand and kissed his fingertips. "We've much to live for, Jack Perkins."

In that moment, he knew it to be true. And tomorrow

would dawn a new day, perhaps one which would end the war for good. Then they could live as he'd always dreamt: with Annalisa by his side. He need only ask her to marry him, but he could hardly do so at camp.

Lying beside her in the darkness of the tent, he whispered, "Would that we were home, that I could please you until dawn and you needn't contain your ecstasy. That we could wake in the morning and drink chocolate together by the fire...our children gathered around us."

"May this war end here. At Yorktown." Annalisa sat upright and took his face between her hands. "I wish to begin our lives, Jack Perkins. Our mundane, quiet lives far from all this."

"I pray it will be so, dear heart," he replied. "We offered ourselves completely to a cause with no bounds. 'Twill will be a life worth living."

❧

COME MORNING, THE FAINT SOUND OF DRUMMING STARTLED Jack awake. Beside him, Annalisa slept. He kissed her.

"My love, there's drumming."

"Drums?" Annalisa rubbed her face and sat upright. "Is it a surrender?"

In the chilly October darkness, Jack covered himself and crept from the blankets. He peered outside, then felt his way to George's tent.

"George?"

His cousin met him at the flap. "Drumming."

The bombardment had ceased, and they lingered in the silent stillness of camp until an officer cried out, "They surrender! Cornwallis has surrendered!"

"Well, I'll be damned, 'tis over at long last." George guffawed and embraced Jack.

"Thank heaven." Jack sighed as more men joined the celebration.

"Go tell Cav," George said.

Jack returned to the tent, where Annalisa sat upright, her shirt open and breasts exposed. "What is it?"

His body surging with elation, he crawled on top of her and caressed her lips, her neck, her jaw with his mouth. "Cornwallis surrenders. 'Tis over. Six years and 'tis over."

Annalisa flopped back and accepted him into her, and he pleased her again with renewed vigor, as though his sight had fully returned to him, as though they'd already arrived home to Topsfield and strummed upon a soft bed and not cold, damp blankets on the hard ground. Yet no such revelation of joy or good news could surmount to British surrender, save for the intimate movements of his beloved at Washington's camp.

Jack peered down at her, his blurred vision revealing a bit more of her face as she bit her lip with unparalleled delight. He, too, nearly forgetting himself, expressed a groan of pleasure.

"Come, let's break our fast." Annalisa rose from the ground and pulled on her breeches.

"'Tis Lord Brunswick to you, my lady." He pulled her back onto the blanket and showered her with kisses.

"Shh." She giggled into his shoulder.

"I've not felt such joy in years."

"Me either. But I do think George will have us court-martialed if we delay much longer."

Jack chuckled. "You're probably right."

He dressed beside her, and they fled the tent, one by one.

THE ENCAMPMENT TEEMED WITH A SPIRIT JACK HAD NOT experienced from camp since they'd ambushed the Hessians on Christmas Day 1776. After a brutal series of defeats in New York that year, they'd needed a victory to revive morale. Now, they held the ultimate triumph.

Annalisa handed Jack a small plate and tin cup. "'Tis a johnnycake. And cider."

He reached for the bland disk of dough baked upon the fire's ashes and ate. "I'll be glad to never again eat firecake, ashcake, johnnycake—what have you—as long as I live."

"Hear, hear," George said.

Jack faced his cousin and lifted his tin cup. "I salute you, Major Howlett. 'Tis hard to believe we came from such humble beginnings six years ago, our first and only battle with the Topsfield minutemen at Concord, to then find ourselves enmeshed at Bunker Hill two months later."

"Aye." George chuckled. "'Tis been a long six years. There's no other I'd rather have fought beside than you, Brother." He leaned closer to Annalisa, "Or you, Cav."

They toasted and drank.

A soldier, garbed in one of Virginia's regimentals, turned. "Did I overhear you say you are veterans of Lexington and Concord, as well as Bunker Hill?"

"Aye, sir," Jack replied.

"And others," George added.

"Have we Massachusetts militia here?" Another soldier near them raised his glass. "The battles that started it all. Here's to you, gentlemen."

The first soldier shouted, "To Lexington and Concord!"

"Huzzah!"

"To Bunker Hill!"

As cheers commemorating Bunker Hill and Lexington and Concord filled the space, others shouted for Bemis Heights and Saratoga, Kipp's Bay, Monmouth, Camden,

White Plains, Trenton, Princeton, the Cowpens, and far more battles and skirmishes Jack didn't recognize until nearly every British encounter, victory or defeat, had been named. The conquest at Yorktown had been won by an amalgamation of veterans who'd fought by Washington's side from the beginning and every year thereafter—men who'd given themselves for one battle and men who'd sacrificed their livelihoods for six years, men who'd survived, and men who'd fallen.

At this, Jack studied his Annalisa. Her figure blurred, though he appreciated the cloak of Benjamin's guise. She, too, stood a veteran of several battles and had earned a badge of courage. She deserved an honorable discharge from all of this. *The women deserve as much recognition as their men.*

Amidst the shouts and cheers, he leaned in and whispered, "Pray, how many more like you do you suspect have fought?"

Her lips taut, Annalisa contemplated the matter. "Dozens, I pray. Mayhap, hundreds. Lives we'll never know, nor acknowledge. They will retreat to their homes, if they survived, and keep the secret of their guise until no one else is alive to remember them, and soon, we, too, shall be lost to time."

Jack blinked away his tears. He didn't want to acknowledge all she said as truth, but the histories were indeed written by men and victors. His darling girl and her courage, her devotion to the cause, her selfless display of martyrdom, would certainly never be known, acknowledged, nor celebrated. Annalisa Howlett would be a woman, a name forgotten to time, with no record of her having served ever documented, nor honored.

Overcome with emotion, he cleared his throat. "We must obtain you an honorable discharge."

Her face colored. "No." She shook her head. "You can't. I'm not even supposed to be here."

"You've earned it, more so than I." Jack turned to George. "How may we obtain an honorable discharge for our dear friend Cav?"

George peered down at his sister with pride. "I know a commander in chief who may oblige."

Annalisa gripped his arm. "No, please. You mustn't."

If there was ever a person more deserving of such an honor, it was her, but Jack swallowed his pride and resisted the urge to take her into his arms. She was his darling girl, his dearest friend, and when they returned home, he would at the very least ask her to be his wife.

65

GEORGE

DOBB'S FERRY, NEW YORK, LATE NOVEMBER 1781

HUNDREDS OF MILES AND weeks of travel separated them from British surrender at Yorktown. Yet as they rode into Dobbs Ferry, a mere twelve miles north of British-held York Island, George still heard the Lobsters singing "The World Turned Upside Down" upon their retreat from Yorktown. Now, the Bloodybacks convened in New York City with Clinton and the troops that had arrived far too late to rescue Cornwallis from devastation.

As he gazed at the Hudson River, his leg aching and swollen, George conjured an image of Admiral Bixby: his only regret. The vow, the reason he'd ventured south to Virginia, sank to the bottom of the river before him, as likely as his uncle's scuttled ships sank upon the York. And yet something of the promise he'd made had come to fruition in British surrender. He may not have challenged Admiral Bixby as he'd intended, but he'd decimated the Bloodybacks under command of the artillery, something he'd not frequented in battle. And he'd accomplished it all with Annalisa and Jack by his side.

Next to Abigail and Louisa, his sister and cousin proved

the two others he most cherished. In the early twilight, they chatted beside him, but their words emptied into the vast openness of the river valley before them, blue and crystalline, reflecting what would become a verdant landscape come springtime. The view left him pondering the farm and Annalisa's oak. Would that the devastation rebirth come April, when the fields meant to be tilled for planting. *Would that her tree offer buds of chartreuse and singing chickadees high in its branches.*

A simple, humble life spread before him, and for the first time since his riotous youth, he welcomed it. Perhaps it was the path meant for every man once war was done. And for that, he leaned back and inhaled the crisp November air. It held the chill of dried leaves, reminiscent of encroaching winter. With the scent, an overwhelming ease settled over him, and George deemed himself satisfied to leave Admiral Bixby behind. *Let him rot wherever he may end up in this life, if he's not already found the locker.* Life was rarely what he thought it to be, and Annalisa had certainly proven it to him these last six years. He, too, had seen it of himself.

For the first time since the massacre in Boston's streets back in 1770, he was ready: to be a husband and father, to run his tavern and his household.

To return to Topsfield.

To return home.

❧ 66 ❧

ANNALISA

TOPSFIELD, DECEMBER 1781

THE ROAD WAS NARROW, just as she remembered it. Snow had recently fallen and thickly lay, covering all things. In her finest winter gown, Annalisa pulled her wool cloak about her against the biting wind and watched Lord Perkins's carriage turn down the drive. The former magistrate stepped from his vehicle and acknowledged her with a small smile.

"Miss Annalisa, it does me so very well to see you."

She embraced him. "Likewise, sir."

Behind his round spectacles, his light grey eyes sparkled in the low winter sun. His white periwig hid the natural hair beneath, which had certainly greyed from the last decade of turmoil. Yet, without his wife beside him, he presented an air of relief. Annalisa supposed such weight may have lifted since the final battles at Yorktown, yet Congress still held much work to contemplate and conjure. Lord Perkins's job proved far from over, unless the gentleman wished to retire in these later years of his life.

"I think there's someone else you'd perhaps rather see, my dear."

He stepped aside, and Jack jumped from the carriage with four-year-old Robby, who bore only a small healed burn to his right cheek. *Much like my own.*

She hugged her nephew. Jane's final request echoed from within and returned her attention to Jack. Time wore well on him. His soft chestnut hair hadn't yet begun to gray, but his gaze held a wisdom that only a man nearing thirty could boast. The fine blue velvet coat embroidered with gold threads, matching breeches, and waistcoat mimicked the marine of his eyes, which had so nearly returned.

Jack's dimpled smile widened as his gaze settled on her figure. She could hardly believe him the same man her thirteen-year-old heart had loved all those years ago and still cherished.

"Annalisa." He reached for her. "You appear radiant, as much as I can tell. That cloak is red, and your dress...'tis green. Like your eyes."

"Yes." She beamed. "The silk one."

They laughed, and he offered her his arm. Robby held his other hand.

From the second carriage, Andrew, Oliver, Tommy, and Sarah emerged. The five-year-old boy, with his blond hair and pale blue eyes, struck her as a perfect amalgamation of Jane and Oliver's union.

Mamma and Papa met them in the foyer, and Liza took their coats and hats and led everyone into the parlor.

Reverend Cleaveland lingered near the fireplace, awaiting everyone to take their seats. Annalisa settled beside George, Abigail, and Louisa, who squealed with delight when she saw her cousins Robby and Tommy. William joined Henry and Andrew since his wife, Martha, was still confined after birthing their son, Samuel, on the twenty-sixth of November.

Annalisa quite approved of the name, which had similarly brought a tear to George's eye upon hearing it.

Reverend Cleaveland began the service by speaking of liberty, freedom, and the goodness of mankind. He even acknowledged the British surrender at Yorktown and the Topsfield patrons who had fallen in battle since the war's commencement. Annalisa bit her tongue, knowing that piece of her, Benjamin Cavendish, belonged.

She required no noble recognition for her efforts. The battles at Yorktown had offered her everything she'd longed for since Bunker Hill: to fight alongside Jack and George as their equal. After all these years, they finally acknowledged her for all she was and all she hoped to be. That, she decided, was worth more than all the recognition in the world. No, the histories of their infant country would never learn her name, but that had never been her aspiration. She had overcome the adversity set before her by a rigid Society and learned to be herself. For this alone, it had been worth each trying task and trauma, for she was no longer that girl of thirteen balancing on the precipice of feminine perdition. She was Annalisa Howlett, a woman, a lady, and a soldier. And she'd earned the love of a man who truly cherished her.

Having accomplished far more than she'd set out to do, therein remained one final endeavor in which she yearned to partake, one that already stirred within her. Annalisa glanced at Jack. He knew nothing of the life growing beneath her stays, one conceived upon the battlefields of Yorktown. She tamped away the building excitement and focused upon her dear sister, Mary, as Papa walked her toward Quinnapin to be married.

After the modest ceremony, everyone congratulated the happy couple. Annalisa and Abigail pulled Mary and Quinnapin beneath a bundle of mistletoe dangling from the entryway.

"You must kiss the bride," Annalisa said.

Mary's cheeks flushed as Quinnapin pecked her ruby lips.

Annalisa and Abigail giggled and sought George and the bowl of wassailing punch. From a table near the fireplace, he and Liza ladled the steaming spiced wine into glasses. Abigail raised hers to toast.

"To you, my dearest Annalisa." Abigail drank the punch and winked at Jack across the room.

Amidst the holly and evergreens, Papa set forth his finest bottles of port and offered Lord Perkins a glass. Liza set out a plate of cheese and bread while, from the kitchen, aromas of roast goose and savory puddings tantalized Annalisa's senses. She finished her cup of wassail as she caught Jack's desirous stare.

He carefully made his way toward her and saluted. "To the bride and groom. May your lives be prosperous, full of life, good health, and laughter."

"Hear, hear!"

"Huzzah," George bellowed.

"If I may." Jack sipped the port, then faced her. "Miss Annalisa, you steal my breath each moment I'm in your presence. Since the day I met you, I've known no other to possess more courage, more grace, more beauty, more devotion...or tenacity." He winked.

Everyone chuckled.

Annalisa smiled, though she felt her face flush. "Thank you, sir."

"I want to do this correctly this time." Jack's dimpled smile widened, and he knelt.

Trembling, she gripped her skirts.

"My darling girl, our story has been anything but linear, but 'tis our story. 'Tis no secret I've only ever wished to be yours and for you to be mine. Our paths took their time in allowing it of us, but the wait is over, dear heart. I've loved you since you first assaulted His Majesty's Regulars with ice and oysters that cold March night, and each night and day since."

Jack removed a sizable sapphire embedded within a gold band delicately etched in tiny leaves. Peering up at her with candor, his gentle baritone offered her the sweetest words uttered. "Marry me, my wonderful, darling friend."

If her she could contain the warmth of the sun within her breast, it would have burst with the adoration of a hundred other suns. "Yes, of course. A million times, yes."

Jack's steady hand slipped the ring upon her finger. He curled his arms about her, and a flood of amber perfume washed over her as he spun her about. Louisa, Robby, and Tommy shrieked and clapped hands until Jack set Annalisa down, blending his lips with hers.

George's laughter filled the room, and he kissed Abigail.

Quinnapin, beaming, kissed Mary, then embraced Jack and Annalisa. "My congratulations, beloved friends."

"Blessings abound tonight," Papa said. "Dear Mary is wed and Annalisa is engaged."

Mamma clasped her hands and addressed Lord Perkins. "Now, we'll have another wedding after Ollie and Sarah."

"Springtime." Annalisa faced Jack. "When the weather is fairest and the lilacs are in bloom—should they bloom."

The fire's damage had burned the cornfields—a huge loss for Papa that harvest—and the oak. Since returning from Virginia, she'd not appreciated the destruction to her tree, but should it flourish come May, it would be beneath those branches she'd finally call Jack her husband.

Smiling, Mary reached for Annalisa and held her. "This is the most...wonderful...wedding blessing."

Abigail moved to the spinet, and music filled the room. Couples paired off to dance, and after sharing a cotillion with Oliver, Annalisa withdrew from the room, tugging Jack with her.

"Let's to the oak."

They fled the house, donning their wool cloaks. Beneath a waxing moon, the snow-covered fields glowed. With moonlight as her guide, Annalisa led Jack to their venerable tree.

Silvery rays wept through the tree's barren canopy, illuminating the blackened bough upon which they'd so often sat. Annalisa ran her fingers over the roughened, charred bark.

"The damage, is it bad?" Jack asked.

Annalisa took his hand and led him to the branch. "'Tis still here. It stands, though injured."

Jack felt for the bough, sat, and drew her toward him. "As we've been ravaged, so do we continue to stand, dear heart."

"Yes." A wintry breeze rustled her cloak, and she pulled it about her. "I'm with child."

In the broken moonlight, his countenance lifted. "Thank heaven." His lips twisted as though to contain joyous tears, and he pulled her into his arms. "Pray, how long have you known?"

"I daresay since the night you planted her within me. I knew."

"Her?" The corners of his mouth lifted.

"Yes."

He fell silent. "May she be fearless, like her mother."

"May she be honorable, like her father."

"Pray, how are you feeling? When do you suspect we'll meet her?"

"I'm well. She should come in July."

Jack laughed. "My God, how did I ever live before you, my Annie?" His thumb swiped the space beneath her right eye, and she shivered at his touch.

"I feel my life began the day I met you."

Wrapped in his arms beneath their tree that had been marred by flames, Annalisa couldn't help but sense an overwhelming love and protection, that despite the raw chaos, life continued, and persisted. And come spring, she knew their tree, too, would endure.

❧ 67 ❧

ANNALISA

TOPSFIELD, MAY 20TH, 1782

TOPSFIELD

O N THE FAIREST DAY of May, when the lilacs were in full bloom, Abigail dressed Annalisa's body, now modestly round in her seventh month of pregnancy, in a simple yet elegant cream silk sack-back gown with sage and ivory ribbons.

"You hardly look pregnant, Annalisa." Abigail marveled at her in the looking glass. "'Tis because you're so tall and slim."

Annalisa smiled at Mary beside her, who massaged her own stomach, which at five months had just started to show. *I pray our children arrive strong and healthy.* Perhaps not a trying task for the girl growing within her, having been conceived amidst battlefields.

"You know, I, too, have missed my courses," Abigail said. "I'll be joining you both in welcoming a baby this year."

"Oh, Abbie!" Annalisa hugged her. "What wonderful news."

"I know...they will all be...so close," Mary replied, smiling.

Beyond the casement, not a cloud littered the azure sky. *I want to see the blue of Jack's eyes in everything.* She returned to the looking glass and conjured the last Strawberry Festival in which both her sisters had readied beside her in this very room. Jane's absence pinched, though her void had been filled by Abigail.

Ten years ago, she never would have recognized the young woman staring back at her. The scars, the battle wounds, both physical and emotional, colored the face and body in that looking glass. But she couldn't help but smile. Everything she sought to do, she accomplished. With her sister-in-law and sister by her side, Annalisa pondered this new journey she was about to embark upon, not alone, but with the family and friends she so cherished.

Annalisa stepped outside, and the delicate beauty of May in Massachusetts greeted her with a pleasant breeze that rustled her lace and curls. Behind her, Mary and Abigail followed with Louisa.

Papa offered her his arm and led her to the oak, where everyone assembled.

The branches, though many blackened, defied death and destruction and burst anew with chartreuse leaves.

Jack, in a light pink silk coat embroidered in delicate ivory, with cream-colored breeches and waistcoat, stood by the base of the tree with George. They both beamed as she approached with Papa. A black-capped chickadee high in the branches whistled a humble melody, and time stood still. Annalisa clutched a bouquet of lilacs from her garden, their sweet perfume overwhelming her senses.

George, an officer and capable of marrying couples, turned to Jack. "Wilt thou have this woman to thy wedded wife?"

"I will." Jack kept his voice intimate and alluring.

George addressed Annalisa. "And wilt thou have this man to thy wedded husband?"

"I will."

"Who giveth this woman to be married to this man?"

Papa smiled. "Her father." He kissed Annalisa's cheek, then shook Jack's hand.

George winked at Papa as he left them to stand beside Mamma. "Please face one another."

Jack offered her his right hand, and she accepted him as George prompted them to take vows. She gazed into Jack's eyes that had nearly returned to their color before the fire, eyes she knew the child within her would bear.

"I, John Jackson Perkins III, take thee, Annalisa Howlett, to my wedded wife." As he spoke, his thumb caressed her hand. "To have and to hold from this day forward, for better, for worse, for richer, for poorer, in sickness and in health."

Jack paused. Blinking quickly, he composed himself to finish. "To *love* and to *cherish till death parts us*, according to God's holy ordinance; and thereto I plight thee my troth."

"I, Annalisa Howlett, take thee, John Jackson Perkins III, to my wedded husband." She spoke clearly, not once removing her gaze from his. And when she finished, she looked to George, who prompted Jack with the ring.

"With this ring, I thee wed, with my body, I thee worship, and with all my worldly goods, I thee endow. In the Lord's name, amen." Jack slipped the sapphire ring upon her finger with ease.

"Forasmuch as Jack and Annalisa have consented together in holy wedlock, and have witnessed the same before God and this company, and thereto have given and pledged their troth to each other, and have declared the same by giving and receiving of a ring, and by joining of hands, I pronounce that they be man and wife together."

They turned to face their families and friends.

George clapped. "I present to you Lord and Lady Brunswick...Mr. and Mrs. John Jackson Perkins III."

Everyone retreated across the fields toward the farm-house. Captain Gould and Elisha Porter supplied fresh ale and cider, and Addy had assisted Liza with the cooking and baking. Martha and Sarah had helped Mamma decorate with white paper chains, garlands of fresh juniper berries, and flowers from the gardens. Mr. Averill and Josiah brought their instruments to play while Abigail and George convened with William and Henry. Mary and Quinnapin took turns playing with the children, and Andrew, Oliver, and Lord Perkins shared in a toast with Papa.

As they slowly retreated from the tree toward their cele-bration, Jack kissed Annalisa's hand. "So shall it be Lady Brunswick or Mrs. Perkins?"

"I'm quite satisfied to be your darling girl," she replied.

Jack's cheek dimpled. "That you'll always be."

"But if you insist, Lady Brunswick has a particular ring to it I quite like. And your aunt was always kind to me."

"Then *my lady* it is."

"And besides, Sarah will be Lady Perkins. I'm quite glad you relinquished your father's title to Ollie."

Jack chuckled. "Ollie's glad of it, too. But so am I. More so that we've reconciled as brothers these last few years."

"He's a good man. And I never thought I'd say it. He and Sarah make a blissful pair. I can hardly wait to meet their little one."

"And Quinn and Mary's babe."

"And Abbie and George's." Annalisa laughed.

"Zounds! Abbie is in the family way, too?" Jack laughed. "Our child is going to have plenty of cousins to play with."

Robby ran about with Tommy and Louisa. He seemed to have recovered well enough from the fire and losing his mother, though the sting of Jane's absence still filled them all with regret.

"I know I'll never replace Jane, but I'll try to mother him as best I can."

Jack shook his head. "He loves you so much already. You needn't try very hard."

"The night Jane passed, she asked me to love Robby, to protect him. 'Tis the least I can do. He is half you, after all. How could I not adore him?"

"I would never ask it of you, Annalisa. I know the pain, the betrayal of that circumstance—"

"'Tis in the past. Let us develop our own relationship. If he should one day wish to call me *Mother* instead of Auntie Annie, I'll not stop him. George does call my papa *Pa*."

Annalisa knew she could never take Jane's place, but she would honor whatever Robby deemed right by him as he grew older.

When they reached the house, Mamma crowned Annalisa in a wreath of freshly picked flowers, and Sarah offered her a glass of Gould's cider.

"You're radiant, Calais," Sarah said. "Would that Gee could see you today."

"Would that Gee could see *you*, Lady Perkins," Annalisa cried. "You're glowing."

Sarah's hand smoothed her round belly, and she smiled. "I can't wait for the baby to meet yours."

On a day so fair, it would be foolish to squander such weather by eating indoors. Liza and Addy, with the help of Henry and Papa, set up a large wooden table in the garden. At its center, Liza served roast mutton, venison, and boiled rabbit; surrounding the meats were mushroom broth, beetroot salad, and an abundance of sweet and savory puddings, including Annalisa's favorite: fish-and-cheese pudding. On a separate table stood two white cakes—a bride's cake and a bridegroom's cake.

After dinner, as twilight descended over the farm, dancing

commenced when Mr. Averill and Josiah took up their instruments. Annalisa laughed and clapped her hands as her parents circled the garden, now lit in lanternlight.

"I've got your shoe." Quinnapin tossed the item to Oliver, who snickered.

George guffawed. "Kiss him to get it back."

"You've got to kiss him, Annie." William laughed.

Annalisa pecked Quinnapin's cheek, and Oliver relinquished her shoe.

Jack joined her. "Pray tell, what must I steal from you to get a kiss?"

"Lord Brunswick, you've stolen my heart. Is that not thievery enough?"

The sound of "Corn Rigs Are Bonny" flew from Mr. Averill's guitar strings, and Annalisa turned to Abigail and George. "George Washington's favorite cotillion."

"Get over here, Little One," George shouted. Unlike Benedict Arnold, who'd kept his leg but was unable to dance with Peggy, George hobbled quite well upon his amputated limb, including keeping up with Abigail's spry feet.

"Let's dance, Lady Brunswick." Jack pulled her to the set.

They danced the cotillion with George and Abigail, followed by a reel. When Annalisa felt she might collapse from joyous exhaustion, Jack took up Josiah's fiddle and played "Flowers of Edinburgh," her favorite reel.

The gleeful song always reminded her of the Strawberry Festival and their beloved little town of Topsfield. And tonight, beneath a starry sky, Jack played for her. She'd know the sound of his fiddle anywhere, and to that day and beyond, would never forget it. Everyone disappeared behind her, and nothing else mattered. Before her, the life they now shared shone brightly as the stars in the sky and the moon. She'd faced war and adversity alone and survived, but she would continue it all with Jack by her side.

❈ 68 ❈

ANNALISA

TOPSFIELD, 1792

THE ROAD FROM THEIR summer home in New Castle was long but always worth the drive. Jack sat across from her in their fine carriage, a handsome man of forty years and sporting strands of grey in his chestnut-brown hair. He still wore his face clean-shaven with side-whiskers long, though now faint creases etched his face in the places he smiled. She peered back at him until he met her regard and grinned. Quickly, she averted her gaze, never quite capable of staring at him for too long, lest she take a seat in his lap. At six-and-thirty and with five children, four of whom she birthed these ten years, she managed to keep her figure, but she no longer wished for another pregnancy. Jack, too, seemed content with their family of five.

"My father will wish to come to dinner, dear heart," he said.

Annalisa smiled. "Of course. We'll have everyone over, as we always do when we return from New Castle."

Jack returned her smile and kissed her hand.

He never spoke of his mother or youngest sisters, but his

relationship with Lord Perkins and Oliver had grown, and for that, Annalisa was thankful.

As their carriage turned down the drive toward their large yellow house in Topsfield, their eldest daughter, Molly, pointed out the window.

"We're home! Mamma, may we visit Grandmother and Grandpapa and climb the oak?"

Annalisa laughed. "Of course,. Let us get settled for one night, then we'll visit the farm tomorrow."

Robby, a strapping boy of fifteen, appeared more like Jack each day. He leaned close to his sister. "When you're old enough, maybe I'll teach you to fire a musket."

Molly's marine eyes widened. "I couldn't."

"And whyever not?" Annalisa shifted her youngest child, a boy of two, on her lap. "You can do anything, my darling. Can't she, Robby?"

Robby grinned back her. "Aye, Ma."

The carriage stopped within the drive, and the coachman opened the door. The children hauled from the vehicle, leaving behind Jack, Annalisa, and their son, John Jackson Perkins IV, the future Lord Brunswick. *Three girls and, finally, a boy.* Jack jumped from the carriage, and offered her his hand. Rather than take it, she handed him their son and jumped out after them.

"Some things may never change, my darling girl." He kissed her and led them inside their house.

That evening, when everyone was settled about the drawing room, Annalisa played the pianoforte Jack had shipped from France—a gift from the Duchess of Devonshire in 1783, the year of the Treaty of Paris, which recognized their new country as the United States of America. Her fingers played old songs from memory and new songs written by the latest composers, but none matched her adoration of Mozart —the late Mozart, who had died just last year.

"Mamma, what is this?" Molly ran into the room with Robby. She held out her hand. Within her palm rested a musket round; Robby carried an old cocked hat and breeches far too small for his father to have worn.

Annalisa stopped playing and glimpsed Jack, who chuckled. "They're your mother's."

"Mamma?" Molly cried. "You wore breeches?"

"And the musket above the kitchen hearth?" Robby asked.

"Your ma's," Jack replied. "Annie, my darling girl, we have more than a remarkable story to one day tell our grandchildren. But first, we must tell our children."

Annalisa smiled, her life having finally come full circle. "Yes?"

"I'm honored to live it by your side, dear heart." Jack tugged her from the pianoforte and kissed her. "We have *our* story."

THANK YOU

Thank you for reading *Muskets & Martyrs*.
Please consider leaving a review. Reviews not only help other
readers find new books, they help readers find which books
may end up being their new favorite!

18TH CENTURY & NEW-ENGLAND VOCABULARY, PHRASES, AND SLANG

- ABRAMS: men/gentlemen
- APPLE DUMPLING SHOP: a woman's bosom
- BAGPIPE: fellatio
- BANNS: (marriage banns) an announcement of impending marriage
- BAWDY BASKET(S): a lady or group of ladies
- BEAR-GARDEN JAW: rude or vulgar language
- BENEFIT OF CLERGY: avoiding the death penalty as a Christian by pleading benefit of clergy; one would be branded on the thumb with the letter of their crime: F for felon, M for murder, T for theft; this was so the benefit could not be claimed more than once.
- BLOODYBACK: redcoat in His Majesty's Army
- BUNDLEBAG/BUNDLING: an old New England tradition in which parents would arrange courting couples to spend the night together. The gentleman would be sewn into a canvas sack to prevent copulation prior to marriage. Other times,

a long wooden board was placed between the couple.

- CHRISTMASTIDE: the twelve days of Christmas, beginning on December 25th and ending on Twelfth Night, Epiphany, January 6th. (Sometimes the dates observed are Dec. 24th – Jan. 5th) Christmas itself was rarely celebrated in New England.
- COCK ROBIN: a soft, easy fellow
- CRIMINAL CONVERSATION: sexual encounter with a married person
- CURTAIN LECTURE: an instance of a woman reprimanding her husband in private
- DANDY PRAT: an insignificant or trifling fellow
- DILBERRIES: excrement stuck to the hairs of one's arse (dingleberries in modern terms)
- DISGUISED: drunk
- DOXIE(S): lady/ladies
- DRESSED TO THE NINES: dressed to perfection
- FARTCATCHER: a servant who follows closely behind their master
- FIE: used to express outrage or disgust.
- FLIP: tavern drink made of rum, ale, molasses, and eggs, then beaten with a hot fire poker to create a nice froth, topped off with grated nutmeg. Each tavern had their own version of flip.
- FOWLING PIECE/FOWLER/FIRELOCK: Smooth bore flintlock, muzzle-loading gun, used primarily to hunt fowl. Was a typical household weapon in New England.
- GAOL: old spelling of *jail*
- GO OFF: to orgasm

- HOOPS (see *panniers*): undergarments worn beneath ladies' petticoats to give wide skirt appearances classic to the 18th century
- INTERCOURSE: conversation
- GREEN GOWN (to give someone): to have sex with a woman in the grass
- GOLLUMPUS: a large, clumsy fellow
- JERRYCUMMUMBLE: to shake or tumble about
- KEIHTÁNIT (*Cautantowwit, Kautantowwit, Keihtán*): The Great Spirit. Spelling varies among the Algonquin nations. Keihtánit is the Wampanoag spelling.
- LA: expression of surprise
- LEAPING OVER THE SWORD: a military marriage
- LET-GO: to orgasm
- LOBSTER/LOBSTERBACK: redcoat in the His Majesty's Army
- LOOKING GLASS: mirror
- MARM: ma'am
- MERRY-BEGOTTEN: a child born out of wedlock
- MORT(S): lady/ladies
- MUMMER(s): masked dancers who cavorted through the streets on Twelfth Night and visited homes unannounced to beg for holiday drinks and treats.
- MUSKET: smoothbore barrel, muzzle-loading gun. Less accurate but was usually used within the military because of quicker loading and the ability to attach bayonet.
- NECESSARY: bathroom/loo/privy/outhouse
- NOOZED: married, hanged

- OWL IN AN IVY BUSH: said of a person who wears a large, frizzed wig
- SPATTERDASHES: made of wool, leather, or linen, they covered a man's leg from mid-shin to top of the foot. Worn by military, sporting, or working men for warmth.
- SPILL: a piece of rolled wood or paper used to light a fire
- PANNIERS (see *hoops*): these were worn beneath a lady's petticoats to give the wide, 18th century skirt silhouette.
- PEGO: a man's penis
- PHYSICK: medicine
- PLUM: a fortune of £100,000 or someone with such fortune.
- POMADE: hair grease used with powder to create desired hairstyles
- PUK-WUDJIE (various spelling): translating literally to 'Person of the wilderness'. Little people of the forest in Wampanoag folklore who are mischievous in nature.
- RECEIPT: recipe, old spelling
- ROGUE: men/gentlemen
- REMEDY CRITCH: a bowl/chamber pot, usually porcelain, in which to urinate
- RUN GOODS (to take): virginity, or, to take one's virginity
- SHENEWEMEDY: some historians believe it is Topsfield's name, according to the Pawtucket, meaning "the pleasant place by the flowing waters." Some believe it was how the Pawtucket pronounced Topsfield's first colonial name of New Meadows. It was changed to Topsfield in 1648, and the town incorporated in 1650.

- SHITTING THROUGH THE TEETH: vomiting
- SHUT YOUR POTATO TRAP AND GIVE YOUR TONGUE A HOLIDAY: to shut up
- SLUICE YOUR GOB: to take a hearty drink
- STAYS (pair of): whale-boned corset that gives conical shape to torso that is classic to the 18th century woman's silhouette
- STRUM: to have sexual intercourse
- SUIT IN DITTO (ditto suit): a man's suit where all pieces (breeches, coat, and waistcoat) are of the same color and fabric
- SQUEEZE CRAB: a sour looking, shriveled, diminutive fellow
- SYMPATHETIC STAIN: invisible ink used during by spies during the Revolutionary War
- TIP THE VELVET: to put one's tongue in a woman's mouth, or cunnilingus
- VICTUALING OFFICE/VICTUALS: stomach
- WHIP JACKETS: men
- WHOLE NINE YARDS: clothing took nine yards to make; to be the whole nine yards meant your outfit was of cut of the same nine yards of dyed fabric, which meant everything matched perfectly; sometimes dyes differed.
- WIBBLE: cheap or bad liquor
- WRAPPED UP IN WARM FLANNEL: drunk with spiritous liquors
- ZOUNDS: an exclamation of surprise or indignation

ABOUT THE AUTHOR

LINDSEY S. FERA is a born and bred New Englander, hailing from the North Shore of Boston. As a member of the Topsfield Historical Society and the Historical Novel Society, she forged her love for writing with her intrigue for colonial America by writing the Muskets Trilogy. When she's not attending historical reenactments or spouting off facts about Boston, she's nursing patients back to health. *Muskets & Martyrs* is her third novel.

www.ingramcontent.com/pod-product-compliance
Lightning Source LLC
Chambersburg PA
CBHW061037310726
48969CB00004B/992